A MINDHUNTERS NOVEL

DEADLY BONDS

AWARD-WINNING ROMANTIC SUSPENSE

ANNE MARIE
BECKER

DEADLY BONDS

THE MINDHUNTERS, BOOK 3

ANNE MARIE BECKER

For Dad, who laid the groundwork for my writing career. I love you.

And for teachers everywhere—you are bright lights that shine on the future.

CHAPTER 1

Late July

F *inally.* Who would have thought an asshole with a broken moral compass would be working this late on a Friday? But then again, maybe the almighty Illinois State Senator Roy Beechum had unfinished business with his piece-on-the-side secretary before going home to his wife for the weekend.

From the floor of the backseat of the bastard's Mercedes, Toxin could see—with only a slight movement of his head—both the side-view and rearview mirrors. In the latter, Beechum's image finally appeared. He stepped off the elevator without so much as a glance at his surroundings. His attention was glued to the screen of his phone as he confidently made his way across the basement-level parking garage, his shiny shoes reflecting the dim yellow light. His steps echoed off the concrete walls.

The guy's suit was tailored to an average-sized body kept in above-average shape. Toxin's surveillance had revealed that

Beechum worked out daily and was careful about what he put into his body. Hell, the senator took care of everything in his life—including this Mercedes with the vanilla-scented air freshener and the untouched leather backseat. He took care of every fucking little thing except defending the helpless constituents who needed him. Yet the majority of Chicagoans thought Beechum was John F. Kennedy reincarnated. There were even rumors of a future presidency in a decade or two.

The guy could be Superman and none of that would matter. Once Toxin's little surprise hit Beechum's bloodstream, his heart would stop beating within, oh, two and a half minutes. Kryptonite in the form of a lethal venom. No amount of healthy living could counter that.

Justice: one. Two-faced politicians: zero.

Besides, Beechum wasn't the only one who'd been working out. In order to carry out his mission, Toxin had been strengthening his body and mind against weakness for months. A warrior had to prepare for anything.

Careful not to make any detectable movement, Toxin's glance slid toward the side-view mirror as Beechum got close. Still clueless, the guy simultaneously texted someone with his right hand and pulled his keys out of his pants pocket with his left. Toxin's quick glance to the rearview mirror showed the garage was still deserted, long ago emptied of cars that belonged to people eager to be home for the weekend.

A distracted target. A secluded, deserted location. *Easy peasy lemon squeezy. This one's for you, Josh.*

Adrenaline flooded Toxin's bunched muscles as he clutched the needle in his left hand. His black hooded windbreaker, carefully matched to the Mercedes' black leather interior and tinted windows, would hide him until Beechum was too close to evade the attack. He ignored the pain in his legs, which burned and cramped from crouching behind the driver's seat. Not much longer now. His breathing quickened and he reviewed the anger management tips he'd picked up in those mandated group therapy sessions, surrendering himself to a focused calm. Good to know those unbearable hours surrounded by miscreants had yielded something useful. Little did that chirpy do-gooder who taught the classes know the skills she'd bestowed upon him would be used to kill. The upshot was Toxin would find much relief for his anger in about twenty seconds.

Beechum stopped at the driver's side and tucked his phone into the pocket of his pants, then shifted his keys to his other hand to unlock the door. Definitely right-handed, as previous observations had indicated. It was a useful tidbit of information when it came to withstanding any attempts by Beechum to deflect the attack.

Toxin wasn't going to fail. He hadn't before. He wouldn't now. He was unstoppable because he was right and these other people were so, *so* wrong.

Beechum pulled open the door. The car's equilibrium shifted slightly to the left and the leather creaked softly as he sat in the driver seat. Keys jangled. Before making a move, Toxin waited for the gentle scrape of metal indicating Beechum had inserted his key in the ignition.

Leaping into action, Toxin wrapped his right arm across the guy's neck and shoulder from behind. He put his forearm against Beechum's chin, forcing his head up and back into the headrest and silencing any attempt to scream or shout. Not that there'd be anyone to hear.

Beechum grunted and tried to open his mouth to bite, but with Toxin forcing his chin up, it was useless and ended in more grunts and groans. As expected, Beechum's hands came up to Toxin's arm, trying to dislodge it.

With his free hand, Toxin jabbed the needle into the exposed left side of the man's neck. His thumb depressed the plunger. Beechum's hands clawed, his manicured fingertips ineffective against the polyester windbreaker and gloves sheathing Toxin. The senator bucked in his seat, but Toxin held firm.

Right makes might.

He hummed a tune that would fill the final two and a half minutes of Beechum's pathetic life.

"HE'S SUPPOSED TO BE HERE BY EIGHT-THIRTY, AFTER STAYING UP late with friends?" Holt made his doubt and suspicion clear. He was having what his nine-year-old son Theo would have called an opposite day—if Theo had been where he was supposed to be this beautiful Saturday morning. Everything that was supposed to go smoothly was as lumpy as his mother's oatmeal, starting with Holt showing up to pick his son up from his parents' house, only to find they'd given Theo permission to sleep over at a friend's house the night before. "Didn't he know I'd be picking him up?"

His mother set down a bowl of steaming scrambled eggs next to a plate heaped with pancakes, freeing her hands to flutter about. "We asked him to be home by ten." Anxiety was evident in the edge in her voice and her jerky movements, but Betty Patterson never let anyone see her sweat. His mother had an agenda—and it smelled suspiciously like an intervention. The expansive breakfast so artfully arranged on the table was the bait.

"Ten?" He could have gotten two more hours of case analysis done.

Betty's gaze went to her plate. "We were hoping to talk to you. We never get a chance to sit down together. You're always rushing this way or that."

Holt's father pushed his plate aside. "Oh, for God's sake, Betty," Ron muttered. "You'd think he was some stranger. Just tell him."

Betty glared at Ron before turning a miserable look on Holt. "We're worried. You're not okay, and it's time you admitted it and let us help you. It's been nearly a year."

Holt laid his fork down on his plate, leaving the rest of his pancake sitting there, soaking up a puddle of syrup. The sweet smell of maple was suddenly abhorrent, and his stomach clenched.

His mother couldn't seem to sit still. She rose and retrieved the coffeepot from its perch on the counter, then returned to the table and refilled everyone's mugs. Just what Holt needed, more caffeine to amp up his racing pulse.

"And in the meantime, Theo is also suffering," Betty continued. "More so, since it seems he's lost his father too."

Theo had lost a mother and Holt had lost a wife and a good friend. Yeah, the world was sometimes a shitty place. But Theo hadn't lost his father. "I'm here for him." Holt was unable to keep the defensiveness from his voice.

"On the weekends, yes. And on nights that you're not working late, which isn't all that often."

"He knows I'm only a phone call away."

"He knows nothing of the sort. In fact, he's been acting out at school, trying to get your attention."

"He's nine. It's normal for kids his age to engage in pranks."

"And Theo is a bright boy who shouldn't have to go to summer school, and yet that's where he's spending his time."

Better there than with his father. Holt smashed the thought. At his elbow, his phone rang, jostling against the table where it sat. Relief flooded him until he realized the call must be from work. On a Saturday morning, that was never a good sign. It looked like today's metaphorical oatmeal had formed another lump. He picked up the phone.

The lines that bracketed his mother's mouth deepened. "Can't that wait? We're talking about your future, your son's future. Sara is very concerned."

Sara. The name set Holt's teeth on edge even as a memory of warm, soft lips slipped past his defenses. He stuffed it away. "It's work. I'll just be a moment."

He went out the sliding door onto the patio and took a deep breath of cool, summer-morning air. Freedom. He didn't want to discuss his future. He was just starting to get his bearings in an Elizabeth-less world. His wife had been a bright light, a firecracker that added spark to the monotony. For the past few months, he'd finally been able to climb out of bed each morning without an anchor weighing his chest down. But flashes of the past and his failure to save Elizabeth sometimes left him curled into the fetal position. Was *that* what his parents wanted to hear? It wasn't something he particularly wanted to share.

He answered the phone before it could go to voicemail. "Dr. Patterson."

"Good morning, Holt. Your assistance has been requested." Damian Manchester's voice was deep and sure and rarely fluctuated. The man was all business, but he was damn good at that business. As one of Damian's employees, Holt appreciated that.

"Where and when?"

"Here in Chicago. Now. The CPD found a body they believe is linked to two other murders over the past several months. They called us because the latest victim is high profile."

Us was the Society for the Study of the Aberrant Mind, otherwise known as SSAM, a private organization that assisted law enforcement agencies in hunting repeat violent offenders. Another function of SSAM was to teach the public to both recognize danger and avoid it. Holt's role as a profiler—a mindhunter who delved into the minds of the criminals they hunted—was more focused on detection than prevention.

"The victim?"

"Illinois State Senator Roy Beechum."

"A politician?" Damn. It would be a particularly sticky case. Profiling potential suspects could be complicated by myriad interested parties with their own agendas.

"I'm sending you the details now. Head over to the scene ASAP. I want you to get the lay of the land while the coroner's still there."

Holt hung up and surveyed the backyard that was as familiar as his hand. Summer barbecues and winter snowmen. Growing up in the suburbs north of Chicago had given him a childhood blessed with all four seasons and oblivious to the dangers in the real world. His mother was a gardener and landscape designer, constantly surrounded by all things lovely. His father, who'd been a police officer with the Evanston Police Department for thirty-two years before retirement, had, one day when Holt was nine, sat him down and told him all about the dangers of the world. *I should do the same thing with Theo.* Holt's throat tightened. Of course, the kid already knew about loss and grief.

"Holt?" His mother stepped out onto the patio. Her eyes brimmed with concern. "Is everything okay?"

His heart softened. He shouldn't have been so hard on his parents. He'd probably given them good reason to worry that he was slipping into a depression. It had been a very real possibility for weeks after Elizabeth's death, especially as it had followed many months of chemo and radiation. But he was getting his feet under him.

"Yeah." He tucked his phone into his pocket. "Just got a new case."

"We don't mean to chase you away by talking about Theo's future."

"It's just hard to think about the future, period. But I'm starting to. I promise."

"We love having Theo here. You know that." They'd set up the arrangement when Elizabeth's health had taken a nosedive after the third round of chemo had failed. Theo stayed with Betty and Ron whenever Holt was working odd hours. Luckily, they didn't live more than fifteen minutes from his place, or from Theo's school.

"I know. And I miss seeing him more. I do," he said when his mother continued looking at him with concern. "But my job is no place for a kid." And what the hell did that say about his life choices? With Elizabeth around, it had been manageable. Sane. But the kind of hours—and cases—Holt worked weren't optimal for raising his son alone.

His mother stepped forward and embraced him. Her lilac scent flooded him with memories of a secure, happy childhood. But the subtle jiggle in his pocket from his phone reminded him Damian's email, with the details of the horror he would be facing today, had arrived in his inbox.

He squeezed his mother and stepped away, bending to brush her creamy cheek with a kiss. "I have to go. Duty calls."

"We didn't get to discuss Theo. Sara says—"

Holt stepped away and moved toward the house. "Sara doesn't know everything." When he'd first gotten to know Sara, she'd struck him as intelligent, thoughtful and funny. He'd sensed something special about her. He'd been wrong.

His mother inhaled sharply, then followed him inside as he retreated from the argument. "She's excellent as the Academy's director. And she really cares about Theo. Since you won't return her calls, I've had the pleasure of getting to know her while we talk about my grandson's issues."

"Theo doesn't have any *issues*. He's in transition, dealing with a major life change. It's normal."

"Whatever happened between you and Sara and Elizabeth is in the past. Having her in Theo's life was what Elizabeth wanted."

But his trusting mother didn't know the full score. Before she'd died, Elizabeth had finally forgiven her former best friend, but he didn't see why he had to.

"Theo needs you. Sara says he's had more issues at school. The fact that a bright kid like him even had to take summer school should have told you something was wrong."

Holt heaved a sigh. "He seems okay to you, though, right?"

His mother hesitated before nodding. "He's okay at home, but at school…"

"Good. Look, I promise if Theo's *issues* worsen, I'll contact his teachers. Right now, I have to get to work." He gave his mother a sheepish look.

She sighed. "You want us to keep Theo for the day?"

"That would be great. If it weren't so important…"

"But it is. One day, though, you're going to reassess your priorities and realize experiencing every aspect of Theo's childhood is— or should have been—important too."

THANKFULLY, THE HEAT OF THE SUMMER DAY DIDN'T PENETRATE THE stark confines of the concrete building, especially on the basement sublevel. The parking garage was cool, dark and smelled of stale motor exhaust and death.

The area had been cordoned off by the CPD, an easy feat since the government building the garage lay beneath was closed up tight on the weekends. There were no other cars, no curious bystanders. At least something was going right today.

As Holt approached the only car and the few people gathered there to process the scene, he nodded to the detective who stood to the side. The other man's scowl wasn't exactly a warm-fuzzy greeting. Of course, he'd probably been stuck in this place for hours and now Holt was treading on his territory. Judging by the cold welcome, SSAM must have been called in by one of his superiors. Holt was accustomed to the lack of appreciation of his talents and let the man's assessment roll off him. In the end, what mattered was apprehending a murderer.

Behind him, the coroner was squeezing into the passenger seat of a black Mercedes, careful of any evidence, assessing the body in the position it was found before it was removed and taken to the morgue. Talk about up-close and personal.

Holt offered his hand to the detective. "Dr. Holt Patterson. My specialty is forensic psychology."

The detective accepted his hand with a clammy grip. He was shorter than Holt's six-foot-two, but the guy's paunch made him twice as wide. "Detective Wayne McDowell. My specialty is catching murderers." His tone held a degree of sarcasm that Holt chose to ignore.

"Then let's get to it."

McDowell jerked his head toward the Mercedes. A crime scene technologist circled, taking pictures of the car and the garage. Judging by the coroner's actions, the body and the car interior had already been extensively photographed and processed. "Victim is Roy Beechum. State senator with an office upstairs. Worked late yesterday. Was found this morning as the weekend cleaning crew arrived. They've been questioned and cleared."

"Any suspects?"

"I suppose that's why you're here. Ask anybody around here and nobody hated the man. Christ, one of the cleaning ladies was actually in tears when she found out. At forty-five years old, Beechum was young, attractive and relatively competent. What's not to like? In fact, recent polls showed he has the highest approval rating of any Illinois state senator in history. Happy marriage too. Nineteen years. Nuclear family with a son and daughter in high school. No rumors of shady side dealings, at least nothing we know of yet."

"Why didn't his wife report him missing?"

"Apparently Beechum was due to leave town last night. She didn't expect to see or hear from him until today."

Holt glanced into the dark recesses of the garage. Sure enough, a camera hung in the corner near the elevator. *Hallelujah.* "Video surveillance should give us more."

"We have someone processing it."

"If you don't mind, SSAM has an expert who can help out too. Einstein has a lot of experience."

"Einstein?"

"Just a nickname. But an accurate one."

McDowell eyed him a moment, then sighed. "Sure. I'll have someone send a copy over."

The coroner was now standing beside the car, pulling his gloves off. The yellowish light of the garage glowed against his bald spot as he joined them. He nodded a hello to Holt before turning his attention to McDowell. "Same signs of struggle, same style wound, same weapon of choice as the previous two scenes. I'd say your guess about this being the same killer has merit."

"Fuck. That's what I thought. Thanks, Rick." The detective dropped any lingering signs of an attitude as he turned back to Holt. Lines formed across his wide forehead. "We found black fibers under a few of Beechum's broken nails, but I doubt it'll lead anywhere. Just like the others. This murderer doesn't leave any traceable evidence behind, except for what he wants us to find."

"Which is?"

"A hypodermic needle and syringe. Other than the weapon, he's careful. Methodical. And deadly. Beechum wasn't the first victim, or the second. And I'm guessing he won't be the last. *That's* why you're here, Dr. Patterson. We suspect we have a serial killer on our hands, and I'll be damned if I have any idea who's next on his list."

THEO PATTERSON'S CREATIVITY WAS OFF THE CHARTS BUT SARA couldn't say that. Not yet, anyway. As director of the Hills Boys' Academy, she had to hide her surprise behind a mask of disapproval as he and his science teacher faced off across the desk from her. It wasn't even ten in the morning and her Monday was veering off a cliff. Summer was supposed to have a more relaxed atmosphere with fewer students around, yet this was Theo's fourth time in her office. There was clearly more going on here.

"This—" Mr. Lockhart, a valued professor at the Academy, shook a spiral notebook in Sara's face, "—is why he's going to be held back and forced to retake fourth grade. Summer school is his chance to finally pass this class, yet he'd rather doodle about nothing than learn something useful."

She bit back the defense that sprang to her lips. The doodles had hardly been aimless. Given Theo's youth and lack of training, they were amazing. In a comic book format, the boy had created an entire cast of unique characters that told a coherent and compelling story. Sure, it had elements of violence, and she would speak to him about that, but at least the notebook was a healthy outlet.

Sara took Exhibit A from Lockhart before he could shove it under her nose again and tucked it into a drawer of her desk. Theo's groan was audible, but one sharp look from her quelled the outburst she knew was brewing. The boy showed signs of his father's intelligence and his mother's devil-may-care attitude. Still, she had a soft spot for the son of her best friend. More than that, she'd made a promise before Elizabeth had died.

"Thank you for bringing this to my attention, Mr. Lockhart. You can return to your class now." Sara's words had the man's jaw dropping.

"You're going to let him get away with this?"

"Absolutely not. He's staying so we can have a little chat."

"Chat?" Lockhart's neck turned bright red.

"I understand how serious this is, and you can be sure I'll be addressing it."

"I've spoken to his other teachers, and we all agree his attention span is equal to a gnat's and nowhere near par for this school. Punishment is the only acceptable recourse."

Sara rose from her chair and came around the desk to stand toe-to-toe with Lockhart. Though he had a few inches on her average frame, he took a step back. "As director, my goal is to act in the best interests of the school as well as its students. I assure you, I plan to. I take my job and the reputation of this school very seriously. Don't ever doubt that. Will there be anything else?"

"No, uh...no." Lockhart glared at Theo. "I'll expect that extra work on my desk by the end of the week."

As the door closed behind Lockhart, Sara retreated behind her desk, then dropped into her chair. She picked up the phone and dialed the outer office, where Cheryl, efficient as always, picked up immediately.

"Shall I hold your calls?" her secretary asked, a hint of amusement in her voice. Sara added mind reader to the list of Cheryl's talents.

"Yes, please. Thank you." She put the phone back on its cradle and eyed Theo.

After a moment of quiet, he lifted his head to meet her gaze. "I thought we were going to *chat*."

She didn't miss the sarcasm slathered in a thick layer over that comment. "We are. But a conversation requires two participants, and our previous experience together suggests you won't exactly be eager to talk."

Theo shrugged. "Not much to say."

"I disagree, but I think you'd rather communicate in other ways." She pulled the notebook from her drawer and laid it on the desk between them. "You're very talented."

"Thanks." His mumble was reluctant, but she caught the glint of pride in his eyes before he glanced down at his lap. When he looked up again, the seriousness of his gaze immediately brought Holt to mind. Her heart squeezed. "Can I have my notebook back?"

"No." Just like that, she felt their tremulous connection break. "At least, not yet. Let's talk about the content. Your story has a lot of violence."

Theo rolled his eyes. "They have to fight. They're an army of mutants who battle the minions of death. They're not just going to lie down and take a beating."

Sara wondered if Theo realized how his comic illustrated his own frustrations, fears, and pain of the past year and a half. He'd probably channeled all those deep emotions into this creative outlet. "You're right. It's hard to fight evil forces without a battle or two. But we don't approve of violence here at the Academy. I have to be sure you don't intend to act out any of these fantasies."

Theo looked surprised. "I would never hurt anyone for real."

"I'm glad to hear that."

"So, can I have my notebook now?"

Sara wanted to give in, but there was no better opportunity to connect with Elizabeth's son. "How about I make you a deal?"

His eyes narrowed in suspicion. "What kind of deal?"

"I'll return your notebook if you promise me one thing."

His response was swift. "Deal."

She held up a hand. "You haven't even heard the deal yet. You'll meet with me on Friday afternoons, after your summer school class, for the rest of the term."

He scowled. "To do extra homework or something?"

"No. You'll be working on a special project with me. I hope you'll share your notebook with me too."

"You *want* me to work on my story?" Surprise chased the frown from his face.

"Absolutely. But if your grades don't improve and your teachers don't stop complaining, we'll have to chat about other ways to curb your distractions—maybe the extra homework or chores you mentioned. Do we have a deal?"

"Sure." Theo accepted the hand she reached across the desk toward him and punctuated the agreement with a tentative smile.

Again, Sara thought of Holt and his reluctant grins. He'd always been serious in a thoughtful, distracted, studious way. But when he smiled, it seemed to be filled with boyish wonder or mischief. She wished she could forget that smile.

"So, that's it?" Theo asked. "That's my punishment?"

"Nice try, but there's more. This is the fourth time you've been sent to my office in the last few weeks—"

"—because my teachers have no sense of humor—"

"—and I'm seeing a pattern here. A disturbing pattern that has to end now, before school rules require I expel you." She stifled a smile as Theo paled. At least the kid wanted to be here. "Pranks, cutting class, and distractions like comic books...I *am* going to have to call your dad. He might decide on an additional consequence."

"He won't answer." Where other kids might have sounded

triumphant at the prospect of getting out of further punishment, Theo sounded sad. Worse, she suspected he was right. That certainly had been the case in the previous instances she'd attempted to reach Holt. She'd ended up discussing things with Theo's grandparents, with whom Theo seemed to spend most of his spare time anyway. At least they'd been concerned and supportive.

Hoping Theo was wrong this time, she dialed the number she found in his contact information. The phone rang and went to voicemail once again. Holt's recorded voice requested she leave a message.

Keep it professional, no matter how much you want to wring his neck. "This is Sara at the Academy. Theo is in my office once again. Please call me at your earliest convenience so we can arrange a parent-teacher conference. It's imperative that you contact me." She left her number, hung up and met Theo's gaze.

To his credit, Theo didn't back down, didn't look away. There was wisdom beyond his years in those hazel eyes, tinged with pain. His shrug was deceptively casual. "Told you."

CHAPTER 2

August

The feel of the H&K pistol in Holt's hand was a comfort. As ex-law enforcement, Ron Patterson had taught his son how to fire a gun—and instilled a healthy respect for the weapon—at an early age. Holt hoped to teach Theo similar lessons one day soon. In the meantime, retreating to the basement of the SSAM building where Damian had constructed a firing range was therapy. Holt had some serious kinks to work out of his mood.

He'd had his hands on the three supposedly connected murder cases for a couple of weeks now, and most of his attempts to profile the killer had involved reading through the interviews already on file and re-interviewing people linked to the victims. Tedium *ad nauseum.*

Add his latest discussion with Theo's science teacher Mr. Lockhart a few days ago to the mix and Holt was not a happy camper.

Theo was a smart kid but apparently very distracted and still struggling to get his grades up. And, according to Lockhart, Sara was compounding the problem by coddling Theo. Perhaps it was time to try a different school. Elizabeth had wanted Theo to attend the Academy, where her friend could help look out for him, and Holt had honored that. But surely she wouldn't have continued to send Theo there if it wasn't the right environment for him.

"Tough day?" Fellow SSAM agent Max Sawyer had to stand at his side and shout the words to be heard through Holt's ear protection.

Holt pulled the gear off and let it circle his neck. "Sometimes I do my best thinking down here." Except today it wasn't working.

Max nodded. His specialty at SSAM was weaponry, and this basement level, which housed the employees' gun safe as well as a target practice area and a gym, was his domain. He kept SSAM agents up to speed on their shooting skills, and sometimes his training extended to the public, particularly in weapon use and safety, but he was also ex-special forces. Though he wasn't a profiler, a sharp brain lay within the good-ole-boy Texan. Perhaps it was time to invite a different perspective.

"Hey, do you have a minute?" Holt asked.

Max flipped his hand up to check his watch. "About an hour, as a matter of fact."

"Meet me upstairs in five." Holt cleaned and put away his equipment, locking the gun away in the community safe. A short while later, Holt used his palm print and a key-code to gain entrance to the west wing, which housed their offices.

"What's this about?" Max followed Holt into the conference room.

"I could use a fresh pair of eyes. Latest case involves three murders we believe are connected."

Max stood at the SSAM conference room table and studied the crime scene evidence Holt had set out that morning, hoping a global look at all the little pieces would help the puzzle slide together. Photos of each of the three murder scenes were laid out in an organized manner.

A few minutes later, Max frowned. "I can see why you're struggling. Victims of different ages, genders, occupations. It's as if he threw some darts at a board and these were the unlucky winners."

Holt was relieved he wasn't the only one to see the complications. A doctorate in psychology, special training with the FBI Behavioral Analysis Unit, and years of experience hunting big, bad killers with various police departments across the United States, and Holt still failed to see a pattern. "A CEO, a doctor and a politician."

"Sounds like a bad joke. A CEO, a doctor, and a politician walk into a bar…"

"Coffee?" Becca Haney entered the room, a tray in her hands. She had the petite frame and graceful movements of a fairy princess, but her short, sassy, blond hair and the gun at her waist quickly relieved one of that impression.

"Thank you." Grateful for the break, Holt took the tray from Becca and set it on a side table. He'd been so immersed in the investigation he was seeing the photos in his sleep. Which meant he wasn't getting enough sleep. He took a cup and dumped in the contents of two sugar packets. Without looking up, Max accepted the cup Becca handed him.

She stood beside Max and scanned the evidence. "The drug?"

"A blend of neurotoxins," Holt said. "Our lab is analyzing it in case there's something unique enough to lead somewhere. From the previous two crime scenes, the CPD's lab determined the components are used for industrial purposes and can be purchased from any of several commercial chemical facilities."

"Scary thought. What about the delivery system?"

"One needle and syringe was recovered from each of the scenes. Hypodermics available at any pharmacy or medical supply company."

"Damn."

"Exactly."

Becca slapped Max on the shoulder, which was at the level of her head. "Well, I'll leave you experts to it then. I'm off to play bodyguard." A SSAM security expert, Becca often guarded at-risk, sometimes high-profile people.

"For?"

"A wealthy business buddy of Damian's who's had a couple of death threats. I've got to go get dressed up for some fancy party."

Max smirked. "Must be hard being you."

"Somehow I suffer through." Becca wriggled her fingers over her shoulder as she walked out.

Holt's gaze went back over the items on the table, landing on the pictures of the hypodermic needles. The real things were locked up in the CPD evidence locker after the crime lab had finished with them. The media was pressuring him for interviews, profiles and answers. Answers he didn't have. "Becca may be on to something. Maybe I should get SSAM's crime lab to hook up with CPD's. Have them go over the older needles one more time."

Max straightened and took a gulp of coffee. "What for? We have a detailed report of the contents, and the chemical breakdown."

"That covers the inside, but not the outside."

"Prints on the needles, you think?"

"No. They tested for those and found them clean. I'm wondering if there are traces of other chemicals. Something that would indicate where these cocktails were mixed. Maybe they were made in a lab that has other specific uses."

"I can check with my street contacts. See if any of the illegal drug labs are known to mix special requests."

"Do that."

Max took out his phone and sent a quick text, then tucked it away again. "I should hear something in the next twenty-four. What else have you got?"

"Let's review the victims." Holt learned more about the killer by profiling the victims and the crime scenes than he did searching for the bad guy. After all, there was a reason a killer chose the people he did, even if the reason was convenience. "The first—"

Max arched a brow. "That we know of."

"—was found slumped in his chair in his office at Tech Innovations in early January. Joseph Kurtz was the CEO. Fifty-three years old. At first, everyone thought the death was natural—heart attack or something—but he had been relatively healthy." The coroner had found a small bruise on Kurtz's neck, which led to the tox screen that showed cause of death hadn't been a simple heart attack. Irregular blood chemistry and the presence of neurotoxins showed Kurtz was poisoned. "When foul play was suspected, police interviewed his coworkers and associates. A cleaning lady admitted she'd found an empty syringe under the desk and thrown it away. Thankfully, they recovered it from the trash. His employees seemed to think Kurtz was competent, but not particularly likeable."

"I assume his family was investigated?"

Often it was someone close to the victim who perpetrated such a violent crime. Sometimes the line between love and hate was a fine one.

"Yes. Married, and though it wasn't a happy marriage, they tolerated each other. His wife complained Kurtz worked too much, but I don't think she'd kill him and then throw suspicion elsewhere by killing two more people. Besides, Kurtz was much taller, heavier and stronger than her, and he was injected in the neck."

"So we're looking for a strong, relatively tall male."

"Yes, and probably someone Kurtz knew."

"Either that or the killer snuck up on him. To get that close in a private office without a fight…"

"Interviews of everyone who'd come close to Kurtz in the weeks before his death didn't lead to any strong suspects."

Max picked up a picture from the table. "And the second victim?"

"Dr. Sheila Brown was found late on Valentine's Day, outside a bar, sprawled on her stomach near her car in the parking lot. Thirty-four-year-old oncologist who worked at Mercy Hospital. Well-liked. Had an active social life, when she could squeeze in the time. Also injected in the neck."

"But she put up a fight."

"The defensive wounds—broken fingernails, bruising across her torso, and a black fiber remnant in her teeth—clued the ME in, so there were extra tests done. Bingo, same neurotoxins found in her bloodstream."

"No sign of sexual assault?"

"None."

Max set her picture on the table away from the others. It was a smiling portrait of a healthy woman, taken from the medical directory at Mercy. "She was an attractive lady."

Holt had thought the same thing. "These attacks aren't sexual in nature. The killer's after another kind of power, or has a different motive altogether—revenge, greed, covering up something else..." Holt had been through the list of possibilities countless times, but the picture was still hazy.

Max lifted a photograph from among those of the third crime. "And then there's the politician. Even though he was state-level, definitely a powerful position. How would killing Beechum give the *killer* power?"

"It might not be a literal shift in power, just something the killer experiences. A kind of post-kill high."

"I get it." As an experienced covert operative, Max would know what an adrenaline high felt like, and possibly what it felt like to kill a person, maybe even with his bare hands.

"Forty-five-year-old Illinois State Senator Roy Beechum was physically fit and could have fought back. I think the killer learned from Dr. Brown's resistance and ambushed him. But he had to have lain in wait for hours. Like the others, Beechum had been stabbed in the neck. The killer was hiding in the backseat of his car and waited for the opportunity to attack with minimal risk to himself. There were no prints in the car or on the door handles. We even checked the rearview and side-view mirrors, assuming he'd turned them to watch the elevator doors from where he'd crouched. Einstein reviewed the video, and the killer had adjusted the mirrors before breaking into the car, but still no prints. No hairs, either. In the video, you can see the killer from behind and he's wearing a hood. Presumably, this also kept him from leaving hairs behind at the scene. This guy is careful, and may even have shaved his body to avoid leaving DNA. Still, we were able to determine he's Caucasian, and estimate he's about five-eleven and one hundred-eighty pounds." Holt tapped a fingertip on the table. "What I can't figure out is why Beechum? He was relatively new to the legislature."

"Hardly had time to make enemies."

"I'm sure he had plenty of time along the road to election, and probably in the positions he held before, since he worked his way up to the State Senate." Holt's gaze traveled over the table. "But how did all three of these people make the *same* enemy?" It was the question that had been bugging him since he'd been handed the case.

As if hearing his thoughts, Max spoke the question. "What leads have you got?"

"Nothing."

"Come on, Holt. You're thinking too hard. What's your gut telling you?"

"This guy wants to be noticed. He's got an agenda he wants known, but on his schedule."

"What makes you say that?"

Holt met Max's curious gaze. "Instinct. Maybe because the method of killing is so dramatic and different. And, despite being so careful not to leave personal evidence, the fact he leaves the needles at the scene…it smacks of someone who wants to be noticed. He wants someone to figure him out."

"A drama queen?"

"Exactly." An idea bloomed. Holt grinned. "Every drama queen craves a spotlight. Maybe I should oblige him."

"WHERE ARE WE GOING?" THEO ASKED, BENDING HIS HEAD TO AVOID a tree branch.

"I thought we'd take our chess game outside today." Sara smiled as he looked back in surprise. "This is our last Friday meeting. Last day of summer school. I thought we could make it special. Are you excited to have a week off before the fall semester starts?" She laid out a plaid blanket beneath a tree on the far edge of the school's property.

He shrugged. "I guess. This is really where you want to play chess today?"

"I was kind of thinking that, yeah." Their chess chats, as she'd come to think of them since she'd begun teaching Theo chess, had become a regular Friday occurrence over the past couple weeks. With the same attention to detail he'd used in creating his comic book, Theo had taken to the game in a flash. She was going to miss the way he chewed his lip as he studied new moves or drummed his finger against his knee when he was thinking particularly hard.

"Where's the board?"

She slid her bag off her shoulder and sat cross-legged on the blanket. "I have a miniature version for travel." She took out the chess pieces as he sat down opposite her in the shade of the elm. "Do you have something for me?"

He fished in his own backpack for a tattered notebook and handed it over with a triumphant look. "I finished it last night."

"How about you set up our game while I read?"

Sara was soon absorbed in Theo's story, fascinated by the chal-lenges he'd thrown at his heroes, and the way they'd united to overthrow the villain. But what most gripped her was the relationship between one of the heroes and the guy who supposedly ran the group. "Agent Z doesn't seem to like his employer, Mister X, much, does he?"

"Yeah, X is kind of a mystery to everyone."

Kind of like Theo's dad was a mystery to Theo? Or was she reading too much into things? Still, she would love for Holt to read this. "Are you going to show this to your dad?"

"Maybe." Another shrug.

"Well, I think you should. It's excellent. How about our game?" The next fifteen minutes was spent mostly in silence as they moved and counter-moved. Theo had her in check but didn't seem to want to take his final turn. He had to have seen the opening she'd accidentally left him. "I think you can capture my king."

Theo nodded but still didn't do anything. "Maybe we should call it a draw and have a rematch in the fall?"

"If that's what you'd like. I bet you'll have more of your story to show me then too. In fact, that's what I'm hoping." Sara reached into her bag and pulled out the leather journal and drawing pencils she'd spied in the bookstore last week.

Theo's eyes widened. He took the gift and flipped through the unlined, blank pages. His grin bloomed. "I think I already have an idea for a sequel."

"Maybe we'll get to know a little more about Mister X?" She had hoped Holt and Theo could spend more time together this summer, especially after Theo's difficulties in class. Unfortunately, Holt hadn't seemed able to make the time. "Is your father coming to the Labor Day picnic?"

Theo's eyes shuttered. "I don't think he knows about it."

"Did you tell him?"

"It wouldn't matter if I did. He's usually busy."

"But the picnic's on a Saturday. He has a day off now and then, right?"

"Maybe. If something doesn't come up."

Sara didn't know if she could safely push Holt into coming to the picnic. They had reached a polite, unspoken truce. He ignored her but was acknowledging weekly updates from Theo's teachers. Sara was trying to stay out of it.

She gathered their things, then stood and brushed off the seat of her pants. "Your ride should be here any minute now to pick you up."

When she and Theo reached the school and entered the cool foyer, Sara was brought up short by the sound of raised voices.

"He simply doesn't have the grades," Mrs. Robertson, the high-school-level English teacher, was telling a parent. John Rochard. The Rochards had a long history of attendance and success at the Academy.

"Can I help with something?" Sara asked. Behind John, a tall boy—Neil Rochard, a rising senior—and his younger brother, Jeremy, stood with identical slumped postures. Theo moved over to Jeremy, who was in his classes.

John's gaze raked over Sara. He immediately dismissed her and turned back to the teacher. "Neil deserves an A in your class. He's done everything you asked."

Sara stepped beside Mrs. Robertson in a show of support. "I'm certain that if Neil deserved an A, that's what he would have received." She looked at Neil, whose gaze skittered away and then locked on the polished wood floor.

"Neil is a good kid," Mrs. Robertson explained, sympathy in her voice. "And yes, he did the work, but not on time. And not to the standards of an A student."

But John wasn't listening. His attention was now fully on Sara, who'd dared to butt in and contradict him. "You may not be aware, but my family has done great things for this school."

"I'm aware." Sara had heard from the board many times about the Rochard endowments. John's father was a prominent politician. "But that doesn't mean Neil gets a free ride." In her peripheral vision, Neil shoved his hands in his pockets. "Nobody does, not even the grandson of a United States Senator."

"You haven't heard the end of this." His cheeks flushed with outrage, John looked as if he would say more. Instead, he pressed his lips together and spun on his heel, heading to the door. His two sons fell into step behind him as if marching to their doom.

CHAPTER 3

Holt rushed up the steps toward the large oak door of the Academy. He was late. Again. Which meant Theo would likely give him more of the silent treatment.

Inside, he found Theo waiting for him, not looking at all upset. Unfortunately, that was because Sara was standing there with him. As she laughed at something Theo said, her blue eyes sparkled with all the colors of the sea. Her hair shifted against her shoulders, reflecting shades of yellow, gold and light brown. Every hair on her head, even her eyelashes, seemed to have been dipped in sunlight. His breath caught in his chest. He coughed to cover the moment of poetic insanity.

"Hey, bud, ready to go?" Holt reached for Theo's backpack.

Sara stepped into his path. "Well, hello, Dr. Patterson. I was keeping Theo company while we waited for you." Her expression was a combination of amusement and determination. Hell, he knew that look. She had an agenda. "Cutting it a little close, aren't you?"

Despite the bite beneath her words, the silk of Sara's voice slid over him like a caress. His gaze moved to her lips and his groin hardened. He chalked the weakness up to male hormones. Then again, no female had aroused his interest since Elizabeth. Sara's combination of quiet intellect, snarky humor, and subtle beauty were a seductive weapon. They always had been. Which was why she was so dangerous.

He jerked his attention away from her lush mouth. "I'm in a hurry."

He avoided the temptation to slip into a familiar pattern of banter with her, especially with Theo looking on with interest. Ten years ago, she'd had a wit as sharp as a samurai sword. He was curious if she still had it. *Curiosity killed the cat.* Better to stay away from the cream. He'd learned his lesson the first time.

"I have to be somewhere, so if you don't mind..." He nudged Theo. Thankfully, his son took the hint and headed out the open door and toward the car. Holt wasn't so lucky. Sara's hand touched Holt's arm, bringing him to a halt before he could get through the door. A memory of those slender fingers gliding along his jaw jolted through him. But she removed her fingers and the memory was gone in an instant.

"I happen to be pretty busy myself, up to my elbows in boys who've been cooped up all summer and ready to unleash themselves on the remainder of vacation. Theo is one of the afflicted."

"What's he done this time, Director? Doodling on his homework?" He arched a brow at her and watched her lips press together in irritation. He probably enjoyed her response more than he should.

She looked away. When she turned back, misery was heavy in her eyes. "Can't we put the past behind us? I don't know why you're still so angry with me, but it doesn't really matter in the grand scheme of things. What matters is Theo."

He took a deep breath and blew it out. "Agreed."

"Good."

He glanced at his watch. Time was slipping away. If he wanted to make the television interview, he had to leave now. His mind was already cartwheeling ahead to what he needed to say. They were going to show the footage from the parking garage surveillance video. Nothing gory. All it showed was someone disguised in a hooded windbreaker exiting the car four minutes after Beechum got into it. What they wouldn't show was the hours the man had lain in wait in that parking garage to kill Beechum. The killer was highly organized and dedicated to his mission, which worried Holt more than anything. He wouldn't be easy to catch. But maybe someone would recognize his walk, his posture —hell, even the windbreaker—*anything*.

He was betting the killer would come to him. Based on the "drama queen" assumption in the profile Holt had developed, this broadcast might be his best shot at catching him before he killed again.

"Look, I really do have an appointment," Holt told Sara. "Could you email me or something?"

She huffed out a laugh. "We both know that would go ignored. I wanted to invite you to...I mean..."

Her hesitance had him raising an eyebrow. He'd never known Sara to dance around an issue. Was she going to ask him out? The idea was both ludicrous—given their history—and enticing... which was also ludicrous. What was he thinking? He had to get out of here. "What?" he asked, not bothering to hide his impatience.

"I thought you'd want to know about the Academy's upcoming picnic. It's a week from tomorrow, and it's shaping up to be kind of a big deal among the students. Games and activities. Lots of food. It's a fun way to welcome the kids back to school, and I'm hoping it will become an annual tradition." She seemed to glow as she rushed through the explanation. When he didn't respond right away, her excitement faded. She frowned. "But if you're too busy to be there for Theo..."

"Ah, there's the Sara I know, trying to manipulate me using my emotions." Why couldn't he stop prodding her? They'd always been able to push each other's buttons, and he usually felt like a louse afterwards, which is why he avoided her.

Regrettably, the blue fire of her eyes dimmed. "And there's the psychologist *I* know. You think you know me...or knew me. It was one night, one mistake. Things weren't what they seemed ten years ago, and you certainly don't have a clue how they are now."

"What? You weren't trying to break up Elizabeth and me?"

She looked away. "I don't want to stroll down memory lane with you. I only deigned to pester Your Almightiness in order to beg you to put your saving the world on hold long enough to attend a picnic that might be important to your son. Theo said he wasn't going to ask you because you wouldn't come. I don't think he can stand another disappointment, not after the year he's had. Elizabeth would want you to come, for your son."

Holt's irritation flared. "Damn, Sara. Don't hold back."

Her chin lifted a notch. "Considering I've been trying to reach you for weeks, I figured I'd better lay it all on the line. I can keep my distance from you at the picnic, if that's what you're afraid of."

"I'm not that shallow." Or was he? Part of his conscience pricked at him. Hadn't part of him been avoiding most activities at the school because of her? And hell, didn't that make him feel like a dick when she was so ready to offer to make herself scarce at her own event, just so he could be there his son. He jerked out a nod. "I'll come. For Theo."

"Pinky swear?" She held up her hand, fingers folded except for her pinky, which stuck defiantly into the air. Her nails were neat and trim, and painted a soft seashell-pink. She silently dared him to commit.

He matched the determination in her eyes with a hard look of his own and linked his pinky to hers. "I'll be there." Liking the sizzle of contact a little too much, Holt untwined his finger and turned away.

He could have sworn she'd added, "It's about time," beneath her breath as he walked out. But maybe that was his conscience speaking up again.

Fifteen minutes later, he'd settled Theo in a soundproof room where he couldn't hear the news broadcast.

"You're on in two, right after the headline stories and a commercial break." The blonde with the heavy makeup—Sherrie or Sharon or something like that—placed her hand on Holt's arm as she spoke to him.

Whoa—a come-hither smile aimed in his direction? It had been years since he'd noticed one. But Shannon—yes, *that* was her name—didn't get his hormones racing. Maybe he was just getting old. At thirty-five, sometimes he felt more like fifty. He felt like he'd lived a lifetime in the past couple years.

Then again, there were certain people who made him feel like a twenty-year-old pulsing with energy again. *Sara. A pinky swear.* Christ, what had he been thinking? Letting any part of her touch him had led to near-constant thoughts of her on the drive to the station.

He forced his attention to the present. The anchorman had already been given strict instructions to ask questions from the script Holt had provided. As directed, the station had included the promise of an expert's profile of Chicago's latest serial killer in the commercial it ran several times a day. Not typically a gambler, Holt was betting his reputation that the killer would be watching along with most of Chicago when Holt finally delivered that profile.

He followed Shannon into the taping area. Some other woman removed his glasses and waved a makeup brush in his face, dusting his skin with beige powder. He resisted the urge to swat her away like a gnat.

Shannon was all business now, rattling off a list of dos and don'ts. "Look into the camera, or at Steve. Speak clearly. Be sure to mention your agency and the tip hotline often, even though the number will be at the bottom of the screen. Make sure to list the points our viewers should look for..."

He tuned her out. This wasn't his first rodeo. He'd delivered profiles of varying types and degrees to many different agencies around the world. This would be his first time on television, but, really, it was no different. He was hunting a killer and his goal was to make the public and law enforcement better prepared to help, or to defend themselves, should the need arise. He simply needed to keep in mind his audience—and hopefully the killer was among them.

He took his seat next to Steve Bollardi, the ageless anchor of Channel 7 News, who was diligently reviewing the questions Holt had prepared, displayed on the teleprompter. Someone immediately stepped forward to straighten the collar on Holt's suit.

A countdown signaled they'd be on the air in three, two, one...

Steve looked into camera one with a grim smile. "Welcome back to Channel 7 Nightly News. A new threat to Chicago citizens has recently been identified by local law enforcement. Tonight, we have forensic psychologist Dr. Holt Patterson here to discuss three murders and the man behind them. Dr. Patterson, what can you share with us about these cases?"

Here we go. One unprofessional asshole coming up.

Holt had decided this persona would be the best way to lure a killer he suspected suffered from severe egocentrism. "First of all, I'm not sure *man* is how I would characterize this *animal*. He is a creature without conscience. A monster. He's killed three innocent people." Calling the killer an *animal* and other names, and referring to his victims as *innocent,* was all part of Holt's strategy, but his pulse accelerated as instinct told him to shut up and run.

"Victim number one was a successful CEO," Holt continued. "I'm certain jealousy was a motive there. And the killer's inability to get victim number two, a female, to accept his sexual advances was most likely the reason he killed her. This final murder, Senator Roy Beechum, who was well-liked in his community, is clearly another example of the killer's impotence. The man we're hunting wasn't able to succeed in his career, or with women, so he's taking his frustration out on others who *are* successful."

"So you believe he's acting out of some kind of inferiority complex?"

"Yes. That, or he's crazy. Delusions of grandeur, probably." Inwardly, Holt winced at using such a nontechnical term as *crazy*.

"What can citizens do to avoid becoming a victim?"

They cued the videotape and showed the obscure image of Toxin getting into Beechum's Mercedes, then fast-forwarded to him exiting the car a few minutes after Beechum got in.

"Be aware of your surroundings," Holt said. "Don't walk blindly into potentially dangerous areas. This guy is too cowardly to strike by the light of day. He attacks at night, or when a place is deserted. And if you know of anyone suspicious, or the man in this video clip looks familiar, please contact our tip hotline at 1-800-555-JUST. Together, we'll find justice for these poor victims."

Steve wrapped up the interview with some parting comments. The interview had gone according to plan. Holt had appeared pompous and described the killer as an impotent, pitiful, sexually frustrated animal. Only Holt, Max and the local CPD knew the truth—that there were no clear ties that linked these victims other than the way they'd died.

Steve sent the show to commercial break and Holt stepped into the wings.

"There's a call for you," Shannon said. "CPD just transferred it from the hotline to your cell phone."

Just like clockwork.

Toxin did a hundred push-ups before calling the stupid hotline. Whoever this Patterson guy was, he was in serious need of straightening out. But Toxin had to be smart. He couldn't rush in, half-cocked and full boil. He'd take a quick breath or two to focus.

Thus, the push-ups. Toxin did fifty more just to show he was in control.

Animal. Impotence. The worst of all was his *innocent* victims. *Like hell.*

He jabbed the numbers into his throwaway cell phone. He wasn't stupid. Calls could be traced. He'd have to replace the phone, but it would be worth it to set the record straight. Besides, it was high time the authorities had an idea who they were dealing with.

"CPD Tip Hotline. Do you have a tip to share?" The perky woman's voice grated on him, but he forced himself to smile and match her hopeful tone.

"Sure do," Toxin said. "But I'll only talk to the good doctor himself."

"Who?"

"Dr. Holt Patterson."

"I'm afraid that's—"

"Nothing's impossible, sweetheart. I know because I've taken those lives he's so intent on glorifying. Be a dear and patch me through."

"Just a moment." Her perky attitude had popped and deflated like a balloon.

Several minutes later, Toxin was about to drop and do another hundred push-ups to keep his cool when someone finally came on the line.

"This is Dr. Holt Patterson. With whom am I speaking?"

With whom... Pretentious fuck. "This is Toxin."

Patterson had the gall to laugh. "Wow, your parents must have hated you."

"It's the name I chose for myself. *I'm* in control of my destiny... and those of many people who aren't nearly as innocent as you indicated."

"And you use poison to kill people. I get it."

"I doubt you *get* anything." Toxin felt better already. The guy was a joke.

"Why don't you clear things up, then?"

"Oh, I don't think so. Since you're so smart and all… But start calling me Toxin, because I deserve some measure of respect."

"Okay, *Toxin,* tell me why you've taken up killing as a hobby."

"Cleaning up the streets of Chicago is a tough job, but somebody's got to do it."

"You killed a CEO, a pediatric oncologist, and a state senator. I hardly call that cleaning up."

"Then you have no clue what's really going on." Toxin hung up, satisfied he had nothing to fear from this fuck-up. "See you around *Doctor* Patterson."

DAMIAN MANCHESTER LOOKED ACROSS THE TABLE AT HOLT AND Max. Antagonizing a murderer hadn't been his strategy of choice, but he trusted the people he'd hired at SSAM.

"It was beautiful." Max grinned. "Too bad it didn't work."

"Not entirely, maybe," Holt conceded. "But I got some valuable information."

"You did your job," Damian told Holt. "And now we know your profile was on the right track. We're dealing with a smart individual. Smart enough to use a throwaway phone." Einstein hadn't been able to trace it.

Holt pulled his glasses off and rubbed the bridge of his nose. "*Toxin.* The fact that he calls himself that confirms he's egocentric. That's something we can use again."

"How?" Max asked.

"You were the one who said that the guy could be a drama queen. You may have been more right than we knew. He responded to my tactics, he believes he's doing what's right. He's delusional, but not in a clinical way because he's clearly functional too. He repeatedly indicated that he believed his victims guilty of something, as vermin he had to clean off the streets."

"But they're not," Max said. "They served the city in valuable roles."

"But not to Toxin. For whatever reasons, he saw a CEO, a doctor and a politician as threats, as polluting society. What's more, he sees himself as someone whose job it is to clean things up."

Damian nodded. "It's our job to figure out what those reasons are."

Understanding what drove people to murder wasn't simple. And understanding the mind—and predicting the next move—of a repeat violent offender such as a serial killer was even more difficult. Sometimes the murder spree continued until a group of people with a unique skillset teamed up to take the killer down. Bringing those professionals together was the reason Damian had started SSAM years ago. The reason he woke up every morning. To find the devils who got their kicks from killing. To find the monster who'd taken his daughter from him. At age thirteen, Sam had been the victim of a serial killer who'd never been caught. Never been brought to justice.

Never.

The word weighed heavy on his heart, but he maintained hope that *never* would become *someday*. But even if...*when*...the killer was found and made to pay, it would never bring back Sam. There was no *someday* where she was concerned.

CHAPTER 4

September

The breeze stirred a stray hair from its clip and sent it dancing against Sara's neck, tickling her skin. The barest chill in the air indicated fall wasn't far away. That, combined with the giddy feeling of success, had her smiling as she surveyed the grounds at the Academy. A winding strip of road led from the gothic architecture of the school perched on top of the hill to the main road a quarter mile away. Tall oaks cast growing shadows across the sloping green lawn where picnic tables covered with red-and-white-checked cloths had been cleared of the luncheon—a Labor Day weekend barbecue with all the trimmings.

Cheryl came over with two red plastic cups of lemonade and handed her one. "Looks like all those months of planning were worth it."

"As were the arguments with the board of directors." Sara took a sip that puckered her lips. Still, it was cool and refreshing. Before long, they'd be trading in iced tea and lemonade for hot apple cider. "Maybe they'll listen to me when I suggest the next change."

Cheryl raised a silver eyebrow. Her matronly appearance was compromised by the twinkle of mischief that was never far from her eyes. "And that would be?"

"You'll see." Visions of shaping the old mansion that had become the Academy decades ago—and hadn't changed much since—got Sara's creative juices flowing.

"I'm not sure the board knew what they were in for when they hired you." Cheryl chuckled, then gestured to a group of people seated at one of the picnic tables, watching the action in play on the football field they'd put in last summer. "But they seem to be enjoying themselves."

Several shouts of excitement rose from the direction of the field, where the students were engaged in a game of flag football. Sara tried to make out Theo. Her heart jumped into her throat as the ball came hurtling toward his face. He caught it, but lost his balance and landed face-first in the grass as he fought to hold onto the ball. She relaxed as he jumped up with a grin and held up the ball. He pulled a blade of grass from his bottom lip.

Her eyes sought out Holt, to no avail. She'd hoped he'd make it here for Theo's sake but his anger toward her was just too large to overcome. Apparently pinky swears didn't mean what they used to.

Cheryl clucked at Sara like a mother hen. "I've watched you talking with the parents, but your wheels are always spinning. Relax. Go play some of the games. Enjoy the kids. I think I'll try the dunk tank."

"I should have canceled that. It's a bit chilly, don't you think?"

"Nah. Lockhart has it comin'." With a wink, Cheryl headed across the lawn toward the booth where the science teacher was perched precariously on a slim wooden board, his khakis and polo shirt totally dry. Sara suspected Cheryl was about to rectify that. She grinned.

"Pretty smug, aren't you?"

Sara spun to face John Rochard, her palm pressed to her chest in surprise. She'd caught sight of him earlier and given him a wide berth. "Excuse me?"

His gaze took a slow trip over her. He smirked when she bristled. "You think you hold all the keys to the futures of these boys. Of *my* boy. Think again. Neil plans to go to an Ivy League college when he graduates. I've worked hard to make sure that happens."

"And earning Cs and Ds in half his classes will undo all of *your* hard work. Is that it?"

After Rochard had confronted Mrs. Robertson, Sara had gone back and reviewed Neil's grades. They'd sunk like an anchor since January. John's disdainful glance showed exactly who he thought was responsible for his son's struggles. *Her.* Unbelievable. There was something deeper going on with Neil.

"Glad we understand each other." John turned to leave.

"I'm afraid we don't." Her words had him swinging back to face her. His face was firm and cold as granite, but she straightened her spine. "I don't rig grades, if that's what you're suggesting. The boys get what they earn. If you want to help, Neil needs to sign up to take the SAT soon. And his teachers are offering to let him retake the classes in which he performed poorly in night school or at the community college, so that he doesn't fall behind. I've already told him this as well as sent the information to you in an email."

John's laugh was harsh. "Night school? During football season? And who do you expect will foot yet another bill? I don't think so."

"His grades have been in a steady decline for months. Has something changed in his home life?" She suspected that *something* was the Rochards' ugly divorce. A divorce that was being kept tightly under wraps yet provided grist for the rumor mill in the teachers' lounge. A divorce that even impacted John's father, Patrick Rochard, a distinguished military veteran who hoped to win re-election to the senate in November. She wondered if John recognized the role of his personal and family drama in Neil's problems.

"That's none of your damn business." He took a step closer and jabbed a finger at her. "Your business is getting the best opportunities in life for these boys. That's what we pay you for. See that you remember that. This school has a reputation for excellence and you're driving it into the ground."

In her peripheral vision, Sara caught sight of Theo approaching. "Miss Sara, are you okay?"

Hazel eyes laced with gold looked from her to John. Sara's lips felt like tight rubber bands that refused to curve, but she fought past it. "I'm fine, Theo. Did you get plenty to eat?" He nodded but his eyes, narrowed and untrusting, remained on John. "Why don't you play some kickball? It looks like they're forming a team."

Instead of leaving, Theo moved to her side. The smell of a boy who'd been outside all day—the scents of grass, perspiration, and fresh air that somehow cling to a child's skin—filled her nose and grounded her.

"Theo, I think you remember Jeremy's father, Mr. Rochard," she said. As if he sensed the anger and unwelcome in Rochard, Theo didn't do anything to greet the man. She nudged him gently with her elbow.

Theo looked up at her. "I'd like you to talk to my dad. He finally came."

"He did?" She resisted the urge to search for him. The thought of seeing Holt again, face-to-face, did funny, unwelcome things to her insides. "You should be spending time with him, then."

"Yes, but you should talk to him too."

She got the feeling he was trying to get her away from John. "I'll be over in a minute, once I finish my discussion with Mr. Rochard."

After a moment of staring down John, Theo moved away. He looked over his shoulder, but she waved him on. Soon, he was trudging down the grassy hill toward a stand of large oaks where Holt stood waiting.

Holt's gaze was on her. She was certain of it, though sunglasses hid his eyes. Tension radiated from his stance. Did he not approve of something? Despite the warm sunshine on her shoulders, she shivered. But as Theo joined him, Holt turned toward his son.

Rochard took a step closer to her and Sara's attention was immediately on him. His face was white with controlled anger. "Just so we're clear, Neil's grades *will* change. There had to be a computation error. Remember, my father is a United States Senator. He has a lot of influence. Neil *will* be getting into Harvard. Anything else would be unacceptable, and, ultimately, detrimental to this school." He got right in her face as he delivered his threat.

Bully. Sara bit her tongue and counted to three, tamping down her anger and refusing to back away.

"Then I guess we'll be seeing Neil in night school this semester." She forced her lips into a smile and turned to follow Theo. The breeze disguised the hitch in her breath. Walking worked the shakes out of her legs. She'd be damned if she'd let John see just how angry he'd made her.

HOLT STOOD IN THE SHADE AND WATCHED HIS SON STAND AT SARA'S side. Even from fifty yards away, he could see she had wriggled her way into Theo's heart. A twinge of jealousy was quickly followed by a pull of longing. He used to have that kind of relationship with Theo. Comfortable and easy. Now, the kid rationed smiles as if they were a limited stash of his favorite jelly beans. The red ones.

In the past few weeks, he'd sensed a shift in his son—a rekindling of interest in life. Theo had been spending an increasing amount of time in his room, working on some journal. Theo refused to show it to him, saying he'd already shown it to Miss Sara, and she'd approved. She'd accomplished what he hadn't, breaking through his son's defenses.

The man who'd been in conversation with Sara turned a glare on Theo. Even across the distance, Holt could sense the anger. It was evident in the stiff set of the guy's shoulders, in the way he leaned toward her, his fists clenched at his sides as he got right in her face. Holt was about to intervene when Theo turned and headed toward him. Holt's gaze, shielded by his prescription sunglasses, met Sara's. Holt thought he saw her shudder.

The breeze lifted Theo's hair as he stopped a few feet away from him. No hug, again. Holt swallowed his disappointment.

"Miss Sara said she'd come over in a minute." Theo's concerned gaze went back to her. The angry man stepped toward Sara and jabbed a finger in her face. Holt felt Theo stiffen beside him and moved his hand to his son's shoulder. She held her ground, as still as stone, stubborn determination shimmering off her. She ended their conversation with a taut smile before turning and walking toward Holt. The edge of her filmy skirt blew around her knees, emphasizing nicely shaped calves and slender ankles.

"You know her pretty well, right?" Theo asked. "Not just because of school, but because of Mom?"

"Yeah." He knew her about as well as he wanted to. *Liar.* At least one part of his body wanted to know her much better.

"But you don't like her?" Theo's question surprised Holt.

"What makes you say that?"

"You're different around her."

Probably because she made him remember. To feel things he didn't want to feel—regret, temptation, guilt. Longing. But as astute as his son seemed to be, there was no way he was going to share that with Theo. "Some things happened, a long time ago. Sometimes it's hard to let go of the past."

Theo seemed to consider that for a moment. "Mom did. She let go. Miss Sara said she was really happy when Mom and her became friends again. She said it feels good to let go of a grudge."

Apparently his son had been spending more time with Sara than Holt had realized if they'd talked about all that. Across the distance, the man she'd been speaking to headed in the opposite direction, his brisk gait and long strides indicating he was ticked off. Sara wrapped her arms around her middle as if to protect herself. If he were profiling the scene, he'd say she'd just survived a serious verbal exchange but suspected there was worse to come. The woman was in serious need of a hug. It shocked him that he cared. She'd always been prickly and annoyingly self-sufficient, like a cactus. But he supposed even a cactus needed a little nourishment once in a while.

Maybe that was what had drawn his introverted son to her. They both needed somebody. Elizabeth's words haunted him.

Theo needs someone who'll be there for him night and day. Your world, filled with serial killers, is no place for kids. Sara will take good care of him. And he'll be good for her.

Sara detoured to pick up a couple of cups from a nearby picnic table, then filled them from the spout on the upright cooler. She headed his way again, her butterscotch hair gleaming in the sunlight as strands of it got caught up in the wind. He tried to ignore the press of fabric against her curves when the breeze stirred again.

Her wide mouth bent into a smile as she reached them, but the smile didn't quite reach her eyes. Because of him, or because of the man she'd been speaking with? She held the cups out to them. "I brought these for you two. Saw Theo playing flag football earlier and thought he might be thirsty." Her blue eyes were warm like the waters of the Caribbean as they turned to his son.

"Thank you." Holt accepted the peace offering, then glanced at Theo. "He can't say enough positive things about you." He hadn't believed most of them.

"I'm glad you made it."

"I promised I'd be here."

"My faith in pinky-swears is restored." Her lips twitched. She seemed to recall their preteen audience and returned to formalities. "Theo's been working hard. I'm proud of him."

There was no eye-roll from Theo this time. She had him wrapped around her little—pinky—finger. Fooled, just as Holt had been once upon a time. "Well, that and five bucks will buy you a cup of coffee. It's hard work that'll pay off, and his teachers don't seem to think he's reaching his potential."

Beside him, Theo buried his face in his cup, attempting to disguise his hurt with a gulp of lemonade.

Shit. He'd blown it. Again. Trying to communicate with Theo this past year had been like negotiating a labyrinth—every turn felt wrong and led to more complications. He'd put his "dad hat" on when he should have been more encouraging.

Holt could see Sara biting back a scathing response that he probably deserved. But when she met his gaze, he was shocked to find empathy there. "Hard work is important. But so is passion about what you're working on. Has he shown you his journal?"

"No," Theo said. "He wouldn't get it. I gotta go. Have a good Labor Day, Miss Sara." He jogged toward the boys gathering on the athletic field for some type of game.

Sara's gaze followed Theo. "Must be tough raising him by yourself." Once again, her understanding shocked him. She caught his look and smiled. "Yes, I'm capable of understanding. Raising a child isn't easy. Alone, it must be much harder. I have a lot of respect for parents."

"Even *that* parent?" Holt tipped his head toward the man she'd been talking to, who was now in deep discussion with a group of starchy people at a picnic table.

Her eyes darkened. "Mr. Rochard?"

"Rochard? As in the U.S. Congressman?"

"Same family. Patrick Rochard is his father. And John Rochard's probably regaling the school board with tales of my incompetence as we speak." The stiff posture he'd witnessed earlier was back, as if she were steeling herself against attack. As the breeze lifted her hair, he had the sudden impression of an ancient Viking princess riding into battle.

"Hard to believe that's how Rochard's wasting this beautiful afternoon."

Her gaze met his. "And yet, it's likely the truth."

"That you're incompetent?" Holt asked in surprise. Sara was many things, but never incompetent.

She laughed—a soft, husky sound that tugged at something inside him. "No. That he's being an ass."

He studied her a moment. "You don't deserve that. You're good at what you do here. You're good with the kids. I've seen it with Theo."

"Thank you. Coming from you, that means a lot."

Because of their history.

Uncomfortable, she averted her gaze, looking at her toes. The same pink polish he'd seen on her fingers adorned the toes that peeked out from her sandals. A strand of hair blew across her cheek and he resisted the urge to reach out and tuck it behind her ear. "I'm sorry," she said.

"For what?" he prompted, curious which part made her feel guilty.

"All of it. Ten years ago, I never should have butted into Elizabeth's relationship with you. I just thought you were…"

"All wrong for her?" He couldn't fault her for that. At the time he'd thought the same thing. And when he'd responded to Sara's unexpected kiss, his doubts had only intensified. But Elizabeth had assured him it was simply nerves, a momentary lapse in judgment, and that all relationships faced challenges. Elizabeth had also convinced him that Sara was jealous of their relationship and was trying to break them up. So they'd cut Sara out of their lives and moved on.

"Yeah." Sara had paid for her mistake. The break in her friendship with Elizabeth had only been mended many years later, after Elizabeth had become sick. "And about the way I invited you to this picnic." She looked away, but a grin pulled at her lips. "You were right. There may have been an element of manipulation to it."

"I accept your apology." He was tired of being angry anyway, tired of wasting energy trying to avoid her whenever he came to pick up Theo or attended a school function.

"Thank you." Just like that, she seemed to shake off the sober mood. "I read in the paper that you're working with the police to find that killer called Toxin."

"True." Had she seen the news footage of him acting like a pompous ass to bait Toxin? He was surprised to find that the thought bothered him.

"Theo's been getting a lot of attention from the other kids because of it."

One reason he'd agreed to send Theo to the Academy was to avoid that kind of thing. "*Good* attention, I hope."

"Yes. He's enjoying it. He's very proud of you."

His head suddenly felt like it might float off his shoulders. Who'd have thought it would be so important to have a nine-year-old be proud of you? It was supposed to be the other way around. "The feeling's mutual."

"You have reason to be proud of him. He's working much harder lately. He's more focused."

"Good." Guilt nagged at him. He hadn't had much to do with the turnaround. Sara and his parents deserved the credit.

She nibbled her lip a moment, drawing his attention to the plump lower half. He remembered the softness of it, and the hopes he'd had that night he'd bumped into her at the bar near the University of Chicago Great Lakes campus and they'd talked for hours.

"I was prepared to spend the night feeling sorry for myself—alone on Valentine's Day, stood up by my best friend who was supposed to commiserate with me—and now here you are." Sara's eyes had seemed full of wonder, like Alice falling down the rabbit hole. But she was half drunk. Holt didn't kid himself that this was anything other than a dream. Things like meeting the right girl—the funny, smart girl—didn't happen to him.

"I'm glad I decided to go out," he said, locking gazes with her. He'd seen her before. The quiet girl in the front row of the Psych 101 course he'd taught as a graduate assistant had drawn his eye more than once, especially when he'd seen the grades she'd earned. Pretty face and a brain. The latter was the sexier of the two in Holt's book.

FROM THE STAND OF TREES AT THE TOP OF A KNOLL, TOXIN COULD see everything without being seen. Kids played games in the field to the north. Parents and teachers mingled at tables and bleachers on the sideline. To the south, under a large oak, was the man he'd followed.

Dr. Holt Patterson, the man who had dared to laugh at him. But his opinion didn't matter. Patterson was apparently some kind of brain at SSAM, which Toxin had been researching. The Society for the Study of the Aberrant Mind. More pretentiousness. As if anyone could understand aberrations.

No, the only thing that had pissed Toxin off was being labeled *aberrant.* If his behavior was so abnormal, how had he succeeded in killing three people without recrimination? And if what he'd done was wrong, then why did it feel so good?

No, what he had done was right. It was *just.* He should be receiving accolades, not admonishments. Three killings and the CPD had to call in a specialist. There was something poetic about that. Finally, he was getting noticed.

Dr. Patterson wasn't what he'd expected. Toxin had been tailing the guy for the past week, deciding their ridiculous phone conversation warranted a personal follow-up. But he'd only seen the man's house in the 'burbs and the building that housed SSAM where Patterson worked. There seemed to be no other facet to the man. The wonder-boy mindhunter depicted in the press was, in fact, dull as a rock. All work and no play...

But today...today had been extremely interesting. Following

Dr. Patterson had led him to a private school for boys. That, in itself, was a notable deviation from the norm. And the surprises kept on coming.

Patterson had a son who attended the school. From the looks of it, Patterson might yet have a healthy libido too. He was smiling at the pretty blonde, his gaze covertly moving over her body whenever the breeze pinned her skirt against it. She was nicely formed. And she had a genuine smile.

Yes, Patterson was a complex guy after all. Toxin liked that. Perhaps the guy wasn't a total dick. Toxin wanted a worthy adversary. A challenge. A nemesis who could, perhaps, come to understand him with a little help. Every superhero needed a counterpart who would drive him to perform at his best.

His lips twisted into a grin. The mindhunter, the man who hunted him, was about to become the hunted.

CHAPTER 5

"Got some news for you." Max sat across the desk from Holt. "I scouted out a lab my street contact mentioned. Typical meth lab, though the guy who runs it is legendary for his creativity."

Holt felt a prickle of excitement. "So he could cook up something Toxin might have injected, if someone paid the right price?"

"Sounds like it. The guy's name is Henry. He's way too small to have committed the murders. He's maybe five-five and one-twenty soaking wet. He survives because he's smart and supplies a need in that area."

"But could he have made the toxic cocktail that's being injected into these victims?"

"Absolutely," Max said. "Did he? I don't know. I only got a look at him from a distance. Didn't want to show our hand yet."

"I got a call from Detective Noah Crandall of the CPD. He's now in charge of the Toxin investigation. I guess they want some fresh eyes on it." And Noah had certainly seemed refreshed. The man was in serious love with an art expert they'd met on a case in New York. Holt missed that feeling. Since the Labor Day picnic a week ago, he'd started having intense dreams of sex with a faceless woman. Unfortunately, that woman's lips were the exact softness and shape of Sara's. He had a sneaking suspicion his subconscious was trying to betray him.

Max snapped his fingers. "Yo, where'd you go?"

"Nowhere." Holt cleared his throat. "Where were we?"

Max's look was speculative. "Is it a woman?"

"What?"

"Only a woman can make a man that spacey this early in the morning."

Holt bit back an automatic denial. "Well, sort of…"

"It's okay if you're getting out there again. Hell, it's been a year, right?"

"Yeah." Holt rubbed the back of his neck. And, if he were being honest, he and Elizabeth hadn't exactly been intimate—not in *that* way—when she was really sick. Or before that, either. They'd been so different, and they'd started to grow apart before her illness. Her cancer had actually drawn them closer together.

"You don't have to be a candidate for sainthood, you know."

"It's not that." Hell, he wasn't sure Max was capable of understanding the depth of a committed love. The man was always charming women, but was careful to avoid complicated entanglements. "She was my friend, the mother of my child…"

Max held up a hand. "Yeah, I get it. But a guy has needs. You can only ignore them for so long before they build into an obsession."

Was that what Holt's dreams of Sara were? Some kind of obsession that could be relieved if he took action? "Let's get back to the case."

"Do you think Toxin's even around anymore?" Max asked, voicing one of Holt's fears. "One murder in early January, one in February, and one a few weeks ago. An odd schedule. We hear from him after the TV broadcast, he seems angry, and then…nothing. It's almost like he's slowing down instead of escalating."

It wasn't likely Toxin was running scared just because Holt had been assigned this case. "Could be stalking his next victim." Toxin was still out there, somewhere. He hadn't simply disappeared forever. They couldn't be that lucky.

"Our focus is on academics." Over the speakerphone, the Academy president's firm tone brooked no argument. A chorus of agreement sounded from the other board members connected via the conference call.

"As it should be," Sara agreed, trying to control her frustration. "But students need a well-rounded education to be competitive in today's universities. A drama program is another way for kids to show their talents. To branch out, to feel comfortable with themselves by feeling comfortable within someone else's skin. It's a way of expressing themselves." John Rochard's angry face came to mind, as did the not-so-subtle phone message he'd left for her yesterday, a follow-up to his threats at the picnic, no doubt. It was for students like Neil and Jeremy, John's sons, who desperately needed an outlet, that she fought.

"There's a reason they're called *electives*." The president drew out the word. "They're a choice."

"Yes, and the university selection committees are looking at our kids' choices. If our students want the best scholarships, the best opportunities, they'll need to show they have more to offer society. They need to show they can earn good marks *and* contribute in other ways. In fact, I also want to start a volunteer program that shuttles the older students off campus one afternoon a week. It'll show them where they can contribute to their community. They can help at the hospital, the library, tutoring at the elementary schools..."

Her words trailed off as she realized the group had fallen into silence. Had she broken through the solid brick wall that was the school's board or had she gone too far, pushing for too much?

Elizabeth had often called her a pit bull—not afraid to fight for what she wanted.

"Let's table this for now," said the president.

Sara bit the inside of her cheek and resisted the urge to hurl something. Her award for Educator of the Year from a few years back, a big block of polished glass etched with her name and presented to her by the school district she'd worked for prior to the Academy, sat on the bookshelf beside her, taunting her. Instead, she curled her fingers into her palms.

Cheryl peeked her head in the door, took one look at Sara's face, and gave her a sympathetic grimace. Through the phone, the other participants chorused their agreement about the adjournment. Sure, *that* they could agree on. She swallowed sour disappointment. They could shelve her for now, but she wouldn't be letting her plans go anytime soon. She disconnected and sat back in her chair.

Cheryl came forward and set a stack of folders on Sara's desk, then planted her hands on her generous hips. "Judging by the look on your face, that wasn't as successful as you wanted it to be."

"No, but I won't let it go, no matter how much they try to discourage me." She'd have to tread carefully, but she would not give up.

"That's my spunky girl. The last kid was picked up an hour ago. I think you should take the rest of the afternoon off. You skipped lunch again, and you've barely taken time for yourself at all for weeks. The Academy will survive the last half hour before the weekend without you at the helm."

"You're one to talk."

Cheryl had been contracted to work shorter hours in the summer, but often stayed the full regular-semester schedule because, she insisted, there was nothing to do at home anyway but cook and clean for grumpy Mr. Cheryl, her husband of forty years. Of course, her grumbling was heavily laced with affection. Now, with the fall semester underway, Cheryl still went above and beyond when Sara or one of the teachers needed assistance.

"Hey, I know when to take a break when I need one. You, missy, need one."

"Yes, Mom." Sara's chest squeezed, then relaxed. Cheryl was the closest thing to family she'd had in a long time. Her parents had died three years ago in a car accident, during the year from hell. Losing her parents and divorcing her husband, all within a nine-month period, had been a major turning point in her life. But she'd survived. Barely.

Perhaps she *would* indulge in a little time off. After closing down her office and seeing Cheryl off for the weekend, Sara turned from the wide oak door that was the grand entryway to the school and mounted the gleaming mahogany staircase. Built on twenty acres as a retirement escape for an eccentric, wealthy Chicago industry magnate, the mansion had been converted to the Hills Boys' Academy a decade later, as designated in the owner's will. It had seen generations of boys grow up to be fathers of future students. John Rochard was one of those legacies who now had his sons enrolled here.

"This is John Rochard. I hope you're enjoying the semester, especially since it may be your last at the Academy."

She hadn't responded to his vaguely threatening and totally childish voice mail message. What was there to say, really? Neil had to do the work. It was as simple as that. But, poor Neil and Jeremy, having a father like that. Wealth didn't excuse people from being polite and playing nice. Maybe the first play by the drama department should subtly emphasize the values of honesty and hard work. Or the Golden Rule. If she didn't live by that maxim, she'd give John a dose of his own medicine.

Her fingers slid over the banister, which was dark and waxy-smooth from thousands of hands passing over it. She kept going past the second floor, where the majority of the classrooms were located. The third floor housed an impressive private library and some additional classrooms, as well as a lounge-type study area. On the fourth floor landing, she turned left. To the right was a door to the attic storage area. Across from that were her quarters, a small apartment that had probably once housed a servant of the industry magnate.

She unlocked the door and pushed it open. She had an inkling of how Dorothy felt when the twister was over and she was finally home. Only there were no uncles or Aunty Em to greet her. No Toto. She refused to be lonely, reminding herself that leaving her marriage had been for the best, and that being alone wasn't all bad. In fact, it provided much-needed peace and quiet at the end of the day.

Maybe she should get a dog. She wondered what the board would think of *that.*

Closing the door, she kicked her heels under the secretary desk and checked her personal phone line for messages, dreading what she might find. Thankfully, there no more angry words from John. She made a mental note to speak to Neil soon, and see how the night classes at the community college were going.

She quickly discarded her skirt and blouse in favor of yoga pants and a soft cotton T-shirt. She scrubbed the makeup from her face and immediately felt lighter.

Once settled on the couch with a beer, a bag of chips and her laptop, Sara perused her emails. A name caught her eye.

HPatterson. Holt? It had been a little over a week since the picnic, when she'd sworn she'd felt the beginnings of a truce between them. She'd apologized. He'd accepted. Not that it meant anything in the grand scheme of things.

Liar. Her hormones were buzzing at the mere thought of Holt emailing her when, until now, he'd gone out of his way to avoid contact with her.

She clicked on the message and felt her enthusiasm turn to concern. Theo had used his dad's account, probably without Holt's knowledge.

Miss Sara, I've been working on my comic. Adding a girl hero too. I think you'll like her. I've also been practicing my chess moves on Dad's computer. Better watch out.

Her restlessness receded as she read Theo's words, focusing on the emotions that lay beneath. He'd lost his mother, and he missed having that important female role model in his life. That much had been clear in her time with him over the past few months.

Sara was tempted to call Theo. Just to check on him. Or to see if he wanted to play chess over the phone. But despite their truce, Holt probably wouldn't appreciate her interference, and the last thing she needed was another parent angry with her. With the school board looking for any excuse to keep her reined in, she couldn't risk any contact that might rattle some cages.

Rochard would be watching too. She'd bet on it. He seemed hell-bent on finding a way to unhinge her.

Holt wasn't anywhere near the same category of father—or man—as John Rochard. John was blissfully ignorant of his children's wants and needs. Holt would want to know that his son was using his email account, trying to reach out to others in his loneliness. But she didn't want to betray Theo's trust.

A knock interrupted and she opened the door. Chad White, the computer tech guy she'd hired last week to update the school's wireless system and teach computer classes, stood on the threshold.

"Sorry to interrupt." Looking uncomfortable at bothering her after hours, he ran a hand over his thick, short brown hair. "You said it was okay to bug you here."

"No problem. How are the upgrades going?"

"Fine, fine. Old wiring here and there, but nothing I can't handle."

"Good." That was a relief. She'd had to urge the board to upgrade the system in the first place. She was certain they wouldn't want to hear of any major issues with the project. "What can I do for you, then?"

"There's a student here. I didn't want to get him in trouble since he seems to be studying and all, but I thought you'd want to know he was here."

Someone was here after five on a Friday? "I appreciate you bringing it to my attention. Where is he?"

"The library. I didn't say anything to him. Didn't want to disturb him if you'd said it was okay to be there."

"Thanks."

"And I'll be out of your hair in another hour or so. Be back tomorrow with the rest of the equipment to finish the job. I may have to turn the power off for a bit, though. The internet will be back online pretty quick."

At least something was going right. "That sounds great. Thank you."

Chad disappeared through the door opposite hers, where he was working on the wiring that ran through the attic space. She marched down one flight of stairs, wondering which of her students had broken the rules. No child was allowed to be on campus without adult supervision. If the board found out about this, it would be one more strike against her.

The library was quiet. A lamp was turned on at one of the broad study tables. Notes and open books were scattered within the ring of light. Neil Rochard's dark head was bent over a legal pad as he scribbled something.

She cleared her throat and he nearly fell out of his chair. His gaze shifted quickly around as if he would duck under the table to hide. His Adam's apple bobbed. "Um, hi."

"Hello." She took a seat across the table from him. Upon closer inspection, she noted the materials were SAT study books and index cards with equations and vocabulary words. "You look like you're studying hard."

He started gathering up the materials and shoving them into his backpack. "Just about to head home."

Shoot. He was going into avoidance mode again. "You must

have quite a workload with those make-up classes. It's okay if you want to stay a little longer."

"Isn't it against the rules?"

"That didn't stop you before." Amusement tugged at her lips. "Besides, there are worse ways of breaking the rules."

One side of his mouth moved toward a half-grin, just for a nanosecond before he drew on his serious demeanor again. "I just needed a quiet place to study...away from home, you know? But I should go. Dad will start wondering where I am."

"Too late. Dad's already here," an annoyed John Rochard said from the doorway. "I finally found the note you left. I was supposed to deliver you to your mother an hour ago. Get your things." He looked at Sara. "May I have a word with you in the hall?"

She dropped her voice to a whisper. "I'm proud of you, Neil."

He nodded once but didn't meet her eyes. Swallowing a sigh, each step heavy as if she were approaching the gallows, she moved into the hallway to face off with John. "He's working hard."

"I overheard you say he broke the rules."

"Technically, yes, but—"

"It is unacceptable for a Senator's grandson, for *my* son, to break any rules."

She hid her incredulity. Was this the same man who'd suggested she fudge his son's grades?

"But of course you'd condone that kind of behavior. It doesn't bode well for the future of this school."

Her jaw dropped. She'd never, ever been labeled as a rule-breaker. She nearly laughed out loud. Elizabeth would have been proud to hear her friend had achieved anarchist status after all this time. "I didn't know he was here until just before you arrived. And he is working hard, as you wanted him to."

"He can do that at home."

"Can he?" She doubted whatever was going on between the Rochards was conducive to academic excellence. Not only had

Neil's grades been slipping and his sullenness growing, but Jeremy had started to show signs of similar issues just before school had let out for the summer.

John lips pressed together until they were white around the edges. She thought he would blow up at her, but instead he seemed to regain self-control. "I'd be very careful what you say, Miss Burns. Watch your step. You'll find your sweet ass out on the street with no hopes of future employment in this field. And you'll find out just what the Rochards are capable of."

"Dad?" Neil's arrival saved Sara from spitting the fiery words she longed to hurl at John. "I'm ready."

"About time." John spun on his heel. Neil didn't even look back, just walked with his head down and shoulders hunched as he was swallowed in the wake of his father's enormous ego.

CHAPTER 6

I thought I should let you know that Theo emailed me using your home account. I'm sure he just misses the routine of school, and I represent that to him, but he may be lonely too.

Holt read and reread the email Sara had sent to his work address. She might be a busybody, but she really seemed to care about her students. Or was it just Theo, and was she acting out of guilt about how she'd almost broken Holt and Elizabeth up years ago?

He closed the laptop on his desk and went in search of his son. He found him plunked on the couch in front of the television.

"How about burgers tonight?"

"Takeout?" Theo didn't pull his attention from the movie.

"Actually, I thought maybe we could cook outside together. It's about time you learned how the grill works."

This time, Theo actually turned to look at him. "Our special recipe?"

"Of course."

"Yeah, okay." He went to the kitchen and washed his hands in the sink.

If he'd known his son would get this excited over grilling something, Holt would have tried this long ago. He led the way outside and showed him how to light the grill. From inside, the doorbell chimed.

"I'll get it," Theo said. He returned a moment later with a grin. And Sara. She'd been near his thoughts all week, but seeing her in the flesh was like a punch to his chest. She was even sexier in jeans that hugged her curves and a button-down shirt than she'd been in her sundress.

"I didn't mean to intrude." She looked at the grill, then sent an apologetic look toward Holt. "I certainly don't want to interrupt dinnertime."

"It's all right," Holt said.

"Can you stay for dinner?" Theo asked.

Sara's gaze turned helpless. "Oh no, I just need to talk to your dad for a moment. Nothing bad, I promise," she hastened to add.

"We're making our famous burgers," Theo continued. He was actually trying to entice her to stay. Holt was both amused at his son's antics and frustrated he and Theo wouldn't have time together on their own. But maybe Sara's presence would be the buffer he needed to break through his son's barriers. She seemed to get along with Theo so well.

"We'd love it if you'd stay," Holt told Sara. "And we can discuss whatever you came by for over dinner."

She smiled and he felt a ridiculous pull in his groin. His attraction to her confused the hell out of him, given their past.

"We'd better get started on those burgers," he said, covering his reaction by moving inside. The others followed.

Theo gathered ingredients from the cupboards, keeping up a surprising stream of chatter. "Our burgers are a family tradition."

Sara leaned against a counter, both to stay out of the way and to watch the show. "Oh?"

"There are only three ingredients—hamburger meat, shredded cheese, and chunky mild salsa." Theo looked from the block of cheese in his hand to Holt. His bangs slid across his forehead, but he didn't swipe them away. "Remember what Mom used to say—that you were the meat, she was the salsa, and I was the cheese."

Holt grinned. "Because you're always cracking cheesy jokes."

Sara laughed. "Now *that*, I can imagine."

"Theo is quite the clown." Or at least, he *had* been a jokester. Most of that spark had dimmed, but Holt hoped it was still there, an ember waiting to come to life again. Elizabeth had added the fun-loving spice to their family unit. Holt had been the meat—important but nothing exciting, until you added the other ingredients.

"It's not the same without the salsa." Theo tossed the pile of cheese into the bowl of ground beef.

Yes, Elizabeth had added all the flavor.

Holt wanted to reach out to hug Theo, but felt the attempt would be rejected. He didn't know if he could stand that right now. Besides, Theo was already moving away from him to grab the jar of salsa from the refrigerator.

"Hey, I should be helping." Sara pushed off the counter, stood up straight, and saluted as if she were a soldier readying herself for action. "Reporting for duty, sirs."

"Yeah, you should be helping," Holt said, grateful she'd taken the edge off a difficult moment. He grinned at Theo. "How about we give her the dirty job."

Theo grinned back. "Sounds good to me."

"Wash up, Cadet," Holt ordered Sara. "And you might want to take those rings off."

She had an engagement-type marquis diamond ring on her right hand, but nothing on her left, and he wondered what that meant.

"Gladly. I'm not afraid to get dirty."

"How about raw meat squishing between your fingers?" Theo said, adding a wicked grin. "Grandma says the only way to cook is to use your hands."

"And get a little dirty." Sara washed her hands in the sink. "I get it. Guess I'm not the guest of honor." But her smile said she didn't mind. She dipped her slender fingers into the mixing bowl and deftly churned the ingredients together, then shaped and molded them into three patties. Holt couldn't seem to remove his gaze from her hands. *"Voila."*

He had a sudden urge to kiss the silly, triumphant grin off her face.

Theo appraised her work as if he were a foreman. "Not bad."

Swallowing his desire, Holt carried the plate of patties out to the grill. He sucked in the night air, trying to cool the fire in his blood.

"That was delicious. I can see why your family keeps the recipe a secret." Sara teased Theo from across the kitchen table, enjoying the way he smiled easily. It seemed he wasn't the only one missing someone the past week. She'd missed him too. She sat back and crossed her hands over her belly. "But I'm full."

Theo slanted her a sly look. "Too full for a chess match?"

"I'm never too full to exert worldwide domination."

Holt raised his eyebrows. "Is she always this cocky?" he asked Theo.

Theo nodded. "Yes, but she has reason to be. I haven't beaten her. Yet."

"I like your confidence," Sara said. "But I need to talk to your dad for just a minute. Then, maybe we can play a game." She looked suddenly at Holt, realizing that she was, perhaps, over-staying her welcome.

"I'd enjoy seeing my son crush you," Holt reassured her. The heat in his eyes when he met her gaze was only partly friendly challenge. There was something more there. If Sara didn't know any better, she might call it lust, or at least sexual interest. But this was Holt Patterson she was thinking about.

"Sweet." Theo rose from his chair and scooped up his empty glass and plate. "I'll be waiting in the den." After plunking his plates by the sink, he rushed off.

Holt shook his head. "He's been studying how to play chess. The kid hasn't shown an interest in anything in months, and now...I don't know how you got through to him." He sighed. "But I'm glad someone did."

Her heart flip-flopped. Was that a compliment? "Me too. Did you get my email?"

"Yes. I assume that's why you stopped by?"

She felt her cheeks heat. She couldn't admit that she'd wanted to see Theo again with her own eyes, to reassure herself that he was okay. He might see that as an insult. But that wasn't the complete story, anyway. She'd wanted to see Holt again. "I was concerned. And since you don't usually answer phone calls from me, I took a risk and stopped by in person."

"I'm sorry I was such an ass to you. Thank you for letting me know about the email, by the way. I'd have understood if you didn't try so hard to notify me, given how I've behaved, but I'm glad you persisted."

"Sure. If I were a parent, I'd want to know. And I know, with our history, why you avoided me, and that it didn't have anything to do with how much you love Theo. But everything seems okay with him now."

He sat forward and folded his arms on the table. "Hell, Sara, I don't know what's okay. One minute, he's ignoring me. The next, he's grinning like the old Theo. On rare occasions, I'll say or do the right thing and we make a connection, but it's always brief." His eyes brimmed with misery as they met hers. "I miss my son."

Before she could talk herself out of the gesture, she reached out to touch his forearm. "You've been through a tough time. Go easy on yourself."

His gaze locked on her hand and she slowly withdrew it. Maybe it was too soon to show that much sympathy. It probably wasn't welcome, but there was such pain behind his expression that she hadn't been able to resist some measure of comfort.

She covered the sudden awkwardness by rising and going to her purse on the counter. "I brought something for Theo. I thought, with your permission, maybe I could give it to him?"

Holt came over to stand next to her, looking at the video game in her hand. "I think he'd like that."

"And then I should probably get going."

His brow crinkled. "I thought you were going to stay for a game of chess."

She hadn't wanted to come between Holt and his son. Truthfully, she hadn't wanted to give Holt any more reasons to be angry with her. "You can play with him."

"Oh, no. You're not putting this on me. He's looking forward to besting *you*. I wouldn't dare disappoint him." He grinned mischievously. "Besides, I'd like to see that myself."

"I'm sure you would. Too bad you won't see it. Because it isn't going to happen."

They found Theo sitting on the floor of the den next to the chessboard. He'd put a couple of floor pillows in her spot and was hugging one himself. Sara sat opposite him, curling her legs under her. She was surprised that Holt hung around. He moved behind his desk, probably getting back to work on some case or other. But every now and then, she felt his gaze on her and she'd look up. Questions lurked there. And still, that heat she didn't understand. Perhaps he was just as confused as she was by their sudden connection after years of distance.

"WILL YOU COME BY AGAIN SOMETIME?" THEO ASKED AS THEY walked Sara to the door an hour later. The game had ended just as Sara had predicted. She'd captured Theo's king, but Holt had been impressed by the way his son had strategized.

"I'll see you every day at school," Sara reminded him. "You'll soon be sick of seeing this face." Her gaze went to Holt's, and he realized she wasn't sure what her welcome was.

"I doubt that," Holt said. Feeling foolish, he backpedaled immediately. "Theo would enjoy a rematch. A chance to reclaim his honor."

"Yeah, since I got my you-know-what handed to me," Theo said, pretending to be disappointed. Holt had never seen his son so focused as when he was hunched over that chess board.

"Language," Holt said.

"What? I didn't say anything bad."

"But it was what you intended..." Holt heaved a sigh as he realized the conversation was quickly turning sour. "Good night, Sara. Thank you for stopping by."

"Thank you for dinner, and I hope we'll see you at Parents' Weekend in a couple weeks." She left the statement as a question, but Holt hadn't even thought about attending the parent-student functions that weekend.

"Maybe." They said their goodbyes and watched until Sara was safely in her car. Holt shut the door. "I do believe we just let our guest escape without helping out with the dirty work."

"The dishes." Theo groaned. "I forgot." A few minutes later, side-by-side at the kitchen sink, Theo washed and Holt dried.

"You're coming for Parents' Weekend, right?" Theo asked.

"I hadn't really thought about it."

"There's some kind of parent party thing after the student-parent dinner."

"There is?" He'd barely glanced at the itinerary that had been mass-emailed.

"Yeah. Jeremy's dad is even staying overnight at the hotel where they're having it."

"Jeremy told you all of this? How?" Holt had just received the email that afternoon.

Theo's bangs slid across his forehead. He swiped them back. "Jeremy and I chat online while we play video games."

"What?" He could have kicked himself. A boy who was savvy enough to figure out his dad's password and email the director of his school was smart enough to figure out how to hook a game system up to the internet.

"I haven't played much this month." Theo's tone of reassurance told Holt that he had caught his worried expression. "I was too into that chess book. That was cool of Miss Sara to give me a computer chess game. Now I can practice."

"I should have gone over some ground rules about online activity. It's not always safe."

"I know to be careful. I don't tell anyone where I live or give away credit card information or anything. Miss Sara taught a personal safety class last fall when she found out someone tried to get Brendan Tucker to meet up at a gas station across from the school."

Holt tried to swallow past the sudden constriction of his throat. SSAM occasionally offered similar courses to the public—usually after there'd been an increase in online crimes and someone had gotten hurt. "Well, Miss Sara should earn a gold star for hyper-vigilance."

"Yeah, she's pretty cool."

He studied his son, surprised to get such a genuine, non-sarcastic answer from him. He wanted to hug him, but he wanted his son to want the hug. Lately, all signs seemed to indicate Theo wanted some distance.

Sara would have hugged Theo. *She* wouldn't have let him retreat behind his defenses. *She* would have marched right over to him and pulled him up against her, rejection-be-damned. Because the only thing he knew for sure about Sara was that she was fearless when it came to doing what she thought was right. Perhaps he could learn some things from her after all.

THE BREEZE CARRIED THE SMELL OF A COOLING GRILL AND RECENTLY cooked beef. Through the window, father and son stood side-by-side at the sink. Theo rinsed dishes. Holt dried them and put them in a neat stack. Like two parts of a whole. Perfect symbiosis.

Toxin enjoyed watching the minutia of everyday life, but it reminded him of what he'd lost. The little things he'd never thought he'd miss. It had been fate that brought Holt and Toxin together.

No, not fate. Toxin was in control of his destiny. It had been his own actions that brought Holt Patterson into his world.

He stiffened as the neighbor's sliding glass door opened and the old lady's dog trotted out. Toxin backed farther along the fence line, glad that Mrs. Mendelson had poor eyesight without her glasses. Glasses she was too vain to wear most of the time, even at home with only her precious dog for company.

Still, his pulse was pounding. Damn, these drugs Henry had cooked up made him jumpy. He'd requested alertness, but Henry had apparently gone a little too far. He'd talk to him about adjusting the mix.

Reaching into his pocket, his fingers wrapped around the treats he'd brought for Roscoe. It hadn't been difficult to make friends with the pudgy pug. And it had kept the dog from barking on evenings like these, when he chose to spend his time observing Holt Patterson from the shadows near the back fence. The narrow alley that ran behind their yards, occupied only by trashcans awaiting pick-up day, was perfect for people-watching.

But Theo would be back at school Monday. And Holt would be back to his boring routine of home, work, home, work, and sometimes, when Theo was staying with his grandparents, not going home but sleeping at the office. *Yawn.* Perhaps he'd have to shake things up a bit.

His blood pumped harder as he thought about the next phase of his plan. He'd savored the details for weeks. He'd taken a break from finding justice, let things cool off until Holt and the police had likely exhausted all their measly leads and were left frustrated. There was only so much time Toxin could allow to pass before he felt the pressure to fulfill his destiny.

He was a hero. Heroes weren't allowed breaks. They didn't get time off. There were things to be done.

CHAPTER 7

Parents' Weekend

A year ago, Theo had been preparing to attend his mom's funeral. He'd worn the itchy suit and neck-strangling tie Grandma had bought him and watched them sink Mom —inside the white-pearl coffin with gold trim—into the ground and throw some shovels of dirt on top of her.

Today, he led his father across the school's lunchroom, crowded with students and parents gathering for a dinner to kick off parents' weekend. He didn't dare bring up the anniversary. He didn't want to see his father shut himself away again the way he had this past year, when Theo had received clear signals that his dad didn't want to talk about any details regarding Mom.

Besides, he had Miss Sara. He'd talked with her about his mom during their chess game a couple of hours ago. He'd pretended not to see her eyes tear up. She'd been at the funeral, though he'd barely known her then and she'd been way at the back. He'd just started going to the Academy. But his mom had told him before she died that, whenever he was missing her, he could talk to Miss Sara.

He liked Miss Sara. She liked his stories. *Really* read them and asked him questions, so he knew she was serious and not just blowing smoke up his ass.

The cafeteria was already full as Theo wove his way toward the far table where his friends sat. Jeremy had held a couple of seats for them.

"My dad couldn't make it to the dinner," Jeremy said, "but he'll be at the mixer later." He sounded disappointed. Theo was glad Mr. Rochard wouldn't be around. He didn't want Miss Sara to be so tense.

Jeremy's brother, Neil, kept his head down and dug into his food, finishing the whole plate in about five bites. Then again, he was a football player, and they all seemed to eat that way. The other parents at their table asked Theo's dad questions about the murders and the investigation. His dad avoided answering most of them, but Theo could tell the parents were interested. As were his friends. That was kind of cool.

"My dad says you've stopped Toxin from killing again," Jeremy said before shoveling a bite of chicken parmesan into his mouth.

Dad poked his fork at the spaghetti on his plate. "I don't know about that. He hasn't hurt anyone in two months, but that doesn't mean we can stop looking. He hasn't paid for what he's done."

Theo wondered how Jeremy felt about that, given Mr. Rochard didn't have to pay for bullying people. People like Miss Sara. Theo looked around the cafeteria but didn't see her. He frowned.

"You okay?" Dad asked.

"Yeah. Just looking for someone."

"I'm sure they'll show up later."

"Right." He ate a bite of butter-soaked toasted garlic bread, thinking over his options. It seemed he didn't have any if he wanted to make sure Miss Sara was okay. "Dad, will you look out for Miss Sara tonight at the mixer?"

His dad paused in the middle of lifting a bite to his mouth. A noodle slid off his fork. "Look out for her?"

"Yeah, you know, since she's alone. I don't want her to be alone, or in danger."

He set the fork down. "Danger? Why would she be in danger?"

Theo looked around to see that everyone at the table was talking or otherwise busy. "We didn't think Mom was in danger, either. But then she found out she was sick. Anything can happen."

"That doesn't mean the same thing will happen to Miss Sara. Or to me."

"I know. Still, there are things you can do to keep safe."

His hand reached out to rest on Theo's shoulder. His wedding ring was missing. Theo's throat closed up, but he swallowed past it. His mom had said they might let go of her one day, and that it was okay. Natural. But nothing seemed natural about it. "I know it's hard to believe after you've lost someone you love, but I'm not going anywhere. You can trust me to take good care of myself."

"Grandma would say that means eating your veggies."

His dad laughed and Theo felt warm all over. "I'll eat my veggies if you do."

"If we want some of Grandma's apple pie, I suppose we'll have to."

Dad checked his watch. "Speaking of Grandma, we'd better get to their house. Grandpa rented a movie for you."

"What about Miss Sara?"

"I don't think she's in danger. And I'm certain she knows how to take care of herself. But if it's that important to you, I'll make sure to check in with her tonight."

PART SPORTS BAR AND PART HAPPY-HOUR VENUE FOR THE PROFESSORS and local government offices that seemed to populate this stretch of town, Heather Hedge Lodge was the perfect place to unwind, and for Academy parents to mingle. The log cabin look and soft music provided a sedate, comfortable setting that stood in sharp contrast to Sara's anxiety level, currently ratcheted up to red alert. John Rochard had been shooting her dark looks since she'd walked in. She felt each glance like a jolt of caffeine to her system.

"Sounds like your son enjoyed the Monterey Bay Aquarium." She inserted the comment as her conversation partner paused for a breath. She'd kept half an ear on the topic and half on her surroundings. The skill came from living with an alcoholic husband with unpredictable moods and a caustic tongue. Yes, she'd learned many things—mostly about herself and what she wanted from life—during the two years she'd endured with him.

Thankfully, not all parents were of the same frame of mind as John or her ex-husband. In fact, most parents were happy with the school's improvements. But John was the squeaky wheel. As such, he was currently encircled by three board members and seemed to have the run of the conversation. She had no doubt he was making an important move in whatever chess game he had going on with her in his head.

"Oh yes, my son loves all things aquatic, so it was right up his alley," the mother in front of her was saying.

She smiled. "I'm glad to hear he was able to feed that passion this summer."

A flicker of movement near the entryway caught her eye and she turned her head, her gaze colliding with Holt's. Her eyes widened in surprise, prompting his lips to twist into a smile that she found an intriguing combination of boy-next-door sweetness and sexy hellraiser. A tug in her abdomen told her to tread carefully. He was attractive, but he'd been Elizabeth's. Sara had stifled any feminine response she'd had to him long ago, but apparently she needed to shore up her defenses.

"Yes, well, passion is important," the woman opposite her said.

Passion? Had the woman read her mind? Sara nearly choked on her drink but managed to recover. As she chatted, she couldn't help but chart Holt's progress around the room. He said brief hellos to a few people but always moved on. No attachments, no deep friendships. If she hadn't known better, she would have wondered if lack of social connection was a casualty of his job. Or a protective layer. Maybe that was why Elizabeth had appealed to him. She'd been his complete opposite and probably shielded him at these kinds of functions.

Sara grew restless. "If you'll excuse me, I'm going to get a drink. Don't forget there's an appetizer buffet along the wall."

She sat at the bar and ordered a fresh glass of white wine. Her limit was two. After all, she represented the Academy. That didn't appear to stop some people. The board members were already knee-deep in the bottle of 12-year-old scotch John had bought them. A shout of laughter came from their direction. A moment later, the hairs on the back of her neck stood at attention.

"They look like they're enjoying themselves," Holt said from behind her. "Maybe more than they should."

She swiveled on the barstool and met his hazel gaze. How had he known the direction of her thoughts? Was she that transparent? She turned back to the bar and toyed with a cocktail napkin. "They're big boys and girls."

He slid onto the stool next to her, so close his thigh brushed hers. She felt a warmth that wasn't due to consumption of alcohol and subtly shifted to break the contact. "I take it you're not happy they're so captivated by John Rochard."

Surprised, she glanced at him. "What makes you say that?"

"I saw the looks between you and him. Whatever happened at the picnic hasn't blown over, has it?"

She avoided Holt's much-too-perceptive eyes. "Nothing I can't handle."

The bartender arrived with her glass of wine and took Holt's drink order. "Put her drink on my tab," Holt added.

"You don't have to do that," she said as the bartender left to make Holt's Jack and Coke.

"You look like you could use a friend, and friends treat each other to a drink now and then."

A friend? Boy, could she. She'd missed Cheryl's advice these past few days while she'd traveled with her husband to a reunion of his retired military friends.

"Am I wrong?" he asked when she didn't reply.

"No, but you and I can't be friends."

"Why not?"

"You know very well why not. You don't really want to be. It would be too much work."

He shrugged as if dealing with their turbulent past was nothing. "Water under the bridge."

"A flood's worth?"

"It's been ten years, Sara. The waters have receded. Besides, you've had dinner at my house, cast some kind of spell on my son and..." He paused in midsentence, then shook his head, discarding whatever he'd been about to say. "You apologized. I'm willing to move on if you are."

She thought about that a moment, wanting to set things right between them but not even knowing where to start. She couldn't be friends with someone who didn't trust her. "Friends, though? That's stretching it a bit. I'm certain you're a good listener..."

"Comes with the job."

"But friendship is a two-way street. It wouldn't be fair for me to do all the talking."

He considered her comments. "Okay. Tit for tat. How about you give me a chance to show you I can give as good as I get. After all, there was that one night...we didn't have any trouble connecting then. I'm sure we can get back to that."

She ignored the shiver his comment generated. He surely hadn't meant anything sexual by it, referring to the night they'd spent hours just talking at a bar, much like this one—the night the sexual tension had been so thick she could almost see it in the air —and yet her body had reacted to his husky words as if he were a lover.

"Okay," she said. "You go first. Let's have a conversation."

"All right." He glanced around. "Good showing tonight."

"One less expense I'll have to justify to the board."

He laughed. *Damn.* She should have eaten something before she'd left. The alcohol had gone straight to her tongue, loosening it. She'd missed the dinner to deal with a problem, and she was paying for it now.

She took a breath and tried again. "What I mean is…this gathering was my idea, and the board shelled out some money to reserve the bar for the night. Not everyone thought it was a good idea."

"Well, I think it's a great idea." He took a sip of his drink.

She slid him a sideways glance. "Right. And you're such a great judge because you *always* attend school functions."

"No, but I'm enjoying this one."

She flushed with pleasure. "Thanks. Could you, maybe, run for the board?" He laughed and she couldn't help but laugh too. "I confess I had an ulterior motive to organizing this shindig."

"Free appetizers?"

"Well, there is that…but I want the parents to get more involved…to help the kids see how important education is. Active families create more invested learners."

"Smart."

She examined him. The light of the bar bounced off glasses that weren't geeky, but intellectual-looking. Actually, she'd always thought his look was understated and bookish. So very unlike Elizabeth. And so much more Sara-like. But she'd been wrong, and she'd severely underestimated Elizabeth's charisma…and her desire to get what she set her sights on.

"He's all wrong for you, Sara." Elizabeth had stood at Sara's dresser, picking up items, seeming to examine them, and setting them down again. Her gaze had met Sara's in the mirror. "But perfect for me. You know it. It's only a matter of time before he realizes it too."

"We had a connection." Before Elizabeth had shown up.

Elizabeth shook her head as if amused by a small child. "But look how long that lasted. I've been on several dates with him in the past few weeks. How about you? Have you even heard from him?" She turned and moved to the bed. She sat in front of Sara and took her hands. "I didn't plan this. I think he's really into me, and he's got that hunky nerd thing going for him. I can see why you like him."

It's not like, it's love, Sara wanted to scream. She'd watched Holt from afar for months, during class and sometimes seeing him on campus. She'd come to know his behavior and how the small quirk upward at the corner of his mouth was an indication of deep amusement.

Elizabeth had squeezed her hands. "Save your heart, Sara. He's not for you. He wants me. In fact, he's already invited me into his bed."

Elizabeth's words were over ten years old now but stung as if they'd just been spoken. And, sure enough, they'd been true. Holt had wanted Elizabeth. So much so that he'd married her a few months later.

"So far this conversation is about me," Sara said, snapping her focus back to the present. "I thought you were going to show me that we could talk about you too. Tit for tat, remember?"

Behind the glasses, his hazel eyes connected with her blue ones and held. "You know what today is, right?"

She swallowed. *Really?* He wanted to go *there*? She wasn't sure she was up to discussing it with anyone, let alone him. "Yes."

"Holt Patterson?" John Rochard slid onto the empty barstool on the other side of Holt, and her intense but fragile bond with him was broken.

"Yes?" Holt didn't hold out his hand to greet the other man, who hadn't offered his hand either. Sara found that odd, and a bit comforting.

"I'm John Rochard. My son Neil is a senior and my younger son Jeremy is in your son's class." He paused as if Holt had heard of them, but Holt let the silence drag on. After a moment, John chuckled. "His grandpa is on television constantly, running for re-election to the U.S. Senate, and all Jeremy can talk about is how his friend's dad is hunting a killer. Isn't that what the media is saying...you're some kind of mindhunter?"

"I profile criminals. Dig deep into their psyche. I'm good at seeing beyond the facade most people present to the world." His gaze was piercing as he looked at the other man. Sara released a breath, uncertain what had caused the tension between the men, other than her brief discussion of John.

John's smile was lopsided. "Well. Sounds like an interesting job."

"It does," Sara agreed. Holt's gaze swung to her and stayed there. He winked as if they shared a secret. Realizing John was watching them with interest, she cleared her throat. "Well, you were right about Jeremy and Theo. In fact, I believe they're best friends."

John looked surprised. A calculated gleam entered his eye as he looked back to Holt. "Guess we'll be seeing more of each other then."

"Maybe." Holt was a man of few words.

Sara hid a smile. "I hope we'll see Jeremy at the tryouts for the Academy's first fall play. It'll be a great fundraiser for the new auditorium."

"Ah yes, I've heard your plans, but there won't be a new theater. The board agrees we need to direct funds toward hiring more advanced instructors."

She stiffened. "I hired three very capable teachers this summer. In fact, the new computer science instructor just updated the entire computer network at the Academy and it works like a dream."

"Many of the teachers simply aren't up to Ivy League standards. It's your job to be more selective."

"I think she's doing a fine job," Holt interjected. Sara hid her shock. After so many years opposing each other, it was a surprise to have him in her corner. "And if you think the school is subpar, why do you keep your kids there?"

John's face turned red. "It's a family tradition. And my sons will get into their college of choice." His gaze met Sara's. "I'm certain of it."

Though her stomach hurt at his subtle threats, Sara refused to be cowed. "Our students won't be up to the standards of those schools unless we give them a well-rounded education."

"With a drama department? Don't be ridiculous."

"Giving them an outlet like that is important, just like adding sports to our curriculum offerings was important. Neil certainly enjoys the benefits of the new facilities."

"Well, I can tell you Jeremy won't be part of it."

Though her face felt as if it might crack, Sara held on to her stiff smile. "But he was so good at memorizing his argument in the debate competition last spring. And he seems comfortable on stage. He'd be a natural."

"He's not interested." John looked over his shoulder. "I see someone I need to talk to." After a brief nod of acknowledgment to Holt, he slid off his stool and walked away without even looking at Sara.

She took a long sip of wine. "Something I said, I guess."

"No." Holt eyed John across the room. "I know his type. He's a bully."

A weight shifted on her shoulders. It wasn't gone, but it felt a bit more comfortable to carry around. Someone recognized what she was up against. Someone sympathized. And it was someone whose sympathy she'd never expected, and therefore was all the more precious. "Guess we might be friends after all."

Holt studied her and gave a slow smile that sent heat through her body. This wasn't how the best friend of a dead woman should behave with the widower, especially on the anniversary of that friend's funeral.

Abruptly, she pushed off her stool. "I have to go."

Holt's eyes widened. "You're leaving?"

"I think I've talked with just about everyone." And she didn't want Holt to remember the topic John had interrupted. "I should get home. Thanks for the drink."

She hurried to her car without a backward glance, gulping in the cool night air. Crickets chirped in a chorus of sympathy.

Elizabeth, I'm so sorry. Sorry Elizabeth was dead. Sorry Sara was the one who was able to enjoy Theo's everyday successes. Sorry she was still, after all these years, attracted to her friend's husband.

She made it to her car before hot tears rolled down her cheeks, and drove to the Academy in a haze of memories. Sara had watched Holt from afar for months, and fallen hard in one night. *One damn night.* A night that had been interrupted when Elizabeth had arrived and stolen the show—as always.

Sara hated the bitterness she tasted when the old jealousy flared. The fact that Elizabeth had seen Holt as her ultimate conquest made it worse. Sara hadn't been aware of the sibling-like rivalry Elizabeth had felt toward her, but once Elizabeth set her sights on something, she got it.

And then Sara had done the unthinkable. She'd wanted to test whether the spark she'd sensed between Holt and herself had been real or a figment of her imagination.

The Spring Break party Elizabeth had organized had been in full swing around them, and people had filled the three-bedroom apartment she and Elizabeth shared with another senior. Sara found herself hiding out in her own bedroom, unwilling to watch Elizabeth wrap herself around Holt one more time. Jealousy gnawed at her belly, a constant ache that was only eased by distance. So Sara tried to take the high road and disappear. It was getting late, anyway, and her head was slightly hazy from the lemonade-and-vodka concoction one of their friends had placed in a cooler on their kitchen counter.

"Oh, sorry," Holt said from the doorway. "Didn't realize anyone was here."

Sara sat up on her bed and crossed her legs under her. "No, it's okay. Were you looking for me?" Surely not, but her heart did a ridiculous pirouette anyway.

"Just needed a bit of quiet for a phone call." He held up the cell phone in his hand.

"You're welcome to make your call here."

Whether he deemed it impolite to leave or was seeking the shelter of a quiet place, he stepped into her room and shut the door most of the way. Boisterous laughter and thumping music filtered through the open crack, but it was muted by Holt's presence. Every one of her senses seemed attuned to him.

"I can leave if you want privacy," she said when he simply stood there, looking at her as if he were trying to solve a puzzle.

"It's okay. I can do it in a minute. Are you okay?" His brow knit with concern as his gaze swept over her.

"Yeah. Just needed a break from—" She waved a hand toward the party.

Holt nodded his understanding. "I've been meaning to talk to you, anyway."

"Have a seat." Her tiny bedroom had no chairs, so he sat next to her on the bed. "What did you want to talk to me about?" *Do you want to run away with me? Because I can pack a bag in five minutes flat.*

"I feel bad about that night at the bar." It had been only a month ago, but everything had changed. He was dating Elizabeth now. "We were having a great time, and I feel like I ditched you."

"Well, you kind of did." She laughed to show it didn't hurt her, but it had. Elizabeth's beauty and natural charisma had dazzled

Holt. Sara had always known her friend was more popular, and it had never bothered her. Until now. Why did Elizabeth want Holt, anyway? Focused and serious, he was the antithesis of the man she typically preferred.

He brushed a hand over the back of his neck. "Yeah, well, I am sorry."

"It's okay. I know I don't have that spark guys are drawn to." Though, like bugs to a flame, that spark often led to their downfall. Would Elizabeth play with him and leave him like the others? It hurt Sara's heart to think that was Holt's fate. But it also made her angry at him that he would fall for that.

"That's ridiculous." His words were just forceful enough to be believed.

"Whatever."

"No, really. Is that what you think, that you're plain next to Elizabeth?"

She stared at him as if he didn't have a clue. Because he didn't. "Yes. But don't feel sorry for me." Pity was the last thing she wanted from him. "I know I have other talents." She slowly leaned forward as she spoke, not sure what she was doing until she'd done it. But she'd dreamed of kissing him for months, even more so since their encounter in the bar. Holt held still, a look of uncertainty and, yes, desire on his face.

And that was when she kissed him. He didn't pull away, but he didn't respond at first. Then his lips moved, ever so slightly. In an instant, they turned hot and questing. His mouth slid over hers, branding her. Heat and need coiled together in her belly. With a moan, Sara opened to him and pressed closer, her breasts brushing his chest. Though layers of fabric separated them, her nipples puckered in reaction. His arms came around her, his hands blazing a trail down her back.

Do it. Touch me. She willed his fingers to lift the edge of her shirt and touch her skin, to pull her closer and make her his. A low moan, almost a growl, sounded in his throat and her heart leaped.

She was breaking through the wall that had gone up between them.

He jerked away suddenly as the noise of the party became louder. Caught off balance, Sara nearly fell off the bed. Elizabeth stood in the open doorway, scowling.

Holt pushed to his feet. "Elizabeth…"

Elizabeth looked from his flushed face to Sara's and her frown disappeared. She turned to Holt and ran a hand over his chest. "Would you get me a glass of that lemonade stuff, honey? I'll be along in a minute."

Without a backward glance, Holt did as he was asked. Sara watched him leave, feeling suddenly adrift. "It wasn't what it seemed. *I* kissed *him*."

"Oh, I know. I just didn't want to see you embarrass yourself by throwing yourself at him any longer." Elizabeth's pity was so thick Sara could choke on it. Tears pricked her eyes. "Just so we're clear. He's ours."

"Ours?"

Her demeanor sobered suddenly and she bit her lip. "I think I may be pregnant."

"What?" The ball of tension in her stomach expanded, threatening to push the lemonade-vodka back up her throat. For Elizabeth to be pregnant…Holt had, indeed, fallen fast and hard for her best friend. The first layer of bricks went up around her heart.

"I haven't told him yet, because I'm not sure. But I'm becoming more sure every day. And I'm scared." Her eyes brimmed with fear. "I'll need him, Sara. He's a stable man. Someone who will keep me grounded."

"Right. Well, maybe you shouldn't be drinking the spiked lemonade then, either."

Elizabeth's look turned hard. "I'll do what I need to. Stay out of it. You've always wanted what I have, but this time you've got to get your own life. Maybe it'd be best if we kept our distance for a while."

A week after graduation, Elizabeth and Holt married in a small church ceremony. Sara hadn't been invited, and hadn't wanted to attend. She'd still been heartsick. Still roommates through the end of the semester, she'd endured enough glimpses of Elizabeth's new life—the prenatal vitamins *innocently* left out on the kitchen counter, the stack of wedding invitations, and the picture of the happy engaged couple ready to be submitted to the newspaper—to convince herself she was a horrible person, and that Elizabeth had been right. She'd wanted what Elizabeth had.

She still did.

It had been a competition, and Sara hadn't even realized it until later, looking back. Despite their brief, intense connection, Holt had been lost to her forever.

She'd certainly felt something in that kiss...but apparently it had been one-sided. Her cheeks flamed with the memory of how mistaken she'd been, and how her tunnel vision had led to the ultimate humiliation when Holt had walked away without another thought.

But she refused to harbor old regrets. She never would have been happy with Holt, as he clearly preferred the sparkle of women like Elizabeth. Vibrant and full of life, Elizabeth had been a free spirit but also flighty and undependable. But always intensely passionate. Sara couldn't compete with that, nor had she wanted to be at odds with her friend.

Sara pulled into the parking lot at the end of the drive and nearly ran inside the school, rushing up the stairs as if her past were chasing her down, nipping at her heels. She slammed her apartment door behind her and took several deep breaths.

An only child, Sara had found a sister in Elizabeth. And then she'd blown it. And then she'd lost her parents a few years later. Another chance blown. Then she'd purposely blown up her marriage to a sycophant control freak who'd never understood her and liked to lose himself in the bottle. It had been a desperate grab for compassion and connection when she'd married Dillon. They'd fooled each other and themselves.

Then she'd finally grown up and found herself.

She moved to the cupboard in her kitchen and took down an unopened bottle of tequila. The good stuff. Top shelf quality— nothing but the best to celebrate the memory of Elizabeth's life on the first anniversary of her funeral. And to chase the bitter taste of jealousy down her throat.

She poured a generous shot into a juice glass and searched the refrigerator drawer for a lime. Putting a wedge on the side of the glass, she was about to carry it to the couch where she could indulge in a good mope when there was a knock at the door. She must have left the front door of the school unlocked in her rush to get to seclusion.

"Yes?" she called through the door.

"Sara? It's Holt." She opened the door to find him there, catching his breath. He gestured to the stairs. "Quite a climb."

Had he run up the three flights? "What are you doing here?"

"You raced out of the bar so fast...I wanted to make sure you got home okay."

"I'm fine."

His glance moved to the glass in her hand and he frowned. "I see that."

She lifted it in salute. "Yeah, and I was about to be a lot finer."

"Or a lot more messed up."

"I figured tequila was the best way to honor Elizabeth's memory."

His eyes darkened and he started unzipping his jacket. "I'm in."

"What?" She didn't point out that she hadn't invited him to join her pity party.

"If you're remembering Elizabeth, I want in. Who understood her better than the two of us? Besides, I wanted to talk to you about Theo. You fled before I could mention it."

"I'm warning you I won't be good company tonight."

"Ditto."

She moved inside to pour a drink for him. He followed her, closed the door behind him and took his jacket off.

"I wanted to thank you again for that email," he said. "And for stopping by the other night...staying to play chess."

"I hope I didn't overstep my bounds." The memory of their past kiss, when she *had* overstepped *several* people's boundaries, had her cheeks flaming. She turned and went to the refrigerator to get a second wedge of lime.

"Not at all. It meant a lot to Theo—" He stopped abruptly, as if he'd been about to say more. But when she looked over her shoulder, he was slamming back a gulp of tequila.

"Hey, be careful. That stuff's more for sipping than shots."

HOLT DIDN'T WANT TO BE ATTRACTED TO SARA. HE DIDN'T WANT IT with everything in him. But as she bent over the drawer in the refrigerator, he couldn't help but notice the fine roundness of her ass. Not wanting to be aroused by her, he lashed out with sarcasm. "*There's* the old Sara. Always did know the *right* way to do things. Elizabeth said that was one of the reasons she broke things off with you. You insisted you knew best."

She handed him a lime wedge, then surprised him by nodding. "I admit I tended to think I knew what was right. Nobody could ever win with me." She arched a brow at his shocked silence. "What? People can't grow? I wasn't trying to be controlling about your alcohol consumption. I was simply suggesting you slow down and pace yourself. And for the record, it was Elizabeth who established a two-shot limit."

"Did she now?" The Elizabeth he'd met had been the life of the party, always flirting and laughing. He'd been shocked and flattered when the woman who'd captured every male eye in the room with her easy laugh and sexy confidence had come on to him. She'd admitted she'd been the partying type but was working to become more studious and focused. She'd told him he'd be a good influence on her. And when she'd become pregnant, it had seemed a natural move to get married.

Sara led the way to the couch, carrying her drink. "Most definitely. Any more than two drinks and you were at risk for some serious sinning or spinning." She sat on one end of the couch, and he sat on the other. She bent her legs, pulling her bare feet up onto the cushion between him and her. Her toes were pink, just like that day at the picnic. Conservative, yet flirty. A reflection of the woman, though he suspected she didn't realize she had that fun side. The hem of her skirt slid up her thigh, but she didn't seem to notice. Instead, her lips curved as if enjoying some wicked memory.

He couldn't help but laugh. "Which did it lead to for you?"

"I'll never tell."

"I'd bet spinning." Sara was too controlled to let out her inner animal. Except with him, a decade ago. It had cost her dearly, he imagined, having lost her friendship with Elizabeth because of her impulsiveness…and he'd seen the price she'd paid on her face whenever he'd happened to bump into her. Between Spring Break and graduation, she'd dropped weight and turned pale. He'd blocked the thought of it…or tried to.

She laughed. "You might not want to place that bet. And you're forgetting that stupid kiss."

"I couldn't forget the kiss." His gaze shot to her mouth. Her lips were definitely meant for sinning. He dragged his attention back to her eyes, relieved she hadn't noticed the chink in his armor.

Sara's demeanor turned serious. "I had been drinking that night I kissed you, but that wasn't why I did it."

"No, it was to break up your best friend's relationship. You saw me as a threat." He hated the raw accusation he heard in his voice and immediately censored it. That was the past. "But we were all much younger back then."

Sara studied him a moment. "Is that what you really believe? Or is that the line Elizabeth fed you?" Before he could form a reply, she shook her head. "Never mind. Tonight isn't about old regrets. It's about remembering Elizabeth." She raised her glass. "Ready?"

"As I'll ever be." He did a quick sign of the cross with his right hand and she laughed again. He realized with a jolt that he liked the sound. How long had it been since he'd heard a woman's laughter?

"To Elizabeth's spirit of fun—may it remind us that life is precious, and meant to be enjoyed." She took a sip of her tequila and he echoed the movement. The burn warmed his throat and tickled the back of his nostrils. He closed his eyes to savor the warmth. When he opened them, Sara was sucking on her lime wedge. She licked her wide lips. The sight stabbed him straight in the gut. "Your turn."

He shook off the image of her lips and raised his glass. "To Elizabeth..." His voice cracked and he simply left it at that, then slammed back a large swallow. Sara's eyes shimmered with sympathy.

"TELL ME A STORY ABOUT HER," SARA SAID. "I MISSED SO MANY YEARS because I was an idiot."

His lips twitched before he gave in to a half smile. "*Was* an idiot? Who says you've changed?"

"I do." She pretended to be offended. "And what I say is always correct."

"Ah, the old Sara."

"The new Sara admits to her mistakes and moves on. Life is too short."

"Hear, hear." Holt saluted her with his empty glass.

She clinked hers to his. The warmth of the alcohol was working its way into her limbs, making them heavy and liquid, leaving her with a pleasant, if bittersweet, sense of reality. Remembering Elizabeth was painful but strangely liberating too. It affirmed what was important in life—spending time with loved ones and pursuing your dreams.

She went to retrieve the tequila bottle from the kitchen, refilled their glasses and placed the bottle on the table.

"So, what mistakes have you moved on from?" he asked.

"Well, there's you."

"What do you mean?"

"I was wrong." She settled on the couch again, braced her elbow on the back and propped her cheek on her hand. "About you, about your relationship with Elizabeth. It was stronger than I'd deluded myself into believing. Besides, it was none of my business."

"You're right on all accounts." His gaze held hers. Five o'clock shadow darkened his cheeks. "But you've already apologized, so let's move on."

"I wonder what Elizabeth would say about this." She gestured between the two of them.

"I think she'd be happy we put our differences to rest. For Theo's sake too."

Sara's heart clenched. She stared into the amber liquid in her glass. "I love that boy. You've done a great job."

"That was all Elizabeth."

Sara stuck out her leg and nudged him sharply in the thigh with her toes.

His gaze went to them, then to her, amusement dancing in the hazel depths. "What was that for?"

"*Now* who's being the idiot?"

"You?"

"Guess again. You're Theo's *father*. I seriously doubt you've had nothing to do with who he's become. Hey." She tipped her head until he met her gaze again. "You've been through the wringer. Not just this past year, but the year before, with all the chemo and radiation and the hospital visits…watching Elizabeth—someone so full of life that you wondered how the human body could contain it—

slip away. It couldn't have been easy." It had to have been hell. Sara had only been around for the last few months of it.

"After Elizabeth's death, I felt him disconnect."

Sara smiled gently and Holt's gaze fell to her lips. Though he hadn't touched her, it felt like a caress. Her breath hitched. "Guys always want to rush out and fix things. Sometimes you can just let them be. Theo will let you know when he's ready. Of course, you have to be around him in order for him to let you know when he *is* ready."

He seemed to weigh her words. "Is that what he's said in your sessions together?"

"Sessions?"

"Your weekly chess games. They've resumed, right? I hope so, because he really enjoys them. He's determined to beat you. He's been practicing every night on that game you gave him."

She laughed. "I thought his technique had improved. The chess was a way to keep him close, get to know him. When he started getting in trouble, I thought I'd failed Elizabeth by not keeping better track of him."

"I know the feeling," he muttered.

Yeah, failure wouldn't sit well with either of their personalities. "And he's so smart and introspective, like you. I thought he might enjoy a game of strategy. So I started it as a way for me to get to know him. It evolved into some pretty good chats, especially about the storylines in his comic books. He's really talented."

Holt frowned. "He still hasn't shown them to me." He tipped his head back against the back of the couch. "I have to find something like that. A way to connect."

"The connection's there, Holt. It's the timing that has to line up." She realized her toes had migrated until they touched the seam of his pants so she bent her knees to pull them away. "He really is doing much better."

"Because of you."

"Maybe...but the passing of time helps too. I'm glad you

brought him back for another year at the Academy, though." She chewed her lip before plunging forward and asking the question that had bugged her for a year now. "Did you approve of Elizabeth's decision to send Theo here?"

"Truthfully? Not at first," he admitted after a long moment. "But looking back, it was a good decision. He needs the stability of a strong school, and a strong female influence. Two years ago, none of this was even on the horizon yet."

"None of what?"

"The notoriety."

"From your current case, you mean?"

"That, but also becoming known for what I do within certain circles."

Her brow crinkled as she tried to understand what he was getting at. "You mean fellow professionals?"

"And serial killers."

"Oh."

"Yeah. *Oh.* Over the past year, a couple of them started writing to me from prison. Nothing threatening. In fact, some were admiring, inviting me to interview them." He gave a half smile, but his grim amusement quickly disappeared. "But it woke me up to the fact that I had a little boy who needed me to be both father and mother now. Being both has been a strain, and I see him pulling farther and farther away from me."

He was becoming increasingly agitated as he spoke and she felt the need to touch him, to comfort him. She leaned forward across her bent knees and laid a hand on his arm. "Being a parent isn't easy. You're doing your best."

"And yet our relationship is getting worse."

She could see that the distance between him and Theo was hurting him. "He still needs you."

"Not as much. Not anymore."

"Don't let his bravado fool you. Inside, he's a scared kid who wants his dad to wrap him in a hug and protect him from the world."

Holt examined her a moment. "You're pretty in tune with these kids, huh?"

"Sometimes too much." John Rochard definitely didn't appreciate her being in tune with his kids. Neil needed a firm hand to hold him in line as he approached graduation. Jeremy seemed overlooked and was desperate for attention. He'd earn it in a healthy way—on stage, if he were allowed to. If he couldn't do that, he'd choose less healthy ways. It was one reason she was fighting so hard. "Some parents don't appreciate my involvement, but I decided long ago that I would be a hands-on, from-the-heart administrator."

"I bet the kids appreciate your involvement."

"I like to think so. And I like to think I've learned some hard lessons, wisdom I can share. I've worked hard to make a life I could be proud of, and that included mending fences with Elizabeth. And with you."

He eyed her for a long moment before raising his glass. "To healing relationships—*all* kinds of relationships."

She leaned forward and clinked her glass to his before they took the final swallows. The room spun a bit and she put her glass down. "I warned you two should be the limit. I think that was the equivalent of number three. Maybe four."

"Guess we'll find out if it'll be sinning or spinning after all." That heated glance was back, but he quickly averted his gaze and she convinced herself she must have been mistaken. Holt Patterson had disliked her up until a month ago. No way was he now looking at her as if he wanted to do tequila shots off her abdomen. Though he was being kind and forgiving, this was Holt My-Moral-Compass-Points-Due-North Patterson, after all.

"What brought you to the Academy?" His gaze was penetrating, as if it could see into her soul. She wasn't sure she wanted to share the intimate details of her failed marriage, and the self-examination that had led her to this point. Even the tequila wouldn't encourage that much revelation.

"The Academy was hiring at a time I was looking to come back home." Even if her family was gone, it still had the feeling of home for her. "Of course, they couldn't say it outright, but the board wanted a woman. Though it's a boys' school, they thought a female might encourage a gentler tone here. Things had gotten a little too competitive and nasty, and morale, as well as enrollment, was dropping. Before this, I'd worked my way up to principal at a public school and had the appropriate credentials."

"Quite a different atmosphere here, I would guess."

"Yes. But I needed a change of scenery after my life went to hell. My parents died, I was married, blinked, and then divorced." Suddenly cold, she sat up and tucked her feet under her, smoothing her skirt over her legs like a blanket. She covered her awkwardness with a laugh. "See, I can admit to my mistakes." One of the problems with her marriage to Dillon had been her constantly comparing him—though only in her mind, and she hadn't even realized she was doing it at first—to Holt. "Dillon and I were completely wrong for each other…but then, I didn't even know who I was at the time."

"Elizabeth missed you, you know. All those years."

"I'm glad she gave me the chance to be her friend again before…" Before she died. Sara shook her head and sent the room spinning again. "Boy, I think I've had enough to drink. I've turned this celebration into a somber occasion. Elizabeth would have had music blaring."

He chuckled. "She would have had me clearing the furniture away to make a dance floor."

Sara snorted. "Yeah, and we would have been propping up the wall."

"Or holding down the couch."

. . .

WAS HE REALLY THINKING ABOUT HOLDING DOWN THE COUCH WITH Sara? Holt put down his empty glass and stood. Time to get back to reality. "I think I should get going."

"No way you're driving. You aren't sober." She jumped up, then swayed. He reached out a hand to steady her and felt the skin-to-skin contact jolt through him. She laughed. "Neither of us is. Stay. Unless, of course, you have to get home to Theo and relieve a sitter. I could call you a cab."

"Theo's with my parents for the night."

"Good, then there's no reason to leave."

There were many reasons, not the least of which was he needed time to process this *friendship* with the new Sara. He was about to opt for a cab, but his niggling conscience and the determined look in Sara's eye swayed him.

He sat down and tugged her down next to him, if only to keep her from tipping over. She wasn't kidding when she'd said two drinks was her limit. "You're right."

She bounced right back up and moved away from him, almost as if she were nervous. "Just what every woman likes to hear. You can sleep in my bed."

"Just what every man likes to hear." He was surprised at the heat that shot through him, landing in his groin, at her innocent invitation.

"You're not every man. You were my best friend's husband. And I was planning to take the couch."

"I wasn't coming on to you," he assured her. But he might very well have been flirting with her, just a little. "Thank you. A place to sleep is a generous offer, and I'll accept only because I'm seeing two of you right now. But *I'll* take the couch."

CHAPTER 8

The hot water ran through Sara's hair and over her face, leaching some of the pain from the pounding headache. Despite a touch of hangover, this morning she felt lighter...happier. It was amazing what some forgiveness could do. She and Holt had made a huge step together last night.

She'd risen early so she could shower and dress before he woke. Then, he could use the apartment's only facilities while she made coffee. That was the plan, anyway, but as she entered the living room, still wrapping her wet hair back into a twist, the smell of fresh-brewed coffee nearly made her weep with gratitude.

"You certainly found your way around quickly," she said.

Holt took two mugs out of the cupboard. "I thought you could use a cup. I know I could."

"It smells wonderful. Thank you." She took the full cup he offered. He looked crisp and fresh, and she was pretty sure he wasn't wearing the same clothing as the night before. "The bathroom's all yours if you want it."

"Thanks, but I had my travel bag in the car. Already brought it in and used the boys' bathroom downstairs to dress." His gaze ran over her quickly before darting away. "Thanks for the couch."

She winced. "I hope it wasn't too short."

"I made do." His expression was hidden as he took a swallow of coffee. Was he regretting what they'd shared with each other?

She ran a finger around the rim of her mug, unsure how to go back to the more comfortable manners they'd had with each other last night.

His next words relieved her anxiety. "I thought maybe Theo and I could sit with you at the family-faculty breakfast this morning."

"That would be great."

He downed the rest of his coffee and rinsed the mug, then set it in the sink. "No dishwasher, huh?"

She set her own cup down and waggled her fingers. "That would be these puppies. Magic fingers." She stuck the fingers in the pockets of her slacks as the mood turned awkward again. But maybe it was all on her end. How had her attraction to Holt Patterson flared up again? She'd managed to shut it down for so long. Apparently, it had been a dormant seed, just waiting for a bit of rain to encourage it to bloom brightly again.

He glanced at his watch and her gaze went to the hair on the back of his hands. Brown, like the hair on his head, with highlights as if dusted with sunshine. "I promised Theo I'd pick him up at eight-fifteen so we'd be at the breakfast on time. I'd better get going."

"I'll see you there."

He paused as he passed her at the breakfast counter. "Thank you for last night. It meant a lot to be able to talk to someone who understands."

"To me too."

In the wake of Holt's departure, the apartment seemed quieter than the normal Saturday morning. Sara hurried to straighten up, washing the mugs and coffeepot, as well as the tumblers they'd drank from the night before. She paused in the process of folding the couch sheets, and resisted the urge to hold them to her nose and inhale Holt's musky scent. She left them on the couch. She was in a hurry anyway, she told herself. She was so good at telling herself what she needed to hear.

The family-faculty breakfast at the Heather Hedge Lodge was located in the restaurant across the lobby from the bar where they'd had the mixer the night before. A fresh flower adorned each table, along with crisp white tablecloths. The students who attended filled up on the buffet brunch—most of them returning two or three times—while the teachers and parents seemed to have no problem engaging in conversation as they ate.

John Rochard passed by, his two sons trudging behind him. There was no sign of his soon-to-be ex-wife, but rumor had it they could barely stand to be in the same room together. Sara knew the feeling. Despite the wonderful smells coming from the buffet, her stomach clenched up tight in protest of John's appearance.

"Hi, Neil. Jeremy. John." Sara smiled at each male in turn.

Jeremy beamed. "We get to eat whatever we want?"

"Whatever your stomach can hold. But I recommend you try a little at a time. You don't have to pile it on all at once."

"We're not heathens," John said. "Unlike some people, we practice manners and good morals."

She stiffened. He'd attack her in front of the kids? As usual, it was an insult disguised as vaguely helpful advice. "Practice makes perfect."

From the corner of her eye, she thought she saw a smirk on Neil's face before he quickly wiped it away and followed his dad to a table. Damn. They were sitting with the president of the board. She should have snagged that seat. But she'd much rather sit with Theo and Holt at a table with friendlier company, anyway.

When Holt arrived a minute later with Theo at his side, he almost looked shy. "Hey."

"Hey," she returned.

Theo looked from her to his dad but didn't seem to note anything odd. He scouted out the restaurant. "I see some friends over there." They found seats with a couple of Theo's classmates and their parents, as well as the elementary-level English and Social Studies teachers. For once, she didn't feel like an outsider looking in. She actually felt like she had a family to sit with.

Don't kid yourself. You don't belong with Holt.

Last night she and Holt had broken through the barriers of their past to form some kind of friendship, but would it last now that the tequila bottle was nowhere in sight?

After they'd filled their bellies—Theo had returned to the buffet three times—they walked to the parking lot together and stopped at her car.

"I'll see you at school Monday," she told Theo. "You two enjoy the rest of your weekend." Hers would be painfully quiet after the engaging company she'd had.

"You too." Holt's gaze held hers over Theo's head. "Thanks again for the talk. It helped."

"Same here." Her heart pulled as they walked away, as if there were an invisible string connecting it to them. Holt had offered friendship. The thought had originally been laughable considering their history, but after a taste of Holt's friendship, she found herself thirsting for it. He was quick-witted and kind.

He's also Elizabeth's. The angel on her shoulder was relentless.

The devil opposite her whispered "*was*." He *was* Elizabeth's.

THE WOMAN LOOKED SO FORLORN THAT TOXIN'S CHEST TIGHTENED with sympathy. His father would have called him a pussy if he'd still been alive. *Emotions make a man weak. Might as well grow a vagina.*

Shit. Now he was hearing his old man's voice in his head, after all these years. He'd have Henry tweak the latest batch. Apparently, he was becoming tolerant to the pleasant effects of the drug, which were intended to enhance the senses and creativity...not *feelings*. *Christ.*

He'd learned the hard way that his goddamn bastard of a father had been *right*. Didn't that beat all?

But the look Sara Burns cast toward Holt as he walked away with his son was nothing short of miserable. He knew that feeling well, and it dredged up old memories. Longing. Loss.

She and Holt had spent the night at her apartment. He'd followed Holt there from the Lodge and watched him go inside. The man hadn't come out in the hours Toxin waited.

But now, Holt left her standing alone in a parking lot, a look of hopelessness on her face? What a jackass. Sara was one ripe woman. Hair like sweet, flowing honey. Eyes without guile. Curvy in all the right places. A laugh that tugged at a man's genitals.

And yet Holt kept walking. All the way to his car.

But, what have we here? Sara got into her car, and in doing so missed the look Holt shot her way over the roof of his own. She wasn't the only one wanting more.

At breakfast, their body language told him everything. They wanted each other but didn't want to want each other. Or maybe they didn't even know they wanted each other yet. What the hell had they been doing all night in Sara's apartment? His studies of Holt told him this behavior was out of the norm.

Toxin smiled. Sara was something special, and she was getting to Holt. The so-called mindhunter hadn't even noticed Toxin following him. He hadn't noticed the prick in the flashy sports car between Toxin's and Holt's, either. Or that said prick had crept into the school and spied on whatever was going on inside. It appeared Holt or Sara had another admirer.

If Holt liked Sara enough to deviate from his self-enforced

celibacy, she was some damn good piece of ass. He'd like to taste a bit of that sweetness for himself.

In fact, Holt's life was a very nice one indeed. Toxin wouldn't mind slipping it on like a comfortable pair of shoes and walking around a while. He'd spent the night imagining that. And planning. He'd already taken the initial steps.

One day soon, everything he'd lost, everything Holt had, would be *his.*

CHAPTER 9

Another body, and Toxin had been brazen enough to call it in to the CPD himself. That Monday, the sun was just appearing as a big orange ball on the horizon when Holt arrived at the scene to which the killer had directed them—an abandoned lot on the south side of Chicago. Thankfully, his father had been available to come over to watch Theo and deliver him to school.

Holt pulled behind a plain vehicle he assumed was Noah's car. Max's pickup was already across the street, parked behind a cruiser. The sharp rap of knuckles on the passenger window startled him. The hand belonged to Max. Holt got out of the car and fell into step beside him as they headed for the small group of people standing in the distance.

Holt shot Max a sideways glance. "You look like you've been hit by a train." Yesterday's five-o'clock stubble was turning into a serious beard. Of course, women probably thought Max looked sexy.

Max grunted. "Long night." Probably partying with the girl of the month.

They stopped at the perimeter of the cordoned-off area and Noah came over to them. "We've been waiting for the sun to come up so we can fully process the scene. Once we were sure we had a dead body, and the officer's flashlight lit up the syringe, we backed away. The CPD crime scene team just arrived."

"Any sign of a suspicious person hanging around?" Holt asked.

Noah shook his head. "As you suggested, we've had undercover officers watching the perimeter since the killer likes a show. But nothing so far." He looked about them. "Of course, if he wanted to observe without being noticed, he picked a darn difficult place to do it." The weed-filled, deserted lot was like an open field. And at this hour of the morning, there was no crowd to hide in.

Noah turned on his heel and led them to the far corner of the lot where three other figures, one in a police uniform and two crime scene analysts, were chomping at the bit to get to the evidence.

"What do you know so far?" Holt picked his way across the broken-glass-strewn dirt and knee-high weeds.

"The wallet on the guy identifies him as Leonard Redding, a sixty-five-year-old retired Air Force captain. The syringe and the bruising around a puncture mark on Redding's neck identify him as one of Toxin's victims."

"Bruising?"

"He went at this guy particularly hard."

"The bruising could indicate that Redding fought back or that Toxin knew him and released his aggression on him."

Noah didn't stop walking, but spoke over his shoulder. "There's another difference. Unlike the others, Captain Redding was killed somewhere else, then dropped at this location."

"How do you know?"

"Coroner says the body temp indicates Redding was killed about eight hours ago, but there's dew on the grass under his body. The part of his clothing he was lying on is damp. When he gets to the morgue, the coroner will confirm the theory that Redding was killed elsewhere once he gets a closer look at the pooling of blood."

"Killed in one location and dropped at another? Killer must be strong."

"The broken and bent weeds and grass in the area indicate the body was dragged from the roadside, but yes, it would take a good deal of strength if he did it by himself."

"It's like Toxin's evolving his methods, trying to figure out what he wants his pattern to be. Or he's trying to throw us off."

Noah stopped as they reached the edge of the circle the technicians had roped off around Redding's body. "There's another difference here. A note."

"Handwritten?" If so, Holt would get the SSAM handwriting consultant on it right away.

"No, printed on printer paper. It's what it said that is interesting."

"Please tell me he signed it with his real name and address."

Noah didn't even crack a smile. "Unfortunately, no. But he addressed it to you."

Holt looked at him in surprise. "Me?"

"It seems you have an admirer. He's been following you since he called the tip hotline last month, from what the note says."

Max looked sharply between Noah and Holt. "No fucking way."

"He mentions an incident from a couple weeks ago too. Sounds like a firsthand account. Some kind of picnic?"

Holt's heart thumped harder. The Labor Day picnic? Toxin had followed him there? Holt took the paper, protected by a plastic sleeve, from Noah.

Dr. Patterson,

I'm sure you missed me. I've been following your—my—case since our little chat, but you don't appear to be any closer to discovering who I am. Must be frustrating to be so inept. I wonder what new clues Buzz's death will give you. I look forward to meeting you one day. You lead an interesting life...when you're not working so hard at being inept. The picnic was a particularly interesting day, wouldn't you say? Interesting enough to finally see your woman again this weekend. Took you long enough. She's sexy and smart...a real catch. And to think you never would have found each other if your wife hadn't died.

Holt had to consciously keep his hands from balling the note up and tossing it across the field. Toxin hadn't mentioned Theo, thank God, but he had seen him with Sara and knew he was a widower. How the hell...? Obviously, Holt hadn't been thinking clearly, hadn't even anticipated that the killer might take an interest in him and—*hell*—follow him through his everyday activities. What exactly had he seen between Holt and Sara? *Enough.* Otherwise, why mention her at all?

"Holt?" Max was studying him. "Are you okay, man?"

Noah was watching him too. "Do you know who the *she* is that Toxin refers to?"

"What's in the note?" Max asked. Holt passed it to him.

"Yes, I know who he's referring to." Holt cleared his throat, trying to relieve the tightness there. "Sara Burns. She's the director at Theo's school."

"And she was with you at this picnic he mentioned, as well as this past Friday?"

"Yes."

Max raised his eyes from the note. "That's it? You're not going to tell us more?"

"I'm sure you're assuming the worst, anyway."

"Or the best. I'm *assuming* she's the one who's got you thinking about abandoning your bid for sainthood."

"Is he right?" Noah asked. "Do you have a relationship with Miss Burns?"

Jesus. He sent a hand through his hair. "She's an old friend of Elizabeth's. We spent one night together—this past Friday." His gaze met Max's. "And it wasn't like that."

Max shrugged. "That's your business, unless a murderer makes it everyone's business."

"What *was* it like?" Noah prodded. "It must have been *something* if it grabbed this guy's attention."

"It was. *Something*. It was…" Special. They'd shared things with each other, things he wasn't sure he'd ever have talked about with anyone who didn't know Elizabeth and Theo as well as Sara did. But apparently, now, he'd have to share it—some of it—with at least two other people. "There was a parent-faculty mixer hosted by Theo's school. We skipped out early to talk. We had a little too much to drink. I spent the night on her couch. End of story."

"Is that it?" Max asked.

"That's it."

Noah eyed him for another moment. "Obviously, you're on Toxin's radar."

Holt felt sick. "He has to know about Theo."

Noah's look was sympathetic. "Better to be prepared than to be caught by surprise. I've got officers watching this area in case he's watching you now."

Holt's muscles bunched, resisting the urge to turn and survey the premises himself. He took a deep breath to steady his mind and relax his limbs. "All those details about my life. He wants me to know he knows all about me. Courses of action?"

Max's eyes turned to flint. "Protect the innocent. And then go on the attack." Spoken like a true soldier.

"Protect the innocent? You mean take Theo out of school? Stick him in my office like some kind of prisoner?" He shook his head. He didn't think Toxin's obsession with him was about Theo. "His words indicate he identifies with me, whereas Sara is a nameless woman and he doesn't even mention Theo." Holt felt a tad better as he reconfirmed his suspicions by studying the note again.

Noah nodded. "Then the best place for Theo is probably at the school, where he can keep his routine and is surrounded by familiar people he trusts. Where anyone suspicious would stick out. But you should notify your friend—both about Theo and that she could be in danger."

Holt found himself looking forward to hearing her voice again. Part of him craved the comfort she'd offered him a few days ago. He couldn't act on those cravings, of course. She'd been put in enough danger simply by seeing him twice.

No, he should keep far away from her until they caught Toxin. If she didn't hate him before, when Elizabeth had cut her out of their lives, she'd surely hate him now, for bringing a killer into her world. Still, he found relief in knowing she was at his son's school. If there was one thing he'd come to know about this new Sara, it was that she wouldn't let anything happen to Theo. She'd protect him with her life.

JOHN ROCHARD RUSHED IN AS SARA WAS EATING LUNCH AT HER DESK. His expression of triumph put Sara on high alert.

"Glad you could make time to see me." His voice dripped with sarcasm.

She glanced pointedly at her lunch. "I *had* made time, but not for another hour yet, at the time you had scheduled."

She'd invited the parents to make personal conferences with her, and many had taken her up on the offer. But seeing John's name on the appointment calendar first thing Monday morning had been a shock. Still, she'd hoped it was a good sign. Maybe they could clear the air between them once and for all. Unfortunately, judging by the way his eyes glittered with purpose, she doubted that was his intention.

"This can't wait any longer," John said. "I have to get back to the city for work. Important business."

"I'm sure you do." Sighing, Sara laid her ham-and-swiss sandwich down. She gestured to a seat, but John remained standing. "I hope you enjoyed the parent functions this weekend."

He smirked. "I was surprised *you* made it to the breakfast at all."

Wariness prickled along her skin like the tiny footsteps of invisible bugs. "Of course I did. Forming a relationship with the parents of this school is important to me."

"Whatever you need to tell yourself to face the mirror each day."

"Excuse me?"

"I saw you. You and him. *Forming a relationship.*"

"Me and *who?*"

"Dr. Patterson. You left the mixer in a hurry Friday night. He left directly after. The both of you were late to the breakfast. You sat together, left together. It doesn't take much to put two and two together."

Sara's cheeks heated with anger and embarrassment. "So you're adding that up and getting, what, twenty-two?"

"Surely the board will find this information interesting."

"You should check your math first."

"I don't need numbers. I know he spent the night with you. I followed him to the school, saw him go to your apartment."

Her first reaction was outrage that John had invaded her privacy. Her second was panic. Sara's throat tightened as her mind flew back over the evening. What exactly had he seen? But no, there hadn't been anything improper. Just two acquaintances having drinks together at her place. But Holt *had* stayed the night with her on school property...oh, God, how would that look to the board if John talked? He wouldn't have to try hard to spin it in a negative direction.

He walked to the bookshelf and fingered her Educator of the Year award. To purposely draw attention to her failings as an educator? It seemed he was more devious and calculating than she'd thought.

Rather than dignify his implied threat with a response, she bit her tongue, waiting. Again, she didn't have to wait long. John Rochard was a man who knew what he wanted, and once that desire was identified, he was impatient to make it a reality...

without troubling himself with the same morals and standards as most of the civilized world.

His lips twisted into a perverse smile. "I propose we come to an agreement."

"Such as?"

"I won't say anything to the board about your inappropriate behavior and ruin your plans for a theater or whatever other nonsense you have planned. *And* I won't get you fired." Sara held her breath as she waited for the price of John's benevolence. "And *you* help Neil pass his classes this semester. In fact, I think he deserves to be on the Honor Roll."

"Nothing happened between Dr. Patterson and me."

"I'm supposed to believe that? What other possible reason would he have for staying all night?"

"And if he did? There are no rules against a faculty or staff member dating a parent."

"There should be. So many conflicts of interest... I'm sure the board will take note if the case were presented properly. And your review period is right around the corner, isn't it?"

"There was nothing improper," she repeated. She hated the squeak that had crept into her tone, but her throat seemed to have closed up over her words.

He stepped around her desk and leaned down until he was in her face. The man liked to use his physical presence to intimidate. "Care to take a lie detector test?"

She looked away from his cold gaze. There was no arguing with him, anyway. He had the board in his pocket. One hint of impropriety and she'd be gone.

"Since birth, Neil was meant to go to Harvard," John said. "Make it happen. I promise, if I'm happy, you'll be happy." He yanked her door open and walked out.

Cheryl hurried in. "Boy, he looked like the cat who swallowed the canary. I almost expected to see feathers sticking out of his mouth. What happened?"

"It's nothing." But at that moment, she felt like a tiny, helpless yellow bird.

YOU ARE NOT DOING THIS BECAUSE JOHN ROCHARD SAID SO.

Sara repeated it to herself as she trekked out to the gym. She'd debated how to handle the Rochard issue for over an hour before deciding it was, at the very least, time to check in with Neil. His schedule said he'd be in Physical Education right now. Ironically, given his father's abhorrence of her new programs, Neil was one of the students who seemed to benefit the most from the new sports facilities. According to Coach, Neil spent many hours in the weight room, ramping up for football, track and basketball. Today, the football team was out on the field in full gear. They'd lost their second game in a row that weekend, and were paying for it with a brutal workout.

She went to stand by Coach at the sidelines. "Are they looking any better?"

"They will by the end of the week. We got a tough opponent coming up. This last one was nothing, and still they lost. We should have had them."

"I'm sure you'll whip them into shape."

"Helps to have a place to practice here on school grounds." Coach's gaze remained on the players doing sprints up and down the field. "What brings you out here?"

"I need to talk to Neil."

"What's he done this time?"

Startled, her gaze shifted from the players to Coach. "This time?"

"Heard he had a run-in with the law several weeks back, during the summer. Daddy's money and Grandpa's rep bought him a reprieve. Plus, he was a first offender."

"This is the first I've heard of it." Clearly, things were worse than she'd thought. "What did he do?"

"Stole a case of beer from a convenience store while his buddies distracted the clerk."

"Beer?" Was he into alcohol and drugs?

"The incident was never made official, so I didn't make a big deal of it." His eyes met hers. "Not *officially*, anyway." He jerked his head toward the far corner of the field where Neil was filling water bottles for the football players from a big orange cooler. His attention, however, kept diverting to the action on the field.

"Looks like he's paying his dues."

Coach nodded. "And he will be all season in some form or another, though he gets plenty of time to practice too."

"That, plus night school?"

"It's a lot, but the kid insists he can handle it. We've got him some extra tutoring on the weekends. And I guarantee you I would have made a big deal of the incident this summer if I thought there was a real problem. He's just a kid working out some kinks."

Sara breathed a sigh of relief. She trusted Coach's opinion of his players, and an addiction would make things a hundred times more difficult, as would a criminal record. "The SATs are in a couple of weeks."

"Got that covered too. Told him a University of Michigan scout would be at the game in a few weeks, so he might want to keep his grades up and his nose to the grindstone if he wants to play for a shot at a scholarship there."

"Sounds like you have it under control."

"Never hurts to have more of us on his back, though." With a nod, he meandered down the field to shout instructions at some players.

Sara made her way around the sidelines to the table with the cooler. "Hey, Neil."

Neil looked up briefly then returned to filling cups, this time from a second cooler, apparently filled with Gatorade. "Hey."

"Just thought I'd check in with you." *Not because your father's a bully.*

"I'm fine."

"I see that. But I hope you know my door is always open if you want to talk."

He didn't look up. "'Kay."

"About anything."

This time, his response was a simple nod. He wasn't in the mood to chat, and probably didn't want his friends to witness it, anyway. "You know where to find me." She turned to leave, but his words stopped her.

"You like this school, right? You care about it?"

She turned back. "I love this school. I care very much about it and all of the students."

He seemed to process this. "That's what I thought."

Coach's whistle signaled the end of practice, and the sweat-drenched team swarmed toward the refreshments. Sara made her way back to her office, hoping her invitation had been enough to open the door—at least a crack.

Cheryl waved frantically to her as Sara passed her desk. *Now what?*

"He's on hold." Cheryl's voice radiated repressed excitement.

"He, who?" *Please don't let it be John or a board member.*

"Dr. Patterson."

Holt was calling her? "Thank you."

"That's it?" Cheryl's smile went flat, like an egg hitting a hard tile floor. "Even from what little you told me, I could tell this guy was special."

"He was. For about a day. He's just like any other student's father." *Liar.* She ignored the voice in her head. She couldn't afford to get her hopes up, especially after last time. *He only wants friendship.* "I'm sure he's calling to check in on Theo."

Cheryl scowled at her. "You could at least try. You don't date, you don't have fun. All you have is this school."

Sara regretted having told her anything at all about her past with Holt. This morning, in a moment of weakness, she'd confided in Cheryl that she'd once had feelings for Holt, and that he now seemed interested in rekindling a friendship. "Sometimes it's way too easy to talk to you."

The scowl disappeared. "Good. Now be a smart girl and at least try." Cheryl tipped her head toward her office. "He's waiting. Line one."

Sara collected her scattered thoughts as she went to her office and closed the door. She lifted the receiver and pressed the button for line one. "Hello?"

"Hi."

That one simple word had memories of Friday night filling her head—the long column of his throat as he tossed back tequila, the scent of him on her spare sheets... "What can I do for you?" Did she sound normal? She certainly sounded like a different person to her own ears.

"Look, I'm sorry to bother you at work..."

Bother? Clearly they hadn't been on the same page last Friday if he thought a phone call from him would bother her. "No worries. I wasn't expecting you to call." Hoping, maybe. Not expecting.

"Still, you've been on my mind."

That gave her pause. "Oh."

"I wanted to call you, but not this way, and not at work."

"So why are you calling now? Not that you're bugging me or anything..."

"There's been another murder."

Concern shoved pride aside. "In the Toxin case? I haven't heard anything in the news."

"It just happened last night."

"Okay..." What did this have to do with her? "Are you okay?"

He paused. "Yes. But I need to warn you..."

"What?" Her pulse was suddenly pounding at her throat.

"The killer left a note. Apparently, Toxin has been watching me. He knows about you."

Sara was grateful her chair was under her, otherwise she might have slid to the floor. "How?"

"Somehow, he knows."

John. Damn, had he spilled the beans to someone?

"Sara?"

"I'm here. Just absorbing this."

"Did you see someone suspicious that night? Think back."

"Not that I remember." She'd been too wrapped up in Holt and memories of Elizabeth. It had been an emotional roller coaster of a night. "But I did hear from John Rochard today. He told me he knew you and I had been together that night. He insinuated I was behaving improperly."

"But we didn't do anything to be ashamed of."

That was what she'd told him, but it didn't matter. John would twist what he'd seen. "It doesn't look that way to the common observer. It's enough that he saw us. Now it sounds like *two* people saw us that night." Her heart stuttered at the thought of a killer like Toxin lurking in the bushes. "Besides, John's a bug in the ear of the board members, who are already looking for any reason to shoot down my projects because they don't want to fund them. John is threatening to provide the ammo. He may have talked to someone already."

Holt cursed, surprising her. "Why didn't you tell me right away?"

"He just came to me a couple hours ago. What could you have done? Besides, did you call *me* about Toxin right away?"

"That's different."

"How? More lethal?" Sarcasm dripped from her words.

"It's an ongoing police investigation. I didn't want to involve you unless I got the go-ahead. Want me to talk to Rochard?"

She smiled grimly. After their last encounter, she'd love to see John squirm under Holt's directness. But John wasn't going to back down, and Sara wasn't going back on her principles. All she could do was continue to encourage Neil to do his best. The SAT was in a couple weeks, and midterms were right after that. Getting Holt involved would only rattle John's cage. She sighed. "It won't help. In fact, it would probably convince him there's something going on between you and me. Please, just stay out of it."

"I have to do *something*. I got you into this mess. Besides, he could very well be a suspect now...and if he has an alibi for the other murders, he may have seen someone else around the school that night."

"You think John could be Toxin?" She laughed. "He's all bark and no bite. But sure, investigate him. It would serve him right. As for Toxin, tell me what I need to do to keep the boys and myself safe. Would he come here, to the school?" He'd already followed Holt here once, maybe twice. Would he come when Holt wasn't around? Fear pierced her lungs, sucking the air from the room. She was responsible for these students. They'd become her family. Her *only* family.

"He's more interested in me, but I wanted you to be aware. I can send someone up there to guard the school. One of our security experts, Becca Haney, will be available by the end of the week, after her current assignment is over."

"I don't want to do anything to panic the boys, or their parents. If you're sure there's no immediate danger, I think I can handle things here. And there's always the local police."

"I called the local PD right before I called you. They're on the lookout for anyone suspicious in the area. In fact, I'll be paying a visit to them to deliver my profile in person." The thought of Holt taking action to protect her and the school was reassuring. Toxin would be crazy to take his murderous tendencies to the middle of the suburbs where he was more likely to be noticed as out of place. But then, maybe he *was* crazy.

Suddenly, she didn't want to talk about killers anymore. She needed something resembling normal on a day that had been anything but.

"How are you doing?" She could have kicked herself for asking.

She should be running the other way, protecting her heart. But she wanted to know. "I mean, this guy is targeting you, right? Are you taking care of yourself?"

Holt exhaled a deep breath. "It's been a long day, but this could be the break in the case we need."

"I didn't mean the case. I meant how are *you* doing? What are you doing to stay safe? I can ask you that, right? I mean, that's what *friends* do. You told me you wanted friendship." Sara could hear her own heartbeat count out the seconds in the long pause that followed.

"After what you've told me about Rochard and after the note from Toxin, I should keep my distance." Which meant he'd stay away from *her*.

"Right." Stupid to think he'd say what her heart wanted to hear, anyway. She'd been willing to settle for friendship, but it looked like that offer was off the table as well. Her laugh was brittle. "Never mind."

"Sara—"

"I'll let you know if I remember anyone suspicious from that night. Goodbye, and good luck." She hung up before she could make a bigger fool out of herself. She wouldn't travel that road again. She sat back in her chair and stared at the wall.

Cheryl opened the door and poked her head in. "Done already?" Her eyes narrowed as she saw Sara's expression. "What's wrong?"

"Is it that evident?"

"The guy's an idiot if he doesn't see what a catch you are."

Sara was pretty sure Holt was far from an idiot. Which meant he simply didn't want her, or Elizabeth's ghost was too powerful to combat. Of course, she'd always been second best. When would she learn? "Thank you for saying that, but that's not what's wrong. It seems that one night with Holt was even more of a mistake than I thought." Now, it wasn't just her heart in danger, but her life.

CHAPTER 10

The throng of students bubbled over with enthusiasm. It was Friday and their normal school-day routine had been disrupted. The hum of conversation rising from the bleachers in the gym threatened to become a roar by the time Holt accepted the microphone from the overly tan, silver-haired guy known simply as Coach.

"Hello." Holt's greeting echoed and the boil of excitement among the Academy students became a low simmer before dying off altogether. "I'm Dr. Patterson and this is Mr. Sawyer. We're here today to talk to you about personal safety."

Despite his reservations about leading Toxin to Sara's and Theo's doorstep, Holt had been persuaded to return to the Academy. Damian had shot down all Holt's arguments against going to the school, reminding him that nothing should keep him from his son, especially since it was quite likely that Toxin had already observed Holt with Theo. Holt had capitulated on the condition that Sara was okay with him coming. With the awkward ending to their conversation a few days ago, he wasn't sure she'd agree.

Indeed, Sara had been a tough sell. Though Holt had been eager to get the safety program underway to prepare the students and staff and ease his own guilt, he understood her need to get parent permission slips and find space in the students' schedules. It had required most of the week, but it had given Holt and Max time to prepare a student-friendly presentation that covered everything from avoiding a fight to an awareness of cyber-stalking—no easy feat given the variance in the kids' ages.

Mainly, though, he was eager to see Sara for himself, to see that she was healthy and whole and untouched. Though the private security he'd hired to sit outside the school had reported that there'd been no unusual activity, it was hard to focus on his job miles away when his thoughts were at the Academy. He'd also prepared his parents for the worst. Thankfully, his father was an ex-cop and understood how to be wary of strangers, watch for tails and be vigilant in general to increase safety.

His gaze sought out Sara as he handed the microphone off to Max and breathed easy for the first time that week. Her blond hair was pulled back into an artfully messy bun. She stood at the side of the bleachers—which held the entire student body, some three hundred boys—and nibbled on a thumbnail. He doubted she was even aware she was giving away her nervousness. Still, she was beautiful in a classic gray skirt and a teal shirt that picked up the blue of her eyes.

Max launched into his spiel about awareness—of both physical surroundings and interpersonal boundaries in relationships. He kept it short and sweet, wanting to hold the kids' attention until he could deliver the details about protecting themselves. The crowd seemed to sit a little straighter as Max called for a couple of volunteers to illustrate some self-defense moves. A sea of hands shot up. Good, they'd gotten their attention.

Sara scanned the crowd. Her gaze met his and her smile faltered. She turned her attention to Max's demonstration.

Max worked with three boys of different ages and sizes to

show firsthand—but with a restraint of force—how they could defend themselves against an attacker. The students' attention was fully on the middle of the gym floor, where mats had been laid out. Max wouldn't be doing anything too physical with them, but a couple of throws and hold-breaks would be included.

Max walked a middle-school-aged kid through how to turn an attack from behind into an advantage by throwing his elbows out and up while dropping to the ground, using dead weight to escape. He also demonstrated how to thrust his shoulder forward and knock the attacker off balance. Max barely touched the kid, but when the boy hunched his shoulders forward as he'd been told to, Max threw himself to the ground and the Academy student body erupted in applause. The boy's grin covered his entire face.

Max rose slowly, holding his back as if he'd been hurt, then grinned and patted the kid on the back in congratulations. While Max showed a few other moves, Holt took a turn with the microphone, discussing the techniques and interspersing other information. He reinforced what Theo had said Sara taught them last spring—how to avoid cyber-stalking or unwanted online attention. The world was so different from when he'd grown up.

As Holt summed up, he found himself wanting to snatch up Theo, who sat in the middle of the front row, and wrap him up in a safe cocoon. He could come out when he was twenty-one. *Scratch that. Thirty-one.*

Of course, life didn't get easier as you got older. As the decades flew by, that was when all the other truths of life hit you, such as what it felt like to lose a loved one. Theo had learned that one early too.

Sara began ushering the students by row out of the gym. She bent to listen to one of the smaller kids, smiled at something he said, then moved him along with the rest of the crowd. Holt's eyes tracked her hand as it tucked a stray hair back behind the delicate shell of her ear.

Theo came over and presented him with a fist, knuckles out.

Holt accommodated him with a fist-bump. "That was pretty good, Dad."

Holt's chest swelled. "Did you learn something?"

Theo nodded and his bangs slid into his eyes.

Max finished congratulating the volunteers, giving them the pins Damian had made with the SSAM logo so that they could have something to motivate young kids when they did talks such as these.

"That was a good group," Max said as he joined them. "You must be Theo."

"Yeah," Theo said. "That was a cool presentation."

"Which part, watching me get thrown to the ground?" Max chuckled.

Sara had seen to the emptying of the gym and couldn't avoid them any longer. She came over, wariness lurking in her eyes. "Thank you for coming. Theo, you should head to the lunchroom. You don't want to be last in line."

Theo looked at his dad. "It's pizza Friday. Want to stay?"

"Sure," Holt said. "Save me a spot. I need to talk to Miss Sara for a moment." He dared Sara to reject him in front of the others. Her chin went up a notch.

Max's gaze moved between Sara and Holt, reconnoitering the situation like a proper ex-Navy SEAL. He wisely chose a hot lunch over a tense conversation. "Lead me to the chow line, Theo." After he'd passed Sara, Max glanced back at Holt and gave him a thumbs-up behind her back.

Holt ignored the gesture and turned his complete attention to Sara. "Would you like to join us for lunch?"

"On Pizza Friday? Wouldn't miss it. But if you're just asking to be polite..."

"I wasn't." He was somewhat surprised to realize his words were true. He wanted to spend some time with Sara. He wanted her easy banter and soft laugh. Besides, she had to have had a rough week, mostly because of him. He hated feeling responsible for her current predicament. "Sorry about all of this."

Sara huffed out a laugh. "Which part? Turning my life upside down or worrying me to death about my kids?"

"Well, technically it's Toxin who turned it upside down."

"No, it was you. We'd better get to lunch before it's all gone." She turned away before he registered what she'd said.

He reached out to snag her hand. "Hey, wait a second."

"What?"

"You don't drop a bomb and leave. What did you mean by that?" His heart was thumping so loud she had to hear it.

"By what?"

"Don't play stupid, Sara. We've known each other too long. I thought we were done with the games."

She pulled her hand away. "You're right. I was more than attracted to you ten years ago. Kissing you wasn't about breaking you and Elizabeth up. I had feelings for you."

"That's it? Hell, that was a long time ago." And he'd suspected there could have been something, if he'd pursued it. But attraction was fleeting and he could deal with her past feelings. Especially since he was starting to think Sara could be a good friend. She'd proven she was good for Theo, and could be someone Holt could talk to about parenting issues. She was a goldmine. The thought brought his attention to her gleaming hair. Despite the harsh lighting of the gym, it looked incredibly soft. But her eyes had filled with hurt.

"I thought it had been long enough, but apparently not." The last part of her sentence drifted off and he had to lean forward to hear it. She shifted her weight as if she might turn and bolt, but the new, confident Sara took over. Deep pools of blue met his gaze. "One of the reasons I stayed away from Elizabeth and you was because of my reaction to our kiss, not because I wanted to prove you two were wrong for each other. I only used that as an excuse."

"I'm not taking the blame for your failed friendship."

"I'm not blaming you. I take full responsibility. I couldn't believe I was so horrible as to want what my friend had. And I still do."

A thick silence fell around them, as if they were the only two people on a stage, playing out a drama. The audience waited, breathless, for the next act. Only Holt had no clue whether this was a tragedy or a comedy, or if there was another act.

Sara must have sensed his confusion. "I'm not expecting you to solve my problems, Holt, so relax. This is my issue, and I'll deal with it. I just wanted all the cards on the table, so you'll understand if I'm moody around you, or snap at you, or simply avoid you. Since you're not keeping your distance from the school anymore, I figured I should let you know."

"Okay..." He didn't know what to say that would make things better.

Luckily, she didn't seem to need a response from him. Shaking her head as if to reset her emotions, she linked her arm with his. Even through the barrier of his shirtsleeves, he was keenly aware of her fingers resting on his forearm. "Now that that's off my chest, let's go get some pizza."

SARA PATTED HERSELF ON THE BACK. SHE'D SURVIVED LUNCH WITH Holt without dying of embarrassment, even managing to eat a few bites. She'd dared to open up to him in the gym, and she had to admit, she felt better now that the past was off her chest.

Now the ball was in Holt's court, not that she expected him to lob it back to her. They'd probably go back to business as usual—which meant no business at all, unless it was school or Toxin business.

A knock sounded on her office door. "Come in." She hid her surprise when Neil Rochard poked his head, with its fashionably shaggy mop of dark hair, through her doorway.

"You busy, Miss Sara?"

"I have time. Have a seat."

He closed the door behind him and dropped into a chair. But his casual slouch didn't match the way his glance darted around her office or the up-and-down bouncing of his knee. Something was bugging the kid and, with teen boys, she often found direct honesty was the best policy. "I have to say, I'm glad you came by. Surprised, but glad."

"Yeah, well..." The tempo of his knee-bobbing increased. He nibbled on a thumbnail. Sara waited patiently. He'd come this far. He'd talk when he was ready. "I thought that seminar today was good. Really good."

"Oh?" Of all the things she'd thought he'd come to talk about, this was last on the list.

"I'm glad someone finally talked about it—bullies and bad people—how to stand up to them, fight back."

"So many people don't know they have power until they choose to stand strong." At her words, his leg stilled and his hand dropped to his thigh. His gaze met hers, then flitted away.

"Yeah. That's why I'm here."

"Are you being bullied?" She hadn't heard anything about it. In fact, as one of the most popular kids in school—a football player from a wealthy family who could be handsome and charming when he chose to be—she'd be downright shocked if someone had targeted Neil.

"No, but I know bullies."

"Are you here because you're worried about someone?"

"Sort of."

"And this someone doesn't want to step forward on his own?" It was like dropping breadcrumbs to lead him into a conversation.

"They don't have anyone to stand up for them."

"That's sad. You want to share who it is? Maybe I can help."

Neil looked her directly in the eye. "It's you."

"Me?"

"I know my dad hasn't been nice to you. I'm not blind. And I overheard him talking to someone about you. I think he was trying to get you fired, saying you're incompetent."

Sara strove for diplomacy. "Sometimes people don't say nice things, but it doesn't always make those things true."

"I know. And I wasn't sure what to believe for a while. My dad's pretty smart about most things. But...I've decided he's wrong about you. You're okay."

Was there any more glowing recommendation from a teenager? "Well, thanks. I'm glad you can form your own opinion. And I'm glad you felt you could come talk to me."

"I didn't want you thinking I was like my dad."

Oh, no, she'd never think that. John Rochard was in a class all by himself. "Neil, when I look at you, I don't see your dad at all. I see a young man who's going through some normal growing pains, ready to get out there and take on the world. There may be some things in your life you're learning to deal with, but I have every confidence you'll get where you need to be when you're supposed to be there."

The knee-bobbing resumed. It was a tell—a hint that he was dealing with some emotion deep brewing inside. "You heard about my parents' divorce?"

"Yes. Is that what's got you doing things like stealing beer?"

He winced. "I don't know. I won't do that again, though. I promise."

"That's good enough for me."

"Did you ever take the SATs, Miss Sara?"

"Yes, they had those back in the Dark Ages."

He grinned. It transformed his face and she had a glimpse of the handsome young man he was becoming. "How'd you score?"

"Above average, but not as high as some people."

"And you survived."

"Yes, I did. I am a fairly well-adjusted person who even contributes to society now and then."

He snorted. "My dad needs me to get close to a 2400 to get into Harvard."

"What do *you* need? Or, more importantly, what do you want?"

"I *don't* want to go to Harvard. I *don't* want to be a lawyer like him, who works on people's lame lawsuits all day." His tone had turned fierce. "I'm not sure what I do want, though."

"Have you tried talking to the school counselor?"

"I don't need a shrink."

"He's not that kind of counselor. He's good at helping people find what direction they want to go. Otherwise, they're just spinning their wheels, wasting time and energy. Life's too short for that."

Neil would have a hell of a time with his dad if he chose any other path, but she didn't want to mention the stumbling blocks. He was on the verge of exciting things. She was proud of him for acknowledging what it would take to deviate from his dad's plans, and evaluating the pros and cons on his own.

Neil stood. "Thanks, Miss Sara."

"You're welcome. Come see me anytime, especially if you need help." *Talking to your dad,* she wanted to add. He slung his backpack over his shoulder and, with a brief nod, was gone.

It seemed she hadn't been the only one carrying around a burden she'd had to get off her chest. She wondered if Holt was feeling as stunned as she was right now.

The Evanston Police Department served the Academy and everything within a several-mile radius. Holt's father had worked here for decades, and stopped by his old stomping grounds to hear Holt's profile of Toxin.

"The killer known as Toxin killed four people over the past nine months. Based on his identification with me in his latest note and certain aspects of the crime scene, he's in his mid-thirties, Caucasian and college-educated. We haven't found the connection between him and the victims yet. He's most likely a successful businessman, and most definitely likes to be in control."

"A puppet master," his father added. "He likes to run the show."

"Yes, that's an apt description. He even named himself Toxin. We're still trying to trace the chemicals found in the victims' systems, though we think he may be using a lab in south Chicago. That he uses a neurotoxin is telling."

A hand went up and Holt acknowledged the officer. "So we should look particularly close at people who have a science background, or people with interests in poisons?"

"That's possible. Detective Noah Crandall has been investigating that angle, particularly by questioning employees of chemical companies in Chicago as well as professors, researchers, etc. We're also keeping an eye on suspected drug dealers and their sources. If you run across someone suspicious, give Noah or me a call."

"What about the note on the most recent victim?"

"The fact that Toxin focused on me, and my association with a female here in the area, Sara Burns, indicates he is in an unhappy relationship with someone, or has recently lost a relationship he valued."

"Hard to believe someone like him cares about anyone," one guy muttered, loud enough for the room to hear.

"He cares enough to take lives," Holt's father said.

Holt felt his father's frustration. "He's clearly expressing a sense of entitlement, but quite possibly due to the loss of an important person in his life as well." Holt knew all too well what a loss could do to a person's perception of the world. "While he's intelligent and sane enough to restrain his impulse to kill for long periods of time, to make plans, and to fit into society, he's acting out of misguided notions of heroism."

"So watch out for a man in a superhero cape?"

"I only wish it were that easy."

The men chuckled but quickly sobered. Laughter was welcome in lightening the mood, but everyone knew what was at stake. Innocent lives.

"I don't have that kind of money." The lie fell easily from Toxin's lips because Brady Flaherty was an asshole and a lazy SOB. Apparently, he was also a desperate SOB if he was reaching this far out on the family tree, hitting *him*, of all people—a guy who was barely even a leaf on a branch of that tree anymore—up for money.

"I'll pay you back," Brady insisted. "I'm good for it."

Yeah, right. The guy was no good to anyone except as a hired gun. Yet...maybe there was a way Brady *could* pay him back. A plan began to form, one that would get both Brady and Dr. Holt Patterson off his back...and then he could focus on his new plan of taking over Patterson's life. The unfortunate side effect of his latest kill had been giving Patterson more insight into Toxin's life. Now Patterson was interviewing Buzz's family...which could, though unlikely, lead to him.

Buzz. Toxin felt a rush of power remembering the kill. He'd been patient, waiting months to make his move, because this one was personal. But when it was right, he'd struck quickly. At least he'd still had time to enjoy the recognition and the surrender in Buzz's eyes. The guy had always thought Toxin was weak and amoral. In the end, Buzz had acknowledged who was right and who was wrong. The old battleax wouldn't be passing judgment again anytime soon. Not ever, in fact.

"Sorry, Brady." Toxin interrupted the guy's list of reasons why he needed the money. "No can do. Maybe try getting a real job and contributing to society for a change?"

Brady cursed at him and hung up. Toxin grinned. Brady had just given him the perfect out. One call to his ex-girlfriend Gloria and the wheels would be in motion. And Patterson would be off his trail for a while—long enough for Toxin to set up the next phase of his plan. As for Brady, the stupid SOB wouldn't know what hit him.

CHAPTER 11

October

"This is the place," Noah said as Holt joined him on the sidewalk outside an apartment building.

"And you're certain this Brady Flaherty is our guy?" Holt asked.

"Following your recommendation, we closely investigated Leonard Redding's family."

Because Toxin had referred to his victim as *Buzz* in the note, which indicated a certain level of familiarity, Holt had told Noah to pay special attention to the people closest to Redding. "And someone talked?"

"The victim's daughter Gloria said that Buzz is a nickname her father earned in the military. His family began calling him by that name years ago, but most people outside of the family would call him Leonard. When I hinted that a family member might be involved, she mentioned that one of her cousins could be a suspect. Brady Flaherty. According to her, Buzz refused to loan Brady money just days before his murder. I've got a warrant to search the premises, based on the guy's record and Gloria's suspicions. The landlord says Brady is likely at the gym. He sticks to his afternoon workout schedule as if it were his religion."

Noah mounted the stairs leading to a door that looked like all the others. The landlord stood waiting for them with keys in hand. He let them in and left. Noah scanned the living room and kitchen area, then strode to the doorway that had to lead to the bedroom. He disappeared inside but quickly returned.

"He's not here," Noah said. "We should have a good half hour or so until he returns."

The furnishings were sparse, a sagging couch that had seen better days, a nicked-up coffee table, and a single barstool by the kitchen counter. A couple of empty liquor bottles and dirty dishes filled the kitchen sink. "You said Brady has a record?"

Noah donned latex gloves and started picking through drawers. "Assault and battery. Armed robbery. Typical thug stuff."

His record could explain the lack of personal touches and furniture, especially if Brady was still engaged in criminal behavior and anticipated the possibility of future jail time. It also fit Toxin's MO. The killer never left a trace of anything personal at the crime scenes. But would Toxin be so sloppy as to leave clues that would lead them right to his door? "What did you think about Gloria? Do you believe her?"

"I'm no psychologist, but I'd say she's depressed. Or maybe she's just in shock at the loss of her father."

"Is Brady linked to the Academy at all?" *To Sara?*

"I haven't had time to dig deep enough, but I'm sure we'll find the connections. Anything on the repeat background checks from the Academy?"

Damian had agreed with Holt that they should cover any possibility, including using SSAM resources to re-examine the backgrounds of the teachers and support staff at the school. "So far, no red flags other than one who had a misdemeanor for smoking weed in college. She's sixty now, though, and has taught there for decades. And she's *female*. I don't recall seeing Brady Flaherty on the list."

Noah grunted. "If he'd been associated with the school, it would have been under an alias. Otherwise, his criminal record would have prevented him from getting hired." He closed the last kitchen cupboard. "There's nothing unusual out here. Let's try the backrooms."

Holt followed Noah into the single bedroom. Another door led to the bathroom. "I'll start here." It didn't take long. In the cabinet under the sink, a box of hypodermic needles, alongside a bottle of something Holt suspected was the chemical cocktail injected into Toxin's victims, was tucked behind a couple rolls of toilet paper. "Noah, I've got something."

But the sound of the front door opening, followed by the scratch of keys as they slid across a flat surface kept Noah from observing the find. Brady was home.

Noah jerked his head toward the door and withdrew his gun. Holt nodded and followed as Noah moved into the living room. "Police! Put your hands where I can see them."

Brady was still taking his jacket off by the open front door. He bolted.

"Shit." Noah cursed and they took off at a run.

The hours spent in the gym paid off as Brady took the stairs two at a time and raced to his motorcycle. He didn't bother snatching his helmet off the back, but reached in his pocket for his keys—the keys Holt had heard sliding across the table where Brady had thoughtlessly tossed them. Caught in the sights of Noah's pistol with no way to escape, the man put his hands in the air.

THREE HOURS LATER, HOLT TOLD HIMSELF REPEATEDLY THAT HE WAS *not* driving to the Academy to drink in Sara with his own eyes. He told himself he hadn't missed seeing her or hearing her voice these past couple weeks. It was simply a courtesy to tell her in person about arresting Toxin, since it impacted her life too. Besides, visiting Sara would allow him to tell Becca her job at the Academy was done and she could move on to other cases.

When Holt left the station, Brady was still giving them the silent treatment, refusing to speak a word until his lawyer got there. But the incriminating evidence had been under the sink where Holt had seen it.

Exhilaration filled him. He'd finally apprehended a killer who'd eluded him for months. Holt wanted to share that feeling with someone. The first someone who'd come to mind was Sara.

He practically raced up the steps to her apartment. His knock was answered almost immediately, and Sara stood there in yoga pants and a T-shirt. His breath caught in his chest, but he managed a syllable. "Hi."

"Hey," Sara said, her eyebrows raised in surprise. He hadn't thought to call first, thinking of nothing but getting to her as soon as possible.

Becca, who'd been staying on Sara's couch most nights as added protection, came up behind Sara. "Is there news?"

"Good news," Holt told her.

Sara moved aside and waved him in. "Well?"

He grinned. He hadn't felt this good in ages. "We caught him."

Becca's jaw dropped. "Toxin?"

"That's fantastic!" Sara caught him up in a spontaneous hug, her breasts pressing against his chest, and desire flared up within him. She stiffened against him and began to pull away, as if remembering her resolution to leave him alone.

Not wanting the contact to end, he brought his arms around her. His body ached with physical want. When had he last been hugged? Something inside him, like the pulling of a drawstring, brought a sense of closure. He was sorry when he had to let go, but Becca was standing there, watching them with interest.

"So, who is he?" Sara asked. The huskiness in her voice indicated she had been affected by their embrace too.

"Brady Flaherty. The latest victim's nephew. Found evidence of the neurotoxin in Brady's apartment after Buzz's daughter pointed us in his direction."

Becca's brow knitted. "But why would he kill those other people?"

"While we were processing him at the station, Einstein continued to dig for connections. He found Brady used to work for the first victim. He was a night janitor at Tech Innovations where Joseph Kurtz was CEO, but only for a few months before he was fired. In Brady's apartment, there was a matchbook from the bar where Dr. Brown was murdered. And on his hard drive was a hate letter addressed to Senator Beechum. So far, Brady's not talking to police. He probably knows that the moment I hear his voice, I'll know he's Toxin."

"Does he fit the profile?"

"He's white, within the early-to-mid-thirties age bracket I'd identified, and had a trigger event. He was fired from Tech Innovations just before the first murder. When Buzz refused to lend him money a few weeks back, he apparently snapped again. He has a history of violence. Brady is the black sheep of the Redding family—always in trouble, sometimes in jail, and usually out of a job—and Buzz made it clear what he thought of his no-good nephew. The only part that doesn't fit my profile is he's a career criminal, not a successful career person."

"Guess I'm out of a job, then." Becca grinned, not looking the least bit sorry. "I'm sure you two can manage here." She snatched her bag from beside the couch and hugged Sara. "I've enjoyed getting to know you."

"Me too." Becca left and Sara, looking uncharacteristically shy, avoided Holt's gaze. "Looks like we both have things to celebrate tonight."

"Celebrate?"

"One of my students is scheduled to take the SAT tomorrow, and it looks like he'll do well. But that's nothing compared to what you've accomplished. You deserve some kind of party for hauling in Toxin. Hell, you deserve the key to the city."

He slid her a doubtful look. "I didn't do it with my own two hands."

"Don't sell yourself short like that. You're one of the smartest people I've ever met, and if you hadn't come up with a profile, the police might never have caught him." The defensiveness in her voice—on *his* behalf, despite everything—pleased him. She looked away. "But I suppose you need to get going."

He took a step closer, putting her within arm's reach. He remembered what she'd felt like in his arms just moments ago, and wouldn't mind feeling that again. "How about a drink? You said we both had things to celebrate."

She looked up at him from beneath her lashes. "You sure?"

"Positive."

After another moment of consideration, she nodded. "Okay. We'll have a drink to toast our success."

His gaze moved over her face. "I'd like that." He leaned forward suddenly, wanting to taste her.

SARA PULLED AWAY, HER SURPRISED GAZE COLLIDING WITH HIS. AT some point, she'd put her hand against his chest. Did he want her —truly want her—or was he simply caught up in the thrill of success? Then again, she was tired of overthinking things. She curled her fingers into Holt's jacket and pulled him close, then pressed her lips to his. His arms automatically went around her, holding her against him. Never removing her mouth from his, she slid the zipper down his chest and pushed her hands inside until she was stripping his jacket off.

As kisses went, it was sweet, both literally and emotionally. But the tentative sampling didn't satisfy the ache that had throbbed inside her for months. Seeking relief, she pressed her body closer, her breasts to his chest, her hips to his. His heat suffused her.

His hands came up to either side of her face, cradling her. She opened her mouth to him, encouraging him to investigate further. His tongue swept inside and she nearly gasped with pleasure. He slanted his mouth over hers, moaning as he seemed to let go of something that held him back. The air became charged with a new kind of energy, sizzling along her skin.

In a split second, his mouth turned from curious and tasting to hot and wanting. His hands slid into her hair, anchoring her in place as he explored. His chest pressed against hers, and her nipples ached beneath her shirt. As her skin came alive, her muscles went liquid. Feeling weak in the knees, she moved backward toward the couch. Holt came with her, not leaving any gaps between their bodies. The backs of her knees hit the couch and she sank down, pulling him with her, feeling his weight on top of her, anchoring her when she thought the fizzy feeling inside might make her float away.

SWAMPED BY URGES HOLT NEVER THOUGHT TO FEEL AGAIN, HE GAVE in to his baser needs. As he pressed into her, wishing their clothing could simply evaporate, the taste, the smell, the feel of Sara filled his senses.

He pinned her arms above her head, and his mouth moved across her jawline and toyed with her sensitive ear. She interlaced her fingers with his—just like he'd held Elizabeth's hand when she'd received the news that weeks of radiation hadn't worked. The sudden memory was like a bucket of ice water thrown on his head.

Holt pulled away and sucked in several breaths. At some point they'd moved onto the couch and he was stretched out on top of Sara. Hell, his erection was pressing into her thigh. One more minute and he would have yanked her pants down and buried himself inside her. How had he lost himself so completely?

But the sight of her, flushed and rosy and panting beneath him, nipples peaked against the T-shirt stretched across her heaving chest, stirred a war of wills within him. Desire versus rationality. His needs nearly had him leaning in again to recapture the passionate moment.

"Whoa." Coming from Sara, the word was full of wonder.

He propped himself on one elbow and pushed a hand through his hair, finding it had been thoroughly mussed by her fingers. He'd been so wrapped up in her that he hadn't even noticed. The thought had his groin hardening even more, to the point of delicious pain. "Sorry about that."

"Sorry?" Her abdomen shifted under his as she redistributed his weight. She exhaled on a laugh. "Did I give you the impression it wasn't okay with me?"

"I should have asked. It's too much too fast, for both of us." And yet he was still on top of her. His body seemed unwilling to obey his brain's commands.

She pressed farther into the couch cushion, shifting to pull her body out from under his. Her body language indicated he'd said something to put a barrier between them. He moved so that he was safely seated on the other end of the couch. He subtly adjusted the still-hopeful erection straining for her.

But she'd pushed him away, making the decision for them both. His gut twisted when he should have been relieved. He wanted her, but he didn't want to want her. He felt he was betraying his wife, yet she was gone and had urged him to go on living. But with *Sara?* It was too complicated...wasn't it? He hated this war of needs within him.

"Well, I for one enjoyed kissing you." Sara's smile was back, but her eyes were tinged with hurt. "But if you need time, more than these past couple weeks, to think about it..."

"I'm sorry, Sara."

Her laugh had an edge to it this time. "That's the second time you've apologized in less than a minute. Just stop, okay. I'd rather not be a regret, thank you very much. I'm fine. We had a moment. It was fun. We survived. No harm, no foul."

Fun? Frustration burned in his gut. "It was one hell of a moment."

A furrow formed, wrinkling her smooth brow. "But you just said…"

He rubbed his temples. "I'm horrible at this. I'm sor—"

She held up a hand. "Do *not* say it again. Look, let's agree that the kiss took both of us by—"

"—surprise?"

"—storm."

He released a strangled laugh. "Yes, that sounds about right."

"It's okay. Really. If you still have feelings for Elizabeth, it's understandable. But I thought…I mean, when you came all the way out here to give me the good news, and responded to my hug, I guess I thought you wanted something more. With me."

His response was immediate and strong. "Hell, Sara. It's pretty obvious that I want you." He lifted his hand to brush a strand of blond hair from her face. He dropped his hand before it could linger to sample the softness of her cheek. "I have the past, and one important thing in my present, that I have to consider."

"Theo."

"Yes. And I still think about Elizabeth sometimes, and what she'd think…" He shoved impatient fingers through his hair. "I don't want to carry any baggage into a new relationship."

"Everyone has baggage. We worked around it just fine a minute ago." Her gaze went to his mouth.

He stifled a groan and looked away, physically turning his body so it was no longer facing hers. He prided himself on logical conclusions drawn after logical arguments. Sara wasn't logical. She wasn't a rational choice. And yet he wanted her.

She touched his hand. "I don't care about your baggage, since I carry it too. But I do care about Theo. I would never do anything to hurt him. And I've already told you I care about you."

Holt looked away. "Half the time I don't know who I am anymore. How the heck would I know what I want?" He lifted his gaze to meet hers. "I know I want you."

"But you don't know for how long, or if it's just some physical reaction. Or maybe it's just been a really long time for you."

He winced. Was his body simply on hormone overdrive, led around by his dick to the first warm, willing woman it came into contact with? The thought was unwelcome, since he prided himself on being an intellectual. But he was a man too. One thing was certain. He didn't want to make any false moves, any promises, before he figured out what he wanted…what was best.

"You're right. We should back off from this for a while."

Her expression turned stiff, as if she were holding in emotions she didn't want him to see. "From what? It was one night of talking and a couple kisses. Don't read too much into it. I haven't."

"I just don't know if I'm ready to be in a relationship."

"I'm not asking for that. You're off the hook. Honest." She looked at him sadly. "Go hunt your murderers and find justice for strangers. Maybe it'll be enough."

He could tell by the look on her face that she didn't believe that. Worse, he was starting to doubt it himself.

CHAPTER 12

Jeremy's bony elbow jabbed sharply into Theo's stomach.
Theo looked up. "Hey!"

"Shh. Someone's coming," Jeremy whispered.

In the time between the end of class and when they'd be picked up, they were hiding out in the janitor's closet tucked under the staircase on the first floor of the Academy, with the door cracked only slightly for fresh air. But apparently they'd been discovered. Unfortunately, it wasn't the kindly old janitor who opened the door, but Miss Sara.

The splintered wood along the doorframe caught at her blond hair as she ducked inside and held out her hand. "Fork it over, boys. You know the rules."

Theo gave the handheld gaming system to her. "Sorry." It was an apology to both Jeremy and Miss Sara.

She glanced at the screen. "Death Files Two. Huh. I didn't know they had another one out. I haven't even finished the first one."

"I've heard Scorpion's Sting will be better." Theo couldn't wait.

Jeremy nodded, his face becoming animated. "I've asked for that one for Christmas." With his parents getting divorced, he was enjoying the spoils of their war for custody. A gaming system was one of those perks. He was sure to get whatever he wanted for the holidays—especially since he was having two separate Christmases.

Miss Sara rolled her eyes. "It's barely Halloween."

"But only fifty-seven days until Christmas."

She handed the system to Jeremy. "Put this in your backpack. It's only for use at home or to and from school. It's not allowed out of your backpack while on campus. You know the rules."

"Yes, ma'am." Jeremy eagerly accepted the electronic gadget, along with the implied reprieve.

Miss Sara's look was stern, but her lips twitched, like she was trying hard not to smile. "The janitor's closet is off-limits. Besides, you two have a science test on Wednesday, don't you? If you're waiting for your rides home, you should spend the time studying."

"We're ready," Theo said. This semester, he'd been working hard, and it was starting to pay off.

They filed past her into the foyer. As Miss Sara closed the door and they moved back down the hallway, the front door of the school opened. Jeremy's father entered and walked toward them in weird, jerky strides. The guy was a spaz, but not the entertaining kind. Something about him made the hairs on Theo's arms stand up. Mr. White, the school's computer science teacher, entered behind him, then closed the door against the chilly mid-October afternoon.

"Thank you, Chad, for closing the door," Miss Sara said to Mr. White. She looked right past Jeremy's dad, who definitely wanted her attention. It was that adult way of pointing out what one person was doing wrong by emphasizing what another person was doing right. Using shame to teach right and wrong. *Classic.* But Mr. Rochard didn't seem to learn his lesson. Probably because he had no sense of shame.

"Hey, Dad," Jeremy said, but his dad ignored him.

"A word, Miss Burns." Mr. Rochard barely opened his mouth as he spoke.

Miss Sara had gone all rigid, like Grandma did when Theo forgot to put the milk back in the refrigerator or tracked dirt in the house. She touched Theo on the shoulder. "You guys go study for that science test. I'll see you tomorrow." She turned back to Jeremy's dad and gestured toward her office. "If you'll follow me…"

"See you in a few, Dad?" Jeremy's tone was hopeful.

"Sure." Mr. Rochard was already walking away, following Miss Sara into her office.

Theo's jaw hurt, and he realized he'd been grinding his teeth. "I know he's your dad, but I don't like the way he talks to people."

Beside him, Jeremy shrugged. "You get used to it."

"You heard her," Mr. White said. Theo had forgotten the guy was standing there. "I hear that test is going to be tough."

"Yes, sir." Theo tugged his backpack higher on his shoulder and moved toward the door. Someday, he would do what he wanted, when he wanted. Like protect Miss Sara, even if she told him to go away. If his dad were here, Theo would have made him step up. Maybe his dad *could* do something. Now that Toxin was behind bars, if Theo pointed out that Miss Sara needed him, maybe he'd drop everything and help. Theo ran outside, not stopping until he came to a grouping of trees that offered some privacy. Cell phones were allowed in school, but only for emergencies. This qualified.

"Hey, wait up!" Jeremy caught up to Theo and gulped for breath. "Boy, you're sure eager to study." He settled on the grass and pulled a textbook out of his backpack while Theo brought out his phone and dialed.

His dad answered on the first ring. "Hey, bud. What's up? Did Grandma pick you up?"

"Not yet." He chewed his lip as he tried to decide how to ask for the favor.

"Is something wrong?" Dad actually sounded worried.

"It's just…" He hadn't wanted to bug his dad with stuff this past year. He had enough on his plate, and Grandma had told him to take it easy on him. So he'd avoided telling him most stuff. But this problem was bigger than Theo. "It's Miss Sara."

There was a pause. "What about her?"

Overhearing the conversation, Jeremy shot him a questioning look, but Theo pressed on. "I think she could use your help."

"Is something wrong? Is she hurt?" Dad's tone had turned even more worried.

"No, it's just…" Theo stopped as Jeremy shook his head once. He should have taken the phone somewhere else before making the call. Apparently, Jeremy cared about his dad even if the man was a bully.

On the other end of the phone, Theo's dad sighed. "Miss Sara is a grown woman. I'm sure she can take care of herself."

Theo remembered the look on Mr. Rochard's face and wasn't so sure. "I know, but sometimes people need help. You said that sometimes we can't take on everything by ourselves."

"Theo, she knows she can ask for help if she needs it. Unless she's hurt…"

His chest felt tight, like it had at Mom's funeral. He felt a burning in his throat. "No," he choked out. Not yet, anyway. Maybe he was blowing things out of proportion.

"Look, bud, if you're truly worried, I can check in with her. Or maybe Grandma can talk to her when she gets there?"

"Never mind."

"Theo—"

"I'll handle it. *I'll* watch out for her." He hung up, trying to swallow past a tight lump.

"My dad won't hurt her or anything." Jeremy picked at a blade of grass that had turned to a brown, dry crisp in the cool autumn weather. "He likes to get his way, that's all."

. . .

SARA JUST WANTED THE MAN OUT OF HER OFFICE. JOHN HAD BALLS OF steel if he thought he could control her and the rest of the world.

"He'll never get into Harvard with these scores." John waved a paper with Neil's SAT results in front of her face. She would have backed up if she weren't already pressed against her desk. Max and Holt's presentation on bullies and attackers came to mind. She wouldn't give John the upper hand. Besides, Neil's SAT scores weren't that bad.

"He'll get into a respectable school," she said, appealing to his rational side. "Not Harvard, likely, but that's not where he wants to go, anyway."

John scowled. "He's seventeen. He doesn't know what he wants."

"Have you ever taken the trouble to ask him?"

"I'm his father. I know best."

"You don't know *anything* because you don't want to know the truth." The air between them froze as John's icy glare slid over her.

"Your time here is done. You had your chance. Several, in fact." He spun on his heel and tossed the wadded-up score sheet into the trashcan on his way out of her office.

It took Sara several minutes before she could breathe beyond the tightness in her chest. Her fingers ached from gripping them into fists. The phone on her desk began to ring. Had John already succeeded in bending the ear of a board member? Was she about to be fired?

She snatched the receiver off its cradle. "The Hills Boys' Academy."

"Sara?"

The sound of Holt's voice squeezed her chest harder. "Yes?"

"Are you okay? I heard...Theo called me because he was worried about you."

Holt wasn't calling of his own volition because he wanted to talk to her. He was simply doing his son a favor. "I'll be fine."

"You sure? You don't sound okay."

"Not a scratch on me." Just a bunch of scars on the inside.

There was a long pause. "Okay. I hope you know you can call me if you need anything."

"Sure." But just because she could didn't mean that she would. She refused to give Holt any reason to think she was manipulating him...the way Elizabeth once had. And yet, he'd fallen immediately in love with Elizabeth. Fun, spunky, sparkly Elizabeth. Of course, everybody had loved her. But with Sara...Holt hadn't fallen in love with her. She was the runner-up, second best. A means to an end... the release of sexual frustration.

"Okay, well, if you're sure..."

"I just said I was. Goodbye, Holt."

Toxin grasped at the reins of his temper. That sonofabitch Rochard had practically dragged the older boy out of the school to his sports car, then revved the engine to proclaim his asshole status to the world. The younger boy had run from a cluster of trees out into the road just in time for Rochard to *remember* to take him home too. Poor kid had to squeeze onto his brother's lap because Rochard hadn't thought about taking two kids home when he left the house in a two-seater.

Dicks like John Rochard thought they were God's gift to society, the privileged elite, and then treated everyone else like crap. Kinda like Gloria or Buzz...or his own dad, the devil take his soul. When Toxin had no longer been useful to Gloria, when their bond had been broken in the worst, most painful way possible, she'd kicked him to the curb like yesterday's trash. Same thing with his dad, only the piece of shit had always made it clear Toxin was a loser and wouldn't amount to anything. If only the bastard was alive to see him now, he'd see Toxin had made himself useful to society.

He'd bet all of the Rochard millions that John would miss his kids if they were gone. Yeah, Rochard would realize what was truly important then. He would be scared shitless. His heart would be ripped out of his chest and put through a meat grinder. His lungs would freeze up as if he'd never suck in another breath.

But Toxin had gone to great pains to throw the police and Patterson off his trail by leading them to Brady. Risking his freedom for a vendetta that wasn't part of his original plan would be stupid. He'd have to think long and hard…and maybe use some of Henry's new batch to aid in the decision-making process.

Ultimately, a hero didn't turn his back on someone in need. Sara Burns was in need. As were the Rochard kids. Even Theo needed help. And where was the hero from the local news? Dr. Holt Patterson was holed up in his little cubicle, investigating killers who had nothing to do with his own family.

Which left the heroic acts to Toxin. He felt adrenaline flood his system, preparing him for the next step in his mission. A hero never rested for long.

CHAPTER 13

November

Sara set up the chessboard for their Friday chess game. Theo had continued to open up to her in their time together this semester. Today, she was counting on that hard-won rapport to help her figure out what the heck was wrong with him. He'd been moping around the school all week, barely lifting his head to return her greetings in the halls.

Theo came in and dropped his backpack on the extra chair, then sat at the small table against one wall of her office. Seated across from him, she lined her pawns up in their places, using the activity to hide her concern that he hadn't come in with his usual hello. Theo echoed her actions with his own pawns, ducking his face from her gaze.

"How was your week?" she asked.

"Okay."

"And Halloween?"

"All right."

Time for more probing questions. "What kind of candy did you haul in?"

"Candy bars and sour gummies, lollipops…the usual. Plus a few things like raisins and pencils." Some of the tension dissipated as he warmed to the subject. "Grandpa weighed it on the kitchen scale. Three pounds."

Her finger and thumb pinched the head of a pawn and lifted it in her opening move. "Wow."

His brown eyebrows drew together. "I should have brought you some."

"I'm glad you didn't." She leaned forward as if confiding a great secret. "I'm swearing off sugar for a couple of weeks." She'd decided to go to Acapulco for Thanksgiving break—her first vacation in years, and first time ever alone—and wanted to get bikini-ready. A whole week in the sun, away from heartbreak and confusion. Heaven. "You must have had an awesome costume."

He shrugged, but she was rewarded with a smile as he moved a knight into play. "I made it myself. I was a zombie."

"I think I saw you practicing this week."

"What do you mean?" Theo's hazel gaze flicked up to meet hers before moving back to the chessboard. He moved his queen into play. She doubted he realized he was setting himself up to lose in three moves. She'd rattled him.

She scooped up his queen with a bishop. Theo didn't even wince. "You've seemed kind of down. With all that candy, I'd expect the opposite," she teased. Not even a crack of a smile. "So I figure you must have been a zombie-in-training."

It was his move, but he sat back, ignoring the game. "You won't tell something if I ask you not to, right?"

She fought for a careful response. "That's a difficult question to answer. In my position as director, I'm responsible for student safety. If what you tell me relates to that, I might have to step in. I would do everything in my power to keep your confidence, though."

Theo thought for several long moments, then nodded. "That makes sense."

"I hope so. And I hope you'll share whatever's bothering you. I really am here to help."

"I know. And Mom told me I could talk to you. She said it would be like talking to her."

"She did?" A sudden welling of emotion made her skin tingle and her chest tighten.

He nodded. "Before she died. She said you used to be her other half. Her conscience, or something. Sometimes, when I'm worried about something, I dream about her, and it reminds me I should talk to you."

She swallowed the lump in her throat. "What about your dad? I think he'd want to help too."

"He's got his own things to deal with."

Sara wondered if Holt had any clue how much his son was trying to protect him. They were so much alike. "Yes, but you'd be number one on his list. You mean a lot to him."

"I know."

"You do?"

"Yeah."

"I don't think he realizes that you're protecting him. I think he's worried you don't *want* to talk to him anymore."

Theo looked surprised. "I just don't want to add to his troubles."

She resisted the urge to go around to his side of the table and hug him. "I think you *not* talking to him is troubling him." Theo seemed to consider this. "So, since you're here and all, how about talking to me? What's bothering you this week?"

"I'm worried about Jeremy, who's worried about his brother. I even started a new story about it in my journal. Mr. R is the villain."

"Jeremy's worried about Neil?"

"Yeah. Jeremy says his dad's been really hard on them this week. Well, mostly he ignores Jeremy, but even more so this week, while he goes after Neil."

"Goes after?" If John was beating Neil, she wouldn't just report him to the authorities. She'd *go after* him herself. She kept her face impassive as anger bubbled below the surface. "What do you mean by that, Theo?"

"Jeremy says his dad's been yelling at Neil every night. Neil locks himself in his room, and won't even open up for Jeremy."

Poor Neil. And poor Jeremy. But Sara reminded herself she only had one side of the story—and that was hearsay. "Not every parent is perfect. They do their best. But it's never okay to hurt someone." She thought of Holt, and how he wanted desperately to be everything for Theo, but he felt he was missing the mark. He was so hard on himself. She had to give him credit for trying, though. Or maybe she could do more than give Holt credit. Maybe she could give him a boost behind the scenes. "You're pretty lucky to have parents who care about your feelings."

"Mom was always there for me."

"But not Dad?"

"Dad tries." Theo looked at his hands, which were gripped together on the table. "But he's busy, and I get in the way. And when we are together, I guess I just don't talk to him as much as he wants me to."

Unable to resist some gesture of comfort, she touched his wrist until he met her gaze. "He's not mad about that, Theo. He understands. You know how you feel when Jeremy opens up to you? Like you're being a good friend?"

"Yeah. He feels better after we talk. Usually."

"Because you're listening to him. You're helping carry his burden. What if I talked to Neil? I wouldn't tell him who told me anything. In fact, I wouldn't tell him anything at all about what you've shared. I've been meaning to check in with him, anyway."

Actually, she'd sent notes to his teachers a couple times this week to send him to the office, but he'd never arrived. She suspected he was avoiding her. Was he ashamed of his SAT scores? They'd actually been pretty good, but nobody was giving him the positive outlook on his future. He could easily get in to most schools, just not the highest caliber ones.

Theo looked hopeful. "You'd do that for me?"

"Of course. Neil and Jeremy are my students too. I want to help if I can."

"Yeah. I think that might help." Theo leaned forward and studied the board. "Boy, that was a bonehead move, huh? I should pay better attention."

And just like that, the chess match continued while their chat replayed in her mind. She'd have to wait until Monday to find Neil, unless she wanted to risk connecting with John again by calling their home over the weekend. She hoped Monday would be soon enough.

SOMETHING ABOUT THE CASE DIDN'T FIT. MORE AND MORE THINGS, in fact, didn't match Holt's profile of the killer. Brady's voice, for one. When he'd finally talked, and when Holt was present to hear his claims of innocence, the deep voice didn't match what Holt remembered about Toxin's call to the tip hotline. And then there was Brady's attitude. Confident, but in a hardened criminal kind of way. Not the boastful Toxin who'd contacted Holt twice. Then again, facing life in jail for several murders would probably cause a guy to alter his voice and put an end to the cockiness.

Though Toxin was supposedly in custody, Holt's doubt had led him to hire a private investigator to keep an eye on Theo—and Sara—from a distance at the school, without Sara's knowledge.

That gut feeling had been steadily building until it was screaming at him. And so, early Monday morning, Holt drove to the prison where Brady Flaherty—aka Toxin—was being held until trial.

The prisoner was led into the room and seated opposite the table from him. The interview room was sparse. Gray walls. No décor. Just two chairs, a table, Holt, Brady and a uniformed officer who stood guard at the door. Brady sported a crew cut and several tattoos across his arms and neck. He sat and sank into a slouched position, his cuffed hands between his thighs. He projected an outward confidence, adding a defiant tilt of his chin for good measure. But his eyes wouldn't meet Holt's. His skin had the pallor of someone who hadn't seen much sun in weeks, and there were fresh bruises and scrapes on his knuckles. Apparently, Brady wasn't playing well with others behind bars.

Noah had opted to observe from behind the mirror. He'd already questioned Brady several times, with Holt covertly observing, and it hadn't resulted in anything. A fresh approach was necessary, so the CPD had given Holt permission to speak to Brady.

"Your trial starts in two weeks and the D.A. intends to prosecute you to the fullest extent of the law." Holt watched Brady for a long moment, long enough for the guy's right eye to start twitching. While what he'd said was true, it was also true that the arm of the law didn't reach as far as Holt and Noah would like. They needed a confession, otherwise the case might be dropped. There was precious little evidence other than the needles and neurotoxins under the bathroom sink in Brady's apartment, and apparently Brady was notorious for leaving his doors and windows unlocked. Which meant the matchbook that linked him to victim number two and the hate letter that connected him with victim three could have been planted as well. He claimed anybody could have framed him, and that there were plenty of people who would want to.

"Let them try to make these charges stick." Brady met Holt's gaze.

Either this guy *was* Toxin and he didn't think he'd done anything wrong, or he *wasn't* Toxin and he knew their case was weak. But if he was Toxin, why wasn't he boasting? The man who'd called the tip hotline and left Holt that letter at Buzz's murder scene was cocky. Triumphant. He believed he was doing important work. Felt he had a special connection to Holt, an understanding of him that transcended other relationships. Brady didn't fit the mold.

"You guys can't break me. There's nothing to break. I didn't kill nobody." Brady's gaze held Holt's. "Bring on the jury."

The guy was telling the truth. He could read it in Brady's body language. But why would the real Toxin pick Brady Flaherty to frame? Because Brady was related to one of the victims, and connected to at least one of the others?

Holt sat back in his chair. "Okay, Brady. Let's say I believe you. How did the evidence end up in your apartment?"

"Like I said before, somebody planted that stuff."

"And who would go to the trouble of doing that?"

Brady lifted his hands, but they fell back in his lap as he remembered they were chained together. "Too many people to count. I haven't exactly been an angel."

"Tell me about your relationship with Buzz."

The guy snorted. "Relationship? He's my uncle by blood but hasn't wanted a thing to do with me since Day One. Didn't like me. Hated me, actually."

"So you killed him." Holt had to try one more time.

Brady slanted him an exasperated look. "Like I said, I had nothing to do with it."

Holt leaned his forearms on the table and gripped his hands together. "So tell me who did. Let's talk about your family. Why would you go to people like Buzz, someone who supposedly *hated* you, for money?"

He shrugged. "It worked before. Mainly, my beloved family members would pay just to get rid of me. Squeaky wheel, you know? And this time I was desperate. Down to my last two pennies."

"Did your cousin Gloria hate you?"

His eyebrows drew together. "Not really."

"She'd have no reason to go after you?"

"No, man."

"Then why would she think you could kill her father?"

"Shit, is she the one who turned you in my direction?" Brady's lack of anger told Holt more than words could.

"If I were falsely accused by someone—especially a family member—I'd be furious," Holt added.

"Yeah, well, I figure she's had enough to deal with lately. Too much grief can make a person do crazy things."

"You think Gloria's crazy?"

"Enough to kill her father? No way. She loved the old asshole, though he was hard as shit on everyone. High and mighty, you know?"

Holt nodded as if he did know.

"I'm not surprised he ticked someone off enough to kill him. But Gloria and me? You're barking up the wrong family tree."

"And you have no ideas which tree I should be focusing on?" *Give me something to go on, dammit.* Brady had to know Toxin in some way. "Anybody you know who's obsessed with poisons, knows a lot about needles, was angry at Buzz? Anything? If you give us the right information, it could get you out of here."

"Don't you think I know that? My lawyer's been all over my case to get you some names. The worst I've done is not return some bitch's call after screwing her. Maybe look at their boyfriends and husbands?"

"What about your associates? The ones who get you jobs?" The jobs that involved illegal acts Brady would never admit to.

Brady smiled with false innocence. "All in the past, man. I'm on parole. Or, I *was.*"

"And the people you've hurt through those jobs...their families? Someone might be looking for a little taste of revenge."

"If they did, they wouldn't bother to frame me. They'd kill me."

NEIL ROCHARD HAD BEEN ON SARA'S MIND ALL WEEKEND, BUT ON Monday he wasn't in school. She steeled her nerves and dialed his mother's number. She'd try Claire first, before going to John.

"His dad had them this weekend." Claire's confusion shifted to worry. "He's not the best at getting them where they're supposed to be on time."

"But Jeremy's in school, on time."

"Maybe Neil's sick. Probably snuck out and went out drinking with his friends again." Frustration and resignation rang in Claire's hard tone.

Drinking? *Again?* Sara's heart sank. This was worse than she'd thought.

"May I have permission to ask Jeremy about Neil?" Sara asked. She hadn't wanted to put Jeremy in the position of tattling on his brother, if it came to that. But if Neil was making poor choices, and possibly endangering himself, Sara was certain Jeremy would want to help.

"Sure. Those two keep better tabs on each other than John does. I'll start calling Neil's friends' parents."

"Let me know if you hear anything, please, and I'll do the same." Sara found Jeremy in the lunchroom, sitting next to Theo. "Hey, guys. How's your Monday going?"

"Not too bad," Theo said. Jeremy toyed with the crust on a sandwich.

"Jeremy?"

"Fine, I guess." The boy spoke to his sandwich.

Sara slid into a chair opposite them. The lunchroom was just beginning to fill up, and many people had opted to eat on the picnic tables outside and enjoy the unusually mild autumn weather. The closest students were a table away. "What'd you guys do this weekend?"

"Dad and I talked about painting my room." Theo's gaze darted sideways at Jeremy, as if he, too, noted there was an issue that nobody was talking about. "It's my birthday soon, and I get to pick a new color scheme. Dad says it has to last me for the next few years. That's *if* he gets around to actually doing it, though. He's been really busy."

"I'm sure he will, especially since it's a birthday present. What colors did you pick?"

"Navy and Chicago Bulls red."

"Sweet." She turned to Jeremy. "How about you?"

He shrugged. The crust of his sandwich lay in a heap on his tray. He hadn't eaten a bite of it. "Not much."

"I hear you were at your dad's this weekend."

Jeremy's gaze shot up. His mouth tightened. "Did you talk to him?"

"No. Your mother mentioned it when I called looking for Neil. I'd really like to talk to your brother."

"So would I." Fear tinged his words and Sara felt a new level of alarm.

"What do you mean? You don't know how to reach him?"

"He ran away."

She controlled her surprise. "When?"

"Saturday night. He and my dad had a fight. Neil doesn't think he's good enough for Dad...not good enough to be a Rochard." Jeremy scooped the crusts into his hand and balled them up. Did he think the same thing—that he wasn't good enough?

"Did your dad call the police?"

"No. He said Neil will show up after he's cooled off."

In the meantime, anything could happen to the kid. Sara hoped Claire was having some luck calling the families of Neil's friends. "Thank you for telling me. I can see how concerned you are."

"I told Neil he's good enough for *me*."

She smiled. "I'm sure he appreciated that. And he knows you love him. He'll be fine."

Jeremy looked at her with hope. "You'll find him, then?"

She gnawed on her lip. She could search from this side of Neil's world, starting with talking to his teachers. "I'll try my best."

After leaving the boys to finish their lunch, Sara found Cheryl at her desk and had her run off a copy of Neil's Friday schedule. She walked through the last day he'd been at the school, asking each teacher what he had been like and who he'd talked to. The picture was sadly the same with each class...he'd been quiet and unusually withdrawn all week. His final class on Friday had been Computer Science. She found Chad White in the teacher's lounge.

Chad's eyebrows drew together in a *V* as she explained the problem. "Sure, I remember talking to him after class. He wanted to do some searching online before his father came to pick him up. I gave him a temporary password. He's a good kid, so I trusted him."

"Did he do that in the classroom?"

"No, the library. I purposely keep the classroom computers offline so there can't be any attempts to goof around on the internet. The library has a couple computers for online research, if the student has the password."

"Any idea what he was looking at?"

"No, but I can find out easily enough."

She mentally crossed her fingers, feeling optimistic for the first time that day. "That would be great."

The library was on the third floor, where large windows overlooked the front lawn and rows of bookshelves housed a generous collection of books. She remembered seeing Neil studying at the large wooden table several weeks ago. He'd been working so hard. Had he given up because he was disappointed in his test scores? They'd been making headway with his confidence too. One week of verbal attacks from his father had knocked all his progress flat.

Chad pulled a chair out at one of the computers and sat down.

"This is where Neil was working when I helped him log in." A few drags and clicks later, Chad had brought up the search history from Friday. The last website address was for a military recruiter in this area of town.

"Could I see that site, please?"

Chad loaded the page in the browser. "Unless he was writing a report on the Armed Forces, it looks like he was thinking of joining the Army."

NEIL HAD MET WITH THE RECRUITER, WHOSE OFFICE WAS IN A corner of the mall only five minutes from the school, on Saturday. They'd had a lengthy chat, and the guy had even taken Neil to lunch. Neil, with his brains, brawn and political connections, was apparently being wooed.

Sara found it alarming—not because the military wasn't a fine choice for a young man, but because Neil was a young man whose emotions were a pendulum. After a week of John's constant berating, she worried that Neil would jump into the first thing that felt good…booze, a cult, or the military…at least the military was a relatively healthy outlet. She just wanted him to have the luxury of making such a life-changing choice under the best possible circumstances. The only saving grace in this mess was that he wasn't old enough to sign up for a few more weeks. The recruiter sounded confident Neil would be back.

Saturday. According to Jeremy, that had been the night he'd fought with John. Where had Neil gone that night, and where had he been staying since? He was a well-liked young man with many friends. One of them had to know something.

"He was with another young man," the recruiter offered.

"Who?"

"The kid didn't want to get involved. Guess he was just there because Neil wanted company, but I did hear Neil call him Lance."

"Thanks," Sara said. "I know him." According to the computer's attendance record, Lance was in school today. He'd likely be heading to the football field for after-school practice. After she hung up with the recruiter, she called Claire Rochard to exchange information.

Claire's voice was thick with unshed tears. "I've been at my wits' end, calling everyone I can think of. I didn't get to Lance's mom yet. I don't know her as well."

"I'll talk to Lance. If he knows something, I'll have him contact Neil right away."

"Thank you. Keep me posted. *Please.*" Her voice broke. It couldn't be easy for Claire. She'd been struggling through a divorce for months now, and John certainly wasn't one to take responsibility or make it easy on anyone.

"Have you talked to John? Does he know what's happening?" Sara had hoped to avoid dealing with the man herself.

"We communicate only through attorneys now. I left him a message."

On the football field it only took a hard look from Sara to have Lance opening his mouth and spilling the details. "I told him he had to call someone by tonight or I would tell his parents where he was. Besides, my parents would have discovered him staying in our guesthouse sooner or later. I want to help, but I don't want to get in the middle, you know?"

Sara was all too familiar with the middle and how uncomfortable it was. "Call him. Tell him everyone's worried and if he doesn't come home, we'll have to involve the police." Maybe Neil didn't care about worrying his father right now, but he was close to his grandfather, who wouldn't be happy about how news of this would impact his campaign.

Lance made the call and, after a brief conversation out of Sara's hearing, hung up. "He'll be here in twenty."

Twenty minutes later, Sara was waiting with Claire in front of the school as a red BMW convertible came up the drive.

"That's him," Claire said. She dabbed at her eyes with a tissue.

"John insisted on buying him a car for his last birthday, but I had strict limits on how much he could drive it. John didn't agree."

Sara was so relieved to see Neil drive up that she nearly ran down the steps and hugged him. Claire beat her to it, but immediately released him and started shaking her finger.

"Don't you ever do that again," Claire said. "The Army? Is that what you want to do, get yourself killed?" The words spewed out of her but stopped abruptly as John's car roared up the winding driveway. He braked just short of Neil and Claire. Jeremy came running out of the building and Sara reached out to grab his arm and pull him to a stop next to her before he could immerse himself in the situation.

"I want to talk to Neil," Jeremy protested. Following on the heels of Jeremy, Theo had reached her other side.

"Me too," she said. "Let's go together." Maybe they'd break the tension and be able to assess the situation as they approached.

John unfolded himself from his car. "Making trouble again?" His icy words made Neil flinch. Jeremy's muscles stiffened.

Neil rounded the car to face off with his father. "I was trying to figure things out on my own. I can't think in that house. You don't approve of anything I do anyway, so I might as well do what I want."

"Is the Army what you want?" Claire asked.

"It was good enough for Grandpa."

Jeremy ran to his brother. "Don't leave." Neil put a hand on his shoulder.

Unfortunately, Jeremy's action had brought John's attention to Sara. "This is *your* fault. You've been trying to ruin things for months now."

"It's not her fault, Dad." All eyes turned to Neil as he stood up for Sara. "She's only trying to help me."

"She's going to help you right onto the streets. You listen to her advice and you'll be a nobody. Look where she's at—alone, divorced, living in an apartment above a boys' school."

"That's enough." Claire spoke up this time, her gaze pointedly surveying the crowd of students and teachers who were beginning to gather on the lawn to watch the spectacle. "Let's go home, Neil. We'll talk there."

"He'll go with me," John insisted.

"Oh, because that worked out so well last time?" Claire's voice was saccharine-sweet. "I don't think so. Starting today, it's my week with the boys, anyway." She reached for Jeremy's hand and tugged her sons toward her car.

John turned his glare from the retreating trio to Sara. "I'll be speaking to the board again first thing tomorrow morning. Light a fire under them. You might want to dust off your resume and start packing."

CHAPTER 14

"You busy?" Neil stood in her office doorway the next day.

"Not really. Come in." Sara closed down the file she'd been composing—a list of all the reasons she wanted to stay at the Academy. All the reasons she would fight John's campaign to have her fired. She'd received several concerned phone calls from the various board members since John's threat. They would be visiting the school next Friday to see her in action for themselves. Her stomach ached, but more from anger than worry. "How are you?"

He took a seat. "Hanging in there. I just have to make it to my birthday in a few weeks and then I'm free, right?"

Tread carefully. The last thing Neil Rochard needed was another adult pushing or pulling him in a particular direction. "If by *free,* you mean you'll be of legal age to make your own decisions, then yes." But legal age didn't always equal mental and emotional maturity. "And those decisions will be legally binding."

"So you don't think I should sign up for the military, either." He narrowed his eyes, as if he searched her face for the answers to life.

"I didn't say that. The military is a perfectly viable option. But it depends what you want. And nobody can make *that* decision but you." She sighed and decided to tell him the truth, John and the board be damned. "I'm worried about you, Neil. You're highly intelligent. You'll be successful when you find something you're passionate about. But is that the military? Or is the Army simply the closest emergency exit?"

Neil picked at an invisible thread on his jeans. "I don't know."

"Then don't rush into any decisions. And for God's sake, finish high school first."

A smile played about his lips. "Yes, ma'am. The recruiter told me the same thing, anyway. I thought you weren't trying to make my decisions for me."

"Well, that one should be a no-brainer."

He snorted. "That's good...considering I have no brain."

Her blood heated. "Is that what your dad's been telling you?" She pressed her lips together to keep from calling John the names she'd been thinking all week. "You've got a fine brain and you'll use it to figure out what you want."

"Did you always want to be a director at a boys' school?"

"Not always. But sometimes life takes you in different directions. I did know, however, that I enjoyed working with kids. The important thing is to follow a passion, and you'll never regret it." She knew then that she didn't need any list. She would fight for her job. No matter what John thought, this was where she belonged.

Neil seemed to think over her comments. "I like sports. And when I hurt my knee last year, I thought some of the therapy stuff was pretty cool. I think I might like to be a physical therapist."

The irony in that was that most parents would love it if their child were considering a health profession. "I know someone at Mercy Hospital. They could probably find you a volunteer position in the physical therapy department on the weekends, after football season and your night classes are over. You could see if it's the type of career you'd be interested in."

"Really?"

"In the meantime, research what education you'd need and which schools offer that curriculum. Especially focus on your math and science classes. Finish strong."

"I will."

"Good."

Neil didn't get up to leave. He looked at the ground, then at her. "I'm sorry about my dad. He's putting you in a tough spot, isn't he?"

A really tough spot. Not that she had anything to hide or be ashamed of, but the thought of four stern faces following her everywhere didn't leave her with a warm-fuzzy feeling. Still, she'd been through tough times before, and her personal motto always got her through. "I'll survive."

HOLT HAD JUST FINISHED PLACING A COUPLE LAST MINUTE CALLS TO set up Theo's birthday surprise when the SSAM receptionist appeared in the doorway of his office. "There's a call for you on line one." It was unusual for Catherine to walk from her desk in the lobby to find him when she could have just phoned him, but the way she wrung her hands together was even more telling. "He says he's Toxin."

Holt immediately sat up and reached for the phone. "Hello?"

"Do I have to hold your hand so you can get things right?" The voice on the line was definitely male, and highly annoyed. The same voice that had called Holt on the tip hotline. It was clear, now that Holt heard it again, that Brady wasn't Toxin.

Holt's heart pumped harder. He pressed mute and looked at Catherine. "Get Max. And is Einstein in the office? Tell him to start a trace." Catherine hustled out as he un-muted the line. "Who is this?" he asked, as if he didn't know.

"This is Toxin," the man on the phone said, as if he were any Joe

Schmo and the entire Chicago police force wasn't looking for him. "I've been waiting."

"For?" Holt was careful to match Toxin's casual tone, but, on the inside, his heart was in his throat.

"For you to make a move."

Tell me where you are and I will, you asshole.

"For you to see Sara again. And this time on a real date. She's a good woman. She deserves better."

Holt had to force himself to think past his shock. A serial killer was giving him relationship advice? This was a new twist, but it did fit with Toxin's pattern of egomaniacal puppetry. And now Toxin had transferred his fascination from Holt to Sara. Holt's heart pounded. He forced his words to convey calm disinterest when, inside, his mind was fast-forwarding to how he would get Becca back in position at the Academy right away. "Yes, she does. But how do *you* know her?"

He drew out his cell phone and set it on the desk in case Einstein had texted him. He hadn't. He should have been on the case by now. The guy was always wired-in. He quickly typed a text to the communications expert. *Tracing?*

"She's the whole package," Toxin said. "Takes care of those boys all day, doesn't go out at all. Barely leaves the school for anything. She's devoted. Not to mention she's a nice piece of ass."

Holt found it difficult to talk past the rage threatening to consume him. "Sounds like you know her quite well."

Einstein texted back. *On it.* Of course, if it was a throwaway phone again…

"I've been watching," Toxin said. "As *you* should have been. I thought I made that clear weeks ago, but that obviously isn't enough for you. So I'm going to have to take measures to see that she's taken care of."

Holt froze. "Taken care of?"

Toxin chuckled. "Not *that* kind of *taken care of.* But if you don't step up, I will."

This had to be the oddest conversation he'd ever had, challenged for Sara's affections by the man he hunted. "What do you mean by *step up?*"

"People lean on a hero for protection because he's strong. He goes after what he wants and he gets it. Wine and roses, man. You were married. You have to know the drill."

Jesus, this guy knew a lot about him. And the more contact he had with Holt, the more Holt was learning about him. "Why do you care what I do or don't do with Sara?"

"I just do."

Was he seriously ordering him to date Sara? "What if I don't follow your directives?"

"I'll show her what she truly deserves in a man. Someone who will take care of her. Show her a good time. Protect her."

That was the second time he'd used some form of the word *protect.* It couldn't be a coincidence. "Protect her from what? From you?"

"From John Rochard."

Alarm coursed through Holt. Toxin really had kept a close eye on Sara. He'd have the private investigator go back through the Academy employee records. He must have missed something. "Rochard?"

"Sara didn't tell you, huh?" Toxin chuckled as if they were two old friends sharing a joke. "He's threatening her job."

Shit. Sara had said she'd handle the issue of John Rochard. When he hadn't heard any more about it, he'd assumed she'd taken care of the matter. Of course, he hadn't given her a whole lot of incentive to come to him if she needed help.

"He needs to be taken care of," Toxin continued. "And this time, I do mean the other kind of *taken care of.*" He paused. "On Sunday, there's a banquet honoring veterans. Fancy dinner. Black tie. Be there, and take Sara. She deserves a night out."

"And if I don't, or Sara doesn't want to come?"

"You'll see. Convince her to go."

"What's in it for me?"

"Besides Sara and an expensive meal?" There was a pause. "A hero does things out of a desire to help. But if you need more, I have something that might interest you. Information about Samantha Manchester."

Holt went still. How had Toxin known about Damian's daughter? More important, how could he have information that Damian didn't already have? It had to be a ruse. "There's no way you know things we don't about her disappearance." Not only had it been twenty years since her murder, but Holt had seen Samantha Manchester's file. The CPD and Damian had used every resource possible to track down the serial killer responsible—to no avail. The killer was still at large.

"You willing to take that chance? I'll give you the information after you take care of Sara. I'll be watching."

TOXIN SMIRKED AS HE DISCONNECTED AND THREW THE CELL PHONE into a trash bin at the edge of the park. *That should do it.* The call couldn't have gone smoother, and despite wanting Sara for himself, now Toxin would know exactly where she was all weekend. He'd need that time to set the wheels in motion for the final stage of his plan.

Soon, Sara and Theo would be his.

IMMEDIATELY AFTER TOXIN DISCONNECTED, EINSTEIN ASSURED Holt he would receive the recording of the call ASAP. In the meantime, Holt summoned Max and notified Noah.

Twenty minutes later, Einstein and Max arrived in Holt's office. Twenty minutes was a long time to mull over the conversation, and to consider how to handle things with Sara. First, though, Holt wanted to analyze every nuance, every word, every pause of the recording.

Max dropped into the seat opposite Holt. "Noah's looking into the cell phone number, and has someone heading to the location from which the signal came."

"But I suspect it's another burner phone and Toxin will be long gone," Einstein added.

Holt cursed. "Unless the call came from the prison, it looks like we definitely have the wrong guy, although I already suspected as much. Noah will have to set Brady Flaherty free." He rubbed at his temple, where a headache was beginning. He'd held out hope his gut had been wrong—for Sara's safety. At least he'd had a bodyguard nearby, just in case. "What the hell could this banquet be about?"

Einstein held up a flash drive. "Recording's on here."

"How much?" Holt asked, hoping they'd at least gotten the last couple minutes.

"We got the whole thing." Einstein's grin was triumphant. He moved to Holt's side, neatly inserting the drive into his computer and pressing a button. Catherine's voice answered the call with friendly politeness and Toxin announced his identity.

"How'd you manage to get the whole thing?" Max asked.

"I can't take all the credit. Catherine thought it might be a good idea to start recording all calls that come in. Since SSAM is known for hunting criminals, she thought we might get threats, and some day it would come in handy."

Holt held up a hand to signal quiet and they immediately hushed. "There it is."

"What?" Max asked.

"He mentioned the word *hero*. And *protect*. Several times, actually."

"And that's important?"

"Absolutely. He's giving us clues, whether he intends to or not. He's got a hero complex. He wants me to be a surrogate hero. Kind of like filling his shoes, probably because doing it himself risks his freedom." He listened another moment, then paused the recording.

"That part about wine and roses. He lets me know *he* knows I was married, and that I should know the *drill*. Which means he probably knows the drill too."

"You think Toxin is married?"

"Is or was—some kind of committed relationship, like I'd thought before. I think that part of my profile is correct. And the fact that he refers to it negatively, as a *drill*, leads me to believe that relationship is definitely over. Yet he wants me to pursue Sara, in his stead."

Sara was a key. He'd tried to leave her out of the investigation, tried to forget about her entirely, though she continued to invade his thoughts, day and night. It looked like he was going to have to include her after all.

"Better get on the phone," Max said, standing. "In my experience, women like some advance notice if they have to get ready for some fancy shindig. That banquet is supposed to be full of big names and big egos—not the vets, but the politicians who'll haunt the place looking for good press."

Holt hadn't heard of the thing. "Then we'll need extra eyes and ears there." He compiled a to-do list in his head. He'd have to depend on Max to handle things from SSAM's end while he kept Sara safe. She might object to spending time with him, but he was going to plant himself on her doorstep until she understood how important this was. "We're going to have to get organized fast. The banquet's only a couple days away."

"I'll tell Damian," Einstein offered.

"No, I'll tell him," Holt said. "I need to warn him about Toxin mentioning Samantha, anyway. I don't want to get his hopes up about any so-called new information." The man had seen them dashed too many times.

DAMIAN LOOKED UP AS HOLT KNOCKED AT HIS OPEN OFFICE DOOR.

The haunted look in the other man's eyes immediately put Damian on alert. "What is it?"

Holt entered and closed the door behind him, ratcheting Damian's alert status up another notch. The man taking the seat across from him had some bad news to share. "We heard from Toxin."

"Just now?"

"About an hour ago. Einstein got me a recording of the conversation and I wanted to hear it a couple more times before speaking with you."

"A recording? That's good, right?"

"It is. But the trace didn't lead anywhere."

"Has there been another murder?" Maybe that was why Holt looked so grim.

"No, but Toxin wants me to jump through some hoops."

"You don't have to do anything he says, you know."

"But if I do…"

"What did he promise you in exchange?"

Holt scrubbed a hand across his jaw, then pinned Damian with his gaze. "Information on Sam's murder."

The air left Damian's lungs in a whoosh, as if someone had punched him in the gut. He sat back in his seat, as if it would help absorb the shock. "*My* Sam? What could he possibly know? You profiled him as, what, thirty-five or so? He would have been a teenager at the time of Sam's murder. Hell, he would have been about Sam's age."

"He says he knows something. And he's willing to offer it in exchange for my cooperation."

"What does he want you to do?"

Holt huffed out a breath. "Take Sara to some banquet."

"That's odd, isn't it? Why would he want you two in a public place?"

"I haven't figured that part out yet."

"If it's too dangerous…"

"It's probably the safest way to try to catch him."

"Right. We could have SSAM agents and CPD in place. We'd scope the perimeters, not get caught unprepared…"

Holt's gaze was unrelenting. "I wanted you to hear about this guy's bait from me…but he could just be yanking our chain."

Damian smiled grimly. "Don't worry about me. He can't promise anything I haven't already hoped for. Funny thing about hope…it never completely dies."

"There's someone here to see you," Cheryl said from the doorway.

Sara glanced up from the computer screen where she'd been looking over the spring schedule. It was always strange to think about spring break and matriculation dates when there was frost on the lawn and Thanksgiving was around the corner. Of course, if next Friday's visit from the board didn't go well, she might not be here in the spring. "Who is it?"

Her secretary's grin stretched from ear to ear. "Dr. Patterson."

She experienced the same reaction whenever she heard his name—a stutter in the pulse, a rush of blood to her cheeks, a hitch in her breath. She liked to think it was from extreme annoyance, but she was afraid it was so much more. That the man could still have such an effect on her after all these years…well, she didn't want to consider what that meant. She stood and smoothed her hands over her skirt. "What does he want?"

Cheryl glanced over her shoulder into the outer office area, then stepped aside.

"To apologize." Holt filled the doorway, a bouquet of bright spring flowers in his hand. Did everyone have spring fever? The dreary fall weather should have smothered those impulses. October's Indian summer had given way to a chilly, damp November that finally fit her mood. There were even rumors of a big pre-winter snowstorm headed their way next week.

All these thoughts were an attempt to distract herself from the visual impact of Holt. He seemed thinner, more jagged around the edges. Her fingers twitched, wanting to smooth the lines that bracketed his eyes.

Holt walked up to her and held out the bouquet. "I need to talk to you. Alone." He'd dropped his voice so that Cheryl couldn't hear. While Sara could ignore the flowers, the entreaty in his eyes was hard to resist.

Sara looked over Holt's shoulder. "Can you close the door behind you, Cheryl?" Still grinning, Cheryl did as requested, leaving Sara and Holt facing each other, so many words unspoken between them. She tried to remain impassive, but Holt shifted his weight and looked away as if nervous, and part of her was hopeful. Had he come to beg forgiveness? "What did you need?"

"You."

Her pulse fluttered so wildly she was sure he could see it jumping at her neck. She fisted her damp palms to control her reaction, but was forced to uncurl her fingers to take the flowers Holt suddenly thrust toward her.

"These are a peace offering."

She laid the bouquet on her desk. "You wanted to take things slow, and then I never heard from you again. Was that slow enough? Or are you just here to pick up Theo and knew you'd bump into me? Don't worry. I wouldn't have made a scene."

The intensity in the set of his jaw, in the line of his shoulders, told her he was primed for battle. *With her?* "I'm here to pick up Theo, but I need you to come home with us too."

Her head was dizzy from trying to read between the lines. "After weeks of not hearing from you, you want me to come away with you for the weekend?"

"No, I *need* you to come."

"I don't—" She stopped as he gripped her shoulders. His nostrils flared, his eyes dilated. If she didn't know better, she'd think he was panicked that she might say no. She should say no. She *would* say no.

Absently, his thumbs stroked along her collarbone. "Come home with me and Theo for the weekend. Stay with us. His birthday is tomorrow. It'll be fun. A new start."

"Don't be ridiculous. You want to go from no contact to staying overnight at your house?" His invitation wasn't one born of passion and excitement. Everything he'd done to date told her he clearly wasn't ready for a relationship, at least not with her. The whiteness around his lips made it clear he was issuing the invitation against his will. But why? She planted her fists on her hips. The movement had him dropping his hands to his sides. "I think you'd better tell me what's going on."

He looked so lost she almost agreed to go with him just to relieve his pain. "Toxin requested our presence at a banquet in downtown Chicago."

She sank onto the desk. *"Toxin?* I thought he was in jail."

"Brady was framed. He's been released. The real Toxin decided to step forward and contact me—a phone call this time. He's getting braver. We just need to do what he wants until we can trip him up."

"We? You *and* me?"

Holt sat down. He suddenly looked tired. "Believe me, it wasn't my idea. He's insisting I wine and dine you."

A bubble of laughter moved up through her chest and lodged in her throat. *"Wine and dine?"*

"He's got it in his head that I should be your hero, and that you deserve a good man."

"Well, at least he got that last half right."

He looked even more miserable. "I'm sorry I dragged you into this, Sara."

"You're not the one demanding my presence."

"In a way, I am. His connection to me, his comfort level with me, is our best lead yet. I need to exploit that to catch him. He's expecting me to take you to the banquet."

"And if I say no?"

"I can't say I'd blame you. Hell, half of me hopes you will. It might keep you safe."

She mulled that over. He cared enough to worry about her safety. That was something, anyway. Not exactly what she'd wanted from him, but...something. "But then you wouldn't catch Toxin."

His gaze met hers and held. Beyond the misery, there was determination. "We'll catch him. Eventually."

Possibly after he'd killed again. Or several times. How many people would die before they got another lead like this?

The thought of spending all weekend in close contact with Holt did strange things to her insides. She wasn't sure it was a good idea while her heart was still healing. "Why would I have to be there all weekend? I could meet you for the dinner. Or I could stay at a nearby hotel."

He started shaking his head the moment she'd asked the question. "I want to make sure you're safe. Toxin is watching. He said as much." His gaze went to the flowers. Her stomach plummeted as she realized what they represented—not Holt's contrition, but that he was currently at the mercy of an evil puppet master. "He could have followed me here. He seems to be watching my every move. Some of the things he said...he's close enough to have been watching you for weeks now too. The school will be empty for the weekend. I don't want you here alone."

"What about Becca?"

"She has a prior commitment this weekend. I've had a private bodyguard nearby for the past few weeks—"

"You *what?*" She hadn't had a clue he'd been *that* worried.

"—but I'd rather have you near me so I can be sure you're safe."

The seconds ticked by as he waited for her to respond. If Toxin wasn't caught soon, the killer could remain near her school, possibly a threat to her boys. If she could stick things out with Holt for a few days, they might catch a killer, but at what cost to her heart and her pride?

The door to her office opened a crack, then all the way. "Jeremy told me he saw you come in here." Theo entered, but didn't move to greet Holt.

Cheryl appeared behind him. "I'm sorry. I asked him to wait outside."

"It's okay." Sara smiled at Theo. "Bet you're looking forward to the weekend, with a birthday and all."

He shrugged. "We're supposed to paint my room." He glanced uncertainly at Holt. "If we can find the time."

"Oh yeah, you mentioned that. Sounds like fun. You'll be ten?"

"Finally." He rolled his eyes as if he'd suffered some long wait. "I could bring you a piece of birthday cake, if you want."

"No need," Holt said. "She's coming home with us. We've got big birthday plans for you, bud."

Sara raised her eyebrows.

"You *do*?" Theo looked at Sara and grinned. "Really?"

She swallowed her anger at Holt. "Why don't you go outside while your dad and I finish our conversation. We'll have our chess game later."

"Yeah, okay, since you'll be at our house and all." Theo seemed confused but interested in the prospect. He left her alone with Holt.

"You'll come?" Holt's hazel eyes were laced with concern again.

"I don't see as I have any choice." He'd found her one weak spot. She wouldn't break Theo's heart now.

"I'm sor—"

"No, please, don't say it. We're not going back to that routine again."

"I'll need you to stay through the night of the banquet. I can bring you back to the school the next morning. Until Toxin is behind bars, I plan to keep you close."

With his statement, a shudder traveled over her body. She turned to hide her response, shutting down her computer and tucking papers into a drawer until she recovered her composure.

"We're going to have to set some ground rules." She met his eyes. "No physical contact." Not that he wanted any from her, but she'd be damned if she'd let him make the rules this time.

"If you're sure."

"I'm sure."

"That's too bad." His words shocked her into stillness. He had to be joking. *He* was the one who had doubts as to whether he wanted her or not. He strode to the door and opened it, pausing to look back. "You'd better get packed. Do you have to stay until all the kids are picked up?"

"Most of them are gone already, but Cheryl and Coach will stay until everyone is accounted for. Just give me twenty minutes to pack." She'd need ten just to calm her frazzled nerves. It would require all her battered defenses not to make a fool of herself over Holt this weekend.

"I'll be out front with Theo."

Sara stopped at Cheryl's desk and handed her Holt's bouquet. "These are for you." The last thing she needed was a reminder who pulled the strings in this puppet show. Toxin was in control of her destiny at the moment, and those kind of strings threatened to strangle her.

CHAPTER 15

Holt spoke briefly with the security guard posted in a car across the street, then trotted back to his son. Theo unlocked the front door and stood aside as Sara and Holt carried in two bags containing their fast-food dinner. The aroma of fries and greasy burgers mingled with the familiar smell of home. Elizabeth's bowl of potpourri on the living room table was oddly out of place now. While Holt had eventually donated the items from her side of the closet, there were still touches of her personality and influence everywhere. He hadn't thought of what it would be like to invite another woman into the home he'd shared with her. A twinge of sadness told him he still had emotions to deal with, but they weren't as overwhelming as he'd feared.

Theo bounded past him to the kitchen, on a quest for sodas to go with dinner.

"Wash up," Holt called after him. He turned to take the bag of food from Sara and caught her looking at a shelf, her attention on a picture of him with Elizabeth and Theo, taken a couple of years ago, before Elizabeth had known she was ill. In it, they were smiling as they hugged on Loyola Leone Beach, one of their favorite destinations for family daytrips. "There's a spare bedroom upstairs. I'll get you guys settled with some food and then get your things from the car."

"No hurry." Sara's gaze went to him, and his heart twisted at the sadness he saw there, a mirror of the grief he'd been facing down for over a year now. "Is it hard to live with all of these reminders of her?"

"It's more comforting than sad, I guess. At least, now it is."

"I was the same way about my parents' things after they died. It was hard, but certainly not as hard as it has to be on Theo, losing his mother while he's so young." She shook her head as if shaking off her mood, like some kind of snow globe in which she could reset her feelings. "Never mind me. This weekend took me by surprise."

That was an understatement. He'd dumped a load of guilt and pressure on her, told her she was being watched by a killer, and yet she'd taken it on without further argument. Sara was full of surprises as well.

"Maybe eating will help." Holt said as Theo came in balancing three cans of soda in his hands. Holt smiled, but watched his son and Sara carefully for signs of strain as they sat on the living room rug, around the coffee table. "Hope you don't mind having a little picnic. Theo has a school project spread out on the kitchen table."

"No, this is perfect." Sara tucked her jean-clad legs under her. "I like casual."

Though there was a formal dining room just off the foyer, Elizabeth's rented hospital-style bed had been set up there in the final weeks, while she received hospice care and had needed more space. Holt hadn't had the energy to return the dining room furniture from storage after the room was emptied. He wondered how Theo felt about that—it must be a constant reminder that his mother had spent her final days there.

But, at the moment, Theo was under Sara's spell. She radiated positivity, laughing with him and talking about his week. Conversation turned to Theo's interests.

"Did you show your dad your comics yet?" Sara asked. Theo shook his head. "Why not? They're really good," she said, more to Holt than Theo. Holt felt a pang of jealousy. "Well, maybe one day, when you're ready?"

Theo shrugged. "Yeah, maybe. At least making comic books doesn't get me in trouble like getting caught under the stairs, right?"

Holt's parental alarms went off. "*Caught?* Doing what?" But the pair was absorbed in a discussion of some game involving an assassin.

"Have you really played Death Files?" Theo asked Sara.

"Yes," she replied. Both Theo and Holt looked at her in surprise. "What? You both play. Why is it a shock that I do?"

"I've played the newer games on occasion with Theo," Holt said. "But those first-person shooter games? Overcomplicated, if you ask me."

Sara grinned. "Well, you don't hang out in a school full of video-game experts day after day without picking up some tips." She winked at Theo. "You'll have to show me what you've got while I'm here."

Theo gobbled down the last of his burger and nearly launched himself off the floor. "How about now?"

Sara laughed and Holt's heart clenched. When was the last time this house had been filled with laughter? "It's all right with me if it's okay with your dad."

Holt grinned at their enthusiasm. "As long as there's no bloodshed. But first, clear your project off the kitchen table. We'll need somewhere to eat all weekend."

"I will." Theo hurried off.

Sara watched him leave. When her blue eyes turned to Holt, her confidence had evaporated. "You're sure it's okay? I know some parents don't like their kids to play."

"It's fine." He cocked an eyebrow at her. "If you're sure you're up for it."

She pretended to look offended. "You doubt my mad gaming skills?"

"Theo's pretty good."

"And his dad? Care to show me what you've got?" Her eyes sparked with wicked humor and his blood heated.

"I'd love to show you." He'd dreamed of showing her many things. At this moment, the thought of pushing her down to the carpet and picking up where they'd left off on her couch weeks ago had his interest stirring.

Her laugh pulled at something in his chest, as if she were reeling him in. He tried to resist the pull, but his gaze locked on her lips, then shifted to the long column of throat that moved as she laughed. His lips twitched, wanting to taste that milky skin. *Oh, what I could show you right now, Sara Burns...* The bolt of lust that shot through him had him looking away.

"Well, you've got a couple of days to put your talents on display," she said, grinning, apparently unaware of his discomfort.

An entire weekend of laughter and fun? As long as he knew SSAM and the CPD had security constantly monitoring the house, and he had the private security guard stationed across the street, maybe he *could* relax just a bit. "I'm glad you came, even if my methods to get you here were slightly devious. This time, I won't apologize."

Her laughter evaporated. "I was going to agree before you told Theo I was coming. You didn't have to coerce me. I don't want anyone else to get hurt."

"You're a generous, brave woman, Sara."

She looked away, balling up her hamburger wrapper and stuffing it into a bag. "Yeah, right. So generous that men can't wait to get away from me." She pushed up from the floor. "Forget I said that. It's been a long week and I'm tired."

Disappointment filled him. How had he killed the playful

mood? And why wasn't he relieved that she was keeping her emotional distance? "I can show you to your room. I'll make Theo understand."

"Oh, no." She wagged a finger at him. "Don't think I'm letting you off the hook that easily. Besides, I think some stress relief via video game is just what the doctor ordered."

"You go ahead. I'll be along in a minute."

A few minutes later, as Holt straightened up the living room, he heard Theo's and Sara's cheers and groans. He checked in once more with the guard outside and unloaded the bags from the car, placing Sara's suitcase in the spare room.

He took Theo's backpack to his room. The outer space theme made him smile. A mix of the things Theo had had as a baby—the glow-in-the-dark stars on the ceiling that Elizabeth had carefully arranged into constellations, the pillow she'd sewn in the shape of a smiling half-moon—and the Star Wars posters and figures Theo had asked for a couple Christmases ago. All of it would be gone tomorrow. Theo had asked to entirely redecorate his room for his birthday.

His son was ready to move forward. Bittersweet emotion had Holt's throat shrinking. Elizabeth should have been here for this milestone. She would have been coordinating the décor, as well as planning a big Thanksgiving feast for the entire family. But she wasn't. And he was tired of waiting for her to come back. The love he'd felt for her had become a deep, tender love during her months of illness. With Sara, he'd felt a spark of passion he hadn't expected. An echo of what he'd suppressed a decade ago. It scared the shit out of him. "What do I do, Elizabeth?"

There was no answer from his dead wife. And since there would be no concrete answers, he'd do what he always did. He'd go with his gut. He'd sworn to protect Sara while she was under his care this weekend. But once Toxin was finally behind bars? Would he be happy Sara was out of his life, no longer stirring unwanted emotions, or would he miss her laughter and passion? Either way, he'd proceed with caution. Theo came first. And Theo was enough to fill his life.

But as he stood in the doorway of his den, watching the play of lights across Sara's and Theo's intent expressions while their cyber characters locked in virtual battle, he was worried his son didn't have the same reservations. Theo had already made room in his heart for Sara. Perhaps Holt's heart was expanding as well. *Game on.*

DESPITE THE NUMBER OF CHILDREN IN HER LIFE, SARA HADN'T BEEN to a children's birthday party since…well, since she'd been a kid. As an only child, she didn't even have nieces or nephews to dote on. Theo knocked on her door as she was pulling her hair into a ponytail.

"Happy birthday," she said.

He sat on her bed. "I can't believe I'm ten. Double digits."

She laughed and sat down next to him. "Take it from someone who's been there for a while, double digits aren't so bad. So, tell me what's on the agenda."

Theo shrugged. "I don't know. Dad's got a whole *thing* planned, I guess." She hid her surprise. When had Holt found time to prepare a kids' party? "He's in the kitchen making my favorite brunch—French toast and bacon. He says we'll need our energy to survive today."

"It does sound like he's ready for some serious partying."

"Yeah. We should start fueling up." He led her downstairs to the kitchen, where Holt was removing a jug of milk from the refrigerator. A birthday cake took up an entire shelf inside.

She recognized the symbol, a mask that looked as if it were made of metal. "Transformers. Any friends coming?"

Holt shot her a look and a short shake of his head. It was obvious she'd said something wrong.

Theo didn't seem upset, though. "Nope. Just Dad, and Grandma and Grandpa Patterson. And you."

"Theo didn't want to invite anyone outside of family," Holt explained. *Family.* Sara tried hard not to feel like a third—or fifth—wheel. "But the cake's for later, bud. We've got breakfast and then the hunt begins."

"I know, Dad." Theo rolled his eyes like a proper ten-year-old.

"Hunt? That sounds ominous." Sara surveyed the food on the table. A plate heaped with slices of steaming French toast. A decanter of syrup. A small dish of powdered sugar and another of fresh berries. Holt had put on an impressive spread.

Holt rubbed his hands together. "And when we get back from the hunt, we'll have the cake and ice cream. Today is all about seeking the perfect sugar high."

As they enjoyed the brunch, Sara observed this new, boyish side of Holt with wonder. Perhaps the video games had unlocked something last night. He'd certainly had a wicked gleam in his eye when he'd trounced her on the virtual battlefield.

As they finished their food, Holt sat back. Sara licked a dab of syrup from her fork. "Who knew your mad skills extended to the kitchen?"

When she looked up, her chuckle lodged in her throat. His gaze was on her lips, and she could feel the air sizzling between them. She set her fork down, aware that Theo was still in the room and she couldn't lean over and kiss Holt the way she wanted to at that moment. It didn't look like Holt would object.

"But it sounds like you'll be showing us a lot of your hidden talents," Sara said. "What, with re-decorating an entire room. That should take up a large chunk of the day."

"Don't forget time for presents," Theo added, then slanted a look at her. His grin stretched from ear to ear. "What'd you get me? Another journal?"

"Theo." Holt's voice held a warning, but reminding him his son was in the room seemed to do the trick. The heat was gone.

Sara hadn't had the opportunity to get a gift, so she'd had to improvise. She thought she'd done well, considering her limited time and resources. "You'll have to wait and see." Holt looked at her in surprise, but she ignored him. He wasn't the only one capable of surprises.

"Grandma and Grandpa will be here any minute," Holt told Theo. "Why don't you go find the first clue to the hunt? It's somewhere in the blackness of outer space."

Theo rolled his eyes. "That's got to be my room. Blackness... probably my closet."

"Then I'll expect you back at the table in T-minus-two minutes with an idea of where we lift off to next."

Theo hurried out of the kitchen, leaving them alone.

Holt turned to her. "Don't get his hopes up."

"Excuse me?" Her good mood evaporated like a drop of water hitting a hot skillet.

"He's attached to you. Promising things you can't deliver will only crush him later."

"And who says I can't deliver?"

Holt arched an eyebrow.

"It's a *surprise*." The silence dragged on, but she refused to give him an explanation. He was suddenly determined to think the worst of her—like he had of the old Sara. Why? To put distance between them? *Too late, Holt Patterson.* If the look in his eyes a moment ago was any indication, he was fighting his attraction as much as she was.

"It had better be the good kind of surprise."

Her temper heated. "You drag me here, insist I take part in your family activities—" A twinge of guilt nagged at her. She'd actually found herself wanting to participate in the family fun.

"Only because you're here anyway—"

Ouch. "—and then accuse me of making Theo become attached to me?" She huffed out a laugh. "You are un-freaking-believable, Holt Patterson."

"Are we interrupting?" Betty and Ron Patterson pushed their heads inside the kitchen doorway. Apparently deeming the territory safe, Betty stepped forward and gave Holt a peck on the cheek. Her gaze surveyed him with a mix of concern and interest before swinging to Sara. "Good to see you again, Sara."

Sara recovered her manners. "Good to see you too. Thank you for sharing Theo's special day with me." She turned to Ron and smiled, struck as always by the resemblance between father and son. Studying her were eyes nearly identical to Holt's and Theo's—hazel with gold flecks.

"Holt told me he'd invited you for the weekend," Betty said. *Did he now?* That was interesting, considering he didn't want her to form attachments to his family. "I can't tell you how nice it is to see he's brought someone home."

"Mom." Like a growling dog, Holt had a way of warning people with a simple word.

"What? I'm not allowed to comment?"

"She's here because of a case."

"Well, a mother can hope, can't she?" Betty grinned at Sara. "I haven't seen this much spark in him in two years." She linked arms with Sara and pulled her toward the living room. "Let's have a chat, shall we?" Helpless against the momentum of the tide, Sara went with Betty.

"Hi, Grandma." Theo came down the stairs and accepted the hug Betty offered. His eyes went to the coffee table where a large box wrapped in navy paper and a red bow sat. "For me?"

"You *are* the birthday boy, aren't you?" Betty gave him a smacking kiss on his cheek. "But I've been warned that you'll have to wait until after you return from your outing."

"Outing? The treasure hunt's going to be outside the house?" Sara asked.

Theo held up an index card. "Yep. I found the next clue in my closet."

Ron came out of the kitchen with Holt following behind.

Judging by the creases in Holt's forehead, the two men had engaged in a brief but intense discussion.

"Happy birthday," Ron said, moving to Theo and offering him a handshake. When Theo gripped his hand, Ron pulled him in for a hug. A brief flash of pain passed over Holt's features and Sara realized that Theo allowed affection from everyone but his father. In fact, she couldn't recall seeing Theo initiate an embrace. Or Holt, for that matter. Holt had patted him on the shoulder once, but she hadn't seen the father and son hug.

None of your business, Sara. This is Elizabeth's family, not yours. They'll work it out.

HOLT'S IDEA HAD BEEN TO MAKE THE PROJECT OF TRANSFORMING Theo's room a big deal. Despite the cheesy phrases Holt had dreamed up and Theo's reluctance to show enthusiasm, Theo eventually seemed to get into the spirit. It probably helped that Sara was on board. Who knew the woman would be Holt's biggest cheerleader?

"Stop calling them cheesy," Sara insisted at their second stop, a furniture store. They were searching for a desk and chair at which Theo could do his homework. His son was thoroughly testing swivel chairs. "*Surround yourself in a rainbow?* That was perfect to lead us to Home and Hearth for all the paint colors. And I thought this one was particularly clever."

He'd snuck a paint swatch into Theo's handful from the first stop and Theo had read the clue Holt had scrawled on the back. He'd even cracked a smile. *The birthday king deserves a new throne.*

"Well, they're not Shakespeare." Holt had enjoyed coming up with the clues, but he wanted to reconnect with Theo, not come off as ridiculous.

"I doubt Shakespeare ever went paint-shopping at Home and Hearth." She gestured to Theo, who was spinning in circles in one of the floor-model chairs. His beat-up sneakers pushed off in a repetitive rhythm. "Just look at him. He's happy. Because of you."

"I wanted him to get what he wanted for his birthday…redecorating the room."

She gave him an odd look. "It's not the room. It's spending time with you. You showed him how much he means to you today. That's the best present ever." She walked over to Theo and tried out the chair next to him. Soon, they were both trying the levers that raised and lowered the chairs.

Earlier his father had warned him about Theo adjusting to a new woman being under the same roof. Though Holt had insisted it was only for the weekend, and it wasn't *that* kind of relationship, his father had shot him several concerned looks. Theo's emotional safety was a primary concern.

Looking at Sara with Theo now, he needn't have worried. The kid loved her. Unfortunately, that would make things more difficult if Holt never saw Sara again after this investigation…except for when he bumped into her at the Academy, of course.

If he never saw her? Was he actually contemplating an alternative?

Holt's phone alerted him to a text, pulling his thoughts back from the daydreams to which they were headed.

Good job. She certainly looks happy.

Holt's pulse pounded like a jackhammer in his head. He glanced around and even walked down a couple aisles, while keeping Theo and Sara in sight. But there was nobody nearby leering at them. Yet, Toxin had sent this. Though the number was blocked, Holt knew without a doubt it had been sent by Toxin…and that Einstein again wouldn't be able to trace it.

He dialed Max. "I need you, man. Toxin texted me. He's watching, but I don't see any sign of him. I'm out in public with Sara and Theo. Can you tail us today?"

"Don't you have a security guy in tow?"

"Yeah, but I'd rather have you." An ex-SEAL and Holt's vigilance should be enough to keep them safe for the weekend.

"You got it. I'm just finishing up the security sweep at the banquet room for tomorrow night, anyway. Give me your location and I'll be there in twenty."

SARA ACHED IN PLACES SHE DIDN'T KNOW SHE HAD. "HOW DO YOU use your glutes to paint a room?"

Holt's gaze went to her behind before moving back to his hands, which he was soaping up under a stream of water in the kitchen sink. She felt her cheeks heat as she thought about those lathered hands slipping over her skin. "Stretching to reach those high places with the roller, I guess. I probably shouldn't have put a guest to work." His raised eyebrows indicated he was challenging her.

"Well, it was worth it." She handed him a towel.

Following the hunt for supplies, they'd returned home to find that Betty and Ron had moved the furniture to the center of Theo's bedroom and taped the edges of the walls. All that was left to be done was rolling on the colors Theo had chosen—a nice Chicago Bulls' Red and a deep navy. She'd suggested some cream-colored accessories to lighten the look. "What do you bet Theo's still sitting on his bed in the middle of the room?"

"He sure was excited, wasn't he?" Holt grinned. He'd done a lot of that in the past several hours, and it warmed Sara's heart to be a part of such a lovely family day. She was honored they'd shared it with her.

But as she followed Holt into the family room where his parents were sipping on the mulled cider Betty had put together, she was reminded of the issues waiting in the wings. On one hand, Betty seemed to be firmly in the pro-new-relationship camp. On the other, Ron's furrowed brow indicated doubt. She wanted to reassure them that this was a temporary arrangement, but she understood their concern. Theo had become attached to her, and that bond was only getting stronger.

"You're not going to let him sleep in there with the fumes tonight, are you?" Betty asked.

"He'll sleep in my room," Holt assured Betty. Ron's frown relaxed.

"He seems so happy." Over the lip of her glass, Betty's gaze shifted between Sara and Holt.

"Doesn't mean it's good for him," Ron said. "Change isn't easy."

"But sometimes it's necessary," Holt said. Uncomfortable, Sara was relieved when she heard Theo's footfalls on the stairs. "Time for cake?" Holt asked as Theo emerged.

"Sounds good to me." Theo grinned as they gathered around the small kitchen table, sang the birthday song, clapped when he blew out the candles, and passed around plates with large pieces of cake and scoops of chocolate ice cream. A few minutes later, they fell into silence as a sugar-induced haze enveloped them.

"I'm so full I don't know if I can get to the living room to watch Theo open presents," Ron teased, patting his round belly. "Maybe we'll have to wait a little longer until I can move."

Theo jumped up and began gathering plates. "If I clear the table, I can bring the presents in here."

Ron and Betty laughed and Sara rose to take the plates from Theo. "The birthday boy shouldn't have to do chores on his special day. Unless it's painting." She winked at him, then quickly looked at Holt, realizing she may have crossed a line. It was all a little too familial, but after the beautiful time she'd had with Theo, she didn't want to hold back her feelings. And that wasn't what Theo needed, anyway. The kid was hungry for displays of affection. Then again, her emotions were raw and too close to the surface. Being with Holt's parents had reminded her how much she was missing her own.

Still, she was in Holt's house, and she wanted what was best for Theo. She should honor Holt's wishes. Unfortunately, he wasn't giving her any cues as to what he thought about her behavior, or which of his parents he agreed with. He was just sitting there quietly, watching her.

As if sensing the sudden awkwardness, Ron pushed away from the table. "I think I can make it a short ways. Come on, bucko. Let's go admire the loot." He, Betty and Theo left to settle in the living room. Holt continued to study her.

"Please let me help," Sara said, holding the plates she'd gathered. "I don't mean to intrude. In fact, I'm fine staying in here and cleaning up and you guys enjoy some family time."

Holt took the plates from her and set them back on the table. Her heart plummeted. But when her gaze lifted to meet his, it wasn't anger but a different kind of heat she saw there. Her heart soared again, making her stomach flip-flop as if she were on a roller coaster.

He reached out and took her now-empty hands in his own. "I know you don't mean any harm." His thumb was warm as he stroked it along her palm. "But you have a way of attaching yourself to people." She stiffened. He tugged her into his lap and she was too astonished to release the defensive words that had sprung to her lips. "It's not your fault. You just have a way of getting under our skins. I've seen it firsthand with Theo." It sounded as if he were trying to work out some kind of puzzle.

"Gee, you make me sound so appealing."

His eyes went to her lips. "You are. Too appealing to resist. Lord knows I've tried."

She held her breath, thinking he would kiss her now. For weeks, she'd dreamed of kissing him again.

But Holt lifted her off of his lap and set her in a standing position just as the kitchen door swung open and Theo stuck his head in. "Are you guys coming?"

"Wouldn't miss it," Holt said. Sara was still regaining her balance emotionally and physically as Holt gathered up the pile of plates and dumped them into the trash container.

Sara needed a moment to gather her senses. "I just need to get my gift."

From the dresser in her room, she retrieved the envelope she'd put together late last night, when Holt had given her access to her email and the internet on his office computer. She was returning to the living room when she heard Theo's words.

"She doesn't have to get me a present. She *is* my present. From Mom."

"Mom?" The tension in Holt's voice indicated he'd gone into high-alert mode.

"Yeah. Mom told me before she died that Miss Sara would look after me, and she has."

Somewhere, Sara found the willpower to set one foot in front of the other and descend the final two steps that put her in view of the occupants in the living room. Holt's parents were exchanging concerned looks after the bomb Theo had dropped. Holt spied her standing there and quickly looked away. But not before Sara caught the tight lines around his mouth.

Sara held up the envelope. "I promised Theo a gift." *Lame.* She felt the words fall flat.

Theo didn't seem to notice anything was wrong. He rushed forward. "I want to open it first."

"It's not much." She suddenly felt nervous. She'd been excited by the idea, but perhaps she'd presumed too much.

Theo took the envelope in both hands as if it were precious and delicate. He slid a finger under the flap and removed the single sheet of paper inside. Sara had printed the website page.

Theo read the paper. "A creative writing course?"

"My friend teaches it online, and normally it's for college-age students, but she agreed to let you into the class. I hope that's something you'd enjoy. I thought, with your talent for creating stories, you might be interested..."

So fierce was his excitement as he hugged her around the waist that she almost toppled over into a nearby lamp.

She hugged him back, laughing. "I guess that's a yes?" She looked to Holt, whose eyes were narrowed on his son. "If it's okay with your dad, that is." She should have run it by him first. She could see that now. But she'd wanted to surprise Theo.

"It's okay with me," Holt said. But he was still avoiding looking at her. "You clearly know what my son likes."

CHAPTER 16

"Dad, do you have a minute?" Theo stood in the doorway of Holt's home office.

"Of course. Come in." Holt closed his laptop, on which he'd been reviewing the latest communication among SSAM agents. They'd done everything they could think of to ramp up security for tonight's banquet. He'd combed through the guest list for Toxin's next possible target, but no name was jumping out at him. But then, Toxin's targets never seemed to make much sense.

Theo was clutching the leather notebook Sara had given him a couple months ago, as well as a spiral-bound one. He seemed hesitant.

"Would you like to show me those?" Holt asked. "Because I'd love to see them...but only if you want me to."

Theo thrust them toward him. "Yeah. If you really want to, that is..." He swallowed. "There's some stuff in there that might remind you of Mom. I was kind of thinking of her...and cancer...when I wrote the stories."

Theo sat on the chair in the corner of the room, apparently

wanting to watch Holt read the stories. Holt pulled his glasses on and spent the next fifteen minutes reading through the journals. His heart squeezed as he read about the trials and tribulations of the hero, who felt alone in the world. Was that how Theo felt?

When he came to the end, he looked at Theo, who was nibbling on his bottom lip nervously. "I can see why Miss Sara was impressed."

"You like it?" Theo came over to the desk. "I wasn't sure…"

"I do." And he was most impressed that his son had come up with a way to express his feelings that felt safe. "Do you think of yourself as the hero?"

"Sometimes. But mostly I pictured you."

Holt was startled. "Me?" Did Theo see him as a loner, taking on grief by himself and closing himself off to the world? He'd thought he'd sheltered his son from his own feelings, but he'd gravely mistaken how much Theo had picked up on.

"You didn't like other people to see your weaknesses. But most of all, you kept fighting. Like the hero in the story."

Holt looked away a moment, then met Theo's steady gaze. "I'm sorry I didn't talk with you more about what your mom was going through. I guess I underestimated how much you saw, how much you felt. Sometimes it's okay for people you love to see your weakness. It binds you together. I'd forgotten that, Theo. Thanks for the reminder."

Theo smiled. "No problem." He shocked Holt by coming around the desk to hug him. His arms encircled Holt's neck. Holt squeezed his eyes shut and breathed in the scent of his son. He could have held him like that for a long, long time.

But Theo pulled away and grinned. "Miss Sara was right. I shouldn't have been afraid to show you these."

"Why were you afraid?"

"I didn't want to remind you of Mom's death. Not when you were finally starting to act normal. I didn't want to make you sad again."

Holt felt moisture pricking at his eyes and blinked it back. "You could never make me sad, Theo. You only make me happy. You are the best parts of me and your mother."

"That's what Miss Sara said." It seemed Holt owed Sara another debt. Theo shuffled his feet, apparently reaching the limit of his emotional sharing for the evening. "I should get my homework done. Got some stuff due tomorrow. And you should be getting ready for your date."

"Date?"

Theo rolled his eyes. "You don't have to hide it, Dad. It's okay if you're seeing Miss Sara. She's singing in the bathroom while she gets ready." He leaned forward conspiratorially. "I think she likes you."

More surprises. "And you'd be okay with that."

"She's really nice. I think she'd be good for us."

Holt was thinking the same thing. Hearing the confirmation from his son was like lifting a weight from his shoulders. He handed the notebooks back. "Thank you for sharing these with me. I think that creative writing class will be perfect for you."

Theo grinned. "Yeah, and I'll be like a college student."

He was growing up so fast. Holt was only glad he'd mentally returned to the land of the living in time to see it. "And maybe we can attend a comic book convention sometime soon, if you'd be interested."

Theo let out a whoop and hugged Holt. Twice in one night. Holt could get used to that.

As his son practically skipped out of the room, Holt felt the need to thank the woman responsible for their breakthrough.

He made his way down the hall toward the guestroom, where Sara was, indeed, singing. "Back in Black" by ACDC. He grinned.

"Are you ready yet?" he called through the closed guest bathroom door.

He tried to distract himself from thoughts of her naked in his house by mentally reviewing today's SSAM meeting and the preparations for tonight. They needed to trap Toxin *tonight*. Anything else was unacceptable. Then Holt could shift his focus to his son. It was way past due. The memory of Theo's arms wrapped around his neck left Holt with a warm glow. He had his son back.

The door opened a crack and Holt caught a glimpse of rose-painted lips before Sara's baby blues locked on him. "I need your help."

"With?"

She opened the door wider and he swallowed hard as he caught sight of the dress hugging her curves. Was it possible to be jealous of a dress? Black satin. Simple. Sexy. Effective.

Back in black. And she had his pulse ratcheting up with every breath. Then she turned her back to him, showing an exposed V of creamy white skin and a glimpse of a bra clasp. Black lace. Holt's pulse sped up. Sara swept her blond curls into her hands and held them up on her head. The glint of a rhinestone-studded hair comb that pinned back one side of her hair winked at him as she glanced back over her shoulder. "Zip me?"

His hands shook as he clutched the zipper but she didn't seem to notice when he fumbled. After he'd zipped her, he dropped his hands before they could give in to the temptation to explore the creamy skin near her neck. "Thank you."

Sara released her hair and turned back around. "For what?"

"Theo finally showed me his stories."

Her eyes lit up. "Oh, I'm so glad."

"I think you had a lot to do with it."

She shook her head. "He would have come to you eventually."

"He even hugged me." It seemed he'd been waiting an eternity for a hug from his son.

Her eyes softened in understanding. "There will be a lot more to come."

"Yeah. When we catch Toxin, I'm hoping to take some time off with him. Winter break is just around the corner."

"You work too hard." Her fingertips traced the dark circles under his eyes. He sucked in a breath at the contact.

"Until I catch Toxin, I won't sleep well anyway." And when he did sleep, the image of exploring Sara's lush body had him tossing and turning.

She put on what he'd come to know as her let's-do-this face. "So you'll drive me to the Academy early in the morning?" Classes would start again tomorrow, but not for long. The students had a full week off for Thanksgiving.

Was she so eager to leave him? He should be relieved. He wouldn't have to worry about examining his soul any longer without her there to tempt him. But instead of relief, he was thinking of how empty the house would seem without her laughter.

A frown tugged at his mouth, but Holt fought it. "Don't worry. We'll get you back in time. We can pick up Theo at my parents' on the way." Becca was camping out at his parents' house overnight to help watch out for Theo's safety. By tomorrow morning, he hoped he'd be heading to the jail cell that held Toxin to demand some much-needed answers, including what the guy thought he knew about Damian's daughter's disappearance.

THE LACE BRA AND PANTIES SARA HAD PACKED FOR THIS OCCASION itched against her skin as she mingled during cocktail hour at the banquet. But the discomfort was worth it. The fancy undergarments, like the hair comb, gave her confidence and a much-needed boost of courage. Or maybe some part of her subconscious had wanted to feel sexy around Holt. She didn't want to feel like second best anymore.

Executing a subtle wriggle, she was able to ease the friction. The elderly gentleman speaking to her barely noticed. He was too engrossed in his story. But beside her, Holt's hand went to her elbow as if to steady her. Her skin heated at the contact, building to a simmer when he left his hand there.

"That must have been an intense situation," Sara said when the vet with a chestful of ribbons paused. "Behind enemy lines with no way of communicating with your base." She shuddered. "I can't even imagine."

"No, I don't suppose you can." The colonel glanced around at the other people gathered in the large banquet hall. "Most of these people can't imagine, but there are a few here who know that kind of fear."

"I, for one, am glad you fought on *our* side. Thank you." Her compliment made the pale gentleman's cheeks flame red against his white whiskers.

"If I were twenty years younger…"

She laughed, charmed by his flirtation. "I wouldn't have a chance."

"No, you wouldn't," he assured her with a wink. He looked at Holt. "And I would have given *you* a run for your money."

"I don't doubt it," Holt said. Though he smiled, it was guarded. They'd been like oil and water lately, mixing but never quite merging. His cool gaze assessed her in a quiet but intense way that shot straight to her core. He could slip past her defenses so easily.

HOLT TRAILED SARA AND OBSERVED IN BEMUSEMENT. SHE SEEMED determined to personally speak to each person in attendance, probably trying to ferret out the killer from among those attending. He admired her defiant attitude. The simple elegance of her dress indicated a practical woman, but the flash of diamonds in her hair reflected an impulsiveness, a fiery sensuality, that would have grabbed his attention even if he weren't watching her carefully for other reasons. Her ripe-berry lips were quick to smile or part on a laugh. She was so…*vibrant*.

He wanted to unlock all her secrets. What would it be like to indulge himself, to let himself travel down the road he'd wanted to weeks ago, days ago, hours ago…hell, almost every moment of the past couple months? Instead, he'd chosen safety and run back to familiar territory. He'd claimed he needed to consider Theo's feelings, but his son was obviously in love with Sara. Holt was reluctant to dig into his own feelings and discover why he still avoided taking Sara into his bed. All his reasons for avoiding her had been obliterated this weekend. He could no longer deny that either the old Sara was gone or he'd never really known her.

"See anyone who fits the bill?" Damian asked, his voice loud and clear through Holt's earpiece. Holt almost jumped at the intrusion. Damian had planted himself in a car parked across the street from the venue. He was observing the people come and go, as was Noah from his post near the main doors.

Holt's gaze traveled the room and he gave a subtle shake of his head, knowing Damian and Einstein could see him via the camera Einstein had set up. The crowd all seemed to be interacting as normal people would—and nobody had *psychotic killer* tattooed on his or her forehead. Toxin was a highly intelligent and patient man. He'd bide his time and calculate the perfect time to strike.

"Why would he mention this banquet, specifically? He's got to have a target here." Damian was hypothesizing out loud, and not about anything they hadn't already discussed, so Holt didn't speak.

Max's voice came through the party line. "In a room this crowded, the guy could get close to anyone without looking out of place." Holt spied Max across the room, his gaze sweeping the crowd.

As Sara continued to charm the people who came up to them, Holt watched for anything suspicious. His gut told him something wasn't right. *Think, damn it.* What would Toxin do? Who would he target? Why would he want them at *this* banquet? Toxin had to know Sara would be protected at all times.

"Are you okay?" Sara asked him when they had a moment alone.

"Just thinking about Toxin, and whether he has something planned for us. For maximum impact, if he was going to do something dramatic, he would want his target to have some kind of meaning for you. Who in this room would that be?"

"You." She said it in all seriousness, her eyes wide with concern. His heart rate continued to escalate and he wanted to capture her lips under his own and never let them go.

"No. He wants me to be an actor in this for a while longer." Toxin had bonded with Holt on some abhorrent level. "It has to be someone he'd want to get rid of. Someone whose death would make Toxin a hero in our eyes." His gaze landed again on the man who'd made no secret of his disdain for Sara. "John Rochard."

He felt Sara go rigid beside him before she spoke. "Oh, no." Her words were expelled on a rush of breath. "He's here?"

He hadn't been on the guest list, but, sure enough, John Rochard stood beside his father. Though Senator Patrick Rochard had been expected to attend, it hadn't raised any red flags. The senator was a veteran running for re-election in a couple days.

Holt gripped Sara's elbow. "Prepare yourself. Looks like he's making his way to this side of the room." It wouldn't be long before John Rochard spied her and Holt together. A second later, Rochard's gaze swept the room, then landed on Sara. As he took note of Holt's possessive hold on her, his eyes lit up as if he'd found a hidden treasure.

"Didn't expect to see you here," Rochard told Holt as he sauntered over to them. He looked Sara up and down. "Or you. Guess they'll let anyone in these days." His chuckle was caustic.

"I thought we warned you to keep a low profile," Holt said. They'd let him know that a killer had mentioned his name, and in an unflattering light. Toxin had basically threatened the man's life, yet here he was parading around like a peacock.

"He'd be an idiot to attack me here. Not his style, anyway, is it?"

"No, but that doesn't mean he can't change his habit." If he wanted to do away with Rochard badly enough, he'd find a way.

Sara licked her lips and searched the faces of the people passing by. Holt felt the tension radiating off her. He leaned over to whisper in her ear. "It's okay. Rochard's right. This guy tends to strike when there isn't a crowd around."

She nodded, then forced a smile for Rochard. "I hope you're being careful."

Rochard snorted. "As if you cared. That board review is coming up soon. Friday, isn't it?"

"Yes." Her spine was so rigid, it was a wonder she didn't snap.

A waiter reached Rochard's side, delivering a tumbler of scotch. "Ah, there it is. Thank you." The waiter hovered a moment, probably hoping for a tip, then hustled off when it was apparent he wouldn't be receiving one. Rochard took a large swallow and held the glass up to the light. "Manna from heaven."

Holt felt a prickling of unease. Why? Why would Toxin insist he and Sara attend this thing if he wasn't going to show up? And Rochard was right...the killer preferred a one-on-one scenario to killing in a crowd. Perhaps he was lulling them into a false sense of security, waiting to strike when they were alone. But they'd never be alone. SSAM security and the CPD were keeping a watchful eye. Holt turned to scan the crowd again.

"John?" The worry in Sara's voice brought his attention back to her. "John!" The other man dropped his glass. Its contents splashed onto their shoes, but their focus was on Rochard, who was grasping at his throat. His skin had taken on a bluish hue. Sara reached for Rochard, but the man was stumbling away.

"Get back, Sara!" Holt shouted, but it barely broke through the din of the guests who were starting to notice the commotion.

Rochard had dropped to the floor, still clutching at his throat. He began to writhe in pain. In Holt's peripheral vision, Max pushed his way through the crowd to get to them. From the far end of the room, Noah was trying to make his way to them as well.

Sara ignored Holt's command and dropped to her knees at Rochard's side. Holt bent down beside her and pushed her hands aside. "Don't touch him."

"We can't just watch him die." Her eyes were wide with shock and panic.

Holt loosened Rochard's tie and shirt, but it wouldn't matter.

"The drink," Holt explained as Max and Noah joined them. "It must have been poisoned. Get that waiter!" He knew Damian, listening from his post in the parking lot, would have heard the commotion and would be sending paramedics in. Noah was also calling for reinforcements.

"I'll go," Max told Holt as he took off. "Stay with Sara."

Noah pushed toward the doorways to prevent people from leaving before they could be questioned and cleared.

"Medical personnel are on their way," Damian said over the mic. They'd been on standby in the parking lot. Moments later, Damian escorted the hustling paramedics to their side. Rochard was turning a dangerous shade of gray, his mouth opening and closing like a carp's.

Holt shifted to make room. "Use protection. I believe he's ingested poison."

Sara's hand reached out and took his as they watched them work on Rochard. "Was that waiter Toxin?"

"I don't think so." Holt squeezed some warmth into her fingers. She was in shock. To hell with who was watching, he wanted her in his arms. He pulled her close and wrapped her up tight against him, turning her face away from Rochard. The paramedics were doing their best, but it was too late.

"Why not?" Her words were muffled against his suit.

"Too young. I think Toxin was pulling more strings, getting someone to do his dirty work this time."

"Is my boy going to be okay?" Senator Rochard asked the medics. "Please...please help him. Do something!"

At the senator's anguished cry, Sara's nails curled into Holt's back. The paramedics moved quickly, trying to revive John, but it wouldn't be any use. Toxin moved swiftly and surely. He'd taken another life. And why? To impress Sara? She was certain to blame herself once the shock wore off and she was thinking again. Apparently, the senator was a couple steps ahead of him.

"This is your fault." The senator pointed a finger at Sara. She pulled away from Holt and faced the man. His body shook as he glared at her. "John told me about you, about how you're determined to destroy my grandson's future before he even has a chance at one."

Sara paled.

Holt angled himself so he was in front of her. "If you're going to blame anyone, blame me. I'm the reason she's here."

"No, Toxin is," Damian said.

"Toxin?" The senator shook his head. "The serial killer? But the news says he uses a needle."

"Apparently he's widening his repertoire." Holt jerked his head toward Damian. "We've got all of SSAM's resources at our disposal, and this is our specialty."

"We're going to catch him," Damian assured the senator.

The senator's eyes narrowed on Damian. "If you catch the bastard that did this, I will donate a million dollars to your agency." As he leaned in closer, his face was mottled and his voice quivered with rage and grief, but his eyes were calm and hard. "And if you kill him, I'll give you two."

"We'll get him." Damian motioned to another set of paramedics who'd just entered the room. "Can you check out the senator, please? He's had an awful shock." Damian's phone rang, and he moved away to accept the call.

Others took over Senator Rochard's care, and Holt pulled Sara away from the scene, finally breaking her gaze from John Rochard's inert body. Her arm trembled beneath his hand and she was biting her lip so hard Holt was afraid it might bleed.

"Take her home," Damian urged as he rejoined them a moment later.

"What about the investigation?"

"That was Max on the phone. He found the waiter, but it was too late. He was left in an alley not too far from here with an empty syringe by his side."

CHAPTER 17

Holt gladly accepted Damian's directive to take Sara home and keep her safe. Max and Noah would handle things at the banquet hall. Sara, on the other hand, needed to get out of there. And *he* needed to be home with Sara, even if it was only to watch her pack her bag in preparation to return to the Academy in the morning. He refused to think about how she wouldn't be under his roof, under his protection, any longer. He wanted to run his hands over every inch of her body and check her for damage. He wanted to keep her from biting her lips to the point of drawing blood by kissing her senseless.

And, really, what was stopping him? None of the excuses he'd used before seemed important. There was evidence of her love wherever he turned—she looked after Theo's needs, wanted to protect Rochard tonight despite all he'd done to her, and went straight to Holt's kitchen when they returned home and poured two glasses of water, handing him one before taking any for herself. Despite their rough beginning, somewhere along the way he'd come to know her selfless, warm-hearted side. Or maybe she'd always been that way and he'd tried not to notice, especially after Elizabeth had become pregnant and his future had become clear. Sara had told him she backed away from him and her friendship with Elizabeth to keep her attraction to him from hurting them. Had she sacrificed her own needs and desires for their good?

Besides, Elizabeth hadn't been some dewy rose, totally innocent and guileless. They'd had their issues. All couples did. And she'd once, in a moment of uncharacteristic low confidence, admitted she'd been glad they'd gotten pregnant right away, so that he would be guaranteed to stay with her. Yet Holt had emphasized her positive characteristics. With Sara, he'd highlighted shortcomings. Looking back, he realized how unfair that had been.

Sara leaned against the kitchen counter and took several gulps of water. She was still too pale. "Did you check in with Theo?"

"Dad says he's just fine. Sleeping soundly. Becca's on the floor by his bed."

"Good." Relief softened the hard lines of worry for a brief second before they formed again. "Do you think I killed John? I mean, not with my own hands, obviously..."

Holt's anger at Toxin flared anew. "You mean, because a killer was watching *you*, John was on his radar? Toxin wanted to impress you, Sara, but never, ever believe that you're the reason John's dead. Using that logic, I'm just as much to blame as you are. I'm the reason Toxin found *you*."

She reached up as if to touch his cheek, but quickly dropped her hand. *Not this time.* This time, he would allow himself her comfort. He reached for her and pulled her into his arms. She buried her face in his chest and he felt her warm breath through his tuxedo shirt. He let go of her hand and sank his fingers into her hair, holding on for dear life. The locks were wavy, eager to spring free after being trapped by a comb all evening. He turned his nose into the softness. The smell of flowers filled him like the promise of spring during a desolate winter.

"Holt?" Sara's question held a note of confusion but also one of hope.

"I need to hold you a minute."

She was softness, warmth, vitality. He absorbed all of it like a dry sponge. Her arms tightened around his waist. She melted against him as her initial surprise gave way to acceptance. After several minutes, she pulled away enough to tip her head up to look at him. "What's wrong?"

"Nothing." Nothing was wrong. That was what was different. This time, holding her felt right. "I shouldn't have pushed you away before." The huskiness in his voice gave away his arousal.

Her pupils grew large, indicating her own interest. "You're not pushing me away now."

"No."

"So what now?"

His laugh feathered her hair. "What do you mean?"

Her lashes fluttered, hooding her eyes. "I'll give you a hint. I'm not pushing you away either. In fact, I really, really like being this close to you."

He leaned down, taking her lips beneath his own. She parted for him, letting him in. A moan of relief laced with desire escaped him and he sank into her, trapping her between him and the kitchen counter. His hands slid down her sides and locked onto her hips, holding her in place so he could show her what he wanted.

At first, he ran his tongue over her bottom lip—the lip that she'd bitten earlier. But as his hunger grew, the kiss grew fierce and wanting. He needed this, needed *her*—more with every breath he inhaled. Her light scent filled him, making him boneless with weakness for her, yet stronger somehow. Sara was fire and heat, but also security and understanding. His fingertips dug into her hips, inhibited from touching what he really wanted by her dress, but he didn't let go. He wasn't letting Sara slip through his fingers this time.

.   .   .

SARA SHOVED ASIDE ANY DOUBTS AS TO THE WISDOM OF HER ACTIONS and let herself feel something good without overanalyzing it. She'd always maintained a strict hold on her needs. Even when she'd been married, she hadn't fully been able to embrace her desires. Maybe her body had known her mind was locked on one man, the man she'd fallen in love with years before.

He tasted faintly of the champagne he'd taken a few sips of at the banquet. Crisp and clean. She sensed that he, too, wanted to lose himself tonight. No questions asked. No consequences. Just two consenting adults finding a night of escape, and a reminder that they were alive. Safe. But a niggling doubt insisted she find out whether he'd push her away again.

She took one more taste then pulled away to gulp for air. His hazel eyes glinted with heat and purpose as he scanned her face. "You're sure?" she asked. "I don't want to stop this time. I mean, I won't expect anything later…"

"I'm sure, and you're talking too much." He nipped at her lips.

She flicked out her tongue and he took it into his mouth, eagerly sucking on her. She drifted a hand slowly around his waist to the front of his jeans, slipping the hand between their enmeshed bodies so she could cup his erection. Stroking a thumb up and down the hard shaft, she enjoyed the way he shuddered in response.

He hissed out a hot breath against her mouth. "Wicked woman."

She rubbed her hand against him again. "Teach me the error of my ways."

"Oh, I didn't say they were wrong. Bedroom?" The air between them nearly sizzled as he waited for her answer. He didn't have to wait long.

"Yes."

She only got a quick look at his bedroom before he pulled her into his arms to bring their lips together again. She was about to wrap her arms around him when he released her and spun her in an about-face so he could unzip her dress.

She laughed as the room swayed and then righted itself. "Trying to knock me off my feet?"

"The sooner, the better. I've been dreaming about seeing you buck-naked all night. Ever since that glimpse of lace when I zipped this earlier." The crackle of the zipper and wisp of his hot breath just before he pressed his lips above her bra clasp weakened her knees.

She reveled in his hunger. Finally, he wanted her. Finally, he'd left his doubts behind.

His hands skimmed her with delicious roughness as he pushed the garment from her body into a sleek puddle on the floor. He turned her to face him again, this time more slowly. His gaze drank her in, pausing on the lace bra and panties. His throat worked as he swallowed.

His fingers moved along her body from her hip upward, lingering at the side of her breast. Sara couldn't help the way her body reacted, instinctively arching against him so that she filled his palm. His thumb decided it could be wicked, too, flicking against her nipple through the lace. As she sighed with pleasure, his other hand moved to include her other breast. Still cupping her, he nudged her backward to the bed.

Sitting on the mattress put her at eye level with his abdomen. "You're way overdressed for this party."

She reached for his belt buckle and undid it, then made quick work of the button and zipper. He tugged his tie and shirt free and, in a flash, they joined her dress on the floor, a swirl of white and black like a yin and yang symbol. Unable to resist tasting his exposed flesh, she pressed her mouth to his bare stomach. The muscles there clenched at the contact and he hissed out a breath. Salty skin and musky male swamped her senses. The dark hairs that dusted his belly tickled her nose and she smiled against him.

"God, Sara, it's been so long."

She took another nip at his belly.

With a groan, he shucked the rest of his clothing and gently pushed her back onto the mattress. But he didn't join her. He stood over her, his gaze heating every inch of her skin. Her nipples tightened beneath her bra. The lace no longer itched, but instead created an arousing friction with each breath.

He lay down on his side and trailed a fingertip from her lips, between her breasts, down to her belly button. He circled there once, then dipped his fingers beneath the edge of her panties. His gaze lifted to meet hers, connected, and held. She let him see everything there—her entire soul laid bare.

He moved his fingers against her moist heat. Hot tension gathered in her core and built and built to an aching need for release. And still his gaze held hers captive, his fingers pushing her to the edge. She hung there, immobile. With one more swipe of his finger, she fell off the cliff. She splintered, her core bursting into a million shards of light as she cried out. His palm pressed to her stomach, as if he could absorb the shockwaves that rushed through her.

She pressed her face into his neck as she rode out the pleasure. It wasn't just a physical sense of exhilaration, but an emotional one of losing control with someone—with *Holt*—even if just for a few moments. But she craved a deeper connection. She reached for him, cupping his erection and stroking it until he pushed against her hand. Her fingers circled the length and her thumb brushed the tip once. Twice. He moaned and rocked against her. She let go of him, lifted her hips and removed her panties, making it clear what she wanted. Him. Inside her. *Now.*

He moved on top of her, pressing against the apex of her thighs where she throbbed and ached for him. Needing him to ease the ache, she opened to him and wrapped her legs around his waist. She kissed the hard line of his jaw and nibbled down the column of his throat as he pressed into her. He went slowly, panting with the effort. His breath was cool against her flushed cheeks.

"I need you." And she wanted to push him over the edge with her this time. Her hands gripped his biceps, then trailed down his back to his buttocks. He filled her completely then, and Sara gasped with the incredible emotion that swamped her. *Holt. Finally.* A drop of moisture at the corner of her eye trickled down into her ear.

He increased the rhythm as heat coiled inside her again, ready to strike. His muscles bunched. Their climax struck, and he bent his face into the crook of her neck and muffled his shout against her skin. His exhalation sent shivers radiating to the extremities of her body. The shiver was quickly replaced by a warmth that seeped into every cell.

They lay together that way for several minutes, as if neither of them wanted to break the spell. Her arms locked him in place on top of her, his body a welcome weight, filling the places that had been empty for so long. After several long minutes, he rolled to his back, bringing her with him and tucking her against his side. His arm wrapped around her protectively. She couldn't resist running a hand down his chest. This was Holt. He was with her. She thought maybe she should pinch herself, but if she was dreaming, she didn't want it to end.

The quiet intensity was interrupted minutes later by frantic barking outside. As the barks turned to wails, Sara lifted her head. "Does your neighbor have a dog?"

"Yeah." Holt pulled away from her and rose.

At the window, his nakedness was hidden from the rest of the world by the curtain, but open to Sara's curious gaze. After being deprived of him for so long, she couldn't get enough. Her eyes traced the curve of his shoulder and the strong line of his thigh in the moonlight. Fear—not of any outward threat but an inner one —pierced her. She'd fallen deeper in love with Holt. And though he'd made love to her body, she didn't fool herself that she'd reached his soul. But maybe, in time…

He twitched the curtain back in place and strode to his closet.

"He's not usually a barker. Something must be wrong. I should check on Mrs. Mendelson."

Sara sat up and held the sheet up to her chest to ward off the sudden chill. "Do you want me to come with you?"

He pulled on jeans and a shirt. "No, stay here. I'll lock the front door behind me. Don't open it for anybody. I'll be back soon." He cursed.

"What?"

He sat on the bed to pull his shoes on. "Do you know how to use a gun? I meant to show you, or have Max…" After shoving his feet into shoes, he sent a hand through his hair, setting it askew. "I'll leave it with you anyway." He disappeared into the closet and returned with a pistol.

A gun? Did he even know how to use one? "But you have a child in the house. It isn't safe."

His gaze locked on her. "If it means protecting Theo… protecting you…then it's safer to have it than not. I usually leave it at SSAM, but I've been keeping it nearby lately. Just in case." His gaze moved to the windows.

"I've never held a gun."

He laid it in her hands, the deadly end pointing away from both of them. He gave her a quick lesson in releasing the safety, aiming, and pulling the trigger. She had to admit the weight of it was reassuring, given the circumstances.

"If you think you need it, just be sure it's not me returning." He grinned, but she felt the blood draining from her head at the thought of accidentally shooting him. Thank God Theo was at his grandparents' home.

"Maybe you should take it. You don't know what's going on over there, anyway."

"There's an armed security sentry posted in a car outside. I'll get him to go with me. Don't worry. I'll be back before you know it." Holt kissed her hard on the lips and rushed out, leaving Sara feeling cold from more than just exposure to the air. From outside, the dog continued to bark and wail as if the hounds of hell were after him.

THE STREET WAS DARK, THE MOON BEHIND THE CLOUDS, AS HOLT picked his way across the strip of grass that separated Mrs. Mendelson's house from his.

"It's probably nothing," the guard said from behind him. "I didn't see anyone come or go."

"Just keep your gun drawn." Holt continued toward the front door. A perfectly round orange pumpkin was flanked by two pots of purple mums on the porch.

"You think Toxin would go after an old lady?"

He hoped to hell not. He hoped she was simply injured. But if Mrs. Mendelson was in trouble… He racked his brain, trying to remember her first name. He *should* remember her first name. They'd been neighbors for years. Elizabeth had always been friendly with her. The woman had brought over a casserole for Theo and Holt after Elizabeth passed. And she walked her dog Roscoe every evening at precisely five-fifteen.

So why couldn't he remember her name?

Holt stopped at the door and turned to the security guard. "Make your way around back. See what the dog's barking about. I don't want to scare Mrs. Mendelson if everything's okay. And keep an eye out for anyone approaching my house." Sara was strong. She would use the gun if she needed to—he just didn't want her to have to take a life to save herself.

As the man disappeared around the edge of the house, Holt knocked on the door and waited. Counted to thirty. Told himself that would be plenty of time for a healthy woman to get out of bed and to the door.

The doorknob turned easily in his hand and the door swung inward. The hairs on his neck rose as his brain silently raised the alarm. Mrs. Mendelson was always good about locking her doors.

They'd even had a conversation about it, when she'd found out what he did for a living. She'd picked his brain about the monsters who masqueraded as normal people in society. She hadn't trusted easily, yet her door was unlocked.

The kitchen was dark, but the sliver of light from the window indicated nobody was there. It was the soft light coming from the living room up ahead that drew him. And the silence. Roscoe had stopped barking, and Holt hoped to hell it was because the guard had calmed him. He hoped even more that it was because there was nothing to bark about.

But the stillness indicated something was horribly wrong. As if there was no life in the house, but there should be. Or somebody was holding his breath, waiting for him to discover something. His gaze was in constant motion, surveying the corners and doorways as he moved toward the light. There, his fears were realized. In the circle cast by a table lamp, Mrs. Mendelson lay, facedown, on her living room carpet. A pool of blood had formed around her head. The edge of the pool nearly touched a hypodermic syringe.

A tapping on glass had him looking up. A dark figure stood outside the sliding back door, with Roscoe's shaking form pressed against his leg.

The guard slid the door open. "Unlocked. Must be how he came and went since I didn't see him out front." His gaze landed on Mrs. Mendelson's body.

Whimpering, Roscoe pushed his way past the guard's legs. The pug headed straight for his owner, but Holt scooped him up before he could get to her. "Poor Roscoe," he murmured, stroking the quivering mass. "I'm sure you would have destroyed Toxin if you'd had the chance." He turned to the guard, who still had his gun in his hand. "Check out the house. He may still be here." But he doubted it. Holt withdrew his cell phone from his pocket and dialed 9-1-1 to report the murder. Then he phoned Noah. "Toxin killed my neighbor, this time in a fit of rage."

Noah cursed. "I'm stuck at another scene but will be there as soon as possible. Are you okay?"

"Yeah." Except his stomach was twisting and his head was spin-ning. It could so easily have been him—or Sara—who Toxin chose to release his rage upon. It wasn't any better that it was the inno-cent Mrs. Mendelson. "I've got to check on Sara. Call me when you get here."

With Roscoe still wriggling in his arms, Holt hung up and raced out, his only thought on making sure Sara was safe. He planned to hold her against him until this horrible feeling—this premonition he would lose everyone he cared about—was gone. She seemed the only one capable of restoring the bright light of hope.

THE LIGHT AND SHADOW IN THE ROOM SHIFTED AS THE SCREEN'S image changed. There, the animated woman with an accentuated hourglass figure kissed her buffed-out hero, rewarding him for saving her life. *Success.* But temporary victory over a video game didn't relieve the angry ache that gnawed at Toxin. And beating an old woman to death with a fireplace poker hadn't worked, either. Had Holt discovered her yet? Was he smothered by guilt?

Toxin turned his attention to a different computer screen and scrolled through the images he'd captured earlier that night, having to settle for hacking into the security cameras SSAM had set up and recording events at the banquet. He couldn't very well be there in person when Holt would be watching for him.

But the waiter had done his job. And the poor schmuck hadn't known what hit him. He'd died with his palm outstretched, waiting for his payment in that dark alley. He'd even demanded extra for his *trouble.* His payment had been delivered via syringe.

On the screen, Toxin again watched Rochard drinking the poison. When he toppled to the floor, Sara rushed to the asshole's side, her body movements conveying concern. His breath caught, as it had many times, as he came to the image of her bending over Rochard, worry etched in the lines of her face—worry for an egomaniac who had wanted to ruin her. Tender and compassionate, she was the perfect complement for a hero like Toxin. Together, they could save the world and avenge his son's death.

Unfortunately, Holt had chosen tonight to finally stop being a pussy and try to be Sara's hero. The memory of what Toxin had seen through Holt's kitchen window…and the image of what must have followed that passionate embrace…made Toxin's blood boil.

It should have been *him* kissing Sara. *He* deserved her. *He'd* orchestrated everything that led to the intimacy he'd witnessed.

Though Toxin could no longer see them when they'd gone upstairs, it hadn't taken a genius to know what was next.

Everything—*every goddamned thing*—Holt possessed was because of *him*.

He threw the game controller across the room. It landed next to the box he'd brought home earlier that day. The shipment was ready. Syringes and the neurotoxins Henry had prepared were ready for the final act in this play. He had to see it through. It was the only way. True heroes never rested until full justice was meted out.

Poison. The world was full of it. All that was good and right had been sucked out of reality, and it was his job to show certain people how they poisoned everyone else's existence. He would be the toxin that wiped out all the others. With the amount of venomous shit being injected in the world, he didn't think his mission would ever be complete.

One thing at a time.

He deserved some happiness after what he'd done. With Sara and Theo by his side, he would tackle the rest of the world more easily. And *he* would appreciate them.

Toxin smiled. He would have to wait to claim Sara, but not for much longer. He was ready, and what he had planned would wow her in a way that would win her heart. The grand gesture, like in the movies. The payoff for hours of hard work, like completing a video game.

In the meantime, Toxin knew someone who could make the pain go away, even if for a few brief hours. His reliance on Henry was becoming a liability. Someday, when he didn't need him any longer, he'd rectify that. For now, though, Henry was part of the big finale.

And tonight...tonight he'd find oblivion with Henry's help. He'd be with Sara and his son, a family, in his dreams. Soon, he'd make it a reality.

"THREE MURDERS IN ONE NIGHT," DAMIAN CONFIRMED OVER THE phone.

Holt touched a hand to his aching head and sat at the end of his bed. He'd returned from Mrs. Mendelson's home to find Sara where he'd left her, though dressed now in pajama bottoms and a tank top. His gun had been left on the bedside table, within reach. She was sitting propped against her pillows, trying to read, but the lines in her forehead told another story. She'd heard Damian.

Three? she mouthed. He nodded and she shuddered.

"Mrs. Mendelson, John Rochard, and the waiter," Holt said.

"If Sara's there," Damian said, "you might save some time by putting me on speaker phone."

He pressed the button so Sara could hear Damian too. "We're listening. Go ahead."

"How do we know Mrs. Mendelson was one of Toxin's victims?" Sara asked.

"Toxin left his calling card." Holt recalled the horror of finding Mrs. Mendelson's body. Though still melancholy, Roscoe's shock seemed to have diminished somewhat, and the dog was currently settled on the cozy rug at Holt's feet.

"But why Mrs. Mendelson?"

He had a feeling Sara was going to take this next bit of information hard, so he reached out and took her hand. "Remember when we were in the kitchen?"

"Yes." Her tone was questioning. Suddenly, shock widened her eyes. "Toxin was watching us?" He saw the exact moment when she realized what he'd probably seen. Her skin paled.

"Probably from the back fence."

"But if he wanted you and me together, why get angry? Why kill Mrs. Mendelson?"

"Either he didn't like what he saw, or he changed his mind." Something had made him angry enough to deviate from his normal methods and kill a woman with his bare hands.

"Noah's been apprised of the situation," Damian informed them. "He'll take over processing the scene at the Mendelson home and interview neighbors, then meet us at SSAM later today."

"I'll drop Sara and Theo off at the school in a few hours and be at SSAM in time for the meeting with an updated version of Toxin's profile."

"Get some rest until Noah gets there. It's going to be a long day."

Holt hung up the phone and reached for Sara, who immediately folded herself against his side. She was shaking and he held her tighter.

"I don't know how you do it."

With a finger, he lifted her chin to look into her eyes. "Do what?"

"Deal with violent, sadistic killing on a regular basis."

"It doesn't always hit this close to home." He looked away, dropping his hand. "Just recently. And any kind of death is hard."

"Elizabeth," Sara said, empathizing with the complexity of his emotions. "It must be tough, all of this loss."

"No tougher than when you lost your parents."

"It's different."

Yeah, she hadn't had a little boy to console. Then again, she'd been Theo's rock this past year. "Still difficult."

"I wish I could help." Her earnestness had him pulling away. He couldn't put her through any more, especially not tonight.

"You can help by getting some rest. Theo's going to need both of us when he learns about Mrs. Mendelson."

"What are you going to do about Roscoe?"

The dog's head lifted off the carpet at the mention of his name and sent a sad gaze their way. Reassured that they were still with him, he sank back down again. Holt couldn't leave the dog by himself all day. "I don't know."

"Did Mrs. Mendelson have any relatives who would take him in?"

"No." She'd been a lonely woman. And Roscoe had been great company for her. He deserved a devoted, loving family.

She curled her feet under her on the bed. "Bring him with us."

"What?"

"I'll keep him at the school until we can find him a home."

Her generous heart continued to surprise him. His chest swelled with some unnamed emotion he was afraid to examine. It was too much like love.

HOLT'S PHONE VIBRATED AGAINST HIS HIP, WAKING HIM FROM A LIGHT doze to a foreign feeling. Contentment. He should have been exhausted, but the short rest, combined with his eagerness to get back to the crime scene and find justice for Mrs. Mendelson, had him alert in no time. Noah's text indicated he'd gained clearance to have Holt at the scene. He slipped his arm out from under Sara's neck and resettled her on the pillow. She moaned lightly but curled into her pillow without waking. Again he left his gun for her on the bedside table.

Locking the house behind him, he crossed the dark yard to the neighboring home. He moved past an officer in uniform and found Noah, the coroner, and a detective from the Evanston Police Department standing near the body.

"You discovered the body?" Noah asked.

"I heard her dog barking and came over. The door was

unlocked."

"Coroner says the blows to the head likely killed her. Not his usual MO. What do you make of that?"

Holt knew exactly what to make of it. "He was angry. He probably hadn't planned to commit another murder tonight. He may even have been impulsive enough to leave fingerprints."

"The crime techs will be here any minute to dust for prints. What made him so angry that he killed your neighbor? Why not you, or Sara?"

"Mrs. Mendelson was easy pickings. I think he has other plans for me. In fact, he probably knew *this*—knowing I was responsible for someone dying—would hurt me more than quickly ending my life." Just as Sara felt after Rochard's death.

"But what drove Toxin over the edge?"

"Dissatisfaction with how things went between me and Sara tonight."

"I thought you did what he wanted."

Remembering the feel of Sara's hips beneath his fingertips, and her mouth beneath his, Holt knew without a doubt what had driven the man into a rage. Raw jealousy. "I don't think he knew *what* he wanted. Not until he saw it, just out of reach."

HOLT FOUND SARA IN HIS BATHROOM, PACKING UP HER TOILETRY bag.

"Hope you don't mind me using your shower." She caught his eye in the mirror and a furrow formed on her forehead. "Are you okay?"

Her hair was still wet from a shower, her skin pink, but she was dressed and looking refreshed despite only a few hours of sleep. "I'll be okay. I just want to get you back under Becca's watch so I can hunt this guy." And maybe beat him into the ground. Perhaps a couple hours in the SSAM gym was needed to work off some of this adrenaline.

"I'll be ready to head out in a couple minutes, but if you want to grab a shower first to revive yourself..." She was watching him with concern. He probably looked like hell. "I can make us some coffee."

"I don't have much in the way of breakfast food, but there's still a bit of birthday cake left if you're hungry."

"Starved. Especially for chocolate cake." She padded over on bare feet and wrapped her arms around his neck. She pressed her lips to his, her warmth seeping into his system. She tasted of the mint from her toothpaste and smelled like his shampoo. The combination made his heart rate skyrocket. "I was hoping you'd have time to rest a little more. Did you bring Roscoe's food over?"

"No."

"Do you know what brand Roscoe likes? We can pick some up on the way."

Talking about mundane, daily necessities after all that had happened, and all that *could have* happened to her, caused something inside to snap. "No. Contrary to popular belief, I don't know everything. And I'm sure as hell not perfect." He let his fear and frustration out in his curt tone. Realizing he was responsible for a sweet, elderly woman's death was too much to take. Imagining Sara or Theo as next among the victims threatened to send him over the edge.

She pulled away, confusion and hurt reflected in her eyes. "Why don't you get ready while I let Roscoe out?"

He gathered his shaving materials, thankful for the quiet after Sara left. But the smell of her remained in the steamy air. He couldn't help feeling he'd missed some vital opportunity. It was just as well. In the short walk from his neighbor's house, he'd realized something—he had to break things off with Sara, or at least make it look to Toxin like, despite last night, they weren't on the greatest of terms. Besides, if he could lure Toxin with a sense of victory, yet keep an eye on Sara from a distance, they might be able to trap the killer.

He let a quick shower wash away his doubts. It had to be done. He'd been through enough pain, losing one woman he loved. He couldn't go through losing someone else he cared about.

Sara returned as he was shaving and set down a mug of coffee on the counter beside him. Her glance quickly took in his towel-slung hips and the shaving cream that covered his jaw before meeting his eyes. He squelched the stirring of interest her visual caress had evoked. "Roscoe and I are, um, ready to go. Theo called. I hope you don't mind that I answered, but it came up with his picture on the screen."

He met Sara's gaze in the mirror and pulled his armor around himself. He had to do this. He had to make her walk away. "You answered my cell phone?"

"I knew it was Theo and I didn't want him to worry. I thought it might be better if he heard about Roscoe from me or you..."

He set his razor down on the sink and rounded on her. "You told Theo about Toxin killing Mrs. Mendelson? How irresponsible could you be?"

Involuntarily, she backed away a step, shocked at his anger. Good. She'd be hurt, but she'd be alive. And if Toxin was as close to her on a daily basis as he seemed to be, she needed to be on her toes all the time. The only way to do that was to push her away for good. For real. He could no longer be a distraction.

"Of course I didn't tell him...not all of it. I told him Roscoe would be with us today. And I told him we'd be in a hurry so you could get to work this morning and catch the bad guys. I was going to let *you* explain the rest to him. God, you *still* don't know me at all." She spun on her heel and left. He quickly finished shaving, wincing as the blade nicked his jawline. He yanked on clothes, ignoring the tightness in his chest. When he found Sara, she was already leading Roscoe to the front door. Her suitcase sat waiting in the front hallway. She didn't spare him a look.

Another woman was leaving this home and possibly never

coming back. The reality hit Holt like a wrecking ball to the ribcage.

"Time to get back to reality," she said as she tossed him his coat and slipped into her own. It was still dark as they stepped out and walked to the car. The air had taken on a distinct chill.

"Hey, Miss Sara." Theo slid into the backseat. Holt's parents waved from their doorway. "Hey, Roscoe. We get to hang out together today." Theo rubbed Roscoe's neck and the dog turned in a circle once before settling on the seat next to him with a whimpering sigh.

Sara choked down her hurt as Holt got behind the wheel. He hadn't wanted her to come in to say hello to his parents, asking her to wait in the car instead. The request had followed a silent car ride that had her nerves on edge. With monosyllabic replies, he'd shut down any attempts at conversation until she'd taken the hint and sat quietly.

"Where's Becca?" she asked.

"She'll be a few minutes behind us. Dad wanted to talk to her about how he can increase security."

"She'll be taking up her post at the school again?" Sara had hoped everything would be over after this weekend, but it looked like they were back to square one—with Toxin and with Holt. He acted as if they'd never made the leap to intimacy. Perhaps he was regretting opening up to her. Her throat clenched.

"Yes. As will I."

"What?"

"We're both going to be watching you and Theo. And the rest of the school."

The thought of having him around, day in and day out, but just out of reach was depressing. What had she done now that made him back away? She replayed the morning in her mind and came up with no answers. "For how long?"

His gaze slid to her briefly before returning to the road. "As long as it takes."

She looked into the backseat, but Theo had slipped his headphones on and was listening to his iPod, his head bobbing to the music. She turned to Holt. "Why was Toxin so angry? We went to the banquet like he wanted."

Holt glanced in the rearview mirror. "Apparently it wasn't enough." His gaze met hers briefly.

"Or maybe it was too much?" she guessed.

The pulse in his neck jumped. "Don't try to figure out a killer."

"No, that's *your* job."

"I made a mistake involving you." His lips pressed into a thin line.

Understanding dawned. "You think pushing me away will save me."

His gaze again flicked to the rearview mirror but avoided her. "Let's drop it, okay?"

The gothic structure of the Academy came into view, framed by her window. She was almost home. Except that brought a whole other range of problems. She'd have to seek out the Rochard boys this morning—if they were even at school—and express her condolences. "What do I say to Neil and Jeremy about John?"

"Whatever you say, they know you care. You got Theo through some tough times after Elizabeth died. In fact, if you could talk to Theo, too, I'd appreciate it. Jeremy is a close friend. What he's going through might remind Theo of losing his mother. And then there's Mrs. Mendelson's death…"

"You're going to drop this bomb on Theo and then leave? I thought you were sticking around to be added security."

"I have to run to SSAM for a meeting today, but I'll be back. Besides, you'll be here to look out for Theo."

He was right, of course. No matter what was going on between her and Holt, she wouldn't let Theo down. Holt, on the other hand, was apparently going to perform another disappearing act.

CHAPTER 18

Holt glanced at the caller ID as the cell phone on his desk vibrated and lit up.

Sara.

He let the call go. After all, what could he say after days of keeping her at arm's length?

Sorry I'm such a jackass, but it's better this way, me keeping my distance. At least for a while.

One side of his mouth lifted. No, she'd have stopped him at *sorry.*

Then she'd have chewed him out for treating her like a yo-yo. One minute he was enjoying having her in his house and in his bed, and the next he was sitting in the cold in his car outside the school, refusing to talk to her when she spotted him and came over to his window to talk.

He was just as frustrated as she was. His body stirred whether she was yelling her exasperation or trying to coax him inside the school with hot chocolate. And his mind...the past few days in the car had given him way too much time to remember. To imagine what the next time he made love to her would be like. And the time after that. It would take a century to make love to her in all the ways he'd daydreamed about.

Making love? The words shocked Holt. It shouldn't have. He'd never been the type to have affairs. With Elizabeth, he'd fallen fast, and when she'd gotten pregnant, the end result had been evident. Without Elizabeth...well, she hadn't expected him to waste his life grieving for her. She'd always been fun-loving, but also practical.

"You need someone to look out for you. Let Sara help." Elizabeth had stroked the back of his hand where it rested on her blanket. Soft fleece beneath his palm and paper-thin skin on top. He'd turned his hand over to grasp her fragile one. Her over-bright eyes had sought his. "You try to save the world, but who will save you when I'm gone? And if you work yourself to death, who'll be there for Theo?"

When his body was involved, so were his mind, heart and soul. Sara had captured all the above. Even more shocking was that he was okay with that. No, he was more than okay with loving Sara. He craved her and couldn't wait to see her again. In fact, the only reason he was at SSAM now, instead of parked in his car in the Academy's frigid parking lot watching for a glimpse of her, was because Max had told him to get here, *pronto.*

Holt frowned at his watch. The guy was supposed to meet him twenty minutes ago. Perhaps he should get back to the school...

Max rushed into his office, his face animated. "Sorry to pull you away from the Academy, but I've got a live one."

"A lead?" Holt felt his heart leap.

"Einstein got a hit on one of the online forums he's been monitoring. Henry posted a message for Toxin, saying his order was ready and he could pick it up at three today. It's got to be the same Henry."

"You tell Noah?"

"Left him a message, but he's tied up...or tasting more wedding cake samples. Time to pay a visit to Henry?" The grin on Max's face left little doubt as to what he wanted to do.

Holt ignored his phone as the vibrations started again. *Sara.* A moment later, a final hiccup-like vibration told him he'd missed another call.

Max tipped his head at him. "You gonna answer that some time in this millennium?"

"If it's important, she'll leave a message. Becca's at the school and would have called us if there was some kind of urgent issue." Besides, he'd see Sara this afternoon. And then he didn't intend to leave her side...in fact, he'd been toying with the idea of inviting her to come stay with him and Theo for another weekend, maybe even through Thanksgiving. Toxin was still on the loose, after all. Until then, Becca would be close to her.

Max's eyebrows rose. "In my *considerable* experience, ignoring a woman only pisses her off."

"I'll make her understand." Once he understood it all himself. The mixed feelings of exhilaration and loss were confusing as hell. How could he feel loss over his relationship with Sara—something he'd only held in his hands for the blink of an eye?

Ten minutes later, Max glanced at him from the driver's seat of the truck. "What're you looking at?"

"Text from Theo." Holt read it again. *"Looking forward to Thanksgiving break."* His heart squeezed. He'd pushed his son away so many times over the past year, and yet Theo didn't hold it against him. He'd even hugged him again when he'd dropped him off today, before disappearing inside the school under Becca's watchful eye.

"He's okay?"

"Yeah. Lately, I've felt like I've got my son back. Sara's worked wonders with him." He'd been as honest as possible with Theo about Mrs. Mendelson's death, leaving out the gory details but explaining that the killer he'd been hunting was trying to get Holt's attention. He wanted his son to be careful, but not fearful. Sara had insisted on meeting with Theo every day this week to be sure he had someone to talk to, if he wanted it. So far, Theo was coping well.

"And with you."

She'd made him feel alive again, and once revived, his body craved more. But he couldn't have more until he closed this case. "She'll understand if I wait to call her back. I'll see her in a couple hours, anyway."

Max snorted. "Man, for a guy who was married, you know nothing about women."

He scowled at Max. "And as a guy who flits from one piece of eye candy to another, *you* do?" His answer was an arched eyebrow.

"Yes, I do."

"I haven't dated in over a decade." At Max's horrified look, he laughed. "This may come as a surprise to you, but being happily married will put a damper on your dating life."

"Nope, no surprise. It's why I've avoided it this long." Max parked in front of a derelict house. Drops of rain mixed with snow dotted the windshield, obliterating the sad view before the wipers pushed them away. The sky beyond was a slash of gray.

Holt immediately thought about Theo. Sara would have her hands full with the storm the weathercasters had predicted for their area this afternoon. Thankfully, it would be evening when the worst hit and the kids would be safe at home. His parents had flown to Hawaii to spend Thanksgiving with friends there, and Holt would be picking up Theo—and hopefully, Sara—today.

All this time to think had led him to one conclusion—he needed Sara in his life. He'd kept his distance all week to give the illusion that they were no longer connected, but he was out of patience. And with the school empty over break, he couldn't let Sara stay there by herself. He would convince her to come home with him for the holiday and keep her safe.

Once Toxin's apprehended, Sara, Theo and I will move on together, as a family.

"Noah's meeting us here, right?" Max scanned the street.

Holt texted Noah and received an immediate response. "He's twenty minutes away yet."

A scrawny young man, whose pants were hanging so low it was a wonder he could walk, came out of the house and looked both ways as he tucked something in the front pocket of his jeans. He spied their truck parked across the street and skittered in the opposite direction down the sidewalk.

"Is that Henry?" Holt asked.

"Henry's a white guy, mid-thirties."

Wrong race, wrong age. As they watched, the young man pulled out his phone, glancing back at Henry's house. "Looks like we just lost the element of surprise. No time to wait for Noah."

Max and Holt reached for their door handles at the same time. They crossed the street and moved up the walk to the tiny house with the brown patch of lawn.

The revving of an engine from behind them was followed by the squeal of tires and the sound of a gunshot, followed by another.

"Get down!" Max's shout was barely heard over the noise, but Holt was already diving to the ground as survival instinct took over. Crisp, dry blades of long-dead grass poked into his cheek. Max's body hit the dirt next to him. Holt felt a moment of alarm, fearing his partner had been hit. But, from a prone position, Max steadied his pistol and aimed it at the car roaring by Henry's house.

The thud of Max's bullets hitting metal rang in their ears. Their assailant fired back and wood from Henry's house splintered. The window that faced the street shattered. The noise died down as the car squealed around a corner and disappeared from sight.

Holt lifted his head, and Max grunted with pain. A dark stain was spreading on his left biceps. Max followed his gaze. "Just a flesh wound. I got lucky."

The whine of rusty hinges alerted them that someone was

exiting the shot-up house. A person matching Henry's description bolted toward the scraggly hedge that separated his house from the neighbor's. In unison, Holt and Max pushed off the ground and raced after him.

BREATHLESS FROM RUSHING AROUND, MAKING SURE THE KIDS GOT matched up to their parents before the sleet turned to ice on the streets, Sara shoved the hood of her winter jacket off her head, creating a shower of cold sprinkles. She'd kill for a cup of something warm and rejuvenating. The stress of the impending storm on top of impressing and entertaining the school board members who'd shadowed her all day had her exhausted. But she'd finally tucked the last board member into his car and could now breathe. There were only a few more students to send on their way and she could relax.

Cheryl stood to take Sara's jacket from her. "Holt just returned your call. I'll take over with student pick-up duty."

"Becca's out there helping, too, and almost everybody is gone, but I'll take all the support I can get today. Thanks." Sara entered her office and rounded her desk. She lifted the receiver and pressed the blinking light that indicated Holt was on hold. "Are you on your way? Theo's waiting downstairs. There's only a handful of kids left."

"That's what I'm calling about. Something came up." He sounded preoccupied.

"Another one of those leads that don't pan out?" She hated the censure in her voice, but she'd spent the day defending herself against John Rochard's accusations as to her unfit character.

Holt had been right outside her office all week, sitting in his car like an obstinate mule despite her quest to get him inside the building. And now, when he should be picking up Theo for a long holiday break together, he was miles away. A snowstorm was expected any minute. If Holt and Theo were *hers,* she'd stop at the grocery store to stock up on firewood, cocoa, marshmallows and popcorn. They'd watch the flakes pile higher and higher outside the window as they sipped cocoa and made plans to build a snow fort in the morning. That was what a normal family would do.

But she wasn't part of their family. And their history made them far from normal. Sara's mouth tightened and a throbbing began in her head. A throbbing that echoed in her chest, around the vicinity of her heart. "What came up?"

"You guessed right about us having a new lead."

"Did you catch Toxin?"

"Not yet, but it's a solid lead. We have an accomplice of his in custody and may have Toxin behind bars by evening."

"May have?" she asked. He was making the world safer, but at what personal cost? She'd learned the hard way to appreciate every day with her family as a gift.

"Sara?" Holt's voice held a note of pleading she'd never heard from him before.

"So are your parents coming to get Theo?"

"They're away for the holidays, and Elizabeth's parents retired in the southwest years ago."

"There's nobody else?"

"No. Everyone else I would trust with something like this is working on this case. And if Becca takes him home, that leaves you unguarded." He paused and she could imagine seeing the thoughts flitting across his face as he composed his argument. "Look, I know it's a lot to ask, but is there any way Theo can stay with you and Becca, just overnight? It really is important." There was another voice on Holt's end of the line and the conversation became muffled. Still, the tone sounded as urgent as he'd indicated.

What bothered her most was that he didn't think twice about imposing on her. "You're assuming *I'll* be here tonight. What if I have plans for the holidays?"

"Sorry. I really am, Sara—about so much. But even if you have plans, you should cancel. The weather's going to take a turn for the worse. I don't want you traveling in this weather."

Her grand plans had been to watch a movie and snuggle under the blankets as the snow came down. She also had yet to pack for her trip to Mexico. She was supposed to leave tomorrow afternoon. And, as he'd mentioned, it really wasn't safe for Holt to try to come now. Outside her window, a mix of rain and snow was falling. She sighed. Above all, she wanted both her boys safe and warm. "That goes both ways. Stay put. I'll watch Theo."

"Thank you."

"If the roads are clear, be here to pick him up by noon tomorrow." Or she would personally hunt him down and kick his butt for deserting his son and making her miss her flight. The weather forecast predicted a foot of snow, but their area was usually prepared for such a large amount and the snowplows would be working nonstop.

"I'd like to talk to you too," she added. Things had grown awkward, and she couldn't let them continue that way. Otherwise, she'd be carrying a hell of a lot of baggage with her to Mexico.

"I'll be there. You can count on me."

She suppressed a snort. He'd been avoiding a serious discussion over the phone, or in his car, for days—and face-to-face? Forget about it. He wouldn't sit through a conversation without a liberal amount of Duct Tape.

"Thank you, again. And Sara, I really am going to catch Toxin, very possibly tonight."

"Just...please be careful. I don't want you to get hurt."

There was hesitation on his end. When he spoke, his words were firm with conviction. "I won't let him hurt any of us again."

As she hung up, Cheryl appeared in the doorway to her office, tugging on her parka and scarf. She was scowling. "You heard?" Sara guessed.

"Enough."

"I have to hope he'll come through."

"In the meantime, Jeremy will have someone to play with."

Sara looked up. "What do you mean?"

"Jeremy and Neil are still here, as well."

"What?" Alarmed, Sara looked toward the window. The sleet grew heavier and would soon be a solid wall of white. If they didn't get home now, they risked getting into an accident.

"Neil said you were supposed to administer a test?"

Damn. She'd forgotten all about that. Due to the death of his father, Neil had missed almost the entire week of school and wanted to make up a test before Thanksgiving break. It seemed the kid who'd avoided academic responsibility was suddenly determined to succeed. "Is he in the library?"

"He was headed up there, along with Theo and Jeremy. Said he'd wait for you. Jeremy was going to hang out until he was done and then Neil was supposed to drive them both home." Cheryl's forehead rippled with worry lines. "You've seen that car they gave Neil, haven't you? That thing's a death trap when the roads *aren't* icy."

It was a convertible with rear-wheel drive—the least ideal mode of transportation in a storm expected to lay down a sheet of ice beneath the snow.

"I'll handle it. You get going before the storm gets worse."

Cheryl grabbed Sara and hugged her hard. Her white bob smelled of rose petals. Cheryl swiped gloved fingers at her eyes as she pulled away. "I don't like you being alone for the holiday. You sure you won't join me and Mr. Cheryl, at least for Thanksgiving dinner? I do all the traditional trimmings. You can bring Becca if she's still shadowing you."

Sara forced a smile. "I'm Acapulco-bound. No killers trailing me there, and it'll give Becca a break so she can be with her family. For me, it'll be beaches and sunshine and I'm happy about that. But I'll miss you."

"Yeah, right. Enjoy yourself, but be safe."

"Yes, Mom." Sara winked, but now they were both getting

misty. Damn, dealing with the board members and then talking to Holt had left her drained and emotional.

The moment was broken by a knock at the door. "You ladies need any help in the parking lot?" Chad White stood in the doorway, stomping flakes off his boots, a snow shovel in one gloved hand and an ice scraper in the other. Only his eyes and nose were visible beneath his wet coat and fur-lined hood.

Sara's eyes widened. "You came prepared."

"I was a Boy Scout in a former life." There was a twinkle in his eyes.

"Well, I'll take you up on that offer, young man." Cheryl linked arms with him. "If I don't get home soon, Mr. Cheryl will worry a trench in the floor."

"Drive carefully," Sara called.

The front door of the school closed after them, leaving her with the rustle of bare branches and the howl of the wind outside, and the utter stillness of a near-empty school inside. Though it was only four o'clock, the gray clouds had turned to a smear of charcoal reminiscent of twilight and the wind had picked up. The sleet had turned to snow, which now fell in thick sheets. Perhaps the expected precipitation would be more than the forecasted twelve inches. A chill moved across her skin and she rubbed her arms.

Turning from the window, she went to the address book on her computer and found Claire Rochard's information. Unfortunately, it led straight to voicemail. Sara left a message explaining the situation and telling her not to worry.

As Sara passed the front hallway on the way to the stairs, Becca came rushing in. She closed the door against the wind and snow and immediately veered toward Sara. "I just got a text from Einstein."

"And I just spoke with Holt," Sara said. "He said they were close. Did they find Toxin already?"

"Not yet, but they've identified him as Brady Flaherty."

"Isn't that the guy they already arrested and let go?"

"They found a snitch who gave them more evidence." Becca showed her the text. *Drug supplier ID'd Brady as Toxin. Be on watch for Brady or his vehicle—dark 4-door SUV. En route to his apt. now.*

The first genuine smile of the day touched Sara's lips. "Sounds like Holt was right. This really will all be over soon." Better yet, she'd seen pictures of Brady Flaherty on the news. She hadn't seen that guy near her students. Theo would be safe, her students would be safe. Perhaps it would be a relaxing holiday after all.

The roar of an engine out front had her and Becca running outside. The porch and circular drive were empty of cars and people except for a dark blue SUV.

Becca pushed Sara behind her. "Inside!"

The passenger window went down and a man resembling Brady aimed a gun at them from the driver's seat.

Becca pulled her gun. Sara scurried backwards, keeping low, until she was completely inside. The sound of gunfire had her moving faster. She got behind the heavy wooden door and stayed down, but kept it open a crack so Becca could dart back into the building and find cover, if necessary. Becca was returning fire. The SUV fishtailed as it sped around the drive and headed back toward the main road.

"Lock all the doors and stay inside," Becca ordered. "Stay away from the windows. Call the police and have them send backup here. I've got to keep Brady in sight." Becca took off at a run toward her vehicle and was soon driving into the gray afternoon in pursuit of Brady.

As Sara said a quick prayer for Becca's safety, she shut and bolted the front door. She turned to find the three boys rushing down the stairs.

"What was all the noise?" Theo asked.

Jeremy was right on his heels. "Was that gunfire?"

"Yes, but we're okay," Sara assured them. "Becca and the cops are chasing the guy now. He's far away from here. Go on upstairs while I finish down here."

"Was it the guy who killed my father?" Neil asked when the younger boys returned to the library. "The guy Dr. Patterson has been looking for?"

"Yes." She put a hand on his arm. "They'll get him, probably tonight. Would you mind keeping an eye on Theo and Jeremy while I call the police and make sure we're locked up tight? I left a message for your mother, but…"

"Oh, she probably won't get it. She's at my aunt's house. Reception's lousy there. We were supposed to join her."

"That probably isn't going to happen. Do me a favor and leave her a message at your aunt's number so they know you'll be safe here overnight. Tell your mom you'll be there tomorrow."

Neil moved away to make his call and rejoin the boys. Sara tried to call the police to report the shooting and get more support for Becca, but the phone in her office was dead. A broken tree branch had probably knocked down the lines. With the tall trees and propensity for wind and ice storms in the area, it happened at least once a year. She took her cell out of her desk and was relieved to find a text from Becca.

Got him, but I'll be a while. Stay locked up tight.

She was about to call Catherine to see if she had further information, but her signal dropped to zero. The cell tower went out too? Or perhaps it was overloaded with emergency calls. Holt wouldn't want the distraction of her calling to check on them, anyway. And he would be here soon enough.

Deciding her time would be best spent keeping the boys occupied, she made quick work of checking the locks around the school. On the third floor she found Theo, Jeremy and Neil in the library. She took a calming breath, telling herself they were safe and this would all be over—finally. The sight of the boys healthy, even if subdued, reassured her. Theo had brought out a deck of cards and looked to be engaged in a game of War with Jeremy. A lock of hair fell into Neil's eyes as he bent his head over his book.

"Looks like we're all tucked in for the night, guys. Theo, your father called."

"I know. He texted me a little while ago."

"Ah." She was surprised, but glad, Holt had found the time to personally contact him. He'd seemed eager to rush off to follow their latest lead. "Do you still have a signal? The landlines aren't working and my cell just lost signal."

"No." Neil frowned at his phone. "I left a message with my aunt, like you said. But now? No dice. At least Mom will know we're here for the night, safe."

"So what now?" Jeremy nibbled at his lip. This past week, it had turned red and chapped from constant worrying.

Sara pulled on a cloak of cheerfulness. "Ever wonder what it would be like to stay at the school when nobody else was around? You get to find out...at least until the roads are clear enough to drive. But first, we'll give Neil his test. Might as well make good use of our time."

TOXIN WATCHED FROM HIS HIDING SPOT BEHIND THE PANTRY DOOR as Sara moved between the cupboards and the counter in the Academy's large industrial-style kitchen. She hummed to the music on the radio, which conveniently covered any slight sound he might make. She stacked a package of graham crackers and a jug of milk, along with paper cups, on the counter. Her next trip added a few Hershey chocolate bars and a bag of marshmallows. She set about pulling things from the refrigerator to make sandwiches.

How sweet. She and the boys were planning to make s'mores, but only after they ate a healthy dinner. She'd make a good mother.

After finishing the sandwiches, she laid out plates and began layering graham crackers, chocolate and marshmallows, and topping it with another graham cracker. One by one, she microwaved them until the treats were gooey. He grew hard as she licked the lingering stickiness from her fingers. Not only was she a good mother, she was sexy as hell. She was perfect, and she was his for the taking. Whatever had happened between her and Holt on Monday night, the passion had cooled. Or it had all been for show. Toxin had seen Holt lurking outside the school this week, but that was as a SSAM agent, to protect her. He hadn't dared to cross the threshold, even when Sara tried to talk to him. Again, perfect.

Four plates. Only Sara and the three boys left. Two more boys than he was expecting tonight, but he could handle it. One nudge and his entire plan had been set into motion—like flicking over that first domino to set off the chain reaction. An anonymous payment to Brady, a timely hack into the SSAM phone system to obtain the SIM card information and send a text to Becca implicating Brady as the true mastermind, a disconnection of the school's phone lines and jamming device to prevent cell phone use, and now Toxin had Sara and Theo right where he wanted them. Becca was chasing down Brady, and poor Holt would be in the morgue by now while *he* was here with Sara and Theo.

Sara laid the plates and cups on a tray and lifted it. She paused at the door, looking back at the jug of milk, most likely wondering how she was going to carry it. As it was, she had to use a leg to kick the swinging door open, and zipped through before it hit her cute, tight ass.

It was time. Enter the hero.

"WHY DOES TOXIN SUBJECT HIS VICTIMS TO DEATH BY NEUROTOXIN?" Holt turned away from the darkness outside the conference room's window. "I mean, he could use any number of over-the-counter poisons, but goes to *Henry* for a special mix. Why's he risking getting involved with someone else? And to use a public message board...it doesn't make sense."

Holt didn't expect an answer to the question they'd asked many times these past few months, but he found it helped to think aloud.

Max forgot about his injury and tried to shrug. His features tightened for a brief moment, the only sign that he was hurting. His arm was bandaged, but otherwise he was intact and denied being in any pain. The bullet from the dark SUV had, indeed, only grazed him.

They were waiting at Holt's desk, giving Henry time to ruminate on his situation in the Chamber—SSAM's interrogation room —before they questioned him. One of the perks of working for SSAM was access to the latest state-of-the-art equipment. The computer screen on Holt's desk showed the Chamber and the one person they hoped could answer Holt's questions. The rumpled, scruffy man sat alone, brightly illuminated by a florescent light that flickered every few seconds with an electrical hum meant to unsettle. The overall effect was harsh and unwelcoming.

"When I get through with him, he'll be begging to give me every detail of his pathetic life." Max was eager to get into the Chamber with Henry.

"I can't allow that." Noah stood in the doorway. He took off his coat, scattering drops of melting snow.

"Why not? He knows he's not under arrest."

"He's just waiting us out," Holt added. "Just like we're waiting him out. He's probably feeling safer here than on the street. Once Toxin learns he failed to lure me to my death…"

Noah looked at the bump on Holt's forehead, sustained while diving to the ground to evade bullets, then at Max's bandaged arm. "You two okay?"

"We'll live," Max said. Damian had immediately called a doctor to come take a look, but Max had refused to let go of Henry until they had him locked away in a room.

Noah's attention moved to Holt. "Does Sara know you were hurt?"

"I didn't see any reason to worry her. It was just a bump on the head from hitting the ground so fast." The bump felt more like a mountain and throbbed like a sonofabitch, but he could take it. "Besides, she doesn't need to know what's going on with me. After the way I treated her this week, whatever we had is probably over."

"Right," Noah said. "Might as well pack you up and send you to the monastery today."

Max smirked. "I can see you in that brown robe now."

Holt grew uncomfortable with their analysis of his love life. "Let's get back to Henry."

Noah came to Holt's side and glanced at the computer screen where Henry alternated between pacing the room and flopping into the chair. "Did he ask for a lawyer or his rights?"

"Nothing." Max grinned. "Guy isn't thinking straight. Probably all those drugs."

"The minute he asks, or asks if he's been formally arrested..." Noah's voice held a warning.

"We have to shut down," Holt said. "I know."

"We don't have any charges against him. Legally, he was just in the wrong place at the wrong time."

Max's look was incredulous. "The guy's house is a meth lab."

"We didn't find anything there."

"What?" Holt and Max asked simultaneously.

Noah shook his head. "We have no reason to arrest him. The house had been cleared out. He appears to be just as much a victim as you two."

"That's because he was expecting the shooting on his front lawn. He'd had a warning from Toxin. Shit." Holt ran a hand over his face, then gestured to the screen. "But we don't have to show him all of our cards."

Noah's eyes narrowed. "What do you have in mind?"

"The longer he sits there, the less clear he's thinking. His defenses will be lower as his energy goes toward keeping from falling apart. He'll be hurting for his next hit. And if he thinks we have something on him, he'll be desperate as that hit looks less and less attainable. I can convince him we have enough to arrest him for conspiracy to murder. I'm betting he's the one Toxin convinced to post that message Einstein found on the forum. The one that led us there at that time."

"So, you and Max *were* the intended targets?"

"Me, at least," Holt said. "Let me have a crack at questioning him. He's seen me on the news, I'm sure. He knows I'm after Toxin. Maybe I can get him to give up his so-called friend."

Max and Noah looked at each other. "We haven't located the car or the driver who shot at you. I guess Henry's our best shot. But back away if he asks for a lawyer."

A minute later, Holt entered the Chamber. "Ready to talk yet, Henry?"

"Nope." Henry leaned back in his chair so far, Holt thought he might tip over. "Besides, I know you're not the cops. You have to let me go or I can charge you with kidnapping."

Holt sat down across the table from Henry. "Pretty confident for a guy who brews meth in his living room. You really think we wouldn't find any traces of it?"

"Hey, I gotta pay the bills." Henry's eyes darted to the corner of the room, evidence of a thread of fear beneath his nonchalant façade.

"Some people find legal ways to do that." Holt leaned forward on his elbows. "I don't really want to put you behind bars. I've got bigger fish to fry."

"Yeah, right. That's why you've locked me up for over an hour, wasting your time—'cause I'm the little fish. I have rights."

Holt could picture Noah flinching at that subject. "I figured a smart guy like you, in your line of business and all, might know how to bargain."

Henry looked up from the table, interest sparkling in his eyes. "What do you want?"

"I want to know something about this guy who's been sticking people with needles, poisoning them."

Henry's chair legs snapped to the ground. "Toxin?"

"So, you've heard of him." Of course Henry had heard of Toxin. He'd posted a message on the forum leading them to his house at that time. Unless Toxin had posted that message...

The rapping of Henry's hands against the table began again. "Sure. I mean, all of Chicago has. I even saw your piece in the news a couple months back."

"He's got some pretty sophisticated stuff."

"You think so?" Henry's fingers stilled and he met Holt's gaze. *Pride goeth before a fall.* "Yeah. Whoever created that death cocktail is pretty smart. Like, *PhD* smart. But, given your customer base, you probably don't know him. You're right. I'm wasting my time here."

"Wait!" Henry's angry exclamation halted Holt. "I'm not saying I'm involved..."

"Of course not. You couldn't be."

"I could be." Henry's tone was indignant. "Maybe *you're* the one who's not so smart. Toxin always said so." He pressed his lips together and looked away, realizing what he'd revealed.

"Well then, enlighten me."

The silence was thick, and then Henry laughed. A calculated gleam entered his eyes. "I know a lot of things, but I'm smart enough not to talk about them. Unless it gets me something."

"Let's just say the police might be willing to give you leniency for your involvement in setting me up to die today."

"Setting you up?"

"We saw the supposed message from you to Toxin, on a forum the police suspect is used to link up criminals, telling him the stuff was ready."

Henry paled. "I didn't post anything." But he wouldn't meet Holt's gaze.

"Still, it could look like you were baiting me, which you were."

Henry shoved a shaky hand through his hair. "I had no idea what he had planned. I just knew to be ready for anything." Henry shook his head. "There's no proof I wrote that. Anybody could have posted on that forum, posing as me."

"I have no doubt the necessary proof will show up if Toxin wants you to go down for this. He's got resources. He already set up one person to take the fall for him, and that guy spent weeks in jail. What makes you think Toxin wouldn't do the same thing to you? You think you can't be replaced?"

Henry's legs jostled to the beat his fingertips rapped on the table. Still, he didn't talk.

Holt targeted the most immediate, most uncomfortable need. "And my guess is you have about two more hours until your craving gets so bad that your skin itches like rats are crawling all over it."

"You can't keep me here. It's illegal. You didn't find anything in my house."

"Then leave." At Holt's words, Henry looked toward the door. Holt said a prayer his tactic would work. "Go to the police. We have a detective right outside, in fact. When they discover who you've been protecting they'll detain you for questioning. Of course, you could always take your chances on the street, with Toxin."

Holt's expression didn't shift as he continued. "In one breath, you boast about being smart enough to create the most complex death cocktail the CPD has seen, then in the next you say the police found your house clean. Which is it, Henry? Are you smart or aren't you?"

Henry smirked. "Doesn't take much to place an order at a chemical company for what you want, especially when you have the credentials of a researcher at a major university."

"And you do?" Holt made his doubt clear.

"I was a grad student once, yes."

"Is that where you met Toxin?"

A smile played about Henry's lips but he didn't answer.

Holt leaned forward, lacing his fingers together on the table.

"How about I phrase this another way? How much will your friendship with a killer cost you? If he finds out you failed to kill me, and he knows that *we* know you're a link to him, what will he do to you? Think he'll keep you around when he can ask any number of other drug dealers to help him score his poison? As you said, doesn't take much to place an order at a chemical company. On the other hand, if you were to play for our side, maybe we can keep you alive. It's your call."

CHAPTER 19

Though he was upset his dad had to work again and hadn't come to pick him up, Theo tried to focus on the good stuff. He was with Miss Sara and Jeremy. Even Neil was pretty cool when he finished his test and joined them in playing cards. Theo would get to stay in a big, hulking castle-like school while all the other kids were gone. His mind reeled with all the nooks and crannies he'd always wanted to investigate. But, so far, Miss Sara wouldn't let them out of the library.

"I'm back." Miss Sara returned with a heaping tray. The smell of chocolate and marshmallow had his mouth watering.

She was wearing a sweatshirt, jeans and sneakers. *Miss Sara, in jeans and sneakers, at school?* It was kind of like last weekend, when she'd been at his house and helped paint his room. She glanced at the large window that was best part of the library. Usually, a large branch hung close, part of an equally large tree. Now, all you could see was a blur of white and black. Snow and night.

"And look who I found in the kitchen." She set the tray down on the table and looked over her shoulder.

Mr. White entered the library, a grin on his face as he raised a jug of milk. "Can't have sandwiches and s'mores without a glass of milk."

"What are you doing here?" Theo's gaze narrowed on their computer science teacher. He was an okay guy, but was he interested in Miss Sara? Theo had hoped, after last weekend, she might want to be part of *his* family. His dad had seemed interested in that, too, and had even lightened up and enjoyed himself for the first time in months.

Mr. White raised his eyebrows at his rudeness, but Theo didn't care. He'd lost his mother, and he didn't want to lose Miss Sara. "I was caught in the storm too."

"Then where've you been? Why didn't you come out when you heard gunfire?"

Miss Sara sat the tray of food down on the table. "Now, Theo, that's rude."

Mr. White smiled and held up a hand. "It's okay. It's my own fault, really. I was checking the computers to make sure they were okay in case the power went out during the storm. I decided to do some grading so I wouldn't have to take it home with me over the holiday. Lost track of time and wasn't paying attention to how bad the weather was getting. By the time I was ready to leave, the radio was saying people should avoid traveling if possible. Figured I'd better just wait it out like the rest of you smart people. Guess I didn't hear the gunfire over the sound of the radio." His eyebrows drew together. "Is everyone okay? Was something going on down by the road?"

"Closer than that. He came right up our driveway."

"He, who?" Mr. White's questioning glance went to Miss Sara.

"A suspect in an ongoing investigation," Miss Sara answered as she laid out the plates.

Mr. White's grin was a little too big as he watched. Theo looked to Jeremy for validation, but his friend was sitting in a chair with his arms crossed. Though they could normally exchange thoughts without saying a word, he seemed to be in his own world since his dad died. Theo could respect that. Neil was standing by the window, alternately holding his phone up to see if he could get reception and looking out at the storm. No help from that corner, either.

"Maybe the storm's letting up and we can leave soon," Theo said hopefully.

Miss Sara sighed. "I don't think so. We'll be fine here, though. Warm and dry. Plenty of food and water. And we have nowhere to be until it's all cleared up, so we're lucky. It could be a lot worse." She smiled brightly, and Theo felt his tension ease. "We'll have an old-fashioned campout. Scrounge up blankets and flashlights and make a cozy fort."

Jeremy rolled his eyes. "A *cozy* fort? Geez. Maybe, after that, we can make daisy chains." Theo was angry with his friend for making fun of Miss Sara, but he couldn't be mad for long. Theo had done and said some pretty stupid things after his mom died too.

But Miss Sara surprised both of them by laughing. "Maybe. But I think s'mores would be more fun, and it'll be hard to find daisies this time of year."

Jeremy pushed off his chair and came to stand near Theo, dropping his voice so no one else could hear. "She thinks she's so smart, but my dad was right. She doesn't know anything. Everyone knows you have to have a campfire for s'mores."

Theo's insides warred between defending Miss Sara and keeping on his best friend's good side. "You're just sad about your dad."

Jeremy responded with a middle-finger salute. "I've got more important things to do." He stomped out of the room. Theo was fairly certain his friend didn't have anything better to do than try not to cry. Neil met Theo's eyes, then followed his brother.

THEY'D GIVEN HENRY A LITTLE TIME TO THINK OVER HOLT'S WORDS, but time was getting short. And Holt was feeling a prick of unease over not speaking to Sara or Becca directly for the past couple hours. Damian had said Becca checked in via text message to say all was quiet, but Holt would have preferred more personal contact. He took comfort in the fact that, despite the unlocked door, Henry hadn't walked out of the SSAM facilities. His fear of Toxin kept him a prisoner.

Holt reentered the Chamber, pointedly leaving the door wide open. He took his seat across from Henry. "Why are you protecting someone who almost shot you to death and destroyed your home? SSAM and the CPD are on Toxin's trail. Once we catch him—and we *will* catch him—what do you think he's going to do? You can bet he'll take any deal the district attorney offers, including naming accomplices. He'll turn on you so fast you'll think you just snorted a gram of coke. He probably hoped you would die in the shootout too."

Henry had started nibbling his stub of a thumbnail at the mention of Toxin taking a deal. And when Holt mentioned drugs, his leg started jostling again.

On cue, Noah entered. "SSAM is done with you, Henry. It's the CPD's turn. We found enough evidence of drug production in your home to hold you for twenty-four hours."

Henry sat up straighter. "But—"

"We've got what we need. Caught Toxin driving the vehicle— you know, the car that sped away after your house got all shot up? He's done. Case closed."

"That's not Toxin."

Holt shook his head. "Don't act like you want to talk now. We've got our man." He glanced at Noah. Getting Henry to talk depended on making this ruse work. "Except that he's trying to bargain. Says he can give us information that you were in on it."

"He's not Toxin. He doesn't know anything."

"But he's willing to talk, so we'll listen." Holt rose and headed for the door.

Noah made to remove a pair of cuffs from his pocket. He read

Henry his Miranda rights, and Henry acknowledged them. He licked his lips nervously as Noah brought the cuffs toward his hands.

"Wait," Henry said suddenly. "Brady Flaherty isn't Toxin. He's just a hired gun."

Brady Flaherty had been the one to shoot at them? They'd made up the part about apprehending the driver who'd shot at them.

"I can give you Toxin's real name," Henry said.

"You're aware of your rights?" Noah asked again.

Henry nodded. "But I want leniency in exchange for my cooperation." There was no lawyer there to guarantee anything, and Henry was too muddle-headed to ask for one. "Toxin's real name is Chad White. We were in college together. He knew Brady and paid him to try to kill Dr. Patterson today."

"Chad White?" Holt said. Pinpricks of alarm traveled up his neck. "He *works* at the school. I remember his name from the personnel we did background checks on. He was clean."

Henry smirked. "He would be. Never been arrested or anything like that."

"Sara knows him. She'd trust him." What he wouldn't give for immediate proof that Theo and Sara were okay.

Noah put the cuffs back in his pocket and sat down. "What does Brady know? Where does he fit into this?"

"He only knows someone anonymous paid him to do a job… shoot at you all and then go to some school and do the same thing. He doesn't know Chad was behind the payment. I was just supposed to be the bait to get you guys to the right place. I had no idea how this would play out." He laced his hands together to stop their shaking and stared at his bloody thumbnail.

"Brady went to a *school* after shooting at me? Was it the Hills Boys' Academy?" Holt felt his muscles bunch as if he could run to the school.

Henry looked up. "Yeah, that sounds right. Why?"

Heart pounding in his ears, Holt left Noah with Henry as he

raced to Damian's office. "Sir, we've got Toxin's name—Chad White—and possible location as well as the name of today's shooter—Brady Flaherty. Contact Becca at the school right away. Toxin has plans for them there tonight. Because of the weather, Theo and Sara are there with her."

"I'll get her on the phone," Damian promised, picking up the receiver and dialing. But a moment later, he looked up, worry etched into lines on his face. "Becca's not answering." He dialed the outer office. "Catherine, get me Evanston PD on the line."

Holt grabbed the phone away and tried to dial the school's direct line. His attempt resulted in the *this number has been disconnected or is out of service* spiel. Sara's cell phone went right to voicemail. So did Theo's. He swallowed the sour taste of fear as he hung up.

"Maybe Einstein has another way to get in touch with Becca," Holt said.

But before they could call him, Catherine's voice came across Damian's intercom. "Lieutenant Anderson from Evanston PD is on line one, as requested."

"Thank you." Damian took the receiver from Holt's shaking hand, his concerned gray eyes remaining on Holt as he pressed line one. "Lieutenant Anderson. Thank you for taking my call. You must be battling weather emergencies left and right but we may have an emergency of our own. Have you had contact with anybody at the Hills Boys' Academy?…Any of those accidents involve a dark blue sedan?" His brows drew together. "I assume you're sending a cruiser around to check it out?…I realize you're stretched thin, but send someone out there ASAP."

As Damian hung up, Holt leaned forward. "What did he say?"

"The police have been tied up with several accidents and other emergencies but haven't received any distress calls from the Academy, so they're not making a school drive-by a priority. One of the car accidents involved a dark SUV. The driver was going at a high rate of speed on an icy road. Caused an accident with two other vehicles and then fled the scene on foot."

"Could be Brady. Was it near the school?"

"A couple miles, but headed away from the Academy. There's more. Another car was involved. The description fits Becca's vehicle."

"If she's pursuing Brady, who's with Sara and Theo?" Holt tried calling all the numbers again. Still no answer. With each failed call, the sick sense of powerlessness that had filled his gut so many times during Elizabeth's battle with cancer flared up again. *No.* He wouldn't let it suck him under again. This time he would fight. He would take control.

SOMETHING ABOUT CHAD WHITE BEING AT THE SCHOOL DIDN'T FEEL right.

Sara toed off her tennis shoes, curled her legs under her, Indian style, and tried to pretend her nerves weren't strung as tight as piano wire. She would have felt so much better if she could just touch base again with Holt, Becca or the police. She wasn't sure whether she could trust her gut, or if the storm and being responsible for the boys had skewed her perception, increasing her anxiety so that everything was amplified. And then there was the text from Becca that said they'd already apprehended the killer. Chad had every reason, and some pretty damn good excuses, for being here.

And yet...his smile was a little too bright. His gaze was almost possessive when it fell on her. Then again, he looked at Theo that way too. Perhaps it was simply his normal demeanor and she hadn't noticed before.

She picked up a s'more from the near-empty plate in front of her. The ham and cheese sandwiches had gone over well with the boys—especially because consuming them had been a prerequisite to dessert. The large blankets she'd retrieved from her apartment had been strung between two large tables in the library to create a cocoon of warmth and safety, and they all sat together now in the makeshift tent. She handed Theo a napkin as marshmallow stretched down his chin. He swiped at the sticky spot, laughing when the napkin then became stuck to him and dangled like a beard.

"What's next, scary stories?" Theo asked. As the evening grew darker, only the soft glow illuminating them, Sara switched on a couple of flashlights.

"Or maybe a sing-a-long," Jeremy said, his tone only half snark this time.

She licked the marshmallow from her fingers. "I thought, maybe, some homework time?"

Their groans descended into laughs as she made a face and tossed a balled-up napkin at them. Even Neil grinned. His head brushed the blankets overhead, but he'd stuck close to them and made the most of the situation. For that, she was grateful. Chad sat across from her, licking chocolate from his fingers.

He was a decent-looking man. Charming, for sure. He'd definitely come out of his shell since she'd first interviewed him. He'd seemed downright shy at the time. Now, though, his smiles and direct looks were sending her a different vibe. *Interested male.* Was that why she was feeling uncomfortable? There was only one man who interested her.

"We don't have homework over the holidays." Jeremy's words were without attitude this time. *Progress.*

She gave him a look of mock shock. "No homework? But you have a whole week until school resumes. Your brains will turn to mush."

He frowned and looked down at his lap. "We've got a funeral instead."

She immediately sobered. Her stomach ached for him, the sugar she'd ingested churning. "That must be very difficult. I know how hard it is when a parent dies."

"You do?"

"Your parents died a couple years ago, right?" Neil looked sheepish. "Sorry, a classmate was digging up information on you. He thought you were hot."

Her jaw dropped but she promptly recovered. "Well, aren't you guys industrious students, doing all that research. Kind of like you did on the Army, huh?" At her teasing, Neil's glance shot to Chad.

"I think I'll head out for a bathroom break," Chad said. "Be right back." He exited through a gap in the blankets.

What had that brief, shared look been about? Had Chad not told Neil the truth about having helped her locate him?

She brushed a blanket aside and glanced around the library. "Surely, there's a math book around here. Or history. *Something* we can work on." She laughed as a pillow hit her squarely in the chest, then shook a finger at Theo. "Don't start a mutiny."

"You're just kidding about the homework," he said. He was in need of a haircut. But that wasn't her job. Holt would surely notice over the next week.

"Yep, just kidding."

The lights flickered. The boys looked at each other, then at her. Then the lights went completely out, leaving them with only a couple of flashlights. From one floor above, where Sara had left Roscoe napping earlier, they heard frightened howls.

"I forgot he's afraid of the dark, especially when he's alone," Theo said. "Mrs. Mendelson always brought him in at night, and during storms. He's not used to being by himself."

They crawled from the tent. Sara pointed a flashlight at the door, so they could see potential obstacles. The beam fell across a face in the doorway and she clutched at her chest. She bit back her scream as she realized it was Chad.

"Don't worry," Chad said. "I'll go check out the fuse box, just in case this is fixable. If not, there's a generator in the computer room. Boys, why don't you come with me?"

"Maybe they should stay here where it's warm," Sara suggested.

"Nonsense. They'll learn something useful about survival. Besides, they've got coats if we have to go outside for a moment. We'll be back, after we've saved the day. Don't go anywhere."

"Just to check on Roscoe," Sara said.

"Maybe I'd better stay with her," Neil said. "I don't think she should be alone."

Chad's mouth thinned before he nodded, but perhaps she'd imagined it in the dim light and shadows.

Jeremy and Theo pulled on their coats and followed Chad out into the hallway. As their footsteps faded, Roscoe howled again. Neil followed her up the flight of stairs to her apartment. The beam of her flashlight bounced off the steps as they climbed.

"There's something odd about Mr. White," Neil whispered, as if someone might overhear.

Both relieved and worried that someone felt the same way, Sara tread cautiously. Chad was, after all, Neil's teacher. Her imagination was running wild, but his reputation shouldn't have to suffer for it. She'd done the necessary background checks before hiring him, so there was definitely no reason to be suspicious. "Maybe he's anxious about being stuck in a storm too."

She opened her unlocked apartment door and Roscoe nearly bolted down the dark stairs. He stopped as she called to him. "Here, baby. Come here. It's okay." Sitting on the landing in front of her door with the flashlight cutting through the darkness, she patted Roscoe's back and stroked his neck until his quivering stopped. The light she'd left on in her apartment suddenly came on. "See, we're okay." She looked at Neil. "Mr. White has been very helpful."

Neil sat down next to her and absently petted Roscoe. "That's just it. Mr. White was the one who *helped* me search for Army recruiters."

"I know. He gave you the password."

"It was more than that. He helped me search for information too. He told me not to tell anyone. I can understand him not wanting Dad to know, and he thought he might lose his job if I told someone he let me use the school computers to search the internet when it wasn't for a school project. Still..."

"What?"

Neil paused in petting Roscoe. "You know when someone is trying too hard and it comes across desperate? That's what it felt like with Mr. White. Like he was trying to impress me, or become my best bud or something."

Sara digested Neil's information. Had Chad's goal been simply to make a connection with a struggling student? Or were his motives less noble? Before she could ask more questions, though, they heard Chad and the boys coming up the stairs.

Theo's voice was excited. "The way you repaired that wire was so cool. I should tell Dad to add that tool to his toolbox."

"Just because you have the tools doesn't mean you know how to use them," Chad said. "I've been working with wires and stuff like that all my life." As they appeared on the landing, Chad patted Theo's shoulder. Under her hand, a rumble began in Roscoe's chest and then emerged as a growl. Chad frowned at the dog. He reached out a hand to soothe Roscoe but jumped back when Roscoe snapped at him.

Shocked by the easygoing dog's aggressive behavior, Sara stood and brushed off the seat of her pants. "I should take him back inside my apartment. He's probably shaken from the storm." She took Roscoe's collar and tugged until he went with her. She led him to the dog bed she'd gotten for him—a circular pillow on the floor at the foot of her bed.

"Power should stay on now." She jumped at the sound of Chad's voice behind her. He'd followed her into her bedroom and seemed to fill the doorway. He looked at a snarling Roscoe and set his toolbox down by the bedroom door. "Maybe he's afraid of a guy with a big, heavy metal box."

"Or guys in general," Sara offered, still trying to make sense of things. "He was used to a sweet old lady. It was just the two of them. She died recently." Steeling her nerves, she made herself meet Chad's gaze.

His brown eyes didn't flicker. "That's a shame. But I bet he'll be happy here with you."

How had she not noticed how tall Chad was before? And wide through the shoulders. To leave, she'd have to move past him. She shifted her weight, trying to decide whether to bolt, but that would be ridiculous. He was one of her teachers. She'd liked him enough to hire him. In the months since then, he hadn't done anything malicious.

Roscoe snarled again, as if sensing her uneasiness.

"May I?" Chad held out a hand toward Roscoe. "Maybe he'll feel better if he knows me." Sara knew that was true for her. He squatted at the dog's level and continued to hold out a hand.

"Theo wanted to check in with his dad," Chad said. "His phone isn't working. I checked the landlines earlier, but they seem to be out too. Want to check your apartment phone?"

"I hadn't thought of that. That's a good idea." Sara turned away to check the phone on her bedside table and found it dead. She took her cell phone out. Sure enough, still no bars. "Nothing." She tucked it back into her pocket and turned to him. "Where are the boys?" She moved toward the door, and Chad didn't make any move to stop her. He was stroking Roscoe now, and the dog was definitely looking more relaxed, which calmed her a bit.

Chad looked up, a sheepish expression on his face. "I introduced them to my lair."

"Lair?"

"It's probably against the school rules, but…" He grinned. "I've got a little getaway here at the school. Every superhero needs one —along with a secret, boy-next-door identity and a passion for making the world a better place." Roscoe leaned against him, his lids growing heavy. "Whoa, looks like bedtime. Poor guy got all stressed out by the storm. Now that the lights are on, and things aren't so scary, maybe he can sleep." Chad gently hoisted the dog and carried him to the dog bed. He settled him in and petted him for a moment. Roscoe immediately closed his eyes, his breaths smoothing out as he drifted off to doggy dreamland.

Well, if Roscoe trusted Chad, maybe he wasn't all bad. Maybe Chad was simply socially awkward and his earnestness came across wrong. He'd probably just been trying to help Neil with that internet search. After all, there was nothing devious about encouraging someone to consider joining the Army. Ultimately, it was Neil's choice.

"What were you saying about a lair?" she asked.

Chad straightened and crossed the room to her. His eyes twinkled. "Come on. I'll show you. I set it all up last weekend, while you were gone."

HOLT STARED STRAIGHT AHEAD AT THE ROAD, MISERABLE. HE AND Max were making slow progress because of the storm. The cell in his hand rang and he immediately answered. "What have you got?"

"Like you, I wasn't able to get through to the Academy via any of the usual communication methods. And there seems to be someone blocking my more *unusual* methods." Einstein didn't sound happy about that at all. "In fact, the bastard hacked into my computer."

"Hacked in? What was he after?"

"SIM cards."

"Why would he want that?"

"Apparently, he's been impersonating our agents, sending texts that appear to be from agent phones."

"Let me guess," Holt said. "Becca received one of those messages." It was the only explanation for why she'd leave her post at the school without a good reason. Someone had given her a good enough reason.

In his peripheral vision, Holt caught the question in Max's eyes. Holt clamped down on his worry for Becca. She was well qualified to handle danger. Sara and Theo, on the other hand, could be at the mercy of a killer.

"She's still not answering her cell," Einstein said. "But the Lo-Jack shows her vehicle's at the scene of the accident Lt. Anderson mentioned. They're starting a search for her and Brady there. She was in pursuit of him, thinking he was Toxin."

"Who told her Brady was Toxin? And how do you know?"

"The SIM card info that was hacked. I tracked recent communication and Becca received a text a couple hours ago from SSAM, only it didn't originate from us. Apparently, *we* told her Brady is the real Toxin."

"And that text from Becca an hour ago, saying everything was okay?"

"That could very well have been White too."

"So when Chad White paid Brady to show up at the school…"

"She thought he was the threat and took off after him."

"Leaving Sara and Theo alone. What are our alternative communication options with the Academy?"

"Smoke signals?" Einstein blew out a breath. "Seriously, it's an old place. The records I looked up show that there are internet connections and the regular phone lines, but all of them are down. Whether that's due to the storm or someone purposely cut them, I don't know."

"Your best guess?"

"Given what this guy has already done? They were tampered with, so approach the school with extreme caution."

Shit. "That shouldn't affect a call to a cell phone though, right?"

"No, unless the tower is out. It isn't. I checked. But there are other ways to scramble those, if you have the right device and know what you're doing."

"Let's assume White has connections and is savvy enough to know what he's doing."

"Then we're back to smoke signals. Maybe carrier pigeons. If this guy cut phone lines, interfered with cell signals and is blocking my search methods, he knows what he's doing when it comes to electronics. But I think we already established that with the SIM card thing. Genius, really."

"We're still about ten minutes away."

Max shook his head. "In this weather, twenty."

"Damian's arranging for a snowplow to drive in front of you," Einstein said. "It'll help a little."

"We'll take whatever help we can get." Holt said a quick prayer that the people he loved were okay. He couldn't lose Theo or Sara, not when he was so close to having a life again. He'd have no life at all without them.

CHAPTER 20

"I sn't it great?" Theo sat on a floor pillow, gazing up at a full wall of flat-screen televisions. Parts of gaming systems and controllers were strewn about the floor, their cords leading in all directions like the Borg in *Star Trek*.

"And all of this was right across the hall from you." Jeremy's voice was full of awe.

"Yes, it's quite amazing," Miss Sara said, but when Theo glanced at her, she was still standing by the door. Her arms were crossed over her stomach and her eyes were on Mr. White. She looked stunned. Theo knew how she felt. When Mr. White had unlocked the attic door across from Miss Sara's apartment, telling them it was okay to go in and take a look around, he hadn't expected anything but dust and spiders.

Instead, he'd found *this*. Heaven. "He even has a bootleg copy of Scorpion's Sting," Theo said. He and Jeremy had already figured out the object of the game and were busy making the hero—a six-foot man-scorpion hybrid with a poisonous tail that curled and hung over the guy's head but could strike his enemies down with a whip motion or with venom—kill off his enemies. It was pretty cool. The ultimate goal was to save the prince and his mother, but that would take days of fighting. These games weren't over in a few hours. They kept you hooked for weeks.

"Yeah," Jeremy chimed in while he continued to play. "This Scorpion guy, Deathstalker, fights against the forces of oppression and evil. He's actually mostly man, but has all the cool parts of a scorpion...an extra set of limbs that are pinchers and, of course, the tail that can kill."

"Sounds pretty elaborate." Miss Sara had taken a few steps into the room and her attention was now on the screen.

"It is," Neil said. He was leaning against a wall, watching them play—when he wasn't watching the door. He'd wanted to go after Miss Sara when Mr. White had followed her into her apartment, but Mr. White had told him to stay with them here. In the low-ceilinged space, there'd been nowhere to sit but the floor pillows, but Neil seemed to prefer to be on his feet anyway.

"Wanna play?" Theo asked.

"Um, no," Miss Sara said. "Not right now. I'll just watch you two."

SARA'S INTERNAL ALARM BELLS WENT OFF AGAIN, AND THIS TIME SHE was listening. Something was seriously off about Chad White.

She glanced at Chad, but he was grinning like the Cheshire cat, as if nothing was wrong with an employee setting up something like this on private property. He seemed to genuinely enjoy the boys' pleasure.

She looked to Neil, who was, perhaps, the only other person in the room who would understand her concern right now. He met her gaze and gave a small shrug. He didn't know what to make of this either.

"Isn't this game supposed to be released at Christmas?" she asked Chad, determined to find out what the hell was going on. "Aren't bootleg copies illegal?"

His eyes narrowed on her a moment before he regained his smile. "Yes, they are. But I was a developer on the game, so I was shipped an early copy to try out. Make sure there are no kinks, you know?" He turned to the boys. "Hey, Theo, you can help me out with that. I haven't had the chance to play it through to the end myself, though our beta-testers did." He pulled another floor pillow from the corner and set it on the wood-plank floor beside Theo. "I'll show you some of the secret moves."

"Cool. Hey, your username is JoshCW?" Theo asked as they watched Chad log into his account on the screen. "We played online together a few weeks ago."

A chill tripped across Sara's skin. Chad was Toxin. There were no longer any lingering doubts. And he'd been so close to her, and Theo—*all* of her boys—for months. This *lair* was why Toxin—Chad—had wanted her away from the school last weekend. He'd needed privacy to set this up. Seeing Deathstalker—the animated half-man, half-scorpion—in action on the screen only confirmed her fears. He had staged this whole thing, probably even rigging the power to go out so he could come across as a hero. But why? What was his plan?

Chad grinned at Theo. "Yeah, and you kicked butt at Death Files."

Theo's brow crinkled. "I thought your first name was Chad."

"Josh was someone special, just a couple years older than you. I play in his memory, since he loved video games." Chad's gaze went back to the screen. "He would have really liked Scorpion's Sting. In fact, it's based on his fear of scorpions, and the way he handled chemo, with all those needles. I made a hero out of the scary parts."

"Kind of like making a strength out of a weakness?"

Chad gave him a thoughtful look. "Yeah, just like that."

Seeing their distraction, Sara took the moment to lean next to Neil against the wall. She kept her head near his as she spoke, keeping her voice low. "I want you to stay very calm and act like nothing's out of the ordinary, but listen to me...if you get the chance when Chad's not looking, you take the boys and run."

Neil turned a startled gaze to her before jerking it away again. "You think he's dangerous?" His whole body went rigid and his hands fisted, but he kept his voice low. "Is he Toxin? Did he kill my dad?"

She didn't want to tell him the entire truth. She needed Neil focused on getting the boys to safety, not on what Chad had done to his father. "I don't know for sure, but better safe than sorry. And if he's been playing online games with students...something's not right about that. We have to get the boys out and then we can figure out the rest."

"But the roads..."

"Would be less deadly than White if he is who I think he is. My keys are in my purse, which is still in my office desk drawer. My car's safer than yours. Take it and get far away, fast."

Neil shook his head. "I can't leave you here alone with him."

Sara calmed the fear that wanted to run rampant through her mind by focusing on the boys. She slipped her cell phone out of her pocket and into his hand, covering it with her own. "Take it and tuck it away. If you get a signal, call Theo's dad, and then SSAM headquarters. The numbers are in my contact list. They'll help. But first, get away." She looked him directly in the eye. "If you don't, Jeremy is in danger. And you too. Neither of you can afford to lose another family member. You see a chance, you get them out. Get to safety and you can send someone back for me."

"I can't—"

"You *can*. I have faith in you, Neil."

"Hey, what are you two talking about over there?" Chad's question made Sara jump. He was looking back over his shoulder at them.

"I was just asking Neil how he thought he did on the test he just took." She smiled. "He's doubting his chances, but I told him I believe in him." She had to hope Neil would take her advice and run with the boys. But in order for them to have a chance, she'd have to find a way to distract Chad.

"Looks like we've left the two of you out of the fun. Grab a controller and play a different game on another screen."

"Oh, I don't know. I'd rather watch for a while." Watch for a way to get the boys to safety.

A moment later, Theo shouted in triumph. He'd conquered the first level. Chad handed his controller to Neil. "Here, have a go. I have something to show Miss Burns."

Neil looked from him to her, then took the controller. He sat on the pillow by the other boys, tucking his long legs under him. "Game on." He sounded like a teenager eager to play, with nothing on his mind except fun.

Chad came to her side and stood so close she could smell almonds—from his soap? She racked her brain for details that would help them all get away from a killer like Toxin. What had Holt told her? He wanted to be a hero...he was a type of puppet master. She'd play to that.

She turned her body toward him, even though it put her way too close. "Well, these games will sure pass the time." She tried to sound pleased. *Pass the time until what?* her brain screamed. What was Toxin's plan for them? Surely, he hadn't counted on the boys being here, at least not Jeremy and Neil. So, would he kill them and do something with Sara and Theo? The thought of Theo with a needle in his neck made her pulse race and her body flood with adrenaline so fast she felt dizzy. But she'd use it to protect them. "I don't know how to thank you, Chad. You saved the day, what with fixing the power and, now, entertaining the boys."

He reached out and cupped the side of her neck. She jumped slightly but covered her initial shock with a forced smile. Chad had never touched her before. He brushed his thumb across the sensitive skin beneath her ear. "I'm happy to help. All I've wanted for months now is for you to notice me. For you to let me take care of you. I'll handle everything. I'll keep you and Theo safe. Always."

Get Chad out of here. Give the boys a chance. "You mentioned you had something to show me? Is it here, at the school?"

"Yes, but I need a computer. It's a video clip."

They couldn't use the computer in her office or Neil wouldn't be able to grab her keys. "My personal laptop's in my apartment."

"Perfect. Bring it here."

"If it's a video you want me to see, I think I'd rather watch it in my apartment. Less noise there, and I doubt we could tear these boys' attention away from the game, anyway."

Chad reached into his pocket and pulled out a flash drive. "Everything we need is on here. Lead the way."

Sara looked at the trio of boys, engrossed in their game. Neil kept looking up at a blank screen, where he could see Sara and Chad's reflection. He'd been watching.

"Hey, guys?" Sara called. "We have to get something from my apartment. We'll be just across the hall, and will be back in about ten minutes." She looked questioningly to Chad.

Chad nodded. "That'll be enough time."

It had to be.

CHAPTER 21

"Hey!" Theo looked up as Neil put a hand on his controller. "I almost had an extra life."

"Be quiet and listen," Neil hissed. Apparently Jeremy noticed the tension in his brother's whisper. They both went still. "Mr. White isn't who you think he is."

"He's much cooler," Theo said. He would never have expected all of this stuff, right here in the school.

"Who has all this stuff and then shows his students? Who seeks them out after school hours to play games online? It's creepy. Like he's trying to set us up. And the scorpion...what does that remind you of?"

Recognition dawned. Theo tasted acid in the back of his mouth. "Toxin? The guy my dad's been hunting?"

"Yeah. Miss Sara thinks so."

Jeremy jumped up but Neil restrained him with an arm around his waist. "He killed Dad!"

"I know," Neil said. "Keep your voice down. I want to get him, too, but not until we get the police. Miss Sara needs us to get help."

Theo couldn't stand the thought of losing her. "I'm not leaving without her."

"We have to. She got Mr. White out of here so we can get away and get help. We're not strong enough to overpower him. Not without one of us, or maybe all of us, getting hurt. He could have a weapon. If this is going to work, we have to move *now*."

As quietly as possible, they followed Neil down the stairs to Miss Sara's office. Neil went straight to the desk drawer and got the keys to her car. Theo paused on the threshold of the Academy, torn between finding a weapon to attack Mr. White and doing what Miss Sara had told them to do. He'd vowed to protect her, but Dad had told him before that she could take care of herself. "I promised to be her hero."

Neil turned back to him. He looked exasperated but tried to speak calmly. "You will be. By getting her help from adults."

"We'll get out the gate and call the police as soon as we get a signal, right?"

"Absolutely," Neil said. "Or I'll drive straight to the police station. It's our best chance, and hers."

HOLT LEANED FORWARD OVER THE DASHBOARD, PEERING THROUGH the haze of snow.

"Almost there," Max assured him, keeping the car as close to the snowplow as possible.

"Not soon enough for me," Holt said. They'd made good time, but even with the snowplow Damian had arranged, it had taken them ten minutes to cover the last couple miles. To protect Theo, he would have trekked through the snow on foot, or stolen a snowmobile if one had been nearby.

They'd lost cell signal a mile ago, and there would be no reaching out for other help. The sense of urgency that filled him, coiling in his gut, had him thinking expletives the entire way. He'd been so focused on the road, so tense at the conditions and the need to go faster, that pain radiated from his wrists up his stiff arms and down his shoulders and back.

One fist still gripped his phone—his much-too-quiet phone. He willed it to ring, for someone from SSAM to call him with updated information. Or better yet, to hear his son's voice, or Sara's sexy way of putting him in his place, chastising him for his *laissez-faire* parenting style or his ridiculous notion that he couldn't have her without betraying Elizabeth. He wouldn't ignore her call this time, or ever again.

When he saw them again, he'd wrap them up in his arms and squeeze until Theo couldn't doubt his love and Sara couldn't utter another frustrated word. He'd hold her until she forgave him. She had to be angry, and had every right to be, but she loved him. She'd shown him as much in so many ways he hadn't wanted to recognize before today. But the truth was smacking him in the face today as he realized how afraid he was of losing her.

She loved him. He loved her. And love could overcome anything.

"Finally." Max relaxed his grip on the steering wheel.

The wrought-iron spikes of the fence that lined the perimeter of the Academy came into view outside Holt's window. He couldn't see the school through the swirling snow. Only dark night waited beyond the twin spears of their headlights.

"Still no signal," Holt said, glancing at his cell phone. "Einstein must have been right about a local signal jammer."

Max flashed his high beams at the city's snowplow in gratitude and took a slow turn into the long drive that led to the Academy. The snow was about six inches deep and untouched. There was no sign anyone had driven here tonight, which meant Sara and Theo should be near. The car skidded around a tight turn. In the dark, pristine wonderland, they couldn't even make out the path of the road.

"We'll have to park and hike in." Holt reached under his seat for his gun and checked that it was loaded before tucking it into a holster beneath his coat and pulling on gloves.

They'd only taken a few steps when the crunch of snow and slash of headlights across the terrain alerted them that another vehicle had pulled up behind theirs. A police cruiser. An officer got out and frowned at the ankle-deep snow. "You two Max and Holt?" he asked them.

"We are," Holt said.

"I just received a message for you from someone named Einstein. Guess your cell phones are out. Dispatcher told me to pass it along if I saw you."

"And?" Max asked impatiently. Holt looked toward the dark form of the school. A few lights were on in the upper floors and in the vicinity of Sara's office. A slight orange glow reflected what light there was from the city off the clouds, and bounced back off the snow. That, plus the cruiser's headlights, were the only illumination.

"He said he's tracked you here with your car's Lo-Jack. He figures, since he couldn't get through to you, he was right about the signal jammer. He also wanted you to know there's still no sign of Becca Haney or Brady Flaherty. Detective Crandall put Henry in jail and is en route to investigate further." The officer squinted through the falling snow. "I suppose all of that means something to you two."

"Have a seat." Sara gestured to her couch. Though she tried to sound friendly, she worried that Chad—*Toxin*—could detect the tremor in her voice. The longer she could keep him here, in her apartment, and delay watching the video he seemed so excited to show her, the more time the boys had to get to safety and to send help for her. In the back of her mind, she was also worried about Roscoe. He hadn't woken when they entered, and come trotting out with his usual greeting. "Do you want something to drink?"

"No, thanks." Chad sat down.

"Mind if I have something?" She moved toward the kitchen before he could object.

"Not at all." But his mouth had tightened slightly. Was he annoyed she wasn't as eager to view the video as he was?

She pulled a glass from the cabinet and opened her refrigerator. The path of her hand deviated from the soda she'd been reaching for to a bottle of beer. "I don't know about you, but storms give me the heebie-jeebies. I could use a little something to take the edge off, you know? Sure you don't want anything?"

"No, thank you." His gaze moved toward the door as if thinking about the boys across the hall.

To pacify him, she led him closer to his objective, though she really didn't want to see his video. What could be on there? Footage of his last kill, maybe. A snuff film. "My laptop is stashed under the couch. Why don't you get it set up?"

He located the computer and set it on the coffee table in front of him. Turning it on and letting it start up would take a couple minutes, giving the boys a little more time. With a shaky hand, she set the beer bottle next to her glass and pretended to fumble in a drawer. "Damn. I thought the bottle opener was here. Must have left it in the other room." She began walking toward her bedroom.

"I can get it." Toxin began to stand, but she held out a hand.

"No, I'll get it." Out of his sight in her room, she rushed to the phone and lifted the receiver. Still no dial tone. She hurried to Roscoe and ran a hand over the sleeping dog. He didn't stir, but he was warm and his ribcage rose and fell in a normal rhythm. Drugged? Chad must have given him something when she'd turned her back on him earlier. It was just as well that Roscoe slept through this. She was sure the Toxin she'd heard about would kill anything that got in his way.

"I know why you growled at him, boy," she whispered. The dog must have remembered Chad from Mrs. Mendelson's murder. "I'll take care of everything."

"Sara?" Toxin called.

Ignoring her shaky legs, Sara returned to the living room. "Not sure where that bottle opener went. Guess I'll switch to soda." She felt his eyes on her as she crossed to the fridge and took a few more seconds replacing the bottle and selecting a can of soda.

She passed the window in the kitchen and thought she saw the flash of headlights against snow four stories below, right about where she'd parked her car. She prayed it was the kids and that Neil was driving them to safety. Another flicker of light, this time red. Brake lights? Through the thick snow, it was impossible to tell for sure what she was seeing.

She had done what she could. She had kept Theo safe, just as she'd promised Elizabeth. Just as she'd promised Holt.

The thought of Holt had hot moisture pricking her eyes. So tender was his touch and so selfless his attention to her the night they'd made love, he had to care about her on some level. But those telling moments had been fleeting. Perhaps she'd read too much into them. The boys would be safe. That was all that mattered. She blinked back the fear and regret and focused on the relief coursing through her like a tidal wave. Everything else would be gravy... including getting herself out of this mess.

"I've got the video cued up." Excitement glittered in Chad's dark eyes. "You ready?"

"Can't wait." She sat near him, as he would have expected in order to watch the video, but was careful not to touch him. Still, his arm brushed hers as he reached forward to press Play. She hid her sudden jumpiness by opening the soda and taking a sip.

"This is a gift for you," Chad said. An image of the school appeared. His voice narrated as he did a walking tour of the halls, speaking highly of the school and even interviewing students about Sara. The five minutes of praise for her from staff and students made her uncomfortable, but she hid it.

"If I were running for election, you'd have made a terrific

campaign manager," Sara said. She let her confusion show. "But what is this for?"

"The real question is *who* is this for? The school board. I emailed a copy to each of those idiots a few hours ago. They should be viewing it soon, if they haven't already. And then they'll see what I've seen all along...what a terrific woman you are." His lips pressed into a flat line. "John Rochard was a snake, and he wouldn't know perfection if it walked up and gave him a lap dance." Chad's hand moved to Sara's knee. "But I would."

Sara felt panic well up in her throat but clamped down on it. "Wow." The word came out on a whoosh of breath. She hoped he perceived it as appropriate gratitude. "You did all of this, for me?"

Were the boys far enough away yet? She didn't know how much longer she could keep up this charade. Acid churned in her stomach as she sat there with Toxin's hand on her body. She had to fight the urge to jump up and run.

"You like it?" Toxin's look was hopeful. "All I want is to be your hero. Yours and Theo's."

CHAPTER 22

Darkness surrounded Holt as they moved away from the car and began the hike toward the school. The slight incline and deep snow had his legs burning in no time, but he barely acknowledged it. Snowflakes bombarded them at a steady rate. Their sharp sting against his face was welcome, keeping him alert. Awareness was key. If he made a mistake or got hurt, he couldn't help Theo and Sara.

The crunch of snowfall from up ahead, indicating they weren't alone, was loud in his ears. Max held out a hand to stop Holt, but he'd already halted. Max jerked his head toward a nearby stand of trees and Holt, Max and the police officer moved behind it for cover. There was nothing they could do to hide their footprints, though, which scarred the otherwise smooth sheet of snow.

"How far do we have to walk, do you think?" a boy's voice asked.

"Shhh," another person hissed.

Light reflected off the snow, giving the night an eerie orange glow, but they couldn't see the owners of the voices. Holt's gaze found Max's. *Boys?* Holt mouthed. Max nodded. They hadn't expected any students other than Theo. Was his son among them?

Holt put his lips together and did the special whistle he'd worked with Theo to learn for a Boy Scout project. It had become a fun way of calling to each other, but they hadn't used it in over a year. Would he remember?

"Dad?" The whispered word was Theo's.

Relief was a roar in Holt's ears as blood pounded in his head. He stepped out from behind the tree. "Theo?"

"Dad!" Theo forgot to be quiet and careful and took off running toward them. He stumbled and righted himself. Trusting Max to look out for danger, Holt met Theo halfway and scooped him up into his arms.

"Are you okay?" His words were muffled by his son's cold, damp shirt, but Holt couldn't let go.

"Yeah, I'm okay."

Snow continued to swirl around them and he felt his son shiver. Theo wasn't wearing a jacket, and his shirt was nearly soaked through by the wet snow. Holt set him down and pulled off his own jacket, wrapping it snugly around Theo. His son's eyes went wide at the sight of the gun strapped to his shoulder.

"Who do you have with you?" Holt asked. Two boys, one about Theo's size and the other much taller, stepped forward from the deeper shadows.

"Neil and Jeremy Rochard, sir," the older boy said. They didn't have jackets either.

Rochard's boys. "You two okay? We need to get you somewhere warm."

"We're okay," Neil said, "But we're supposed to be well away from here by now. Miss Sara told me to get them to safety." He sounded upset that he hadn't succeeded.

Holt swallowed a resurgence of fear. Sara wasn't with them. But neither was Chad White. She'd gotten the boys away from danger. "You did a good job, son. You're safe with us."

272 ANNE MARIE BECKER

"We tried to drive. The car skidded off the road up there." Neil jerked a thumb over his shoulder. "Almost hit a tree. Snow was too deep."

"We've got cars down by the road, where the snow has been plowed. If you can hike a little farther, you'll be home-free."

"But Miss Sara..." Neil looked back toward the school.

"Is she hurt?" Holt thought his heart might leap out of his chest, it was pounding so hard.

"No, but she's alone with *him.* Any minute now, he's going to discover what we did when he wasn't looking."

Holt looked from the school to Theo.

"It's okay," Theo told him. "I'll go with the police officer. Help her, please. I don't want her to die too."

"So, you liked it?" Chad asked Sara.

She pursed her lips, striving for the most positive truth she could find. "It was extremely thoughtful of you."

He grinned. "I knew you'd understand."

She didn't understand at all, but she'd play his game if it meant giving help a few more minutes to arrive. But when Chad closed her computer and stood, she knew her time was up.

"We should check on the boys." He moved toward the door.

"I'm sure they're fine," Sara said, catching up to him at her door. "We can have a little more quiet time together first."

He turned and stroked his fingers down her cheek. By sheer force of will, she controlled a shudder of revulsion. "We'll have plenty of time for that soon enough. I want some time to bond with Theo too. We're going to be a family."

"A family?"

"With you happy, and Theo happy, we'll be a happy family." The conviction in Chad's voice chilled her to the bone. He truly believed his delusion.

"A video plus some game time don't equal lasting happiness."

He frowned. "Of course not. It'll take more than that. But we'll be there for each other, no matter what. Besides, Theo will need a new father figure."

Her heart stopped. It had to have. The whole world had gone silent. "What do you mean?"

"Holt Patterson died in a drive-by shooting tonight."

No. It couldn't be true. "How do you know that? Was it on the news or something?" She thought her legs might buckle, and found herself gripping Chad's arm. She forced herself to straighten and let go of him. *He* was responsible for this. He had to be. Who else would want Holt dead?

He examined her face. "It's okay, Sara. I'll take care of you both. Forever." He turned to go into the attic and she knew she had to get herself together. If Holt—*oh, God, please don't let him be dead*—wasn't coming, and if help wasn't here yet, she would have to escape on her own.

And if Holt *were* dead...Theo would need her all the more, so she'd better damn well get herself out of this mess.

Chad turned his back on her to enter his lair and she spun the opposite direction, toward the stairs. Taking them two at a time, she raced down as fast as she could, clutching the railing for support. She was on the third-story landing when she heard Chad's bellow. He'd discovered the boys were gone, and that she was no longer behind him. Angry footsteps pounded above her. She rounded the second-floor landing. Chad was gaining ground, but he was still half a flight of stairs above her.

"Sara, stop!" Chad's shout was angry. Hurt. "You're ruining everything. We're going to be a family. Stop! We'll find Theo."

He sounded like he was only a few steps behind her, but she didn't dare waste precious time turning to check. She was four stair-steps from the front hall when she felt his hand on her shoulder. He shoved her, knocking her off balance. Her socks slipped on the wood step and she slid the last few steps to the bottom, landing on her right knee and ankle, and twisting her wrist as she lost her grip on the railing.

Despite the aches and shooting pain, she scrambled backwards like a crab to the wall near the school's front door. "Stop right there." It was a pathetic plea, and holding her hand out in front of her to stop Chad was as ineffective as waving a flyswatter at an alligator.

"I don't want to hurt you," Chad said, now at the bottom of the steps and walking toward her. "I just wanted to stop you and make you listen. You're behaving irrationally."

She continued backing away, pushing with her legs as she scooted on her butt toward the door. Her ankle throbbed, but she would run on it if she could get to her feet. The snow would numb the pain, anyway, for a little while. But Chad could move faster than she could. He maneuvered himself between her and the door to the outside world.

"You don't have to hurt me," she said, trying to appeal to reason. "That would be your choice. Just because you killed those other people, doesn't mean you have to kill me."

He shook his head. "Kill? I never wanted to kill you. You're not one of them. Not one of the people who killed my son through greed, ineptitude and negligence." *His son?* "You're my future. You and Theo. You're going to replace what I lost." He looked toward the front door and frowned. "Where did the boys go?"

"I don't know."

He took another step forward. "Don't lie to me. Did you hide them?"

When he reached for her, she scrambled the other direction, backing around the base of the stairs and into a corner by the janitor's closet, where she'd discovered Theo and Jeremy playing video games weeks ago. She hoped the boys were far away, because if Chad killed her, he'd be hunting them next. Outside the window, the snow continued to fall, forming a thick white blanket. The longer she could keep Chad busy, the more chance snow would cover their tracks.

"How could I have hidden them? I was with you."

"You must have some idea where they went. You're ruining everything. You're just like the others." Anger flashed in his eyes a second before he roared and lunged for her. His body came down on top of her, pinning her to the floor before he straddled her and wrapped his hands around her throat. She waited for the pain of a needle piercing her neck, but it never came. His weapons must be in the toolbox...the same one he'd brought from fixing the power. The toolbox he'd had on hand when he'd helped soothe Roscoe. The toolbox that was currently upstairs in her apartment.

She brought her good knee up, trying to aim for sensitive tissue, but Chad was guarding against that and twisted to shift his weight. His hands squeezed her throat until she began to see spots. A rush of frigid air and the bang of the door against the wall as it was thrown open told her help had finally arrived. She only hoped it wasn't too late. *And, oh God, don't let it be the boys returning.*

"Stop!" Holt moved swiftly toward them with a gun pointed their way.

Holt? He was *alive.* Apparently, Chad had believed Holt was dead too. The pressure on her neck lessened as he turned with surprise.

"Those idiots," he muttered. He got to his feet, hauling Sara with him, and holding her in place like a shield. "If I want something done right, I'll have to do it myself."

HOLT HELD HIS WEAPON STEADY DESPITE SARA BEING CAUGHT IN THE crosshairs. The gun was the one thing that gave him the upper hand at the moment. Despite her paleness, and a pained expression as she shifted her weight onto one leg beneath Toxin's grip, she looked relatively unharmed. Her tousled blond hair spilled out of a ponytail holder. Wearing a sweatshirt emblazoned with *Hogwarts* and with only socks on her feet, she looked more vulnerable than ever. But determination blazed alongside the fear in her eyes.

Max had gone around to the back of the school, in case Toxin tried to flee from another door. In the meantime, Holt focused on increasing the distance between Toxin and Sara.

"Some hero, using a defenseless woman as a shield," Holt said. "Since you're so powerful, come out and face me like a man."

Chad snorted. "She's not defenseless. And she's not the woman I thought she was."

Sara was looking toward a door only a few feet away. *Good girl. Watch for a chance to escape.* But the door was under the stairs. He doubted it led anywhere significant. Maybe a basement? Still, if she could lock herself inside until Max arrived, she'd have a better chance of survival.

"This is between you and me, Chad." Holt refused to put the killer at a glorified level by calling him Toxin. He was plain old, delusional Chad White. "You've wanted my life all along. You can't take it because I'm still living it."

The spark in Chad's eyes flared. "You were supposed to be dead by now. You don't deserve your life. You don't deserve *them.*"

"And *you* do?" Holt edged to the side, hoping he could get the other man to switch positions with him if they circled. It might give Max a better angle with which to take down Chad. But Chad only held Sara tighter, causing her to wince. "You won't be able to win over Theo," Holt continued. "He's a smart kid. He wouldn't trust you."

"He already does. He was playing video games with me just a half hour ago, just like we've done online for weeks."

The thought of this man anywhere near his son filled Holt with rage, but he kept a lid on it. "He ran into my arms outside. He and the other two boys are with the police. Looks like they caught on to you pretty fast."

Sara smiled, her eyes filling with tears of relief.

"Only because of *her*—" Chad yanked up on Sara, his arm

threatening to choke off her air supply. Holt's grip on the gun tightened, but he was still several feet away. Chad could snap Sara's neck in a blink if he made one false move. With his free hand, Chad reached behind him for the door. "Does this go somewhere?"

Sara tried to nod, and he loosened his grip slightly. He pulled open the door, still keeping her between Holt's gun and his body, then pulled her inside.

SARA WOULD HAVE ONE SHOT AT FREEING HERSELF. HOLT WOULD never risk shooting her, and Chad knew that. The closet was her salvation...or, rather, the hammer she remembered seeing hanging on a pegboard just inside was her salvation. As he dragged her inside, she used one of the moves Holt and Max had taught in the self-defense seminar, making herself dead weight as she thrust her elbows out and up to dislodge herself from his grip. Caught off guard, Chad scrambled to get a grip on her as she grabbed the hammer and came up swinging.

"Sara, move!" Holt's shout seemed as if it came from far away. "I can't get a clear shot. Just get away from him."

She swung her hammer and hit soft tissue, but in the dark closet, she couldn't see clearly. Chad yelped and a rush of air like the sudden creation of a vacuum indicated he'd dropped to the floor.

She stumbled backward out of the closet. One of Holt's arms came around her waist, pulling her beside him, and then tucking her behind his solid strength. Her muscles felt jittery, and she gladly moved behind him and the big black gun.

"Come out with your hands up," Holt shouted. There was a rustling of clothing in the shadows, and then...nothing. "Is there really another way out through there?" he asked her.

"No. It's a closet." The front door opened, but Holt kept his attention on the closet door ten feet away.

"Need any help?" Max Sawyer asked, his gun trained on the closet as his gaze swept the foyer, assessing the situation.

"Chad's in there. Sara says it's a closet."

Max took a flashlight from his waistband and aimed it at the doorway, then stepped closer to inspect the space. "Shit." The space was empty. Chad—Toxin—was gone. Holt stepped forward and pulled a string that brought a bare bulb to life.

Sara gasped. "The crawl space. I forgot all about it." A square opening near the floorboards was just large enough for a man to squeeze through. The board that had served as a barrier had been set to the side, leaving a gaping hole with more darkness beyond. "Chad knew about it because he upgraded our wiring. He knows this place from top to bottom."

"I'll walk the perimeter again and see if I can find where he came out," Max said. "Stay with her and keep watch in case he comes back this way."

Once Max was gone, Sara turned and folded herself into Holt's side. His shirt was wet with melted snow, but she didn't care. He was warm. *Alive.* His arm came around her, while the other kept his gun at the ready, in case Chad should pop his head out of the hole like a whack-a-mole.

"Are the boys really with the police?" Sara asked.

"Yes. They're all okay," Holt assured her. "I watched them leave for the station."

"Oh, thank God. Then they're nowhere near here. What about Becca? She took off after Tox—" She shook her head. "She was chasing the guy we thought was Toxin."

"Noah's found her by now, I'm sure. It looked like she and Brady ditched the cars in the storm and it turned into a foot chase. Chad set Brady up to take the fall again. *He* sent her that text."

"He said you were dead." Moisture pricked at her eyes.

With his free hand, he cupped her cheek. "I have too much left to do, so I refused to die."

CHAPTER 23

"C had never did stick his head back out of the hole," Sara told Becca as she sipped a hot cup of tea at Holt's house hours later.

It was nearly two in the morning, but she couldn't sleep. The relief that her friend was okay, combined with the adrenaline rush from a roller coaster of a night, had left her both giddy and exhausted. Gripping the mug was possibly the only thing holding her together right now. Worry for Holt, who was still out with law enforcement looking for Chad, threatened to rip her apart.

"Max found tracks in the snow that led away from a rear door to the Academy's kitchen," Sara said. There had been another square hole in the kitchen, where the crawl space let out.

"I'm just glad nobody was hurt." Becca absently touched the strap of the sling that encased her left arm. She'd tracked Brady for nearly an hour until she'd caught up to him trying to break into an empty lakefront home. Without her cell phone, which had gotten lost in the snow back at the site of the car wreck, she'd had to cuff Brady and march him back toward a populated area where she could finally make a phone call. Brady was in custody for attempted murder, among other charges. He claimed to have no idea who had hired him—that it had been a random job from a twisted referral source. He insisted he certainly wouldn't have worked for Toxin.

Sara said a silent prayer of gratitude. They'd all come through the night relatively intact. "Even Roscoe's okay, thank God." The head veterinarian of the CPD K-9 unit had been called in to check out Roscoe, who was spending the night in an animal hospital to ensure his safe recovery. Sara had been assured they would receive a call the moment he woke up. She could pick him up in the morning if he was well enough by then.

Becca smiled. "I'm so glad. The kids at the school seem to love him."

"He's become a sort of mascot."

"How are Theo's friends?"

"Neil and Jeremy are safe with their mother. Another thing to be thankful for." Claire had burst into the police station like a mother lion soon after Sara had arrived. She'd hovered over her boys, and couldn't seem to stop touching them. There was always a hand on their shoulders, their hands, their heads, as they answered Noah's questions. Damian and Noah had agreed that, since they weren't the primary targets, Claire, with a police escort, could take the boys to her sister's home an hour away.

Sara took another fortifying gulp of hot tea. "The only thing left is to make sure Max and Holt are safe." They were still out there, along with the CPD, looking for Chad. The storm had let up, but the roads were still treacherous.

The sound of a key in the lock and the front door opening had Sara running for the living room. She exhaled in relief as Holt walked in. Without taking his eyes off her, he closed and locked the door then bridged the gap and caught her up against him. His arms were like steel bands and she reveled in the feeling of security, until she felt the tremors shuddering through his body. Sensing he needed to be held, she gripped him tightly. After a moment, she pulled away to inspect him. She ran her hands over his arms, relieved to find he was in one piece, but exhaustion lined his face. "You're okay. Did you catch him?"

His gaze shifted to Becca, who came up behind her. "No, but we've set up shifts so we can get rest and hit the search hard in the morning."

Becca nodded. "I'll do the same, and give you guys some space. Damian set up a guard for out front again, and one to roam the little alley out back too. Call them if you need anything. See you in a few hours." With a salute from her good hand, she let herself out. Again, Holt locked and bolted the door.

"How are you?" he asked Sara.

She gave a short laugh. "Sore, but not anything a hot soak wouldn't cure."

Holt's gaze searched the hallway beyond Sara. "Where's Theo?"

"Sleeping, finally. That call from you really helped put his mind at ease."

"I didn't want him to worry. Sorry it was so short." His hand brushed her cheek. "I wanted to talk with you too."

"I understand." He'd been busy at the time, and his son needed him more than she did...or just as much, anyway.

"Still, I wanted to hear your voice. Hold you." His hazel-gold eyes raked her face. "In fact, I don't want to let you out of my sight. It seems all of my senses crave you."

"You need rest."

"Then I'll have to settle for holding you all night...or at least for what's left of it. But once I hold you, I won't be able to let go." He cupped her cheek. "I'm talking about more than tonight, Sara."

Her breath hiccupped in her chest. "What about Theo? And Elizabeth? The baggage..."

"Are any of those things issues for you?"

"No, I love Theo, and I love you. And I think Elizabeth would understand." The last of her concerns faded. She was completely in love with Holt Patterson. Always had been and always would be. There was no point fighting it any longer.

"I feel the same." He touched his lips to hers and the weight of the world evaporated. The kiss only lasted a moment before he pulled his mouth away and took her hand. "Come with me."

Holt led her up the stairs, stopping to peek in on Theo, who was sleeping soundly in his bed. He pulled Sara to his bedroom, shut the door and pulled her into his arms. Burying his face in her neck, he shuddered and held on as if she were a lifeline.

"Holt?"

"I almost lost you and Theo forever." His words were hot against her skin.

Sara wrapped her arms tighter, absorbing his shaking. "You didn't. We're here."

He pulled back just far enough to look into her eyes. "Because you were smart enough not to trust Chad White."

Not until it was almost too late. "We're okay. We're safe."

"It's not enough." His gaze held hers. "I want you with me, always. I meant what I said. I love you. Theo loves you. You belong with us. Please stay."

Her tongue darted out to wet her suddenly dry lips and his gaze hovered there. With a groan, he pulled her against him and kissed her. His hands ran down her back, then moved still lower to cup her buttocks. He molded her against him from chest to thighs.

He tasted like coffee laced with sweetness. He took his coffee with two sugars. One morning, would making him coffee with two sugars be part of their routine together? No, not one morning...*every* morning. Starting this morning...but not for a few hours yet. She smiled against his lips.

He pulled away to look at her. "What?"

"Yes."

"Yes?"

"I'd love to be part of yours and Theo's lives. Forever."

. . .

HOLT INHALED A DEEP BREATH THROUGH HER HAIR. THE FAMILIAR smell of her, the feel of her body pressed to his…it was so right. This was what he'd been denying himself for so long. He'd almost lost his second chance at happiness and he didn't intend to let go anytime soon. Not ever, in fact.

Elation filled him like helium in a balloon, lifting the heaviness from his heart. Careful of her sore leg, he backed her toward his bed. Soon, it would be *their* bed. The way she was looking at him, her face so close he could see the indentations by her eyes as she smiled up at him, brought other things to mind. The little details about her that he hadn't been able to get out of his head since the last time he'd held her close stirred his longing. Details like her knowing smile and the way her body felt sliding over his in the dark, how her soft hair had brushed his nose and cheek as he inhaled her sweet scent. It was an ache that only Sara could ease. He forced himself to take it slow, treasuring her as he peeled her clothing off one item at a time.

She did the same with him. "Tit for tat," she said with a wicked smile.

Skin-to-skin, they fell back onto the bed. He braced his weight so he wouldn't land full force on top of her. She seemed just as hungry for him as he was for her. After months of denying himself a full connection with Sara, he was downright starved for every drop of her. He wanted to bury himself in her heat forever.

Her lips were so hot they burned him from the inside—they traveled over his mouth, down his neck, across his chest. Exquisite torture. Her hands joined the fray. Teasing, touching, stroking, she heated his skin until he thought he might combust.

Tit for tat. She arched against him as his hand stroked down her side, his thumb pausing to circle her nipple. As his mouth took over her breasts, his hand continued exploring along the arc of her hip, stopping at her uninjured knee to bend it. He positioned himself to enter her, delaying the sweet torment a few moments longer. As he sank into her, their gazes collided. She bit her lip. His hand moved lower, teasing her most sensitive parts until she was gasping and digging her nails into his shoulders, trying to pull him closer, urging him to join her. She breathed his name and he found their rhythm, riding the wave until it took him over the edge.

He was falling, but not alone. They were falling, together. They'd land together.

CHAPTER 24

Life had kicked him in the groin again. Toxin had been low before. He'd learned how to use the pain. He was adaptable. He'd survived this long, hadn't he? He'd even outrun Holt and the police and returned safely to the house he rented under a fake identity.

Survival of the fittest. Darwin knew his stuff.

But this time, he wasn't sure he wanted to survive. Pain ripped through his chest. He had failed in his quest. His hand came up to the cheek Sara had smashed with a hammer. Swollen and tender. He almost wished Sara had swung the weapon into his head.

I should have had Sara and Theo half in love with me by now.

Instead, Toxin lay in his bed. The rising sun cast shadows across his ceiling. The scent of Sara's hair still permeated the pillowcase he'd snatched weeks ago from her apartment. The smell of her usually soothed him. Tonight, it stank of betrayal. She'd chosen Holt Patterson over him. What the hell had Holt done to deserve her love?

Toxin had eliminated the threats to her.

He'd been the one to deal with Rochard and the board. Just as he'd dealt with his boss, and Dr. Brown, and all the other threats to Josh.

Only he hadn't been able to deal with the one thing that truly threatened his son...the fucking cancer. Toxin's throat squeezed until he thought it might shut off completely. Good. Except it didn't and he kept on swallowing. Kept on breathing.

Despite his inability to stop the cancer, Josh had seen him as his hero. Toxin would have died for him, if he could have taken his place. The ceiling blurred. He'd made a promise by Josh's grave a year ago, after he'd watched men he didn't know shovel dirt onto his son's coffin, but he wasn't able to keep it.

Oh, he'd righted the wrongs that had been done to Josh. Toxin's CEO who refused to provide more time off or medical assistance for the riskier, unapproved treatments when the regular chemo hadn't worked. The bitch doctor who'd failed to diagnose Josh for months, until it was too late for effective treatment. The politician who prided himself in balancing the budget by cutting funding for important medical programs that would have helped kids like Josh. And Buzz Redding, who'd thrived on self-righteous judgment and had never fully accepted Josh as his grandson because the kid was a "bastard" child of unmarried parents.

Yet, despite all he'd done, somehow Sara hadn't seen him as her hero. What more did a guy have to do to prove his heroism?

He'd had Theo hooked. He'd seen the glimmer of love in the kid's eyes as he'd appreciated what Toxin had created for him. But Sara and Holt had intervened.

If only Brady had succeeded in what he'd been goddamn paid to do and killed Holt...

And Henry had been arrested. The guy had probably flipped so fast, telling the police everything he knew about Chad White, that he'd have permanent whiplash. At least Toxin still had a few doses of the special drug Henry had created.

He rose and stumbled over to his chest of drawers, then located his stash. Soon, he'd be drifting in oblivion, at least for a short while. In his dreamy haze, he'd visit his son. He'd forget the fuckers who'd betrayed him. For a brief time.

But the hurt would return. It always did. There was no escape.

WARM LIPS PRESSED AGAINST HERS, ROUSING HER FROM SLEEP IN THE best way possible. But her eyelids were heavy and gritty. Sara moaned and wrapped her arms around Holt's neck. Her nostrils filled with the fresh scents of musk and mint.

Her eyes shot open. "You've already showered, shaved and brushed your teeth. No fair."

He grinned down at her unapologetically. "And you haven't. I'm sorry I had to wake you. I would have asked you to join me, but you were smiling in your sleep. I like to see you smile."

"I was having some very nice dreams. But I'll forgive you for waking me after practically no sleep, as long as this is your method of choice."

Holt chuckled and brushed a strand of hair from her cheek. His smile dimmed. "Damian is gathering the team here. Twenty minutes."

"Here? Why?"

"I don't want to leave Theo and you alone."

She shot upright in bed, pushing him off of her. She immediately regretted the action as her stiff muscles protested. "I've got to shower, change—" She stood and gingerly tested her right leg, grateful the ankle sprain wasn't as bad as she'd originally thought. Still, the knee was throbbing, reminding her it was time for more pain medication too. She looked down at the floor, where her rumpled sweatshirt lay in a heap along with her jeans. "I have no clean clothes...no shoes, even."

Holt lifted a shopping bag. "Catherine dropped off some toiletries and clothes I asked her to pick up for you."

Sara took the bag and peeked inside. It appeared to have everything she needed. "Bless her."

He took her shoulders and turned her toward the bathroom. "Go. Theo and I are making pancakes. You can gobble them down before the meeting."

She could get used to waking up to Holt and Theo in her life. She stopped at the bathroom door and looked back at Holt. "What about Roscoe?"

"I haven't called the vet yet, but he told me he'd call immediately if there was anything to be concerned about."

A quick shower and a change of clothes later, Sara filled her tummy with blueberry pancakes across from a bright-eyed Theo and a grinning Holt.

"The vet told Dad that Roscoe's okay." Theo drenched his pancakes with a second helping of syrup. "And Dad says we can keep Roscoe. We're going to pick him up this afternoon. You coming?"

Sara realized it was Saturday, but a lifetime seemed to have passed since yesterday. "I'm actually supposed to catch a flight to Mexico this afternoon."

Holt stopped chewing a second, then swallowed. "I forgot about that."

"I was going to spend Thanksgiving vacation there, recuperating."

"Recuperating?"

She wanted to reach out and touch him but didn't know if that was appropriate in front of Theo. She'd let Holt dictate the terms of this new beginning. "Sometimes you need a break when things aren't going your way."

"But now?"

She smiled. "Things are going rather well and there's nowhere else I'd rather be."

Holt took her hand where it lay on the table and threaded his fingers through hers. He reached out with his other hand toward Theo. Theo set down his fork and joined hands with each of them, completing the circuit.

"Does this mean you're finally going to make her an official part of our family?" Theo asked, looking from Sara to Holt.

Holt smiled. "Working on it, bud."

"Guess you should dust off those chess skills," Sara added. After making quick work of cleaning up, they left Theo in Holt's office watching a movie. As they moved back into the living room, Sara chewed at her lip. "No ideas where Chad is, then?"

"Given the weather and the way he disappeared, he had to have somewhere nearby to go," Holt said. "But the address on his Academy employment application was an old one. Police are still patrolling a five-mile radius of the school, now that the roads are mostly clear." The storm had blown through and snowplows were cleaning up in the aftermath.

The doorbell rang and Damian, Noah, Becca, Einstein and Max stood on the threshold. Holt set a fresh pot of coffee and several mugs on the living room table and they all took their seats. Sara was uncertain whether she was welcome there until Holt reached out to tug her down next to him on the couch.

"Einstein, want to start?" Damian asked.

The guy in a Geeks Need Love Too T-shirt looked up from his laptop. He was scruffy in a sexy-Colin-Farrell kind of way. A can of Red Bull sat on the side table, within arm's reach. Sara wasn't fooled by his nerdy image. Beneath the shirt, Einstein had some muscles. And beneath his haphazard hair, a whole lot of brain. "Sure thing. Chad White is, in fact, a real person. He was employed at the Academy using his real name and social security number. There was no reason to hide his real identity. He has no known criminal history."

Max looked up. His jaw was covered with stubble and his eyes were red-rimmed. "So now that we know who he is, he should be easy enough for an experienced hacker like you to find."

Einstein frowned. "Unfortunately, he's got hacker skills too. Granted, he's no match for me, but it's taking some time to track him down. My guess is he's rented or purchased a place to live under a false name, or he's hiding out somewhere off the grid."

Damian looked at Noah. "What have Brady and Henry given the police?"

Noah set down his coffee mug. "Brady lawyered-up quick. But Henry is cooperating, hoping for leniency. According to Henry, the predominant neurotoxin in the mix was scorpion venom from a species known as Deathstalker."

Holt looked to Sara. "Ow. What?" She realized she had a firm grip on his forearm and loosened her hold.

"Scorpion's Sting," she said. "Chad told us he'd helped create that video game. The hero is a half-scorpion, half-human named Deathstalker."

Einstein nodded. "Theo told us about that last night. I've been playing the game, trying to see if there are any other parallels that will help."

"Good thinking," Holt said. "The game certainly illustrates Toxin's need for control of his world as well as his need to be a hero. What's the objective?"

"Deathstalker defeats various enemies across several levels to save his queen and the prince."

"Art imitating life."

"What do we know about Chad's real-life queen?" Damian asked. "I mean, before he saw Sara as a substitute."

"I can help with that," Becca said. "I spoke to Gloria Redding just a bit ago. It took her a while to return my calls, as it was the middle of the night. She didn't answer when I went to her door. Apparently she uses a heavy-duty sleep-aid. And if I'd been through what she had, I would too. Chad White was her son's biological father, but she and Chad never married. Not because he didn't try. Apparently, he tried very hard to move them toward a commitment…so hard that something about him scared her away. It sounds like she caught glimpses of the controlling man he really was underneath his charm. She kept on a friendly basis for their son's sake."

"And yet he killed her father." Max shook his head. "Some friend."

"Things apparently went down the tubes fast after their son died. Twelve-year-old Josh White had leukemia. Toxin started killing a couple months after Josh's death last year."

"Grief drives people to do some pretty crazy things," Holt said. Sara took his hand. Yeah, he'd been through the hell of losing someone. But he'd come out even stronger than the man she'd fallen in love with years ago.

"And sometimes it leads you to do beautiful things," Holt continued. "This man thinks he's saving the world, doing a noble thing. In reality, he's deluded in his grief. I suspect he's also using drugs to numb the pain. That always complicates things."

Noah nodded. "Henry admitted he makes a special concoction that Toxin requests regularly. It's a drug that puts him in a trance-like state so he can tune out the emotions but hone his thinking."

"And his thinking led him to kill seven people."

"The first victim was Chad's employer at Technological Innovations. Chad was hired to help with video game development there."

"What about the others?"

Einstein frowned. "Dr. Sheila Brown was an oncologist at Mercy Hospital. She treated Josh White."

"If you say you figured out Vic Three's connection, you deserve a bonus," Max said.

"I did," Einstein said with a grin. "At least, I think so. A simple online search showed that Senator Beechum didn't support the health care bill that would have given Josh more coverage."

"But Josh died almost a year before Beechum was murdered."

Holt shook his head. "Toxin started with the two people he felt personally hurt his son—Joseph Kurtz and Dr. Sheila Brown. Somehow, killing them wasn't enough. To justify taking other lives, he adopted a hero complex, but that took some time. Eventually, he wanted to do what he thought was right and just for *society*. He likely saw killing Beechum as serving the greater good. And the resulting media attention fed his fantasy and his need to be acknowledged, because that's what heroes deserve."

"Josh White has a social media account. An active one, actually, despite his age and his death. I'm assuming Toxin took it over as a tribute to his son."

"And a way to keep him alive," Holt added.

"There's a mish-mash of posts on Josh's page. But I was able to search where Chad had searched and follow the links he'd clicked." Einstein's eyes lit up as he dove into a subject that clearly fascinated him. "He'd been searching the political postings. Sites that indicate what Congressmen have been voting on, and how. And sometimes he was extremely vocal about his opinions. There are forums out there where people can share their opinions, and Chad —posting as Josh—was vocal about his desire to change the level of health care available to kids in this country."

"So how do we find him?" Damian asked.

"The CPD is scouring the neighborhoods around the Academy," Noah said. "Knocking on every door. We did as much as we could last night, but now that the streets are clear, we can do much more."

Einstein tapped on his computer keyboard. "I plan to search all the forums and do anything else I can think of online until something pops up. I'll also work on cracking the video game, in case there's a hint in there." His eyes sparked with the challenge. It was the same spark Sara had seen in the boys' eyes in Toxin's lair the night before.

Max grunted. "Tough job. Good thing all those years of playing prepared you for this. To think you could have been out meeting people face-to-face."

"You meet some pretty interesting people online," Einstein said in self-defense.

Sara's eyes widened. "You're right. Theo and Chad were talking about that last night, and how Theo hadn't recognized playing online with Chad because of his user ID."

Einstein's gaze was piercing. "Toxin didn't happen to say what that ID was, did he?"

"Yeah, something about his son. JoshCW."

"It fits," Holt said. "He'd want to keep his son's memory alive... or even feel his son *was* alive...by keeping his identity active. Can you trace user IDs?"

"Hell, Damian wouldn't have hired me if I couldn't do the simple stuff." Einstein was already typing.

Nobody spoke. All attention was on Einstein and his laptop. Holt's hand wrapped around hers and she turned her palm over, interlacing their fingers. This had to be the answer. To think Chad would be out there another day, another hour, was unacceptable. She was eager to start her new life with Holt.

"Found him!" Einstein swung his laptop to face Damian, who read the address aloud.

Holt went still beside her. "That's the street behind my house."

CHAPTER 25

Goosebumps rose on Holt's skin as he and Noah pulled up to the curb across the street from Chad's rented house. They'd opted to drive the short distance in case he fled in a vehicle. Max was crossing the alley that ran between Holt's house and Chad's in case he escaped from the rear. The house Chad had rented was only two doors down from Holt's. His skin crawled to think how close Chad had been all this time. To think, Mrs. Mendelson might even have bumped into him on occasion while walking Roscoe.

Noah carefully led the way up the cracked-concrete walkway to the front door and knocked sharply. "Police. Open up."

Nobody answered. Warrant tucked in his pocket and gun in hand, he tried the doorknob. It turned without resistance and Holt's spidey-senses went into high alert. The sound of the music and recorded punches and grunts of a video game came from a back area of the house. In the front rooms, there was a noticeable lack of furniture other than a couple chairs and a table.

Noah did a quick sweep as Holt moved toward the hallway. It

was clear. Noah jerked his head toward the hall that led to the back bedrooms, the direction of the video game combat sounds.

Noah and Holt examined rooms as they passed them, heading toward the noise from the back room. Noah entered through the open door of that bedroom first, his gun at the ready. Holt gripped his pistol and mentally prepared himself to face the man who'd tried to take over his life.

As Noah shifted to the side, Holt got a view of the room from the doorway. Chad sat in bed in sweats and a T-shirt, propped against a bare wall. His eyes were glazed. A large, angry bruise covered one cheek, courtesy of Sara and her hammer. Across from him was a wall filled with television screens and equipment and wires going in every direction. It was a set-up similar to the lair he'd arranged in the attic at the Academy.

"Hands up," Noah said clearly and calmly. "Get off the bed and face the wall."

Chad ignored Noah and briefly turned his attention to Holt. Otherwise, he didn't move except for his fingers, which pressed buttons on a game controller. "Welcome to my home. Wanna play?"

"I think I've played enough of your games." Holt's gaze shifted back to the screen where Deathstalker was taking down a foe. After ending the enemy's life in one quick thrust of Deathstalker's tail, Chad grinned.

"You're under arrest." Noah proceeded to read Chad his Miranda rights.

Ignoring Noah, Chad struggled to focus his hazy gaze on Holt. "How's Theo?"

Holt stiffened. "He'll be fine, with his family."

Chad sighed. "Yes. I suppose he will. And I'll be fine with mine." He made a great show of raising his hands in the air, as if in surrender. The controller still hung from one of them, dangling by the cord, and he slowly moved to put it on the bedside table. That was when Holt spied the tiny capsule there. As if in one motion,

Chad put the controller down, scooped the capsule up and popped it into his mouth. His Adam's apple bobbed. He grinned at Holt. "I'll be with Josh again soon."

"Stop!" Holt shouted. "Call an ambulance," he told Noah. But help would be too late. Chad's body was already shaking with convulsions. "Another gift from Henry. He must have had a Plan B in place all along."

It wasn't supposed to go like this. Families were supposed to be able to face their loved ones' killer in a court of law. But then, perhaps this was the ultimate justice.

Holt hurried to the bedside and checked for hidden weapons within Chad's reach. He needn't have worried. Chad—*Toxin*—was already dead.

DAMIAN LOOKED UP AS HOLT AND EINSTEIN ENTERED HIS OFFICE. "You requested a meeting?"

They took seats across from him. Holt seemed uncertain. His fingers picked at the seam of his jeans. "We have something to talk to you about."

Einstein's hands were clenched together so tightly his fingers had turned white. His laptop, an extra appendage he never went anywhere without, lay across his lap.

"Is this about Sam?"

Alongside a police detective with experience in computers, Einstein had spent the afternoon going through the computer system from Chad White's apartment. On the one hand, Damian was dying to know if Chad had found anything new about Sam. On the other, he'd long ago learned not to hope—it only led to disappointment. Over the past two decades, he'd dreamed of the numerous creative, often deadly, ways he would take down the person responsible for his daughter's death. And yet, day after day, year after year, justice evaded him. Despite success finding some monsters, he'd failed to find his own.

"We discovered a document on White's computer that we thought you'd find interesting." Holt's hesitance was a red flag.

"But?"

"Please, take what we say with a heavy dose of caution."

"I always do." Damian gave a grim smile. "I've learned a thing or two over the decades. One of them is not to count your chickens before they've hatched. But if there's something—anything—to what Chad said he found, I need to follow up on it. I owe it to Sam to pursue any lead possible. And it's been a long time since I've had any leads." Despite his desire to remain impassive, hope flared, so hot and desperate it made his chest ache.

Einstein opened his laptop and typed for a moment. "I just forwarded you the document. It's a journal, of sorts, begun this past summer."

"The first entry is the date of my news segment," Holt explained, "when the press first asked me about SSAM joining the hunt for the killer and he called the tip hotline to proclaim his name was Toxin. That's when his fascination with me began. He journaled almost daily after that. At first, it was mostly about what he'd observed between me and Theo through my windows." Holt looked away a moment, clearly upset by the thought of being under a killer's microscope.

"He only saw snapshots," Damian assured him. "He wasn't living your life."

"Once he got a job at the school, he began writing about Sara and his observations of the Academy. He also made extensive diagrams of the floor plan and crawl spaces of the school. Just as his obsession was spreading from me to her, it was also spreading to SSAM and its members. He indicated it was a hero's duty to understand his enemies. In his notes about SSAM, most of them were about you."

"*Me?* Why?"

"Researching SSAM surely led him to information about why you founded this company. It's no secret that you had a daughter who'd been the victim of a serial killer. Chad White was a father who'd recently lost a child. Just as he thought he could relate to me because we both had sons and had lost loved ones to cancer, he felt a connection with you too. Some kind of bond through a father's grief, but twisted by his mission."

"This research...did it go deeper?"

"In October, he apparently found some interesting information online."

Einstein interrupted. "I've searched the links he found and they're all dead now, the sites obliterated by someone, but Chad copied the information when he found it. He saved it to a computer file."

Damian nearly squirmed with impatience. "What information?"

"It seems he thought Samantha's disappearance could have been linked to human trafficking, and in particular, the sex-slave industry. And I have to say, judging by what I could find, he may have been on to something."

Damian's heart raced. "Sex slave? But she was found dead. Dental records proved it." But due to decomposition, analysis of the scene hadn't been able to determine whether Sam had been sexually assaulted.

"Maybe. Or maybe this ring, which my quick inquiries indicate has been known to operate by stealing healthy, beautiful girls and shipping them to whoever pays the highest price, faked her death and planted evidence that would throw you off their trail when they realized how determined and powerful you were."

"Are you saying Sam might not have been killed? She might be alive?" Forget a racing heart, Damian feared his had just stopped beating.

CHAPTER 26

December

S ara pinned a white orchid in her hair. "Do you like it?"

Theo grinned. "You look beautiful."

She took a deep breath. "I feel great. Like the luckiest woman on earth. I get to officially join a fabulous family today." It had all happened so fast, but, then again, she'd loved Holt for years. Given recent events, there was no reason to wait any longer to begin a new life.

"I'll go tell them you're ready."

"Tell them to give me three minutes. I want to make a quick phone call." Whether it was nerves or excitement that coursed through her veins, she wanted to share the moment with Cheryl.

"Okay, but Dad says if you want it perfect, it should be at sunset, and that big orange ball is getting closer to the water."

She laughed and impulsively leaned forward to kiss his forehead. He looked up at her in surprise, then smiled. His acceptance sobered her as emotion pricked at her chest. Elizabeth had created this special boy, and now Sara was lucky enough to love him. "I'm so blessed to have you."

"Yeah, I'm kind of great. And soon, I'll even be able to beat you at chess." He grinned and she laughed again, the bittersweet moment over. "See you in three."

Theo slid the glass door open and pulled it closed. Her eyes tracked him as he hurried across the small patio of the beach villa Holt had rented in Acapulco. Sand flew up under his bare feet as he ran down the beach toward the pounding surf. Two men waited there—Holt and the official they'd found to perform the ceremony.

Cheryl answered on the first ring. "Is it over? Are you Missus Doctor Patterson?"

"Not yet. Very soon, though."

"Then what are you waiting for?"

Sara sighed. "Just wanted some female support, I guess."

"Did you find the box I put in your carry-on?"

Sara's hand went to her neck, her fingers running across the smooth pearls. "I did. Thank you for the *something borrowed*. It almost feels like you're here."

"Oh, hon. You know I'd be there if I could." Cheryl was watching Roscoe for them, and Mr. Cheryl didn't travel well anymore.

"I know. We'll be home in a few days, anyway."

"Oh!" Cheryl exclaimed. "And I have news for you. You received a letter from the school board. Shall I open it?"

Sara smoothed a hand nervously over her dress. "Sure, I guess."

"Well, I already did, and it's good news. Otherwise, I wouldn't have mentioned it today, of course. The school board is dropping its investigation. In light of how you dealt with the three students when Chad held you all hostage, they've judged you to be quality material." Cheryl snorted. "I could have told them that. There's even talk here of a new drama department. And, apparently Neil talked to them on your behalf."

"Neil? Really?"

"I spoke to his mother a couple days ago and she's proud to say Neil has recommitted to studying hard and finishing high school on a positive note. He's applying to local universities so he can stay close to his family for a bit. Plans to study physical therapy. His backup plan is to go into the Army and train to become a doctor and maybe, eventually, pursue a future in sports medicine. Claire said he was influenced by the Toxin investigation and his dad's bullying and wants a career that will make the world a better place."

"Good for him." She didn't doubt that he'd make it work.

"It's good all around, so go out there and make it the best day ever. Holt's waiting."

And Sara had been waiting forever for him. "I'll call you soon."

"It'd better be as *Mrs.* Patterson."

HOLT'S BREATH CAUGHT AND HE SQUEEZED THEO'S HAND.

"Told you," his son said smugly.

"You were right, she *is* beautiful."

Sara closed the door to their villa and gave a little wave. She was a vision in a white sundress with delicate lavender-colored flowers printed on it. She'd left her hair down and it caught in the breeze, lifting tendrils and sending them dancing across her shoulders and bare arms. Her bouquet of white orchids matched the one in her hair.

"She's ours now?" Theo asked.

"She's ours. Forever."

As she walked down the beach toward him, the hem of her skirt playfully swirled around her slender legs. Just like that day months ago, at the school picnic, when she'd walked back into his life. This time, he'd make sure she stayed.

A SPECIAL SNEAK PEEK...

The Mindhunters Series continues...

DARK DEEDS
(The Mindhunters, Book 4)

Friday, 4:03 p.m., early February
Hoboken, New Jersey

Becca followed the instructions—both parts—to the letter. She'd told no one, and she arrived at the diner alone. The window that separated her from the sleet-slick street outside proclaimed the breakfast specials in ketchup-red and mustard-yellow stencil, which only accentuated the day's shades of gray.

Then again, it was February. In Hoboken.

"Another refill?" The waitress's attitude had gone from cheerful to weary over the past hour.

"No, thanks." Three cups had already shifted her usual state of heightened awareness into downright jittery territory. It went against all her self-protective instincts—and in a personal security specialist and bodyguard, those were strong—to continue to sit and wait, but she wanted this interview. Had worked for months to chase down this lead that might provide new information about Samantha Manchester's disappearance. The trail had been cold for twenty years, which was why Becca needed Selina. So she didn't protest when the tired waitress misheard her and moved to top off her cup yet again.

Her hand shook slightly—adrenaline and caffeine were a potent mix—as she lifted her cup to her lips. She set it down too hard, sloshing a bit over the rim, splashing droplets onto the table. As she reached for the napkin dispenser, the tiny diamond stud in her nose reflected in the metal surface, winking at her like sun on snow. During the weeks they'd exchanged emails, Becca had learned that eighteen-year-old Selina loved piercings, extreme hair color and all things city-chic, so Becca had opted to wear the stud she normally removed for her daily job. Her nearly white-blond hair was a constant. Still a year shy of thirty, Becca was short enough, her appearance young enough, to get away with wearing ripped jeans and a T-shirt advertising a popular punk band.

Another minute ticked by. Resigned, she took out her phone and sent the text she'd been composing in her mind. *So sorry. Going to miss rehearsal but will be at party. Will make it up to you.*

She was, technically, in New York City to serve as a bridesmaid in a wedding, but the proximity to this lead in Hoboken had been crucial to her decision to fly in early. However, she hadn't counted on her lead being late for their appointment. She was going to miss the next train back to the city.

A moment later, Vanessa texted a reply. *Because of Diego?*

Becca's body went still. Months ago, she'd reconciled herself to seeing her ex-lover again, since Diego was the groom's best man. She was dreading it, but she would pull on her big girl panties for the sake of her friends' wedding. Vanessa and Noah deserved happiness.

She texted back. *No. Work.*

I know this weekend is tough for you. If you want to talk, I'm here.

Though Becca appreciated the offer, sharing wasn't in the cards. Her two-week affair with Diego last summer would be forever locked away in a vault in the back of her mind. Unfortunately, her masochistic side occasionally whipped out those memories like little jewels and re-examined them in all their sparkling, stunning detail.

A young woman peeked through the diner's ketchup-and-mustard window and Becca hastily returned Vanessa's text. *See you soon.*

Swallowed up by a trench coat that appeared secondhand, the woman looked all of twelve years old, especially when she rapidly blinked away snowflakes as if she were lost and confused. But the highlights in her hair were expensive—not homegrown, but from a quality salon. She winced as the tinkling of a bell announced her entrance, then she spied Becca in the corner.

With halting steps, as if she were facing a firing squad, she made her way to the table. "Becca?"

"That's me." Becca smiled warmly and gestured to the opposite side of the booth. "Thank you for coming."

After another glance around, Selina slid onto the bench. "I almost didn't, but I had to meet the woman who thinks she can take down the Circle." Selina's gaze flicked over her. "Kind of small, aren't you?"

"The best things come in small packages." It was something Becca's brothers used to say to her, before ruffling her hair. Or trying out the latest wrestling moves on her. Not that they'd dared to attempt such a thing in years, not since she'd shown up to a family dinner wearing her black belt in Tae Kwon Do. "I'm tougher than I look." And at five and a half feet tall, she wasn't *that* tiny.

"Me, too." For an eighteen-year-old, Selina's eyes were hard with life experience, her jaw set in concrete.

"You'd have to be tough, to survive what you've been through."

The waitress approached, some semblance of her cheerful

smile back in place at the prospect of another paying customer. Selina ordered a cup of coffee, then waited until the waitress was at the other end of the diner before speaking. "How'd you find me?"

"I'd been looking for anything about the Circle. You were mentioned in a police report."

Selina stiffened. "There's not supposed to be anything to connect me to them."

"It was under your previous name, not your new one. That took some more digging. The rest you know." "You bribed my friend for my email address."

"Pretty much." There had been weeks of trust-building there, too, during which they'd exchanged increasingly lengthy emails until Becca had convinced Selina she could be trusted.

Selina ducked her head, pretending to be absorbed in stirring her coffee. "You believe the police report?"

Becca sensed her response was critical to the success of this interview. "There was very little to it, which surprised me. You were a witness, a *survivor*, one of a kind, who could have testified against a major crime syndicate. But then you disappeared. I'm guessing the former is the motivation for the latter."

Selina set aside her spoon and met Becca's gaze. "I'm only here because you think you can take those monsters down. I want to help, but…"

"But you're afraid. I don't blame you for not trusting anyone. I know what the Circle is capable of. I've been gathering information on them for months now. I've read every police report I could get my hands on from Chicago to New York to Las Vegas."

"To find out if they took this Samantha Manchester girl like they took me."

"Yes, but she was taken in Chicago, so it's a little different. My boss at SSAM—"

"Damian Manchester… he's Samantha's father?"

Becca nodded. "Sam was thirteen years old when she was taken from a mall in the North Shore area of Chicago twenty years ago. A year later, they found her skeletal remains in a wooded, rural area outside of the city."

Selina shuddered. "That could have been me. If I hadn't been rescued, death would have been the easy way out."

"Except she might not have died."

Selina looked up sharply. "What?"

"Recently, we found evidence that suggests it might not have been Sam's body in that shallow grave after all. The Circle may have taken her, then faked her death and identification to throw the police and Damian off the trail." It was precious little to go on, but it was something new, when hope of finding justice had nearly been lost.

Becca waited a moment and watched Selina absorb her words before she continued. "From what I've learned, I believe the Circle deals in the trading of human flesh, including sex slaves and children for pornographic purposes. You were almost one of their victims." That was only a part of their extensive operation, and looking for information about Samantha had been like trying to chip away at an iceberg, searching for that one bit of helpful information.

"Help me stop them," Becca pleaded when Selina remained quietly thoughtful.

"You don't know for sure that the Circle was involved in Sam's disappearance."

"True. That's why I need your help. You're the only person known to have escaped the Circle and survived." Others had been killed before they could testify. Selina had taken off before she could suffer the same fate. And the police report had been notably vague.

Selina seemed to weigh this, then sat back, her shoulders dipping a notch as she made her decision. "It's not a pretty story."

"In my line of work, few stories are."

"You see this kind of thing at SSAM often?"

The acronym for Damian's agency, the Society for the Study of the Aberrant Mind, was a tribute to his daughter Sam. SSAM's clientele enlisted Becca and her fellow agents to hunt violent repeat offenders when local law enforcement agencies or FBI failed to apprehend the criminals, for whatever reason—often a lack of resources or a case that had gone cold or fallen out of the public eye.

Like Samantha Manchester's case.

Becca leaned forward on the tabletop scarred by water rings and knife marks. "I can teach you ways to protect yourself. You're doing a good job hiding, but I have a lot of experience in staying safe." And plenty in getting hurt, too, and how to avoid it in the future. "My job, my entire world, is all about personal security."

Selina pressed her lips together, then shook her head. "I'm here now, and I'll talk. But then we can't meet again. I can't risk it."

"I understand." Becca hoped to get what she needed and leave this woman in peace.

"I hope so, because it's a matter of life and death... and not just mine." Absently, Selina's left hand rubbed her upper right arm as if warding off a chill.

Who else was she protecting? "I made sure nobody followed me," Becca assured her. "I haven't told anyone I'm here. Not even my boss."

Selina stared out the window for so long Becca wasn't sure she would share her story after all. When she spoke, it was in a bitter, miserable tone. "I was at a party where there was alcohol. I was out beyond curfew. My parents didn't care. I'd run away so many times, they'd stopped trying to get through to me. Besides, I was going to be eighteen in a month. An adult." She huffed out a breath. "As if I knew what that meant. I was an idiot."

Stealing Selina's innocence was yet another of the Circle's crimes.

Selina shook off her self-flagellation and refocused. "My phone's battery died so I went to the car to charge it while I called a friend who was supposed to meet me. Before I could dial, two guys opened my door and yanked me from the front seat." She paused and swallowed. "It was dark, and everything happened so fast. They put something over my head and tied me up so I couldn't see or move. In a matter of seconds, they had me...it was all so *efficient.* I was scared, but that was just the beginning." Remembered fear contorted her face.

"It must have been horrible." Becca resisted the urge to reach out and comfort with a touch of the hand. Her source still looked as if she might bolt at the slightest provocation.

Selina's lips pressed into a hard line, and a flash of warrior-like determination glinted in her eyes. "It was a fucking nightmare. But I got away. And then nobody believed me. Do you know what that's like?"

"Yeah, I do," Becca said quietly. Inside, her heart rate spiked with memories. Years of repressing fear and anxiety, pleading with the authorities to listen to her story. Years of being dismissed. Just when she thought she'd moved past it, the horrible memories would pop up again. And now that the man who starred in her nightmares had been released on parole, those moments had occurred more frequently.

Selina must have seen the truth in Becca's face. She took a deep breath, then continued. "When they pulled the bag off my head, I was in a basement with no windows and barely any lighting. There was a row of cells... maybe four or five metal doors, side by side. They—" She broke off and put a hand to her opposite shoulder... the same one she'd been rubbing earlier. Tears shimmered in her eyes. "They branded me." "Branded?"

Selina traced a circle on the table. "With a hot iron. A symbol that I was theirs. Then they put me in a cell with nothing but a cot and a scratchy blanket. One guy tried to touch me, but the other guy stopped him. Said to *save me for the clients.* I'd bring in more money if I was pure." Her laugh hitched in her throat. "The other guy said I was nowhere near pure. Assholes. Later, a third guy came to film me. I was so scared they were going to send it to my parents or something."

"What did they film?"

"That's just it...I wasn't doing anything interesting. They encouraged me to plead with them, like they enjoyed seeing me begging for my life. It was bizarre."

An introduction to the merchandise, possibly? Something to show potential clients? No doubt, interest from buyers would have led to worse scenarios for Selina. Chills ran down Becca's spine at the thought of what could have happened if the teen hadn't escaped...and what had probably happened to many similar girls, maybe even Sam.

"If Sam was a victim, do you think she could still be alive?" Becca asked. "Or maybe she escaped like you did?" And somehow didn't find her way back home. If there was hope for Selina, perhaps there was hope for Sam, though she would be in her mid-thirties by now. She'd be an entirely different person than the daughter Damian remembered, but at least he'd have closure.

"I don't know. Part of me hopes she isn't alive if she didn't escape early on." Selina's eyes met Becca's. "The things I've read online about human trafficking... these people have to be animals. Fucking *monsters*." Selina glanced away to compose herself, but she couldn't hide a shudder. "When they were taping me, the camera's light was bright. It lit up the walls of my cell. There were names everywhere, like a warning or something. It didn't matter what we did—or who we were before—now we were *theirs*." Her hand moved to her arm again. They'd marked her as Circle property, but she'd reclaimed her life.

Goosebumps erupted on Becca's arms. Had Samantha's name been on that wall? She'd been taken in Chicago. Would they have trafficked her through New York City, maybe to keep the authorities from locating her when Damian was putting the pressure on?

"How did you get away?" Becca asked.

For the first time, a small smile curved Selina's lips. "I was lucky. I had a guardian angel who let me out. Told me to be quiet and follow him. The guard was passed out, snoring. I think my angel might have drugged him." Selina's gaze flitted away from Becca's. "And don't ask me any more about my angel because I don't know. And I wouldn't tell even if I did know. He took me to another man who helped me set up a new identity. He saved my life."

Someone in the Circle risked his life for this one young woman? It had to be an undercover agent. The Circle was known for a wide range of crimes in a number of big cities—New York, Chicago, Miami, Dallas, Las Vegas and Los Angeles were all infected with their influence. This man could be FBI, CIA, ICE or DEA. Or maybe he worked alone.

"The police report says you couldn't remember where you'd been held," Becca said. "Or how you got out."

"That was for my own protection. I was stupid."

"How so?"

"There never should have been a police report. The guy who helped me...my angel told me to forget everything I'd seen. To run like hell and start a new life. But I went home to get some things I thought I couldn't live without...and to say goodbye to my parents. I told them what had happened, hoping they'd care." She pressed her trembling lips together and looked away. "Stupid."

When Selina looked back, she'd wiped her expression of all emotion linked to the memory. "My parents called the police while I was up in my room. Just in case I wasn't lying, I guess. Or maybe they wanted me admitted to the loony bin. I wasn't home more than fifteen minutes before a cop was there, asking me questions. Almost like he'd been watching for me to pop up somewhere. That's when I knew my angel was right. I should run.

"I told the officer I couldn't remember anything. As soon as I could, I snuck out my bedroom window and never looked back. Started a new life with my new identity." She met Becca's gaze.

"Until you found me, I had become Selina. Now I'm back to dealing with the old me again."

"Sorry about that."

"I thought I could keep in touch with a friend or two from high school, but I guess I should stop that, too." Selina's anger faded quickly. "If telling my story will save someone else from the Circle, I'm happy to help. But if you tracked me down via a police report and figured out how to get my email address, then the Circle can do it, too. Or the NYPD mole."

"*Mole?*" Becca was sure her eyes had gone as wide as the rims of their coffee cups. A mole working on the force was leaking vital information to a crime ring? It would explain why the police closed Selina's case so quickly. And why the Circle had operated for decades, seemingly without interference from law enforcement. They were usually one step ahead of police raids. It made sense that they might have a reliable source of information within the NYPD. Besides, money could buy almost anything.

But an undercover agent *within* the Circle *and* a police officer leaking information *to* the Circle? As this investigation proceeded, Becca would have her work cut out for her figuring out who was friend or foe.

"My rescuer said that there was a cop who was dangerous and might kill me to keep me quiet. At the very least, I was afraid the Circle would come looking for me, especially if they thought I'd testify."

"Let me assure you, you're difficult to find."

"And yet you found me."

"I'm very careful. I know my words might not be worth much, but I promise you can trust me. You call me and I'll come running to help." This time Becca did reach out to touch Selina's wrist lightly. She was encouraged when Selina didn't pull away.

"But how can I help you?" Selina's eyes brimmed with misery and regret. "I won't put myself at risk again."

"Do you remember where you were held?"

"I do." Selina took a napkin from the dispenser. "Got a pen?"

Becca promptly handed her one, and a moment later, Selina pushed the napkin toward her. She'd written down an address in Brooklyn. Below it was a name that froze the air in Becca's lungs.

"What's this name at the bottom?" Becca asked, hoping her words sounded normal when she was nearly choking on them.

"That's the name of the mole. My angel warned me not to talk about it, but I figure you'd better know who you can or can't trust."

"Diego Sandoval? You're sure that's the name your angel gave you? That's the name of the guy working for the Circle, betraying the NYPD?" Becca's stomach twisted.

"No way I could forget it."

And there was no way Diego would sell out his brothers in blue. No freaking way.

The Diego she'd known, the man she'd held in her arms, the proud NYPD detective who'd vowed to rebuild his career, would never accept bribes from a crime ring. Unless she'd never really known him at all.

DARK DEEDS is available now!

ACKNOWLEDGMENTS

Words of gratitude can't express how much I appreciate the sacrifices made by my husband and kids. Thank you for your patience, and the gift of time in which to create.

To Angela James and the staff at Carina Press, and Deb Nemeth, my fabulous editor, my thanks for helping bring this book to life.

Arlene Hittle, Rita Henuber, Autumn Jordon and Donnell Bell, I appreciate you lending an ear and a pep talk or two.

And last, but definitely not least, thank you to Andrea and Danny, my beloved beta readers. Your time and input is much appreciated.

ABOUT THE AUTHOR

Anne Marie has always been fascinated by people—inside and out—
which led to degrees in Biology,
Chemistry, Psychology, and Coun-
seling. Her passion for understanding the human race is now
satisfied by her roles as mother,
wife, daughter, sister, and award-
winning author of romantic
suspense.

She writes to reclaim her sanity.

Find ways to connect with Anne
Marie at AnneMarieBecker.com.
There, sign up for her newsletter to receive the latest information
regarding books, appearances, and giveaways.

www.ingramcontent.com/pod-product-compliance
Lightning Source LLC
Chambersburg PA
CBHW032146190626
46814CB00005BA/1858